NIGHTSTALKERS

They're not your average, everyday detectives—and in hair-raising cases like these, you'll find out why....

In William Hope Hodgson's "The Gateway of the Monster," a veteran ghost hunter finds his services requested by a terrified butler—and for good reason.

Take a ride on a very different sort of train in Robert Weinberg's "The Midnight El"—and witness detective Sidney Taine's haunting duel with destiny.

Walk into the black night of Appalachia in "Vandy, Vandy" by Manly Wade Wellman—and watch a 300-year-old supernatural struggle come full circle.

In Lee Killough's "The Existential Man," Sergeant David Amaro has a recurring nightmare and a creepy connection with a very determined corpse.

"Falling Boy" features a shaken pilot who has a sickening celestial encounter—and, as police investigator Bridgid Masterson soon finds out, his symptoms are anything but clinical.

SUPERNATURAL SLEUTHS

SUPERNATURAL SLEUTHS

EDITED BY
CHARLES G. WAUGH
AND MARTIN H. GREENBERG

A ROC BOOK

ROC
Published by the Penguin Group
Penguin Books USA Inc., 375 Hudson Street,
New York, New York 10014, U.S.A.
Penguin Books Ltd, 27 Wrights Lane,
London W8 5TZ, England
Penguin Books Australia Ltd, Ringwood,
Victoria, Australia
Penguin Books Canada Ltd, 10 Alcorn Avenue,
Toronto, Ontario, Canada M4V 3B2
Penguin Books (N.Z.) Ltd, 182–190 Wairau Road,
Auckland 10, New Zealand

Penguin Books Ltd, Registered Offices:
Harmondsworth, Middlesex, England

First published by Roc, an imprint of Dutton Signet,
a division of Penguin Books USA Inc.

First Printing, October, 1996
10 9 8 7 6 5 4 3 2 1

For permissions please turn to page 348.

 REGISTERED TRADEMARK—MARCA REGISTRADA

Printed in the United States of America

CONTENTS

LONELY TRAIN A'COMIN'

William F. Nolan

WILLIAM F. NOLAN is best known for his Logan trilogy, *Logan's Run*, *Logan's World*, and *Logan's Search*, which detail a future world ruled by the young, where the most heinous crime is growing old. However, during his more than forty years as a professional writer, he has turned out over a thousand short stories and nonfiction works, as well as dozens of novels, scripts, and teleplays in all genres and styles. Recently Nolan has concentrated on the horror field, resulting in more successes like this story.

> *Lonely train a'comin'*
> *I can hear its cry*
> *Lonely train from nowhere*
> *Takin' me to die*
> *—folk ballad fragment, circa 1881*

At Bitterroot, Ventry waited.

Bone-cold, huddled on the narrow wooden bench against the paint-blistered wall of the depot, the collar of his fleece-lined coat turned up against the chill Montana winds blowing in from the Plains, he waited for the train. Beneath the wide brim of a work-blackened Stetson, sweat-stained along the headband, his eyes were intense, the gunmetal color of blued steel. Hard lines etched into the mahogany of his face spoke of deep-snow winters and glare-sun summers; his hands, inside heavy leather work gloves, were calloused and blunt-fingered from punishing decades of ranch work.

Autumn was dying, and the sky over Bitterroot was gray with the promise of winter. This would be the train's last run before snow closed down the route. Ventry had calculated it with consummate patience and precision. He prided himself on his stubborn prac-ticality, and he had earned a reputation among his fellow ranchers as a hard-headed realist.

Paul Ventry was never an emotional man. Even at his wife's death he had remained stolid, rock-like in his grief. If it was Sarah's time to die, then so be it. He had loved her, but she was gone and he was alone and that was fact. Ventry accepted. Sarah had wanted children, but things hadn't worked out that way. So they had each other, and the ranch, and the open Montana sky—and that had been enough.

Amy's death was not the same. Losing his sister had been wrong. He did *not* accept it. Which was why he was doing this, why he was here. In his view, he had no other choice.

He had been unable to pinpoint the train's exact arrival, but he was certain it would pass Bitterroot within a seven-day period. Thus, he had brought along enough food and water to last a week. His supplies were almost depleted now, but they could be stretched through two more days and nights if need be; Ventry was not worried.

The train *would* be here.

It was lonely at Bitterroot. The stationmaster's of-fice was boarded over, and bars covered the windows. The route into Ross Fork had been dropped from the rail schedule six months ago, and main-line trains bound for Lewistown no longer made the stop. Now the only trains that rattled past were desolate freights, dragging their endless rusted flatcars.

Ventry shifted the holstered ax pressing against his thigh, and unzipping a side pocket on his coat, he took out the thumb-worn postcard. On the picture side, superimposed over a multicolored panoramic shot of a Plains sunset, was the standard Montana salutation: GREETINGS FROM THE BIG SKY COUNTRY! And on the reverse, Amy's last words. How many times had he read her hastily scrawled message, mailed from this depot almost a year ago to the day?

Dear Paulie, I'll write a long letter, I promise, when I get to Lewistown, but the train came early so I just have time, dear brother, to send you my love. And don't you worry about your little kid sister because life for me is going to be super with my new job! Luv and XXXXXXX, Amy

And she had added a quick P.S. at the bottom of the card:

You should see this beautiful old train! Didn't know they still ran steam locomotives like this one! Gotta rush—'cuz it's waiting for me!

Ventry's mouth tightened, and he slipped the card back into his coat, thinking about Amy's smiling eyes, about how much a part of his life she'd been. Hell, she was a better sheep rancher than half the valley men on Big Moccasin! But, once grown, she'd wanted city life, a city job, a chance to meet city men.

"Just you watch me, Paulie," she had told him, her face shining with excitement. "This lil' old job in Lewistown is only the beginning. The firm has a branch in Helena, and I'm sure I can get transferred there within a year. You're gonna be real proud of your sis. I'll *make* you proud!"

She'd never had the chance. She'd never reached Lewistown. Amy had stepped aboard the train . . . and vanished.

Yet people don't vanish. It was a word Paul refused to accept. He had driven each bleak mile of the rail

line from Bitterroot to Lewistown, combing every inch
of terrain for a sign, a clue, a scrap of clothing. He'd
spent two months along that route. And had found
nothing.

Ventry posted a public reward for information leading to Amy's whereabouts. Which is when Tom Hallendorf contacted him.

Hallendorf was a game warden stationed at King's
Hill Pass in the Lewis and Clark National Forest. He
phoned Ventry, telling him about what he'd found
near an abandoned spur track in the Little Belt range.

Bones. *Human* bones.

And a ripped, badly stained red leather purse.

The empty purse had belonged to Amy. Forensic
evidence established the bones as part of her skeleton.

What had happened up there in those mountains?

The district sheriff, John Longbow, blamed it on a
"weirdo." A roving tramp.

"Dirt-plain obvious, Mr. Ventry," the sheriff had
said to him. "He killed her for what she had in the
purse. You admit she was carryin' several hundred in
cash. Which is, begging your pardon, a damn fool
thing to do!"

But that didn't explain the picked bones.

"Lotta wild animals in the mountains," the lawman
had declared. "After this weirdo done 'er in he just
left her layin' there—and, well, probably a bear come
onto 'er. It's happened before. We've found bones up
in that area more than once. Lot of strange things in
the Little Belt." And the sheriff had grinned. "As a
boy, with the tribe, I heard me stories that'd curl your
hair. It's wild country."

The railroad authorities were adamant about the
mystery train. "No steamers in these parts," they told
him. "Nobody runs 'em anymore."

But Ventry was gut-certain that such a train existed,
and that Amy had died on it. Someone had cold-
bloodedly murdered his sister and dumped her body
in the mountains.

He closed down the ranch, sold his stock, and devoted himself to finding out who that someone was.

He spent an entire month at the main library in Lewistown, poring through old newspaper files, copying names, dates, case details.

A pattern emerged. Ventry found that a sizable number of missing persons who had vanished in this area of the state over the past decade had been traveling by *rail*. And several of them had disappeared along the same basic route Amy had chosen.

Ventry confronted John Longbow with his research.

"An' just who is this killer?" the sheriff asked.

"Whoever owns the steamer. Some freak rail buff. Rich enough to run his own private train, and crazy enough to kill the passengers who get on board."

"Look, Mr. Ventry, how come nobody's *seen* this fancy steam train of yours?"

"Because the rail disappearances have happened at night, at remote stations off the main lines. He never runs the train by daylight. Probably keeps it up in the mountains. Maybe in one of the old mine shafts. Uses off-line spur tracks. Comes rolling into a small depot like Bitterroot *between* the regular passenger trains and picks up whoever's on the platform."

The sheriff had grunted at this, his eyes tight on Paul Ventry's face.

"And there's a definite *cycle* to these disappearances," Ventry continued. "According to what I've put together, the train makes its night runs at specific intervals. About a month apart, spring through fall. Then it's hidden away in the Little Belt each winter when the old spur tracks are snowed over. I've done a lot of calculation on this, and I'm certain that the train makes its final run during the first week of November—which means you've still got time to stop it."

The sheriff had studied Paul Ventry for a long, silent moment. Then he had sighed deeply. "That's an interesting theory, Mr. Ventry, *real* interesting. But . . . it's also about as wild and unproven as any I've heard—and I've heard me a few. Now, it's absolute natural that you're upset at your sister's death, but you've let things get way out of whack. I figger you'd best go on back to your ranch and try an' forget about poor little Amy. Put her out of your mind. She's gone. And there's nothing you can do about that."

"We'll see," Ventry had said, a cutting edge to his voice. "We'll see what I can do."

Ventry's plan was simple. Stop the train, board it, and kill the twisted son of a bitch who owned it. Put a .45 slug in his head. Blow his fucking brains out— and blow his train up with him!

I'll put an end to this if no one else will, Ventry promised himself. And I've got the tools to do it.

He slipped the carefully wrapped gun rig from his knapsack, unfolded its oiled covering, and withdrew his grandfather's long-barreled frontier Colt from its worn leather holster. The gun was a family treasure. Its bone handle was cracked and yellowed by the years, but the old Colt was still in perfect firing order. His granddaddy had worn this rig, had defended his mine on the Comstock against claim jumpers with this gun. It was fitting and proper that it be used on the man who'd killed Amy.

Night was settling over Bitterroot. The fiery orange disc of sun had dropped below the Little Belt Mountains, and the sky was gray slate along the horizon.

Time to strap on the gun. Time to get ready for the train.

It's coming tonight! Lord God, I can feel it out there in the gathering dark, thrumming the rails. I can feel it in my blood and bones.

Well, then, come ahead, god damn you, whoever you are.

I'm ready for you.

Ten P.M. Eleven. Midnight.

It came at midnight.

Rushing toward Bitterroot, clattering in fierce-wheeled thunder, its black bulk sliding over the track

in the ash-dark Montana night like an immense, seg-
mented snake—with a single yellow eye probing the
terrain ahead.

Ventry heard it long before he saw it. The rails sang
and vibrated around him as he stood tall and resolute
in mid-track, a three-cell silver flashlight in his right
hand, his heavy sheepskin coat buttoned over the gun
at his belt.

Have to flag it down. With the depot closed it won't
make a stop. No passengers. It's looking for live game,
and it doesn't figure on finding any here at Bitterroot.

Surprise! *I'm* here. *I'm* alive. Like Amy. Like all
the others. Man alone at night. Needs a ride. Climb
aboard, pardner. Make yourself to home. Drink?
Somethin' to eat? What's your pleasure?

My pleasure is your death—and the death of your
freak train, mister! *That's* my pleasure.

It was in sight now, coming fast, slicing a bright
round hole in the night—and its sweeping locomotive
beam splashed Paul Ventry's body with a pale
luminescence.

The rancher swung his flash up, then down, in a
high arc. Again. And again.

Stop, you bastard! *Stop!*

The train began slowing.

Sparks showered from the massive driving wheels
as the train reduced speed. Slowing . . . slower . . . steel
shrieking against steel. An easing of primal force.

It was almost upon him.

Like a great shining insect, the locomotive towered
high and black over Ventry, its tall stack shutting out
the stars. The rusted tip of the train's thrusting metal
cowcatcher gently nudged the toe of his right boot as
the incredible night mammoth slid to a final grinding
stop.

Now the train was utterly motionless, breathing its
white steam into the cold dark, waiting for him as he
had waited for it.

Ventry felt a surge of exultation fire his body. He'd

been right! It was here—and he was prepared to destroy it, to avenge his sister. It was his destiny. He felt no fear, only a cool and certain confidence in his ability to kill.

A movement at the corner of his eye. Someone was waving to him from the far end of the train, from the last coach, the train's only source of light. All of the other passenger cars were dark and blind-windowed; only the last car glowed hazy yellow.

Ventry eased around the breathing locomotive, his boots crunching loudly in the cindered gravel as he moved over the roadbed.

He glanced up at the locomotive's high, double-windowed cabin, but the engineer was lost behind opaque, soot-colored glass. Ventry kept moving steadily forward, toward the distant figure, passing along the linked row of silent, lightless passenger cars. The train bore no markings; it was a uniform, unbroken black.

Ventry squinted at the beckoning figure. Was it the killer himself, surprised and delighted at finding another passenger at this deserted night station?

He slipped the flash into his shoulder knapsack, and eased a hand inside his coat, gripping the warm bone handle of the .45 at his waist. You've had one surprise tonight, mister. Get ready for another.

Then, abruptly, he stopped, heart pounding. Ventry recognized the beckoning figure. Impossible! An illusion. Just *couldn't* be. Yet there she was, smiling, waving to him.

"Amy!" Ventry rushed toward his sister in a stumbling run.

But she was no longer in sight when he reached the dimly illumined car. Anxiously, he peered into one of the smoke-yellowed windows. A figure moved hazily inside.

"Amy!" He shouted her name again, mounting the coach steps.

The moment Ventry's boot touched the car's upper platform the train jolted into life. Ventry was thrown to his knees as the coach lurched violently forward.

The locomotive's big driving wheels sparked against steel, gaining a solid grip on the rails as the train surged powerfully from Bitterroot Station.

As Paul Ventry entered the coach, the door snap-locked behind him. Remote-control device. To make sure I won't leave by the rear exit. No matter. He'd expected that. He could get out when he had to, when he was ready. He'd come prepared for whatever this madman had in mind.

But Ventry had *not* been prepared for the emotional shock of seeing Amy. Had he *really* seen her? *Was* it his sister?

No. Of course not. He'd been tricked by his subconscious mind. The fault was his. A lapse in concentration, in judgment.

But *someone* had waved to him—a young girl who looked, at first sight, amazingly like his dead sister.

Where was she now?

And just where was the human devil who ran this train?

Ventry was alone in the car. To either side of the aisle the rows of richly upholstered green velvet seats were empty. A pair of ornate, scrolled gas lamps, mounted above the arched doorway, cast flickering shadows over antique brass fittings and a handcarved wood ceiling. Green brocade draped the windows.

He didn't know much about trains, but Ventry knew this one *had* to be pre-1900. And probably restored by the rich freak who owned it. Plush was the word.

Well, it was making its last run; Ventry would see to that.

He pulled the flash from his shoulder pack, snapping on the bright beam as he moved warily forward.

The flashlight proved unnecessary. As Ventry entered the second car (door unlocked; guess he doesn't mind my going *forward*) the overhead gas lamps sputtered to life, spreading their pale yellow illumination over the length of the coach.

Again, the plush velvet seats were empty. Except for one. The last seat at the far end of the car. A woman was sitting there, stiff and motionless in the dim light, her back to Ventry.

As he moved toward her, she turned slowly to face him.

By Christ, it *was* Amy!

Paul Ventry rushed to her, sudden tears stinging his eyes. Fiercely, he embraced his sister; she was warm and solid in his arms. "Oh, Sis, I'm so glad you're *alive*!"

But there was no sound from her lips. No words. No emotion. She was rigid in his embrace.

Ventry stepped away from her. "What's wrong? I don't understand why you—"

His words were choked off. Amy had leaped from the seat, cat-quick, to fasten long pale fingers around his throat. Her thumbs dug like sharp spikes into the flesh of Ventry's neck.

He reeled back, gasping for breath, clawing at the incredibly strong hands. He couldn't break her grip.

Amy's face was changing. The flesh was falling away in gummy wet ribbons, revealing raw white bone! In the deep sockets of Amy's grinning skull her eyes were hot red points of fire.

Ventry's right hand found the butt of the Colt, and he dragged the gun free of its holster. Swinging the barrel toward Amy, he fired directly into the melting horror of her face.

His bullets drilled round, charred holes in the grinning skull, but Amy's fingers—now all raw bone and slick gristle—maintained their death grip at his throat.

Axe! Use the axe!

In a swimming red haze, Ventry snapped the short-handled woodsman's axe free of his belt. And swung it sharply downward, neatly removing Amy's head at shoulder level. The cleanly severed skull rolled into the aisle at his feet.

Yet, horribly, the bony fingers increased their deadly pressure.

Ventry's sight blurred; the coach wavered. As the

last of his oxygen was cut off, he was on the verge of blacking out.

Desperately, he swung the blade again, missing the Amy-thing entirely. The axe buried itself in thick green velvet.

The train thrashed; its whistle shrieked wildly in the rushing night, a cry of pain—and the seat rippled in agony. Oily black liquid squirted from the sliced velvet.

At Ventry's throat, the bony fingers dropped away.

In numbed shock, he watched his sister's rotting corpse flow down into the seat, melting and mixing with the central train body, bubbling wetly. . . .

Oh, sweet Jesus! Everything's moving! The whole foul train is live!

And Ventry accepted it. Sick with horror and revulsion, he accepted it. He was a realist, and this thing was real. No fantasy. No dream.

Real.

Which meant he had to kill it. Not the man who owned it, because such a man did not exist. Somehow, the train itself, ancient and rusting in the high mountains, had taken on a sentient life of its own. The molecular components of iron and wood and steel had, over a slow century, transformed themselves into living tissue—and this dark hell-thing had rolled out onto the Montana plains seeking food, seeking flesh to sustain it, sleeping, sated, through the frozen winters, hibernating, then stirring to hungry life again as the greening earth renewed itself.

Lot of strange things in the Little Belt.

Don't think about it, Ventry warned himself. Just do what you came to do: *kill it!* Kill the foul thing. Blow it out of existence!

He carried three explosive charges in his knapsack, each equipped with a timing device. All right, make your plan! Set one here at the end of the train, another in the middle coach, and plant the final charge in the forward car.

No good. If the thing had the power to animate its

dead victims it also had the power to fling off his explosive devices, to rid itself of them as a dog shakes leaves from its coat.

I'll have to go after it the way you go after a snake; to kill a snake, you cut off its head.

So go for the brain.

Go for the engine.

The train had left the main rail system now, and was on a rusted spur track, climbing steeply into the Little Belt range.

It was taking Ventry into the high mountains. One last meal of warm flesh, then the long winter's sleep.

The train was going home.

Three cars to go.

Axe in hand, Ventry was moving steadily toward the engine, through vacant, gas-lit coaches, wondering how and when it would attack him again.

Did it know he meant to kill it? Possibly it had no fear of him. God knows it was strong. And no human had ever harmed it in the past. Does the snake fear the mouse?

Maybe it would leave him alone to do his work; maybe it didn't realize how lethal this mouse could be.

But Ventry was wrong.

Swaying in the clattering rush of the train, he was halfway down the aisle of the final coach when the tissue around him rippled into motion. Viscid black bubbles formed on the ceiling of the car, and in the seats. Growing. Quivering. Multiplying.

One by one, the loathsome globes swelled and burst—giving birth to a host of nightmare figures. Young and old. Man, woman, child. Eyes red and angry.

They closed on Ventry in the clicking interior of the hell coach, moving toward him in a rotting tide.

He had seen photos of many of them in the Lewistown library. Vanished passengers, like Amy, devoured and absorbed and now regenerated as fetid ectoplasmic horrors—literal extensions of the train itself.

Ventry knew that he was powerless to stop them. The Amy-thing had proven that.

But he still had the axe, and a few vital seconds before the train-things reached him.

Ventry swung the razor blade left and right, slashing brutally at seat and floor, cutting deep with each swift blow. Fluid gushed from a dozen gaping wounds; a rubbery mass of coil-like innards, like spilled guts, erupted from the seat to Ventry's right, splashing him with gore.

The train screamed into the Montana night, howling like a wounded beast.

The passenger-things lost form, melting into the aisle.

Now Ventry was at the final door, leading to the coal car directly behind the engine.

It was locked against him.

The train had reached its destination at the top of the spur, was rolling down a side track leading to a deserted mine. Its home. Its cave. Its dark hiding place.

The train would feast now.

Paul Ventry used the last of his strength on the door. Hacking at it. Slashing wildly. Cutting his way through.

Free! In a freezing blast of night wind, Ventry scrambled across the coal tender toward the shining black locomotive.

And reached it.

A heavy, gelatinous membrane separated him from the control cabin. The membrane pulsed with veined life.

Got to get inside . . . reach the brain of the thing. . . .

Ventry drove the blade deep, splitting the veined skin. And burst through into the cabin.

Its interior was a shock to Ventry's senses; he was

assailed by a stench so powerful that bile rushed into
his throat. He fought back a rising nausea.

Brass and wood and iron had become throbbing
flesh. Levers and controls and pressure gauges were
coated with a thick, crawling slime. The roof and sides
of the cabin were moving.

A huge, red, heart-like mass pulsed and shimmered
wetly in the center of the cabin, its sickly crimson glow
illuminating his face.

He did not hesitate.

Ventry reached into the knapsack, pulled out an
explosive charge, and set the device for manual. All
he needed to do was press a metal switch, toss the
charge at the heart-thing, and jump from the cabin.

It was over. He'd won!

But before he could act, the entire chamber heaved
up in a bubbled, convulsing pincer movement, trap-
ping Ventry like a fly in a web.

He writhed in the jellied grip of the train-thing. The
explosive device had been jarred from his grasp. The
axe, too, was lost in the mass of crushing slime-tissue.

Ventry felt sharp pain fire along his back. *Teeth!*
The thing had sprouted rows of needled teeth and was
starting to eat him alive!

The knapsack; he was still wearing it!

Gasping, dizzy with pain. Ventry plunged his right
hand into the sack, closing bloodied fingers around the
second explosive device. Pulled it loose, set it ticking.

Sixty seconds.

If he could not fight free in that space of time he'd
go up with the train. A far better way to die than
being ripped apart and devoured. Death would be a
welcome release.

Incredibly, the train-thing seemed to *know* that its
life was in jeopardy. Its shocked tissues drew back,
cringing away from the ticking explosive charge.

Ventry fell to his knees on the slimed floor.

Thirty seconds.

He saw the sudden gleam of rails to his right, just

below him, and he launched himself in a plunging dive through the severed membrane.

Struck ground. Searing pain. Right shoulder. Broken bone.

Hell with it! *Move, damn you, move!*

Ventry rolled over on his stomach, pain lacing his body. Pushed himself up. Standing now.

Five seconds.

Ventry sprawled forward. *Legs won't support me!*

Then *crawl!*

Into heavy brush. Still crawling—dragging his lacerated, slime-smeared body toward a covering of rocks.

Faster! No more time. . . . Too late!

The night became sudden day.

The explosion picked up Ventry and tossed him into the rocks like a boneless doll.

The train-thing screamed in a whistling death-agony as the concussion sundered it, scattering its parts like wet confetti over the terrain.

Gobbets of bleeding tissue rained down on Ventry as he lay in the rocks. But through the pain and the stench and the nausea his lips were curved into a thin smile.

He was unconscious when the Montana sun rose that morning, but when Sheriff John Longbow arrived on the scene he found Paul Ventry alive.

Alive and triumphant.

VANDY, VANDY

Manly Wade Wellman

MANLY WADE WELLMAN (1903–1986) got his start in the pulps, contributing science fiction to *Weird Tales* and *Astounding Stories* as early as 1927. He is best known, however, for his fantasy stories, many of which involve paranormal investigators. During the 1950s, several stories about a Southern balladeer simply named John appeared in the *Magazine of Fantasy and Science Fiction*. It is these stories which remain among his finest works.

Nary name that valley had. Such outside folks as knew about it just said, "Back in yonder," and folks inside said, "Here." The mail truck would drop a few letters in a hollow tree next to a ridge where the trail went up and over and down. Three-four times a year bearded men in homemade clothes and shoes fetched out their makings—clay dishes and pots, mostly—for dealers to sell to the touristers. They toted back coffee, salt, gunpowder, a few nails. Stuff like that.

It was a day's scramble along that ridge trail. I vow, even with my long legs and no load but my silver-strung guitar. The thick, big old trees had never been

22

cut, for lumber nor yet for cleared land. I found a
stream, quenched my thirst, and followed it down.
Near sunset time, I heard music a-jangling, and
headed for that.

Fire shone out through an open cabin door, to
where folks sat on a stoop log and front-yard rocks.
One had a banjo, another fiddled, and the rest slapped
hands so a boy about ten or twelve could jig. Then
they spied me and fell quiet. They looked at me, but
they didn't know me.

"That was right pretty, ladies and gentlemen," I
said, walking in, but nobody remarked.

A long-bearded old man with one suspender and
no shoes held the fiddle on his knee. I reckoned he
was the grandsire. A younger, shorter-bearded man
with the banjo might could be his son. There was a
dry old mother, there was the son's plump wife, there
was a young yellow-haired girl, and there was that
dancing little grandboy.

"What can we do for you, young sir?" the old man
asked. Not that he sounded like doing aught—mountain folks say that even to the government man who
comes hunting a still on their place.

"Why," I said, "I sort of want a place to sleep."

"Right much land to stretch out on down the hollow
a piece," said the banjo man.

I tried again. "I was hearing you folks play first part
of *Fire in the Mountains.*"

"Is they two parts?" That was the boy, before anyone could silence him.

"Sure enough, son," I said. "I'll play you the second part."

The old man opened his beard, like enough to say
wait till I was asked, but I strummed my guitar into
second part, best I knew how. Then I played the first
part through, and, "You sure God can pick that," said
the short-bearded one. "Do it again."

I did it again. When I reached the second part, the
fiddle and banjo joined me in. We went round *Fire in
the Mountains* one time more, and the lady-folks

clapped hands and the boy jigged. When we stopped, the old man made me a nod.

"Sit on that there rock," he said. "What might we call you?"

"My name's John."

"I'm Tewk Millen. Mother, I reckon John's a-tired, coming from outside. Might be he'd relish a gourd of cold water."

"We're just before having a bite," the old lady said to me. "Ain't but just smoke meat and beans, but you're welcome."

"I'm sure enough honored, Mrs. Millen," I said. "But I don't wish to be a trouble to you."

"No trouble," said Mr. Tewk Millen. "Let me make you known to my son Heber and his wife Jill, and this here is their boy Calder."

"Proud to know you, John," they said.

"And my girl Vandy," said Mr. Tewk.

I looked on her hair like yellow corn silk and her eyes like purple violets. "Miss Vandy," I said.

Shy, she dimpled at me. "I know that's a scarce name, Mr. John. I never heard it anywhere but among my kinfolks."

"I have," I said. "It's what brought me here."

Mr. Tewk Millen looked funny above his whiskers. "Thought you was a young stranger-man."

"I heard the name outside, in a song, sir. Somebody allowed the song's known here. I'm a singer, I go a far piece after a good song." I looked around. "Do you folks know that Vandy song?"

"Yes, sir," said little Calder, but the others studied a minute. Mr. Tewk rubbed up a leaf of tobacco into his pipe.

"Calder," he said, "go in and fetch me a chunk of fire to light up with. John, you certain sure you never met my girl Vandy?"

"Sure as can be," I replied him. "Only I can figure how any young fellow might come long miles to meet her."

She stared down at her hands in her lap. "We learnt

the song from papa," she half-whispered, "and he
learnt it from his papa."

"And my papa learnt it from his," finished Mr.
Tewk for her. "I reckon that song goes long years
back."

"I'd relish hearing it," I said.

"After you learnt it yourself," said Mr. Tewk, "what
would you do then?"

"Go back outside," I said, "and sing it some."

He enjoyed to hear me say that. "Heber," he told
his son, "you pick out and I'll scrape this fiddle, and
Calder and Vandy can sing it for John."

They played the tune through once without words.
The notes came together lonesomely, in what schooled
folks call minors. But other folks, better schooled yet,
say such tunes come out strange and lonesome because in the ancient times folks had another note-scale
from our do-re-mi-fa today. Little Calder piped up,
high and young but strong:

> "Vandy, Vandy, I've come to court you,
> Be you rich or be you poor,
> And if you'll kindly entertain me,
> I will love you forever more.
>
> "Vandy, Vandy, I've gold and silver,
> Vandy, Vandy, I've a house and land,
> Vandy, Vandy, I've a world of pleasure,
> I would make you a handsome man. . . ."

He sang that far for the fellow come courting, and
Vandy sang back the reply, sweet as a bird:

> "I love a man who's in the army,
> He's been there for seven long years,
> And if he's there for seven years longer,
> I won't court no other dear.
>
> "What care I for your gold and silver,
> What care I for—"

She stopped, and the fiddle and banjo stopped, and it was like the sudden death of sound. The leaves didn't rustle in the trees, nor the fire didn't stir on the hearth inside. They all looked with their mouths half open, where somebody stood with his hands crossed on the gold knob of a black cane and grinned all on one side of his toothy mouth.

Maybe he'd come down the stream trail, maybe he'd dropped from a tree like a possum. He was built slim and spry, with a long coat buttoned to his pointed chin, and brown pants tucked into elastic-sided boots, like what your grand-sire wore. His hands on the cane looked slim and strong. His face, bar its crooked smile, might could be called handsome. His dark brown hair curled like buffalo wool, and his eyes were as shiny pale gray as a new knife. Their gaze crawled all over us, and he laughed a slow, soft laugh.

"I thought I'd stop by," he crooned out, "if I haven't worn out my welcome."

"Oh, *no,* sir!" said Mr. Tewk, quick standing up on his two bare feet, fiddle in hand. "No, sir, Mr. Loden, we're right proud to have you," he jabber-squawked, like a rooster caught by the leg. "You sit down, sir, make yourself easy."

Mr. Loden sat down on the rock Mr. Tewk had got up from, and Mr. Tewk found a place on the stoop log by his wife, nervous as a boy caught stealing apples.

"Your servant, Mrs. Millen," said Mr. Loden. "Heber, you look well, and your good wife. Calder, I brought you candy."

His slim hand offered a bright striped stick, red and yellow. You'd think a country child would snatch it. But Calder took it slow and scared, as he'd take a poison snake. You'd know he'd decline if only he dared, but he didn't dare.

"For you, Mr. Tewk," went on Mr. Loden, "I fetched some of my tobacco, an excellent weed." He handed out a soft brown leather pouch. "Empty your pipe and fill it with this."

"Thank you kindly," said Mr. Tewk, and sighed, and began to do as he'd been ordered.

"Miss Vandy." Mr. Loden's crooning voice petted her name. "I wouldn't venture here without hoping you'd receive a trifle at my hands."

He dangled it from a chain, a gold thing the size of his pink thumbnail. In it shone a white jewel that grabbed the firelight and twinkled red.

"Do me the honor, Miss Vandy, to let it rest on your heart, that I may envy it."

She took the thing and sat with it between her soft little hands. Mr. Loden's eye-knives turned on me.

"Now," he said, "we come round to the stranger within your gates."

"We come around to me," I agreed him, hugging my guitar on my knees. "My name's John, sir."

"Where are you from, John?" It was sudden, almost fierce, like a lawyer in court.

"From nowhere," I said.

"Meaning, from everywhere," he supplied me. "What do you do?"

"I wander," I said. "I sing songs. I mind my business and watch my manners."

"*Touché!*" he cried out in a foreign tongue, and smiled on that one side of his mouth. "My duties and apologies, John, if my country ways seem rude to a world traveler. No offense meant."

"None taken," I said, and didn't add that country ways are most times polite ways.

"Mr. Loden," put in Mr. Tewk again, "I make bold to offer you what poor rations my old woman's made for us—"

"They're good enough for the best man living," Mr. Loden broke him off. "I'll help Mrs. Millen prepare them. After you, ma'am."

She walked in, and he followed. What he said there was what happened.

"Miss Vandy," he said over his shoulder, "you might help."

She went in, too. Dishes clattered. Through the

doorway I saw Mr. Loden fling a tweak of powder in the skillet. The menfolks sat outside and said naught. They might have been nailed down, with stones in their mouths. I studied what might could make a proud, honorable mountain family so scared of a guest, and knew it wouldn't be a natural thing. It would be a thing beyond nature or the world.

Finally little Calder said, "Maybe we'll finish the singing after while," and his voice was a weak young voice now.

"I recollect another song from around here," I said. "About the fair and blooming wife."

Those closed mouths all snapped open, then shut again. Touching the silver strings, I began:

> "There was a fair and blooming wife
> And of children she had three,
> She sent them to a Northern school
> To study gramarie.
>
> "But the King's men came upon that school,
> And when sword and rope had done,
> Of the children three she sent away,
> Returned to her but one. . . ."

"Supper's made," said Mrs. Millen from inside.

We went in to where there was a trestle table and a clean home-woven cloth and clay dishes set out. Mr. Loden, by the pots at the fire, waved for Mrs. Millen and Vandy to dish up the food.

It wasn't smoke meat and beans I saw on my plate. Whatever it might be, it wasn't that. They all looked at their helps of food, but not even Calder took any till Mr. Loden sat down.

"Why," said Mr. Loden, "one would think you feared poison."

Then Mr. Tewk forked up a bit and put it into his beard. Calder did likewise, and the others. I took a mouthful; sure enough, it tasted good.

"Let me honor your cooking, sir," I told Mr. Loden. "It's like witch magic."

His eyes came on me, and he laughed, short and sharp.

"John, you were singing about the blooming wife," he said. "She had three children who went North to study gramarie. Do you know what gramarie means?"

"Grammar," spoke up Calder. "The right way to talk."

"Hush," whispered his father, and he hushed.

"Why," I replied. "Mr. Loden, I've heard that gramarie is witch stuff, witch knowledge and power. That Northern school could have been at only one place."

"What place, John?" he almost sang under his breath.

"A Massachusetts Yankee town called Salem. Around three hundred years back—"

"Not by so much," said Mr. Loden. "In 1692, John."

Everybody was staring above those steaming plates.

"A preacher-man named Cotton Mather found them teaching the witch stuff to children," I said. "I hear tell they killed twenty folks, mostly the wrong ones, but two-three were sure enough witches."

"George Burroughs," said Mr. Loden, half to himself. "Martha Carrier. And Bridget Bishop. They were real. But others got safe away, and one young child of the three. Somebody owed that child the two young lost lives of his brothers, John."

"I call something else to mind," I said. "They scare young folks with the tale. The one child lived to be a hundred, and his son likewise and a hundred years of life, and his son's son a hundred more. Maybe that's why I thought the witch school at Salem was three hundred years back."

"Not by so much, John," he said again. "Even give that child that got away the age of Calder there, it would be only about two hundred and eighty years, or thereabouts."

He was daring any of Mr. Tewk Millen's family to speak or even breathe heavy, and none took the dare.

"From three hundred, that would leave twenty," I reckoned. "A lot can be done in twenty years, Mr. Loden."

"That's the naked truth," he said, the knives of his eyes on Vandy's young face, and he got up and bowed all round. "I thank you all for your hospitality. I'll come again if I may."

"Yes, sir," said Mr. Tewk in a hurry, but Mr. Loden looked at Vandy and waited.

"Yes, sir," she told him, as if it would choke her.

He took his gold-headed cane, and gazed a hard gaze at me. Then I did a rude thing, but it was all I could think of.

"I don't feel right, Mrs. Millen, not paying for what you gave me," I allowed, getting up myself. From my dungaree pocket I took a silver quarter and dropped it on the table, right in front of Mr. Loden.

"Take it away!" he squeaked, high as a bat, and out of the house he was gone, bat-quick and bat-sudden.

The others gopped after him, Outside the night had fallen, thick as black wool round the cabin. Mr. Tewk cleared his throat.

"John, I hope you're better raised than that," he said. "We don't take money from nobody we bid to our table. Pick it up."

"Yes, sir, I ask pardon."

Putting away the quarter, I felt a mite better. I'd done that one other time with a silver quarter, I'd scared Mr. Onselm almost out of the black art. So Mr. Loden was a witch man, too, and could be scared the same way. I reckon I was foolish for the lack of sense to think it would be as easy as that.

I walked outside, leaving Mrs. Millen and Vandy to do the dishes. The firelight showed me the stoop log to sit on. I touched my guitar strings and began to pick out the *Vandy, Vandy* tune, soft and gentle. After while, Calder came out and sat beside me and sang the words. I liked best the last verse.

"Wake up, wake up! The dawn is breaking.
Wake up, wake up! It's almost day.
Open up your doors and your divers windows,
See my true love march away. . . ."

"Mr. John," said Calder, "I never made sure what divers windows is."

"That's an old-timey word," I said. "It means different kinds of windows. Another thing proves it's a right old song. A man seven years in the army must have gone to the first war with the English. It lasted longer here in the South than other places—from 1775 to 1782. How old are you, Calder?"

"Rising onto ten."

"Big for your age. A boy your years in 1692 would be a hundred if he lived to 1782, when the English war was near done and somebody or other had been seven years in the army."

"Washington's army," said Calder. "King Washington."

"King who?" I asked.

"Mr. Loden calls him King Washington—the man that hell-drove the English soldiers and rules in his own name town."

So that's what they thought in that valley. I never said that Washington was no king but a president, and that he'd died and gone to his rest when his work was done and his country safe. I kept thinking about somebody a hundred years old in 1782, trying to court a girl whose true love was seven years marched off in the army.

"Calder," I said, "does the *Vandy, Vandy* song tell about your own folks?"

He looked into the cabin. Nobody listened. I struck a chord on the silver strings. He said, "I've heard tell so, Mr. John."

I hushed the strings with my hand, and he talked on:

"I reckon you've heard some about it. That witch child that lived to be a hundred—he come courting a girl named Vandy, but she was a good girl."

"Bad folks sometimes try to court good ones," I said.

"She wouldn't have him, not with all his land and money. And when he pressed her, her soldier man come home, and in his hand was his discharge-writing, and on it King Washington's name. He was free from the war. He was Hosea Tewk, my grandsire some few times removed. And my own grandsire's mother was Vandy Tewk, and my sister is Vandy Millen."

"What about the hundred-year-old witch man?"

Calder looked round again. Then he said, "I reckon he got him some other girl to birth him a son, and we think that son married at another hundred years, and his son is Mr. Loden, the grandson of the first witch man."

"Your grandsire's mother, Vandy Tewk—how old would she be, Calder?"

"She's dead and gone, but she was born the first year her pa was off fighting the Yankees."

Eighteen sixty-one, then. In 1882, end of the second hundred years, she'd have been ripe for courting. "And she married a Millen," I said.

"Yes, sir. Even when the Mr. Loden that lived then tried to court her. But she married Mr. Washington Millen. That was my great-grandsire. He wasn't feared of aught. He was like King Washington."

I picked a silver string. "No witch man got the first Vandy," I reminded him. "Nor yet the second Vandy."

"A witch man wants the Vandy that's here now," said Calder. "Mr. John, I wish you'd steal her away from him."

I got up. "Tell your folks I've gone for a night walk."

"Not to Mr. Loden's." His face was pale beside me. "He won't let you come."

The night was more than black then, it was solid. No sound in it. No life. I won't say I couldn't have stepped off into it, but I didn't. I sat down again. Mr. Tewk spoke my name, then Vandy.

We sat in front of the cabin and spoke about weather and crops. Vandy was at my one side, Calder at the other. We sang—*Dream True,* I recollect, and *The Rebel Soldier.* Vandy sang the sweetest I'd ever heard, but while I played I felt that somebody harked in the blackness. If it was on Yandro Mountain and not in the valley, I'd have feared the Behinder sneaking close, or the Flat under our feet. But Vandy's violet eyes looked happy at me, her rose lips smiled.

Finally Vandy and Mrs. Millen said good night and went into a back room. Heber and his wife and Calder laddered up into the loft. Mr. Tewk offered to make me a pallet bed by the fire.

"I'll sleep at the door," I told him.

He looked at me, at the door. And: "Have it your way," he said.

I pulled off my shoes. I said a prayer and stretched out on the quilt he gave me. But long after the others must have been sleeping, I lay and listened.

Hours afterward, the sound came. The fire was just only a coal ember, red light was soft in the cabin when I heard the snicker. Mr. Loden stooped over me at the door sill.

"I won't let you come in," I said to him.

"Oh, you're awake," he said. "The others are asleep, by my doing. And you can't move, any more than they can."

It was true. I couldn't sit up. I might have been dried into clay, like a frog or a lizard that must wait for the rain.

"Bind," he said above me. "Bind, bind. Unless you can count the stars or the ocean drops, be bound."

It was a spell saying. "From the *Long-Lost Friend?*" I asked.

"Albertus Magnus. The book they say he wrote."

"I've seen the book."

"You'll lie where you are till sunrise. Then—"

I tried to get up. It was no use.

"See this?" He held it to my face. It was my picture,

drawn true to how I looked. He had the drawing gift. "At sunrise I'll strike it with this."

He laid the picture on the ground. Then he brought forward his gold-headed cane. He twisted the handle, and out of the cane's inside he drew a blade of pale iron, thin and mean as a snake. There was writing on it, but I couldn't read in that darkness.

"I'll touch my point to your picture," he said. "Then you'll bother Vandy and me no more. I should have done that to Hosea Tewk."

"Hosea Tewk," I said after him, "or Washington Millen."

The tip of his blade stirred in front of my eyes. "Don't say that name, John."

"Washington Millen," I said it again. "Named for George Washington. Did you hate Washington when you knew him?"

He took a long, mean breath, as if cold rain fell on him. "You've guessed what these folks haven't guessed, John."

"I've guessed you're not a witch man's grandson, but a witch woman's son," I said. "You got free from that Salem school in 1692. You've lived near three hundred years, and when they're over, you know where you'll go and burn, forever amen."

His blade hung over my throat, like a wasp over a ripe peach. Then he drew it back. "No," he told himself. "The Millens would know I'd stabbed you. Let them think you died in your sleep."

"You knew Washington," I said again. "Maybe—"

"Maybe I offered him help, and he was foolish enough to refuse it. Maybe—"

"Maybe Washington scared you off from him," I broke in the way he had, "and won his war without your witch magic. And maybe that was bad for you, because the one who'd given you three hundred years expected pay—good hearts turned into bad ones. Then you tried to win Vandy for yourself, the first Vandy."

"A little for myself," he half sang, "but mostly for—"

"Mostly for who gave you three hundred years," I finished for him.

I was tightening and swelling my muscles, trying to pull a-loose from what held me down. I might as well have tried to wear my way through solid rock.

"Vandy," Mr. Loden's voice touched her name. "The third Vandy, the sweetest and the best. She's like a spring day and like a summer night. When I see her with a bucket at the spring or a basket in the garden, my eyes swim, John. It's as if I see a spirit walking past."

"A good spirit," I said. "Your time's short. You want to win her from good ways to bad ways."

"Her voice is like a lark's," he crooned, the blade low in his hand. "It's like wind over a bank of roses and violets. It's like the light of stars turned into music."

"And you want to lead her down into hell," I said.

"Maybe we won't go to hell, or to heaven either. Maybe we'll live and live. Why don't you say something about that, John?"

"I'm thinking," I made answer, and I was. I was trying to remember what I had to remember.

It's in the third part of the Albertus Magnus book Mr. Loden had mentioned, the third part full of holy names he sure enough would never read. I'd seen it, as I'd told him. If the words would come back to me—
Something sent part of them.

"The cross in my right hand," I said, too soft for him to hear, "that I may travel the open land. . . ."

"Maybe three hundred years more," said Mr. Loden, "without anyone like Hosea Tewk, or Washington Millen, or you, John, to stop us. Three hundred years with Vandy, and she'll know the things I know, do the things I do."

I'd been able to twist my right forefinger over my middle one, for the cross in my right hand. I said more words as I remembered:

". . . So must I be loosed and blessed, as the cup and the holy bread. . . ."

Now my left hand could creep along my side, as far as my belt. But it couldn't lift up just yet, because I couldn't think of the rest of the charm.

"The night's black just before dawn," Mr. Loden was saying. "I'll make my fire. When I've done what I'll do, I can step over your dead body, and Vandy's mine."

"Don't you fear Washington?" I asked him, and my left fingertips were in my dungaree pocket.

"Can he come from the place to which he's gone? Washington has forgotten me and our old falling-out."

"Where he is, he remembers you," I said.

Mr. Loden was on his knee. His blade point scratched a circle round him on the ground. The circle held him and the paper with my picture. Then he took a sack from inside his coat, and poured powder along the scratched circle. He stood up, and golden-brown fire jumped up around him.

"Now we begin," he said.

He sketched in the air with his blade. He put his boot toe on my picture. He looked into the golden-brown fire.

"I made my wish before this," he spaced out the words. "I make it now. There was no day when I have not seen my wish fulfilled."

Paler than the fire shone his eyes.

"No son to follow John. No daughter to mourn him."

My fingers in my pocket touched something round and thin. The quarter he'd been scared by, that Mr. Tewk Millen had made me take back.

Mr. Loden spoke names I didn't like to hear. "Haade," he said. "Mikaded. Rakeben. Rika. Tasarith. Modeka."

My hand worried out, and in it the quarter.

"Truth," said Mr. Loden. "Tumch. Here with this image I slay—"

I lifted my left hand three inches and flung the quarter. My heart went rotten with sick sorrow, for it didn't hit Mr. Loden—it fell into the fire—

Then in one place up there shot white smoke, like a steam puff from an engine, and the fire died down everywhere else. Mr. Loden stopped his spell-speaking and wavered back. I saw the glow of his goggling eyes and of his open mouth.

Where the steamy smoke had puffed, it was making a shape.

Taller than a man. Taller than Mr. Loden or me. Wide-shouldered, long-legged, with a dark tail coat and high boots and hair tied back behind the head. It turned, and I saw the brave face, the big, big nose—

"King Washington!" screamed out Mr. Loden, and tried to stab.

But a long hand like a tongs caught his wrist, and I heard the bones break like dry sticks, and Mr. Loden whinnied like a horse that's been bad hurt. That was the grip of the man who'd been America's strongest, who could jump twenty-four feet broad or throw a dollar across the Rappahannock River or wrestle down his biggest soldier.

The other hand came across, flat and stiff, to strike. It sounded like a door a-slamming in a high wind, and Mr. Loden never needed to be struck the second time. His head sagged over widewise. When the grip left his broken wrist, he fell at the booted feet.

I sat up, and stood up. The big nose turned to me, just a second. The head nodded. Friendly. Then it was gone back into steam, into nothing.

I'd said the truth. Where George Washington had been, he'd remembered Mr. Loden. And the silver quarter, with his picture on it, had struck the fire just when Mr. Loden was conjuring with a picture he was making real. And then there had happened what had happened.

A pale streak went up the back sky for the first dawn. There was no fire left, and of the quarter was just a spatter of melted silver. And there was no Mr. Loden, only a mouldy little heap like a rotted-out stump or a hammock or loam or what might could be left of a man that death had caught up with after two hundred years. I picked up the iron blade and broke it on my knee and flung it away into the trees. Then I picked up the paper with my drawn picture. It wasn't hurt a bit, and it looked a right much like me.

Inside the door I put that picture, on the quilt where I'd lain. Maybe the Millens would keep it to remember me by, after they found I was gone and that Mr. Loden came round no more to try to court Vandy. Then I started away, carrying my guitar. If I made good time, I'd be out of the valley by high noon.

As I went, pots started to rattle. Somebody was awake in the cabin. And it was hard, hard, not to turn back when Vandy sang to herself, not thinking what she sang:

"Wake up, wake up! The dawn is breaking.
Wake up, wake up! It's almost day.
Open up your doors and your divers windows,
See my true love march away. . . ."

THE GHOST PATROL

Ron Goulart

RON GOULART writes in many genres, often blending different elements together, but is primarily considered a science fiction writer. His worlds range from southern California to a solar system named Barnum, which was serialized in the comic strip *Star Hawks*, with Goulart writing and Gil Kane drawing the strip. Whatever the story, Goulart takes present human trends and fears and extends them to the worst possible degree, often with humorous side effects.

The picket sign abandoned in front of the clinic doorway read: LET'S GET RID OF FREE-LOADING AND BLACK MAGIC. When Max Kearny lifted it out of the way, an empty fortified wine bottle, shielded by a paper sack, somersaulted down the three brick steps of the clinic. Max rested the sign against the green stucco and reached for the door handle.

The door fanned suddenly open and a middle-aged man in a dark suit came bicycling out backwards. The man thumped into Max, and a tall square-jawed man in the uniform of the Northwest Mounted Police reached out for him. The man in the dark suit adjusted his rimless glasses. The mountie waited, then hit the man on the nose and heaved him down to the street. Dusting his hands together, the mountie went back inside.

Max jumped to the sidewalk and gripped the dark-suited man up to a standing position. The man adjusted his glasses and said, "Why don't you get a job?"

"Beg pardon?"

"Do a decent day's work," said the man, "and don't come begging for free handouts. Pay for getting ill like any decent sick American."

Max said, "I have a job. I'm an art director with an advertising agency in San Francisco and I'm driving through San Marco to check on some dog food billboards."

"Oh, one of those intellectuals," the man said. "I knew you had some reason for loitering around Dr. Levin's freeload clinic for bums."

"I wasn't loitering," said Max. "Dr. Levin is a friend of mine and I was just walking in when the mounted police threw you out."

"I haven't time to argue. Captain Pennington's in there and needs me."

Max went up the steps again, beside the man. "Who's Captain Pennington?"

"We get used to such uninformed questions. It's because of the news blackout the so-called lords of the press have imposed on the Freeload Prevention Society. Too, too few know about the captain and our crusade."

"You're protesting Dr. Levin's starting this free clinic in the tenderloin here?"

"We protest any and all free-loading."

The door slapped open and a second dark-suited man, tall and red-headed, tumbled out backwards. A fat, rumpled man with grey hair held him by the collar and crotch. "Scoundrel, scalawag, hyena," said the rumpled old man. He jettisoned the redhead.

Max said to the freeload man, "Is that Captain Pennington who just went by?"

"Yes. If we had a better press, you'd have known him at once."

"Are you guys going to attack again?"

"No. We only went in because one of them grabbed our best placard."

"Off, off, you wrongos," ordered the rumpled man. "You lily-livered scamps." He squinted his left eye at Max. "You another three-suited viper?"

Max said, "Nope. Friend of Dr. Levin's. Is he around?"

"Max?" called a voice from the hallway. "Come on in. Quick."

The pale green corridor smelled of rubbing alcohol and sweet wine. "You have a varied staff, Hal," said Max.

Dr. Harold Levin was thin, with curly dark hair and tortoise-shell glasses. "Step into this disrobing room, Max. We can talk." He rubbed his chin, looked at the rumpled old man. "I told you not to hit any of them."

"I didn't come by my nickname by depending on pansy language."

"Never mind our nickname," said Dr. Levin. "Go away now. I don't need any help."

"That decayed bunch of goons will try again."

"All of you," said Levin. "I'm doing okay. I don't want a big frumus."

"Nobody can browbeat a friend of Roundhouse Widder's," said the old man.

"Hey," said Max. "Joe 'Roundhouse' Widder was a senator from Indiana or someplace. Back in the 1910s and 1920s. He died before World War II."

"He's kidding, Max," said Levin.

"The hell I am," said Widder. "There's only one Roundhouse Widder and I'm it. Maybe a good punch in the snout will convince your dude friend."

"I believe you," said Max. "How come you have this ghost here, Hal?"

"In here where it's private, Max. See, my nurse is in the reception room over there, and she can hear most of what's said in my office. Roundhouse, you and the rest, go away now."

Widder made a mild raspberry sound and melted into nothingness.

"Was the clinic haunted when you moved in?" asked Max.

Dr. Levin opened a pale green door and flicked on a light switch. He went into the small room and sat on a white cabinet. "Max, I know your hobby is occult investigation. You're a ghost detective, okay. But I don't want any help."

Max leaned against the wall next to a scale. "It's only a hobby anyway. Up to you. Who are those others, the Freeload Prevention guys?"

"Did April send you over, Max?"

"No. I haven't talked to her since the last time you two were over to our flat."

Levin said, "Sorry. She lets all this upset her too much. Setting up this clinic, Max, getting the private funds and all. We've been under a lot of pressure. Pennington, the one with the red hair, he and a couple of other guys come around and picket. They picket anything that smacks of socialism to them. The San Marco police shoo them away, but Pennington is an ex-Navy man, and the cops don't lean too hard."

"Has Pennington tried anything physical?"

"Not so far," said Dr. Levin. "You know how California is these days, Max. Pennington is just another lunatic. They'll get tired once the clinic has been here awhile. What brings you to San Marco?"

"Had to take a look at some billboards, so I drove down from the city," said Max. "That mountie. He's a ghost, too, isn't he?"

"More or less," said Levin. "Hey, I think April was going to call Jillian and ask you folks over for dinner this week. Free?"

"I'll see what Jillian says. You in the same house?"

"Right. It's easier to find now because you can follow the signs to Yankee Doodle Acres and then continue on over the rise to our place."

"Yankee Doodle Acres?" asked Max. "Oh, yeah, that's the new patriotic housing development."

Levin shrugged. "You know how California is these days. Pennington lives there, of course." Checking his watch he said, "I've got a backup on patients, Max. Maybe we'll see you and Jill on Friday." A white phone on a white table rang. "Just a second. Hello, Hal Levin here. Mom, I can't talk to you much now. Yes, they were picketing today. They don't hurt me any, Mom. When? Friday, Mom, we can't. April and I will probably have company. What? Max and Jillian Kearny. No, it's only a hobby; he's not a full-time ghost detective. He's an art director, Mom." Levin cupped his hand over the mouthpiece. "It's my mother, Max." Back into the phone he said, "Mom, I can't take you to the wrestling matches Friday. What custom? Mom, I've been married two years and never since then have I taken you. One Friday in August last year? No, Mom. Mom, listen, I have to see some patients. They're fine. Okay, goodbye. Love." He hung up. "My mother, Max. Maybe we'll see you Friday night."

Max started for the door, snapped his fingers and stopped. "Russ Knobler. That's who the mounted police guy was. He was in the movies in the '30s, killed himself about twenty years back. Russ Knobler, sure. We used to see him in Saturday matinees."

"Yes," said Dr. Levin, working Max toward the exit.

"Does he always appear as a mountie?"

"No," said Levin. "Sometimes he's a lumberjack."

The front door opened and closed, and Max was on the steps again.

The Levins' backyard covered nearly a quarter acre of thick grass and wild brush and scattered trees. Twilight was slowly spreading. April Levin stood with her back to the sunset and mixed Max a second gin and tonic. She was a tall, long-legged brunette with short-cropped hair. Max leaned forward in his weathered deck chair and said, "I don't want to intrude."

"He's being haunted, Max. As a ghost detective you can't stand by and watch that. It would be against your code."

"We don't have an oath like doctors, April."

"Hal's your friend."

"Ever since he was working for the agency medical plan," said Max. He glanced at Levin, who was showing Max's wife the Victorian sundial he was refurbishing for the yard. "How many ghosts are there?"

"I've only seen the whole bunch once," said April, sitting on a low wrought-iron bench. "They spend most of their time hanging around Hal's new free clinic. But they were here one time when that nitwit Pennington came by in a red-white-and-blue sound truck. Anyhow, there seem to be three of them."

"What does Hal say?"

"Nothing much."

"They're trying to help Hal," said Max. "Defend him against the Freeload Prevention boys."

"I guess," sighed April.

"One of the ghosts is an old senator, Joe Widder. The other one I saw down in the tenderloin was Russ Knobler, the movie hero. Know the third?"

"William Barbee Platt."

"Platt? He was the physical-culture philosopher. Got killed on his 90th birthday while skydiving." Max paused to taste his drink. "Why these three I wonder?"

"That's easy."

"Oh? Some connection with Hal?"

"They're the three favorite idols of Hal's mom," said April. She rose to start herself a fresh drink. "I've heard considerable about them in the last two years. They're three out of four of Mom Levin's heroes. The fourth of which is still alive."

Jillian and Levin returned to the round metal table that held the liquor and ice bucket. "We ought to have a sundial," said Max's auburn-haired wife.

"With our lease we couldn't keep one in the apartment."

"I had a chance," said Levin, sitting, "to buy a real buggy. The kind country doctors used to ride around in. I let it pass."

"You don't make house calls anyway," said Max.

"Things don't always have to be completely functional," said Jillian. "For instance, we could put a sundial in our living room, Max, and use it as a table."

"The gnomon would get in the way," said Levin. "That's the part that casts the shadow, Jill."

"We could just look at it."

From a distance, through the oncoming night, a voice announced, "There's no place in a free republic for freeloading. No place in a pragmatic society for black magic and witchcraft."

"Pennington?" asked Max, as he stood.

"It's actually Mr. Weehunt," said April. She moved to Levin's side and took his hand. "Pennington drives the truck and Weehunt talks."

"Damn," said Levin. "The cops told them to stop that."

"He's a veteran," said April.

"So am I," said Levin, "and I don't have a loudspeaker."

"Why," asked Jillian, "does he throw in the black magic stuff?"

"He thinks Hal has summoned up all the ghosts," said April.

"Did you?" Jillian asked the doctor.

"It's not a good idea to have your neighbors think you're a warlock," said Levin, not answering Jillian.

"Let's go talk to him," said Max.

April said, "Be careful, Max. They say he's a gun collector, too. Has a whole cache of them hidden at his home over in Yankee Doodle Acres."

"No need for you to fear none, mam," said Russ Knobler, stepping out of a cluster of shadowy trees. He was dressed as the deputy sheriff of Tombstone. "We'll settle this hombre."

"Go away," said Levin, angrily.

Around Knobler came a giant old man in a shaggy lion skin. "Sit yourself down, Harold, and take your ease," he said in a rumbling, rolling voice. "We'll settle those fellows."

"Where do you guys change clothes?" Max asked Knobler when the cowboy passed him.

"I can't rightly bring back no information from the other side of the veil," drawled Knobler.

Levin put the palms of his hands against the chests of Knobler and William Barbee Platt. "Go back on the other side of the veil quick. I can't keep explaining you to the police."

"Trust us, pard," said Knobler. He brushed Levin out of his path and ran around the side of the house, spurs tinkling, toward the street. Platt followed him, and Max followed them both.

Parked at the curb of the tree-lined street was a sound truck painted in patriotic colors and designs. Mr. Weehunt, who was the man Max had had thrown at him in front of the clinic, had stepped out of the truck and was talking over the amplifiers while standing on the sidewalk. "I was deathly sick for five long months in 1964 with a slipped disc, and I paid for it all out of my savings. George Washington would have done the same thing. To say nothing of Warren G. Harding. Let's rid the community of freeloaders, and while we're at it, let's throw out the wizards and witches and softies and people who don't take baths often enough."

A police car slowed and parked quietly nose-to-nose with the Pennington truck. A heavyset, medium tall plain-clothes man grunted carefully out. "Mr. Weehunt, Captain Pennington, please go home."

"Let's also get rid of state and federal interference with the fundamental rights of free citizens," added Weehunt.

Platt adjusted his lion skin and charged the Freeload Prevention man. "Let us see who's a softie, you jowly meat-eater."

"No violence, please," said the policeman. He paused, got out a handkerchief and sneezed into it. "These trees," he said to Max, who was nearest him. "Every autumn."

"Ease yourself on down out of that there truck now," Knobler called to Pennington, whose thin hands were still tight on the steering wheel. "Let's us settle this little fracas, pard."

"I'll get out," said Pennington in a high taut voice. He flung the truck open and began tugging a bazooka out of the rear. "I'll get out."

"Please, Captain Pennington," said the policeman, "put that thing back in there and we'll pretend we didn't see it."

"A bazooka," said Max.

"Fight fair," said Knobler, thumbing the brim of his sombrero up.

Closing in on Pennington, the policeman put his arms on his thin shoulders. "A man with a nice war record like yours, chairman of the board of such nice companies, with such nice friends downtown, Captain Pennington. Please, don't make a fuss."

"He's loosed demons on me," said Pennington. He let the weapon drop back inside his tricolor truck. "Demons and succubi and incubi and worse." He waved a thin hand at Platt and Knobler.

"A couple of eccentrics in costume," said the plain-clothes man. "Take those two back inside to your party, and I'll talk a while with the captain."

"I have more than one arrow in my bow," said Pennington. "Tell your socialized Levin that."

"Don't call my boy names." A plump woman was climbing out of a newly arrived blue station wagon. She was grey-haired, wearing a tan car coat and fawn stretch pants and carrying a small wicker hamper. "Don't call him names in a public street."

"Mom," said Levin, who appeared in the front doorway of his house now. "Mom, you're supposed to be at the wrestling matches over in San Francisco."

"The Portuguese Angel pulled a ligament and

stayed home to meditate," said Mom Levin. "So I drove over to case your situation. I see your lawn's looking sparse, Harold."

"Mom, okay, you can come inside, but you can't stay. We have company, Mom."

"Some entertaining of your friends you can do with cops and lunatics all over your sparse lawn."

"There's really no trouble," the policeman told her. "If everyone will disperse, we'll be fine." He sneezed again.

"Too much time in that dark police car and not enough sunshine," Mom Levin told him. She ticked her plump head at the pair of ghosts and went into the house.

"I reckon as how I'll let this pass," said Knobler.

"There'll be other opportunities to teach you flesh-lovers a lesson," added Platt. He took Knobler by the elbow and they strolled away into the new night.

"The suburbs," said the policeman. "People don't realize what can happen out here." He sneezed into his handkerchief.

Max found Jillian in the backyard, sitting in the dark with her hands folded in her lap. "Mom Levin's inside."

"I know."

"Talking about her favorite philosopher."

In the light thrown from the kitchen, Max found the gin and tonic he'd left unfinished. A mosquito had drowned in it. "Who is?"

"Jorge Barafunda," said his wife, discouraging a gnat from her leg.

"Who?"

"Jorge Barafunda, the Portuguese Angel."

"The wrestler," Max said. He found a new glass and started another drink.

"He's a mystic, too."

"That's right," said Max. "Wrestler, philosopher, mystic. Self-taught. Sort of a cross between Eric Hoffer and Bishop Pike."

"And he's supposed to be," said Jillian, "a medium."

"Yeah, there was a piece about it in the *Chronicle.* Mystic, spirit medium, wrestler. A Renaissance man."

"You know how California is these days," said his slim wife.

"I keep hearing." Max sat on the footrest of her deck chair. "So maybe Barafunda summoned up the ghosts of Mrs. Levin's three favorite departed heroes for her."

"Who are they?"

"William Barbee Platt, Russ Knobler and Joe 'Roundhouse' Widder. A ghost patrol to defend Hal."

"Who were they?"

"You never heard of them?"

"I'm five years younger than you, remember."

"Russ Knobler, Saturday afternoons in the late '30s and early '40s, was the king of the B movies. You never heard of *Timber Rascal, Desert Rogue, Speedway Scapegrace*?"

Jillian shook her head. "You told me about Widder on the way over here. He was a senator. And Platt?"

"Physical-culture buff, vegetarian, philosopher."

"Another Jorge Barafunda," said Jillian. "You going to talk to the Portuguese Angel?"

"I guess I will," said Max. "Nobody around here is going to tell me much."

From the kitchen window Mom Levin said, "Come inside, you two young people, before the insects give you malaria."

The sunlight through the stained-glass skylights made pastel splotches on the bare chest of the muscular old man. "Words," said Jorge Barafunda. "Words are a lousy way to think. These college people, they think in words. You take a look at my book *The Vocabulary Of Muscles,* and it's all explained in there."

"I skimmed it in the library this morning," Max told him. "It was full of words."

"They're not ready yet to publish a book that's all pictures of muscles," said Jorge. "Uhn."

"If you put down that weight we could talk better," said Max.

Jorge grunted and kept the hundred-pound weight over his head. "I lift everyday. It helps me think."

"What I was interested in," said Max, "was your work as a medium."

"Yes. That's why I granted you an interview, Senhor Kearny. I've heard of you. Some of your ghost detective work, for a relative novice, is *muito bem.* Very good."

"Did you summon up some ghosts for a Mrs. Levin?" asked Max.

"Oof," said Jorge. His left hand lost its grip on the bar of the weight, and it swung free and thwacked him in the head. "I believe I will put this down." He let the 100 pounds fall to the padded floor of his attic gymnasium. *"Sim,* Senhor Kearny. I helped Mrs. Levin. She is a great admirer of mine. Once when I battled the Grimm Brothers in a tag match, she leaped into the ring and felled one of them with her wicker basket. *Muito bem,* very good."

"You charge her a fee for conjuring up the ghosts?"

"Sim," replied the wrestler, snatching up a paisley terry towel. "Being a mystic and a philosopher without a college degree, Senhor Kearny, requires you to have many sidelines in order to make a living. You know how that is."

"Right," said Max. "Now, why don't you send those three ghosts back. Dr. Levin really doesn't want them, doesn't need them."

"I suppose he became a doctor by attending college?"

"Yes."

"College boys," said Jorge. "They don't know how to think with their muscles."

"About the ghosts?" Max asked.

The old wrestler shook his head. "I was paid my fee. I have honor, even though I don't have a diploma.

I cannot send them away. No honorable self-taught medium would, Senhor Kearny."

Max said, "Okay. It would be easier if you did. Now I'll have to exorcise them."

The Portuguese Angel laughed. "My magic isn't the usual magic. It has muscles."

"I'll try anyway." Max left his chair. "I'll be getting back. I'm on my lunch hour."

"College boys live to punch clocks and wallow in words."

"I wallow in pictures."

"*Mesmo,*" said Jorge. He bent and raised up the fallen weight with one hand. "If the whole country thought with its muscles, we wouldn't be where we are now."

As Max let himself out of the Victorian gym, he heard the weight thwack Jorge again.

"Turn right at Uncle Sam," said Dr. Levin in the passenger seat.

"I keep telling Jillian not to try exorcising ghosts by herself," said Max, gunning the car up to sixty-five. He slowed again, swung onto the off-ramp next to the thirty-foot tall wooden Uncle Sam.

"They used to have Abraham Lincoln," explained Levin, "but they decided it was too controversial. So they painted him over into Uncle Sam."

"I was wondering why he had a black beard and a shawl."

"Anyway, Max, it wasn't Jillian's fault. She was over at our place, as I understand it from the note April left, trying to console my wife about that mess last night."

"Trying to find out more about the ghosts."

"And, see, my mom came by and said she was tired of Captain Pennington picking on me and was coming over here to Yankee Doodle Acres to have a show-down with him."

"And bringing the ghost patrol?"

"Yes," said Levin. "Max, mom is really thoughtful,

though extreme. My turning thirty still hasn't convinced her I can handle things. That April and I can."

Max said, "April left that note before you got home at five. Its eight now."

"I know," said the doctor. "When I called the Pennington place his houseboy just cried. And I could hear gunshots. Which is why I called the police and then you, Max. I'm sorry. I knew mom was probably using Jorge Barafunda to summon that bunch. I figured, though, if I kept things relatively quiet, the situation would settle down. Eventually."

"What kind of weapons does Pennington have stored at his house?"

"Nobody knows. He has a secret arsenal. The police searched his place twice and couldn't find anything but a Daisy air rifle."

Ahead of them on the road was a replica of Mt. Rushmore. "This the entrance to Yankee Doodle Acres?"

"Yeah. Drive in right next to Teddy Roosevelt's mouth."

There were over a hundred houses in Yankee Doodle Acres, recapitulating American history. Log cabin-style homes, pioneer fort-style homes, California mission-style homes, White House-style homes. "Pennington's is which?"

"403 Liberty Bell Lane. Third fort on the right."

In the warm night, gunfire and shell explosions sounded. "The cops and Pennington must be tangling."

Dr. Levin said, "The captain seems to have exceeded the bounds of conservatism. Even for California."

Around a winding rise and down a gentle incline, they were stopped by a police barricade made of two sawhorses and a Volkswagen. "Little mischief up ahead," said the uniformed policeman. "Nobody can enter this street. We suggest you use Boston Tea Party Drive, two blocks over, as a detour."

"My wife," said Max, "and Dr. Levin's wife. We think they're down at Captain Pennington's."

The policeman flickered his fingers on his white helmet. "The lieutenant was trying to find you two."

"Are the girls all right?" said Max.

"We think so. They appear to be in the house with the captain, and he's gone blooey some. We tried to humor him as usual, but when he and Weehunt hauled out those mortars, we had to act."

"Is my mother okay?" Levin asked across Max.

The policeman said, "She's barricaded behind her station wagon with a guy in a leopard skin and a guy who looks like a lumberjack and some little coot who keeps trying to make speeches. They're all taking potshots at the captain's fort, which is why we figure he started going really blooey in the first place. Though I'm no psychiatrist."

Max parked the car short of the barricade, and he and Levin ran the block to the captain's home. The allergic plainclothes man waved them to duck behind his police car. "The girls," began Max.

"They got here a little ahead of your mother, Dr. Levin. They went in to talk to Captain Pennington, warn him and try to avoid trouble. While they were still inside, your mother and her crew started their invasion. At least that's what the neighbors say." He pointed a thumb at the replica of Monticello next to Pennington's two-story ranch-style wooden fort.

Dr. Levin spotted his mother off in the dark. "Mom, stop this and take those guys home."

His mother called, "Don't sit down on the street; you'll catch cold."

"She stopped shooting a half hour ago," said the lieutenant. "But Pennington and Weehunt have kept them pinned down there with rifle fire."

"Is Weehunt berserk, too?"

"You know how it is in the suburbs, one starts and they all follow."

"Death to all freeloaders," broadcast Captain Pennington from his house.

"Look," said Max. "His lawn is opening up."

A great long trench was growing across the front lawn. "The gun cache," said Levin.

"That's where he's got his armory," said the plain-clothes man.

"He's rising up out of the lawn with an antitank gun," said Max.

The lieutenant bobbed his head and waved to the policemen dotted around in the darkness. More spotlights came on and illuminated Captain Pennington as he set up his weapon. "Captain," shouted the lieutenant, "we ask you to surrender or we'll have to use tear gas."

"Pension-loving lackey," replied the red-haired captain.

"Okay," said the plainclothes man.

As the first tear-gas guns thumped, Max left cover and zigzagged toward the side of the house, leaping the mechanized trench in the lawn. Things were growing clouded and blurred, and Max's eyes began to burn. He leaped the captain's flower beds and banged into the side window with his shoulder and tucked-down head.

When he landed on a hook rug, Jillian said, "Max, is that you?"

"Yes," said Max, sneezing and coughing.

"I thought maybe it was Knobler, entering that way."

"Mom Levin is keeping the ghosts near her for protection," said Max, coughing. "Out." Jillian and April were crouched behind heavy wooden chairs.

"Is that tear gas they're using?" asked April.

Max sneezed again, nodded. "Back way."

"Mr. Weehunt went climbing up on the roof with a bazooka, and he took the houseboy to help him," said Jillian. "First time we've been alone."

"Up, out," said Max and followed the women through the house and into the patio. "Jill?"

"Yes," said his wife.

"Can you read? My eyes are going bad from the gas."

"I seem to be okay. Read what?"

Max felt his coat, pulled a small leather book out of his breast pocket. "Page 24, I think. This is a ghost raising and exorcising book written by a 19th-century Spanish circus strongman."

"From our library?" Jillian took the book and Max heard the pages turning. "I don't recognize it."

"From Jorge Barafunda's library. I swiped it while he was lifting weights in the attic. Seems like the kind of muscle-oriented spells he'd pick."

"Do we have to get up close to the ghosts?"

"No, should be able to work the spell from here," said Max. "April?"

"Right here."

"Burn this powder in the barbecue while Jill reads the spell to get rid of the ghosts. There is a barbecue?"

"Of course." April took the packet of yellow powder from Max.

When Max and Jillian reached the street, the police were putting Captain Pennington into the barred part of a police car and trying to coax Weehunt off the roof. "Any ghosts?" asked Max, who still couldn't see too well.

"Gone," said Jillian. "Not behind the station wagon or anywhere in sight. Mom Levin is up the road arguing with the plainclothes cop and Hal. April is running up to join them. You ought to do something about your eyes."

"Might as well get some free advice from Hal," said Max.

"Okay," said Jillian. She took his hand and led him uphill.

THE ADVENTURE OF THE BALL OF NOSTRADAMUS

Mack Reynolds and August Derleth

AUGUST DERLETH (1909–1971) wrote everything from award-winning short stories to regional history pieces to true-crime essays. Over one hundred of his supernatural fiction stories appeared in *Weird Tales,* beginning with "Bat's Belfry," being published when he was just sixteen. Besides being known for his short stories, he was also part of the Arkham House Publishers, which popularized such pulp authors as H. P. Lovecraft, Robert E. Howard, Robert Bloch, and Algernon Blackwood.

MACK REYNOLDS (1917–1983) approached science fiction from a socioeconomic viewpoint with dashes of adventure and detective fiction thrown in for an offbeat mix which became quite popular with the readers of *Galaxy* and *If* magazines. Often extrapolating a future world that is either a pleasant but stagnating utopia or run by totalitarian governments and/or computers, Reynolds always tried to impart the sense that whatever the future may hold, it will be more different than anyone can foresee.

My friend, Solar Pons, the private enquiry agent, has a tendency to be highly dubious of all coincidence—but was it only coincidence that he should refer to the singular adventure of the late Abraham Weddigan on the very day that I had determined to set down the facts about this horrible affair which shocked a continent and, on its successful termination, brought Pons the profound gratitude of millions of people as well as the personal felicitations of His Majesty? From the moment of its conclusion, Pons began to entertain some doubt about Abraham Weddigan, that strange, unforgettable monster—a description of my own which Pons will not countenance—and soon his doubts grew, so that often, when I saw him sitting in profound and troubled thought, and knew no problem had come in to enlist his keen mind, I was aware that he was once again pondering the meaning of the motives of Abraham Weddigan.

On that day in the 1920's that Pons entered the case, in the second decade of our sharing his quarters at Number 7B, Praed Street, I had been reading about the murder of a child—the second in the streets of London. Pons was standing at the window, his long thin hands clasped behind his back, his eyes fastened on the street below.

"I observe that you, too, my dear Parker," said Pons suddenly, without turning, "have begun to wonder— not without some indignation—about the child-murderer in our midst."

"How could you know which account I was reading?" I asked in surprise.

He turned, his ascetic face briefly alight with a smile. "My dear fellow, surely it is elementary. You are agitated, you rustle your paper indignantly, you squirm your disapproval of the police methods in the case, indeed, you all but snort in irritation. What else in the morning paper could stir to such indignation a man who has always been interested in the crime life of London?"

"Ah, you have read of it then!"

"You know my habits, Parker. Little escapes me."

He came over to stuff his pipe with shag from the slipper tacked to the mantelpiece, and sat down in his favorite chair, a frown on his high forehead.

"I fear I neglected to tell you," he went on, "but I am expecting our friend Jamison at any moment. He sent word by messenger this morning before you awoke that he wished to see me on the matter, and it is now some minutes past the hour set for his arrival. Since he is customarily so prompt, I fancy some new facts may have come to light."

"Or another child murder," I put in.

"God forbid! This shocking chain of child murders is far more extensive than Inspector Jamison may know." He listened a moment and added, "But there is the police car now, if I am not mistaken, arriving in Jamison's usual haste."

The outer door opened and closed violently, and Jamison came up the stairs as rapidly as his rotund bulk would permit.

"Dear me," murmured Pons, "I would far rather Jamison glum than Jamison in such good spirits."

I opened the door to Jamison and saw that he was indeed in good spirits, for a broad smile sprang into being on his chubby face, his eyes twinkled, and his mustache fairly trembled with delight at sight of us.

"This time, Pons, we have done it without you!"

"My congratulations! But what is it you have done?"

"We have our man for the murder of Terence Allen and Tomas Kanczeny."

"The child murderer!" I cried. "I thought the crimes clueless."

"Ah, so they were," Jamison went on, rubbing his hands together. "We did not set out to arrest Captain Martin Verne for murder—we went only to question him."

"Pray begin at the beginning, Jamison," interrupted Pons patiently.

"Very well. I need not go into detail about the

crimes themselves; you are familiar enough with the shocking shooting-down of two defenseless children on the city streets. We have been interested—remotely, it is true—in the activities of Captain Martin Verne—"

"One-time soldier of fortune, gun runner, assassin for hire, last heard of in Morocco, after some years in Nicaragua, in China, and on the Continent," said Pons.

"That's him. Well, Pons, he's our man. When he came to England three months ago, he was living close to the bone. We knew as much, and spread the word that the Yard was interested in Verne. So one day he moved from the hole he lived in out Wapping way, set himself up in Park Lane, no less, new wardrobe, and new night life—all the more expensive restaurants and theaters. A nark passed us the word, and two men went over last night to ask him some questions. Verne must have suspected they were after something else. He tried to put them off, then he tried to shoot his way out. He put a bullet into Police Constable McEachern's shoulder, but Constable Leeds put him out with his truncheon. Leeds hit him harder than he ought to have done, and Verne died half an hour ago. But not before we got down what he said in delirium; and, when we had him conscious for a little while before the end, and put it to him: *did he kill the children?*—he admitted it. Further, the laboratory tests show that a bullet from his gun killed the Allen boy; no bullet was recovered in the case of Kanczeny. So there we are."

Pons had listened with keen interest. Now, however, his eyes darkened, his frown returned. "And the motive?"

"He had no time for that. Still, we thought it might be in what he said. You see, the moment they heard him talking, they started taking down what he said. I wasn't called in until after I'd sent word to you. One look at what they'd taken down, and I knew Verne was our man. I brought along a copy of it for you,

Pons. You've done me a good many favors in the past."

He took a folded paper from his inner coat pocket as he spoke and handed it to Pons. It was hardly the size of an ordinary sheet of manuscript paper and was, as I saw when I rose and walked over to look from behind Pons, little more than a meaningless jumble of disjointed sentences. Nevertheless, Pons read it with the keenest interest, though for my part I failed to see that Verne's utterances in delirium conveyed anything of signal importance. The typescript was commendably short.

"Terence Allen, aged 9 ... Escape tutor ... the ball knows ... savior o' the world ... That damned fortune-teller! ... two hundred gross of Brens ... Look, sir, it's a bit out o' me line ... first the smoke, then the picture ... Christ! how real it is ... Bloody old Mussolini! ... Tomas Kanczeny, Hungarian legation, seven years old ... mad dog, mad dog, mad dog ... Gentlemen, we aims to quarantine, if you please, to prevent ... blast him forever! putting the blood o' kids on me hands! ... A pound never looked better to me, and that's the truth, so help me God, but I didn't bargain for that kind of bloody money.... Guns you ordered and guns you got; I'll look at the color o' your money.... Touch the ball, Mister. Fifty quid to have your fortune told. Knows all, sees all, tells the future, tells the past. Fifty quid, Mister ... My alibi's perfect. Nobody can touch me but me.... And if I wasn't so bad off for money, I'd never take on a dirty job like this.... Guns is my line, sir, guns and contraband. I'm the best."

Pons looked up, his eyes fairly dancing.

"Couldn't have made it clearer in a signed confession," said Jamison, smiling happily. "We know the Allen boy was shot when he ran away from his tutor. Now, just to corroborate, we've sent a man out to discover whether there was a dog at or near the scene, plainly enough in evidence, when the Kanczeny boy was killed."

"And how do you plan to establish the connecting link with—let us choose at random—the death of little Ossip Ciciorka in Prague four months ago?" interposed Pons quietly.

Jamison's mouth fell agape. His joviality faded; he grew wary. "Of whom?" he asked finally.

Pons repeated the name and added, "Or, for that matter, of Georges Murat, aged ten, in the Rue d'Auseil, Paris, on May ninth last year; of Giovanni d'Orsini, aged eight, on a holiday in Naples two years ago; of Timor Gushenko, aged six, on the beach of Cannes with his parents three years ago; or even of the abortive attempt on the life of Ana Rabinsohn, a girl of five, in the streets of Bucharest six years ago."

Jamison had recovered his composure. "Pons, you are joking. And an ill-conceived joke it is," said he.

"I daresay you would think so. I regret that it is no jest. I have never been more in earnest. Let us pause for a moment and examine into the matter. There are striking parallels I believe you cannot fail to apprehend. In neither the Allen nor the Kanczeny case was any attempt to kidnap made."

"No."

"Nor to collect blackmail from the parents of these unfortunate victims."

"No."

"Nor was there any molestation of the children themselves."

"No."

"In both these instances murder alone would seem to have been the object of the attack."

"Quite so. It was in all the papers."

"The pattern is precisely similar to their continental predecessors. All are unsolved crimes. And, of even greater importance, they are seemingly without motive. Or did you discover at the last hour with Verne any trace of one?"

Jamison flushed.

"Ah, you need not answer. I submit, then, that Verne had been hired to commit at least these last two crimes. He may have had a hand in some of the others, but I am inclined to doubt it. Very well then. If not Verne, some other hired assassin. They abound in Europe; each has his price, and most may have been less squeamish than Verne. I put it to you that no one pays a hired assassin to murder a child without some motive, however obscure. No, do not say it Jamison—the psychopath does not hire murder done; he does it himself. We must cast into other waters for our motive, Jamison."

"When word of Verne's death reaches whoever it was who hired him, I'll wager he'll leave London by the fastest means," said Jamison.

"Dear me, I had not thought that Scotland Yard was less intent upon the capture of a murderer than his flight beyond their jurisdiction. I fancy that concept of crime detection will interest the Commissioner."

"Oh, come, Pons, you are taking me too literally. Depend on it, we shall be on the watch for him. But, I confess, we have not the slightest hint of motive."

"I suspected as much," said Pons dryly. "But the picture is not so hopeless as all that, surely. There are several salient facts which are curiously similar in the majority of the murders."

"You believe that those you have mentioned are connected with these in London?"

"Can you doubt it? Consider: the methods in all cases are exactly similar, and so are the circumstances surrounding them. There is a sinister pattern in the very fact that there is no similarity whatsoever—unless we are unable to see it—among the victims of this plague of murder. Those children come from all walks of life. Allen was the son of a poor laborer. Kanczeny belonged to parents in the Hungarian embassy. Ciciorka was the son of a Polish librarian. Young d'Orsini, though of an ancient Italian family, was the son of an artist, Murat of a wine merchant, Gushenko of a petty railroad official. And the abortive attempt in Bucharest was made on the daughter of humble Jewish parents.

"Murder of children for vengeance against the parents is not unknown; it was practised at one time by the Mafia. But it is highly unlikely that these murders have a common origin of that nature; they are too widely separated to make it probable that one terror organization could be responsible for these crimes, and to presuppose others is to enter the realm of pure conjecture without relation to facts. None of the parents involved is important enough to have incurred political enmities. Indeed, they are nonentities—even Kanczeny's position at the embassy is that of a minor clerk. In almost every instance, the children were murdered at a supremely felicitous moment for the murderer—when they had strayed or run away, which suggests either a constant watchfulness or an uncanny knowledge. I venture to suggest that all these crimes were the work of one guiding genius."

"A Napoleon of crime," cried Jamison.

"You do Napoleon's memory no service. A modern Herod, perhaps." Pons made an impatient gesture. "But we are wasting time. I beg you to stand by, Jamison. I mean to find the author of these crimes."

When Jamison had gone, Pons turned to me. "If you were to need the services of a fortune-teller—surely one of position, who asks 'fifty quid' a reading—to whom in all London would you apply?"

"Elementary, my dear Pons!" I cried. "There is surely but one such seer: the consultant—so he terms himself—visited by peers, M.P.'s, even persons close to the court—Abraham Weddigan. His fees are exorbitant, and he is never at a loss for patrons."

But Pons was already looking into a London directory. "Let us see. Ah, here we are. His office is in Southampton Row. Let us lose no time. We shall start with him. If we are in error, we shall carry on from there. None knows to what lengths he may be driven now that his hireling is dead."

"Are you not taking the delirium of a dying man too seriously?" I inquired when at last we were in a cab rolling toward Southampton Row.

Pons sat in his accustomed pose, head sunk to his chest, the fingers of one hand toying with the lobe of his right ear, his eyes clouded and dark, fixed on a point not in space but in time.

"No, no," he said impatiently. "I submit that the last words of Verne, however disjointed, nevertheless pointed clearly to some baleful connection with a fortune-teller. 'That damned fortune-teller!' he said. And twice more, he made reference to 'the ball'—which surely is the crystal globe so much an integer in the impedimenta of the seer. We are quite safe in eliminating the references to guns and gun-running; these would be bound to show up in such a scattering of memories as the situation implies. I submit we are on the right track. 'Fifty quid' for a reading. No small sum. No crossing of the palm with mere silver. No indeed. 'Fifty quid'—and for that someone who knows all and sees all will tell the past and the future. Verne had become obsessed by him—and by the magic ball—to such an extent that a rudimentary conscience made him try to flee when, in actuality, none pursued him, and so brought him to his death."

Abraham Weddigan's suite of offices was in one of the most modern buildings on Southampton Row, one given over to business offices representing some of the foremost industries in all England. There, as sedate as any other, Abraham Weddigan was duly listed as a *Consultant,* and his suite was no secret.

We mounted to his floor, found his number, and were prepared to knock when the door was opened noiselessly from within. There before us stood a Caucasian of dark complexion, a Mauritanian, surely. He wore a turban and complementary clothing. He bowed.

"Mr. Solar Pons and Dr. Lyndon Parker. Step this way, if you please, sirs. The Master is expecting you."

"We made no appointment," I said with asperity.

"The Master knows all save his own fate," said the Mauritanian. "Such is as it was ordained."

He led us down a short corridor to a wide door

at its end. There he stood, his head bowed, making no sound.

Nevertheless, a voice from within called out, "Enter."

The Mauritanian threw open the door and stood aside for us to enter a large, almost unfurnished room. In its center was a low divan; opposite it, a conventional but luxurious easy chair. Between chair and divan rose a small round table of oriental manufacture, supporting a small crystal ball. The occupant of the chair came to his feet and motioned to the divan.

"Mr. Pons, Doctor Parker—pray be seated."

His hands were fine and soft, as delicate as a woman's; his eyes were deep and lustrous; his gray hair was heavy and worn long, the only factor of his appearance that seemed affected, for his dress was conventional—a gray business suit. He was a compelling, extraordinarily handsome man, however old he might have been. As he resumed his seat, Pons and I sat on the divan.

"We came . . ." began Pons, but Weddigan held up his hand for silence.

"I regret the nature of your call. I regret the circumstances which have brought it about. The children, yes. The crystal told me Verne was not efficient. Now he is dead before my work in London is finished. Shall I go elsewhere to pursue it? I cannot say; the crystal is dark, very dark."

"Do you now confess to having compelled the man Verne to murder two defenseless children?" I demanded.

"Gently, gently, Parker," admonished Pons, laying a restraining hand on my arm. "We shall listen to Mr. Weddigan."

Weddigan inclined his head. "Thank you, Mr. Pons. Fate has implacably determined that we must be opposed to each other. I regret that circumstance. I know you will hinder my plans. How shall I speak of them to you?" An expression of great weariness came into his face, and he shook his head slowly from side to

side. "Have I any other course? I think not, gentlemen. I hope and pray that you are not of the race of
doubters and the army of the Philistines. I have the
gift of true precognition." He laid one hand on the
crystal ball before him. "All the myths of mankind,
gentleman, have a root, however remote, in fact—even
the dream of seeing man's future in a crystal ball. This
is no ordinary crystal, believe me. It is old, very old—
it and the strangely wrought base of silver on which
it stands. The inscriptions are in Sumerian cuneiform
characters. It was ancient before the city of Ur. Of its
origin I have no knowledge, but many years ago, in
the year 1550, a traveler from Greece, who had found
this crystal in the ruins of Delphi, sold it to a Frenchman named Michel de Nostredame."

"The crystal ball of Nostradamus," murmured Pons.

"At least *he* is not strange to you, Mr. Pons. And
was not Nostradamus the most famous seer of all
time? Did not his prophecies, one upon another, come
true—centuries after he had set them down?"

"The fulfillment of prophecies, like beauty, is too
often only in the eye of the beholder," replied Pons.
"But I concede that the French physician offers as
nearly adequate evidence for prevision as I know."

"This is the original crystal ball and from it stems
the information you seek. It was because of what I
saw in the future that it became necessary for me to
serve my race by destroying the young persons in
whom you are interested."

"You wish us to believe that you hired assassins—
Verne in London, others elsewhere—to murder harm-
less children because of what you saw in the ball of
Nostradamus?" asked Pons, shaking his head gently.
"Sir, I am no seer; I am but an humble practitioner
of the art of ratiocination. This is beyond reason."

"Indeed it is," agreed Weddigan. "I repeat it. These
children, Ossip Ciciorka, Terence Allen, Timor Gushenko—but I need not name them; you know their
names—these children, I say, were destined to become

the oppressors, the dictators, the mad dogs of tomorrow, the Mussolinis of their generation, to fire the earth with war and pestilence, to subjugate and degrade mankind to its lowest level. I failed in the case of the girl, Ana Rabinsohn; perhaps I shall have opportunity to try again. There is but one more in London—Josef Zollern. With your permission, I shall personally execute him."

"I regret our inability to aid your crime, Mr. Weddigan," said Pons.

"Stay a moment, sir. Will you look into the ball? Pray have no fear of chicanery. And you, Dr. Parker. And tell me in a moment or two what you see there."

Pons and I turned to the ball. And in a moment, scarcely more, the crystal had begun to cloud up, as if smoke had somehow entered the glass. I flashed a glance at our monstrous host, and saw him bent above the ball, his hands flat on either side of it, his head bowed, an expression of infinite sadness in his features. Then the ball drew me again, and I saw a scene beginning to take shape, as of a vast concourse of people, before whom stood a fair-haired young man wearing a scarlet tunic, haranguing them passionately and receiving their ovations. The impassioned orator bore a sabre-slash on his right cheek. All about hung the paraphernalia of tyranny. The scene held but briefly; then the clouds swirled up and it was gone.

"I know only too well what you saw, gentlemen," said Weddigan. He rose, clapping his hands.

The Mauritanian appeared almost instantly.

"Forgive me," said Weddigan, bowing once more, his eyes fixed upon some goal far beyond us. "I am an idealist, a perfectionist. I wear a curse upon my soul." And to the servant he said, "Detain Mr. Pons and Dr. Parker for twenty minutes. I leave to protect the future."

The seer stepped behind the servant and vanished into the dark hangings along the wall. The Mauritanian resolutely barred our way, standing with folded

arms before us, his sudden menace seeming to make
of him a giant. And indeed, his shoulders were as
broad as any I have seen, and his girth was in keeping.
He weighed well over fifteen stone, and his aspect
was formidable.

Neither of us made a move for several moments.
Then suddenly Pons reached out, took up the crystal
ball of Nostradamus, and at the same time came to his
feet and flung the ball with all his might. The surprised
Mauritanian fell without a cry, and the ball shattered
when it struck the floor beyond the divan.

Pons leaped over the fallen servant and, without
turning to see whether I was following, ran out into
the hall to the elevators. In the foyer he found what
he sought—a telephone directory of London.

"There is but one chance we may save the boy,
Parker," he said. "Twenty minutes, Weddigan said.
Let us just see . . . Z . . . *Zollern*. Clapham, Loughbor-
ough, Norwood—these Zollerns are well over twenty
minutes from Southampton Row. Camden Town.
Count Helmut von and zu Zollern—he alone is within
twenty minutes of these premises. Now, if only we can
reach Jamison in time . . ."

We sped toward Camden Town in a fortuitously
discovered cab, and turned into a middle-class residential street just as the tall figure of Abraham Weddigan
passed the flats housing the Zollern family we sought.

"Slow down, driver," said Pons.

Weddigan, having reached the end of the street,
turned to walk back.

At that moment a small figure emerged from the
flats and started across the street. At sight of him,
Weddigan changed his pace to swerve toward the boy.

"Now!" cried Pons. "Pray heaven we are not too
late! Driver, get down there at once."

Just as the driver started up, a Flying Squad car
raced around the further corner and bore down upon
Weddigan. The white face of Abraham Weddigan

came up, his eyes widening as he saw the two cars coming toward him. His hand darted into his coat and brought out a stub-nosed pistol. He began to run toward the eleven-year-old.

The bulky figure of Inspector Jamison leaned from the window of the police car, heavy Webley in hand. Within the second it spoke sharply, once and again. Weddigan spun around and dropped to the street, his weapon skittering from his hand.

Pons, myself, and Jamison were out of our respective vehicles in a moment. We ran forward, while young Josef Zollern, who had turned at the excitement to look back, began to walk toward Weddigan's body. The four of us reached the scene almost together.

"Done in," said Jamison curtly. "Acting on your information, Pons. We've traced some of Verne's payments to Weddigan. A madman."

"It would seem so," replied Pons, gazing thoughtfully down at the fallen body. "Even if I find it difficult to forget how he spoke of Mussolini. There are more important things in government than making the trains run on time. . . ."

Josef Zollern, a pale, pinch-faced youngster, looked down at the corpse almost with contempt. Momentarily, a fire seemed to flash in the depths of his dark eyes.

"Young man, you were in danger," said Jamison with bluff heartiness.

The boy's lips were touched with disdain.

"I suppose that before my destiny is fulfilled, I shall see a good deal of this," he said shrilly. There was a cutting edge of fanaticism in his voice.

Pons gazed at him as if he had seen him for the first time.

The boy looked back with eyes that were proud and insolent. Then he turned and walked, quite self-possessed, back to the apartment house from which tenants were coming toward the scene.

*   *   *

Happily, that was the end of the inexplicable sequence of child murders which had shocked the Continent. With Weddigan's death, the case was closed, and so it is marked in the police files, despite Pons's annoying, "Only the future will tell, Parker."

THE GATEWAY OF THE MONSTER

William Hope Hodgson

WILLIAM HOPE HODGSON (1877–1918) was a lieutenant in the Mercantile Marine before he turned to
writing fiction. His stories have a central theme of
man versus the supernatural, with the supernatural
often represented by fungus and decay. His novels
often feature the sea as backdrop, on which his pro-
tagonists wander to find horrific creatures rising from
the watery depths. Hodgson's lighter side came out
in the tales of Carnacki, a detective who investi-
gated the supernatural.

In response to Carnacki's usual card of invitation to
have dinner and listen to a story, I arrived promptly
at Cheyne Walk, to find three others who were always
invited to these happy little times there before me.
Five minutes later Carnacki, Arkright, Jessop, Taylor
and I were all engaged in the "pleasant occupation"
of dining.

"You've not been long away this time," I remarked
as I finished my soup, forgetting momentarily Carnacki's dislike of being asked even to skirt the borders
of his story until such time as he was ready. Then he
would not stint words.

"No," he replied with brevity, and I changed the subject, remarking that I had been buying a new gun to which piece of news he gave an intelligent nod and a smile, which I think showed a genuinely good-humoured appreciation of my intentional changing of the conversation.

Later, when dinner was finished, Carnacki snugged himself comfortably down in his big chair, along with his pipe, and began his story, with very little circumlocution:

"As Dodgson was remarking just now, I've only been away a short time, and for a very good reason too—I've only been away a short distance. The exact locality I am afraid I must not tell you; but it is less than twenty miles from here; though, except for changing a name, that won't spoil the story. And it *is* a story too! One of the most extraordinary things I have ever run against.

"I received a letter a fortnight ago from a man I will call Anderson, asking for an appointment. I arranged a time and when he turned up I found that he wished me to look into, and see whether I could not clear up, a long-standing and well authenticated case of what he termed 'haunting.' He gave me very full particulars and, finally, as the thing seemed to present something unique, I decided to take it up.

"Two days later I drove up to the house late in the afternoon and discovered it a very old place, standing quite alone in its own grounds.

"Anderson had left a letter with the butler, I found, pleading excuses for his absence, and leaving the whole house at my disposal for my investigations.

"The butler evidently knew the object of my visit and I questioned him pretty thoroughly during dinner, which I had in rather lonely state. He is an elderly and privileged servant, and had the history of the Grey Room exact in detail. From him I learned more particulars regarding two things that Anderson had mentioned in but a casual manner. The first was that the door of the Grey Room would be heard in the dead of night to open, and slam heavily, and this when even the butler knew it was locked and the key on the bunch in his pantry. The second was that the bedclothes would always be found torn off the bed and hurled in a heap into a corner.

"But it was the door slamming that chiefly bothered the old butler. Many and many a time, he told me, had he lain awake and just shivered with fright, listening; for at times the door would be slammed time after time thud! thud! thud! so that sleep was impossible.

"From Anderson, I knew already that the room had a history extending back over a hundred and fifty years. Three people had been strangled in it—an ancestor of his and his wife and child. This is authentic, as I had taken very great pains to make sure, so that you can imagine it was with a feeling that I had a striking case to investigate, that I went upstairs after dinner to have a look at the Grey Room.

"Peters, the butler, was in rather a state about my going, and assured me with much solemnity that in all the twenty years of his service, no one had ever entered that room after nightfall. He begged me in quite a fatherly way to wait till the morning when there could be no danger and then he could accompany me himself.

"Of course, I told him not to bother. I explained that I should do no more than look around a bit and perhaps fix a few seals. He need not fear, I was used to that sort of thing. But he shook his head when I said that.

" 'There isn't many ghosts like ours, sir,' he assured me with mournful pride. And by Jove! he was right, as you will see.

"I took a couple of candles and Peters followed with his bunch of keys. He unlocked the door, but would not come inside with me. He was evidently in quite a fright and renewed his request that I would put off my examination until daylight. Of course I laughed at him, and told him he could stand sentry at the door and catch anything that came out.

" 'It never comes outside, sir,' he said, in his funny, old solemn manner. Somehow he managed to make me feel as if I were going to have the creeps right away. Anyway, it was one to him, you know.

"I left him there and examined the room. It is a big apartment and well furnished in the grand style, with a huge four-poster which stands with its head to the end wall. There were two candles on the mantelpiece and two on each of the three tables that were in the room. I lit the lot and after that the room felt a little less inhumanly dreary, though, mind you, it was quite fresh and well kept in every way.

"After I had taken a good look round I sealed lengths of *bebe* ribbon across the windows, along the walls, over the pictures, and over the fireplace and the wall-closets. All the time, as I worked, the butler stood just without the door and I could not persuade him to enter, though I jested with him a little as I stretched the ribbons and went here and there about my work. Every now and again he would say:—'You'll excuse me, I'm sure, sir; but I do wish you would come out, sir. I'm fair in a quake for you.'

"I told him he need not wait, but he was loyal enough in his way what he considered his duty. He said he could not go away and leave me all alone there. He apologised, but made it very clear that I did not realise the danger of the room; and I could see, generally, that he was getting into a really frightened state. All the same I had to make the room so that I should know if anything material entered it, so I asked him not to bother me unless he really heard something. He was beginning to fret my nerves and the 'feel' of the room was bad enough already, without making things any nastier.

"For a time further, I worked, stretching ribbons across a little above the floor and sealing them so that the merest touch would break the seals, were anyone to venture into the room in the dark with the intention of playing the fool.

"All this had taken me far longer than I had anticipated and, suddenly, I heard a clock strike eleven. I had taken off my coat soon after commencing work; now however, as I had practically made an end of all that I intended to do, I walked across to the settee and picked it up. I was in the act of getting into it when the old butler's voice (he had not said a word for the last hour) came sharp and frightened:—'Come out, sir, quick! There's something going to happen!' Jove! but I jumped, and then in the same moment, one of the candles on the table to the left of the bed went out. Now whether it was the wind, or what, I do not know; but just for a moment I was enough startled to make a run for the door; though I am glad to say that I pulled up before I reached it. I simply could not bunk out with the butler standing there after having, as it were, read him a sort of lesson on 'bein' brave, y'know.' So I just turned right round, picked up the two candles off the mantelpiece, and walked across to the table near the bed. Well, I saw nothing. I blew out the candle that was still alight; then I went to those on the two other tables and blew them out. Then, outside of the door, the old man called again:— 'Oh! sir, do be told! Do be told!'

"'All right, Peters,' I said, and by Jove, my voice was not as steady as I should have liked! I made for the door and had a bit of work not to start running. I took some thundering long strides, though, as you can imagine. Near the entrance I had a sudden feeling that there was cold wind in the room. It was almost as if the window had been suddenly opened a little. I got to the door and the old butler gave back a step, in a sort of instinctive way.

"'Collar the candles, Peters!' I said, pretty sharply, and shoved them into his hands. I turned and caught the handle and slammed the door shut with a crash. Somehow, do you know, as I did so I thought I felt something pull back on it, but it must have been only fancy. I turned the key in the lock, and then again, double-locking the door.

"I felt easier then and set-to and sealed the door. In addition I put my card over the keyhole and sealed it there, after which I pocketed the key and went down-stairs—with Peters who was nervous and silent, leading the way. Poor old beggar! It had not struck me until that moment that he had been enduring a considerable strain during the last two or three hours.

"About midnight I went to bed. My room lay at the end of the corridor upon which opens the door of the Grey Room. I counted the doors between it and mine and found that five rooms lay between. And I am sure you can understand that I was not sorry.

"Just as I was beginning to undress an idea came to me and I took my candle and sealing-wax and sealed the doors of all the five rooms. If any door slammed in the night, I should know just which one.

"I returned to my room, locked myself in and went to bed. I was waked suddenly from a deep sleep by a loud crash somewhere out in the passage. I sat up in bed and listened, but heard nothing. Then I lit my candle. I was in the very act of lighting it when there came the bang of a door being violently slammed along the corridor.

"I jumped out of bed and got my revolver. I unlocked the door and went out in the passage, holding my candle high and keeping the pistol ready. Then a queer thing happened. I could not go a step towards the Grey Room. You all know I am not really a cowardly chap. I've gone into too many cases connected with ghostly things, to be accused of that; but I tell you I funked it, simply funked it, just like any blessed kid. There was something precious unholy in the air that night. I backed into my bedroom and shut and locked the door. Then I sat on the bed all night and listened to the dismal thudding of a door up the corridor. The sound seemed to echo through all the house.

"Daylight came at last and I washed and dressed. The door had not slammed for about an hour, and I was getting back my nerve again, I felt ashamed of myself, though in some ways it was silly, for when you're meddling with that sort of thing your nerve is bound to go, sometimes. And you just have to sit quiet and call yourself a coward until the safety of the day comes. Sometimes it is more than just cowardice, I fancy. I believe at times it is Something warning you and fighting *for* you. But all the same, I always feel mean and miserable after a time like that.

"When the day came properly I opened my door and keeping my revolver handy, went quietly along the passage. I had to pass the head of the stairs on the way, and who should I see coming up but the old butler, carrying a cup of coffee. He had merely tucked his nightshirt into his trousers and he'd an old pair of carpet slippers on.

" 'Hullo, Peters!' I said, feeling suddenly cheerful, for I was as glad as any lost child to have a live human being close to me. 'Where are you off to with the refreshments?'

"The old man gave a start and slopped some of the coffee. He stared up at me and I could see that he looked white and done-up. He came on up the stairs and held out the little tray to me.

" 'I'm very thankful indeed, Sir, to see you safe and well,' he said. 'I feared one time you might risk going into the Grey Room, Sir. I've lain awake all night, with the sound of the Door. And when it came light I thought I'd make you a cup of coffee. I knew you would want to look at the seals, and somehow it seems safer if there's two, Sir.'

" 'Peters,' I said, 'you're a brick. This is very thoughtful of you.' And I drank the coffee. 'Come along,' I told him, and handed him back the tray. 'I'm going to have a look at what the Brutes have been up to. I simply hadn't the pluck to in the night.'

" 'I'm very thankful, Sir,' he replied. 'Flesh and blood can do nothing, Sir, against devils, and that's what's in the Grey Room after dark.'

"I examined the seals on all the doors as I went

along and found them right, but when I got to the Grey Room, the seal was broken, though the visiting-card over the keyhole was untouched. I ripped it off and unlocked the door and went in, rather cautiously, as you can imagine; but the whole room was empty of anything to frighten one; and there was heaps of light. I examined all my seals, and not a single one was disturbed. The old butler had followed me in, and suddenly he said, 'The bedclothes, Sir!'

"I ran up to the bed and looked over, and surely, they were lying in the corner to the left of the bed. Jove! you can imagine how queer I felt. Something *had* been in the room. I stared for a while from the bed to the clothes on the floor. I had a feeling that I did not want to touch either. Old Peters, though, did not seem to be affected that way. He went over to the bed-coverings and was going to pick them up, as doubtless he had done every day these twenty years back, but I stopped him. I wanted nothing touched until I had finished my examination. This I must have spent a full hour over and then I let Peters straighten up the bed, after which we went out and I locked the door, for the room was getting on my nerves.

"I had a short walk and then breakfast, which made me feel more my own man. Then to the Grey Room again, and with Peters' help and one of the maids, I had everything taken out except the bed, even the very pictures.

"I examined the walls, floor and ceiling then with probe, hammer and magnifying glass, but found nothing unusual. I can assure you I began to realise in very truth that some incredible thing had been loose in the room during the past night.

"I sealed up everything again and went out, locking and sealing the door as before.

"After dinner that night, Peters and I unpacked some of my stuff and I fixed up my camera and flash-light opposite to the door of the Grey Room with a string from the trigger of the flashlight to the door. You see, if the door really opened, the flashlight would blare out and there would be, possibly, a very queer picture to examine in the morning.

"The last thing I did before leaving was to uncap the lens and after that I went off to my bedroom and to bed, for I intended to be up at midnight, and to insure this, I set my little alarm to call me; also I left my candle burning.

"The clock woke me at twelve and I got up and into my dressing-gown and slippers. I shoved my revolver into my right side-pocket and opened my door. Then I lit my dark-room lamp and withdrew the slide so that it would give a clear light. I carried it up the corridor about thirty feet and put it down on the floor, with the open side away from me, so that it would show me anything that might approach along the dark passage. Then I went back and sat in the doorway of my room, with my revolver handy, staring up the passage towards the place where I knew my camera stood outside of the door of the Grey Room.

"I should think I had watched for about an hour and a half, when suddenly I heard a faint noise away up the corridor. I was immediately conscious of a queer prickling sensation about the back of my head and my hands began to sweat a little. The following instant the whole end of the passage flicked into sight in the abrupt glare of the flashlight. Then came the succeeding darkness and I peered nervously up the corridor, listening tensely, and trying to find what lay beyond the faint, red glow of my dark-lamp, which now seemed ridiculously dim by contrast with the tremendous blaze of the flash-powder.... And then, as I stooped forward, staring and listening, there came the crashing thud of the door of the Gray Room. The sound seemed to fill the whole of the large corridor and go echoing hollowly through the house. I tell you, I felt horrible—as if my bones were water. Simply beastly. Jove! how I did stare and how I listened. And then it came again, thud, thud, thud, and then a silence that was almost worse than the noise of the door, for

I kept fancying that some brutal thing was stealing upon me along the corridor.

"Suddenly, my lamp was put out, and I could not see a yard before me. I realised all at once that I was doing a very silly thing, sitting there, and I jumped up. Even as I did so, I *thought* I heard a sound in the passage, quite *near* to me. I made one backward spring into my room and slammed and locked the door.

"I sat on my bed and stared at the door. I had my revolver in my hand, but it seemed an abominably useless thing. Can you understand? I felt that there was something the other side of my door. For some unknown reason, I *knew* it was pressed up against the door, and it was soft. That was just what I thought. Most extraordinary thing to imagine, when you come to think of it!

"Presently I got hold of myself a bit and marked out a pentacle hurriedly with chalk on the polished floor and there I sat in it until it was almost dawn. And all the time, away up the corridor, the door of the Grey Room thudded at solemn and horrid intervals. It was a miserable, brutal night.

"When the day began to break, the thudding of the door came gradually to an end, and at last I grabbed together my courage and went along the corridor in the half light, to cap the lens of my camera. I can tell you, it took some doing; but if I had not gone my photograph would have been spoilt, and I was tremendously keen to save it. I got back to my room and then set-to and rubbed out the five-pointed star in which I had been sitting.

"Half an hour later there was a tap at my door. It was Peters, with my coffee. When I had drunk it we both walked along to the Grey Room. As we went, I had a look at the seals on the other doors, but they were untouched. The seal on the door of the Grey Room was broken, as also was the string from the trigger of the flashlight, but the visiting-card over the keyhole was still there. I ripped it off and opened the door.

"Nothing unusual was to be seen, until we came to the bed; then I saw that as on the previous day, the bedclothes had been torn off, and hurled into the left-hand corner, exactly where I had seen them before. I felt very queer, but I did not forget to look at all the seals, only to find that not one had been broken.

"Then I turned and looked at old Peters and he looked at me, nodding his head.

" 'Let's get out of here!' I said. 'It's no place for any living human to enter without proper protection.'

"We went out then and I locked and sealed the door, again.

"After breakfast I developed the negative, but it showed only the door of the Grey Room, half opened. Then I left the house, as I wanted to get certain matters and implements that might be necessary to life, perhaps to the spirit, for I intended to spend the coming night in the Grey Room.

"I got back in a cab about half past five with my apparatus, and this Peters and I carried up to the Grey Room where I piled it carefully in the centre of the floor. When everything was in the room, including a cat which I had brought, I locked and sealed the door and went towards my bedroom, telling Peters I should not be down to dinner. He said 'Yes, sir,' and went downstairs, thinking that I was going to turn-in, which was what I wanted him to believe, as I knew he would have worried both himself and me if he had known what I intended.

"But I merely got my camera and flashlight from my bedroom and hurried back to the Grey Room. I entered and locked and sealed myself in and set to for I had a lot to do before it got dark.

"First I cleared away all the ribbons across the floor; then I carried the cat—still fastened in its basket— over towards the far wall and left it. I returned then to the centre of the room and measured out a space twenty-one feet in diameter which I swept with a 'broom of hyssop.' About this I drew a circle of chalk, taking care never to step over the circle.

"Beyond this I smudged, with a bunch of garlic, a broad belt right around the chalked circle, and when this was complete I took from among my stores in the centre a small jar of a certain water. I broke away the parchment and withdrew the stopper. Then, dipping my left forefinger in the little jar I went round the circle again, making upon the floor, just within the line of chalk, the Second Sign of the Saaamaaa Ritual, and joining each Sign most carefully with the left handed crescent. I can tell you, I felt easier when this was done and the 'water-circle' complete.

"Then I unpacked some more of the stuff that I had brought and placed a lighted candle in the 'valley' of each Crescent. After that I drew a Pentacle so that each of the five points of the defensive star touched the chalk circle. In the five points of the star I placed five portions of a certain bread, each wrapped in linen; and in the five 'vales,' five opened jars of the water I had used to make the 'water-circle.' And now I had my first protective barrier complete.

"Now anyone, except you who know something of my methods of investigation, might consider all this a piece of useless and foolish superstition; but you all remember the Black Veil case, in which I believe my life was saved by a very similar form of protection; whilst Aster, who sneered at it and would not come inside, died.

"I got the idea from the Sigsand MS., written, so far as I can make out, in the fourteenth century. At first, naturally, I imagined it was just an expression of the superstition of his time, and it was not until long after my first reading that it occurred to me to test his 'Defense,' which I did, as I've just said, in that horrible Black Veil business. You know how *that* turned out. Later I used it several times and always I came through safe, until that Noving Fur case. It was only a partial 'Defense' there and I nearly died in the pentacle. After that I came across Professor Garder's 'Experiments with a Medium.' When they surrounded the Medium with a current of a certain number of vibrations in vacuum, he lost his position—almost as if it cut him off from the Immaterial.

"That made me think, and led eventually to the Electric Pentacle, which is a most marvelous 'Defense' against certain manifestations. I used the shape of the defensive star for this protection because I have, personally, no doubt at all but that there is some extraordinary virtue in the old magic figure. Curious thing for a Twentieth Century man to admit, is it not? But then, as you all know, I never did, and never will allow myself to be blinded by a little cheap laughter. I ask questions and keep my eyes open!

"In this last case I had little doubt that I had run up against an ab-natural monster, and I meant to take every possible care, for the danger is abominable.

"I turned-to now to fit the Electric Pentacle, setting it so that each of its 'points' and 'vales' coincided exactly with the 'points' and 'vales' of the drawn pentagram upon the floor. Then I connected up the battery and the next instant the pale blue glare from the intertwining vacuum tubes shone out.

"I glanced about me then, with something of a sigh of relief, and realized suddenly that the dusk was upon me, for the window was grey and unfriendly. Then I stared round at the big, empty room, over the double-barrier of electric and candle light, and had an abrupt, extraordinary sense of weirdness thrust upon me—in the air, you know, it seemed; as it were a sense of something inhuman impending. The room was full of the stench of bruised garlic, a smell I hate.

"I turned now to my camera, and saw that it and the flashlight were in order. Then I tested the action of my revolver carefully, though I had little thought that it would be needed. Yet, to what extent materialisation of an ab-natural creature is possible, given favourable conditions, no one can say, and I had no idea what horrible thing I was going to see or feel the presence of. I might, in the end, have to fight with a material thing. I did not know and could only be prepared. You see, I never forgot that three people had been strangled in the bed close to me, and the fierce slamming of the door I had heard myself. I had no doubt that I was investigating a dangerous and ugly case.

"By this time the night had come (though the room was very light with the burning candles), and I found myself glancing behind me constantly and then all round the room. It was nervy work waiting for that thing to come into the room.

"Suddenly I was aware of a little, cold wind sweeping over me, coming from behind. I gave one great nerve-thrill and a prickly feeling went all over the back of my head. Then I hove myself round with a sort of stiff jerk and stared straight against that queer wind. It seemed to come from the corner of the room to the left of the bed—the place where both times I had found the heap of tossed bedclothes. Yet I could see nothing unusual, no opening—nothing! ...

"Abruptly I was aware that the candles were all a-flicker in that unnatural wind. ... I believe I just squatted there and stared in a horribly frightened, wooden way for some minutes. I shall never be able to let you know how disgustingly horrible it was sitting in that vile, cold wind! And then—flick! flick! flick! all the candles round the outer barrier went out, and there was I, locked and sealed in that room and with no light beyond the weakish blue glare of the Electric Pentacle.

"A time of abominable tenseness passed and still that wind blew upon me, and then suddenly I knew that something stirred in the corner to the left of the bed. I was made conscious of it rather by some inward, unused sense, than by either sight or sound, for the pale, short-radius glare of the Pentacle gave but a very poor light for seeing by. Yet, as I stared, something began slowly to grow upon my sight—a moving shadow, a little darker than the surrounding shadows. I lost the thing amid the vagueness and for a moment or two I glanced swiftly from side to side with a fresh, new-sense of impending danger. Then my attention was directed to the bed. All the coverings were being drawn steadily off, with a hateful, stealthy sort of motion. I heard the slow, dragging slither of the clothes, but I could see nothing of the thing that pulled. I was aware in a sunny, subconscious, introspective fashion that the 'creep' had come upon me, prickling all over my head, yet I was cooler mentally than I had been for some minutes; sufficiently so to feel that my hands were sweating coldly and to shift my revolver, half-consciously, whilst I rubbed my right hand dry upon my knee; though never for an instant taking my gaze or my attention from those moving clothes.

"The faint noises from the bed ceased once and there was a most intense silence, with only the dull thudding of the blood beating in my head. Yet immediately afterwards I heard again the slurring sound of the bedclothes being dragged off the bed. In the midst of my nervous tension I remembered the camera and reached round for it, but without looking away from the bed. And then, you know, all in a moment, the whole of the bed-coverings were torn off with extraordinary violence and I heard the flump they made as they were hurled into the corner.

"There was a time of absolute quietness then for perhaps a couple of minutes and you can imagine how horrible I felt. The bedclothes had been thrown with such savageness! And then again the abominable unnaturalness of the thing that had just been done before me!

"Suddenly, over by the door, I heard a faint noise—a sort of crickling sound and then a pitter or two upon the floor. A great nervous thrill swept over me, seeming to run up my spine and over the back of my head, for the seal that secured the door had just been broken. Something was there. I could not see the door; at least, I mean to say that it was impossible to say how much I actually saw and how much my imagination supplied. I made it out only as a continuation of the grey walls.... And then it seemed to me that something dark and indistinct moved and wavered there among the shadows.

"Abruptly I was aware that the door was opening and with an effort I reached again for my camera; but before I could aim it the door was slammed with a terrific crash that filled the whole room with a sort of hollow thunder. I jumped like a frightened child. There seemed such a power behind the noise, as if a vast, wanton Force were 'out.' Can you understand?

"The door was not touched again; but, directly afterwards I heard the basket in which the cat lay creak. I tell you, I fairly pringled all along my back. I knew that I was going to learn definitely whether what was abroad was dangerous to Life. From the cat there rose suddenly a hideous caterwaul that ceased abruptly, and then—too late—I snapped on the flashlight. In the great glare I saw that the basket had been overturned and the lid was wrenched open, with the cat lying half in and half out upon the floor. I saw nothing else, but I was full of the knowledge that I was in the presence of some Being or Thing that had power to destroy.

"During the next two or three minutes there was an odd, noticeable quietness in the room, and you must remember I was half-blinded for the time because of the flashlight, so that the whole place seemed to be pitchy dark just beyond the shine of the pentacle. I tell you it was most horrible. I just knelt there in the star and whirled round on my knees, trying to see whether anything was coming at me.

"My power of sight came gradually and I got a little hold of myself, and abruptly I saw the thing I was looking for, close to the 'water-circle.' It was big and indistinct and wavered curiously as though the shadow of a vast spider hung suspended in the air, just beyond the barrier. It passed swiftly round the circle and seemed to probe ever towards me, but only to draw back with extraordinary jerky movements, as might a living person who touched the hot bar of a grate.

"Round and round it moved and round and round

I turned. Then just opposite to one of the 'vales' in the pentacles it seemed to pause as though preliminary to a tremendous effort. It retired almost beyond the glow of the vacuum light and then came straight towards me, appearing to gather form and solidity as it came. There seemed a vast malign determination behind the movement that must succeed. I was on my knees and I jerked back, falling on to my left hand and hip, in a wild endeavour to get back from the advancing thing. With my right hand I was grabbing madly for my revolver which I had let slip. The brutal thing came with one great sweep straight over the garlic and the 'water-circle,' almost to the vale of the pentacle. I believe I yelled. Then, just as suddenly as it had swept over it seemed to be hurled back by some mighty, invisible force.

"It must have been some moments before I realised that I was safe, and then I got myself together in the middle of the pentacles, feeling horribly gone and shaken and glancing round and round the barrier, but the thing had vanished. Yet I had learnt something, for I knew now that the Grey Room was haunted by a monstrous hand.

"Suddenly as I crouched there I saw what had so nearly given the monster an opening through the barrier. In my movements within the pentacle I must have touched one of the jars of water, for just where the thing had made its attack the jar that guarded the 'deep' of the 'vale' had been moved to one side and this had left one of the 'five doorways' unguarded. I put it back quickly and felt almost safe again, for I had found the cause and the 'Defense' was still good. I began to hope again that I should see the morning come in. When I saw that thing so nearly succeed I'd had an awful, weak, overwhelming feeling that the 'barriers' could never bring me safe through the night against such a Force. You can understand?

"For a long time I could not see the hand; but presently I thought I saw, once or twice, an odd wavering over among the shadows near the door. A little later, as though in a sudden fit of malignant rage, the dead body of the cat was picked up and beaten with dull, sickening blows against the solid floor. That made me feel rather queer.

"A minute afterwards the door was opened and slammed twice with tremendous force. The next instant the thing made one swift, vicious dart at me from out of the shadows. Instinctively I started sideways from it and so plucked my hand from upon the Electric Pentacle, where—for a wickedly careless moment—I had placed it. The monster was hurled off from the neighbourhood of the pentacles, though—owing to my inconceivable foolishness—it had been enabled for a second time to pass the outer barriers. I can tell you I shook for a time with sheer funk. I moved right to the centre of the pentacles again and knelt there, making myself as small and compact as possible.

"As I knelt, I began to have presently, a vague wonder at the two 'accidents' which had so nearly allowed the brute to get at me. Was I being *influenced* to unconscious voluntary actions that endangered me? The thought took hold of me and I watched my every movement. Abruptly I stretched a tired leg and knocked over one of the jars of water. Some was spilled, but because of my suspicious watchfulness, I had it upright and back within the vale while yet some of the water remained. Even as I did so the vast, black half-materialised hand beat up at me out of the shadows and seemed to leap almost into my face, so nearly did it approach, but for the third time it was thrown back by some altogether enormous, over-mastering force. Yet, apart from the dazed fright in which it left me, I had for a moment that feeling of spiritual sickness as if some delicate, beautiful, inward grace had suffered which is felt only upon the too near approach of the ab-human and is more dreadful in a strange way than any physical pain that can be suffered. I knew by this more of the extent and closeness of the danger, and for a long time I was simply cowed by the butt-headed brutality of that Force upon my spirit. I can put it no other way.

"I knelt again in the centre of the pentacles, watching myself with as much fear almost, as the monster, for I knew now that unless I guarded myself from every sudden impulse that came to me I might simply work my own destruction. Do you see how horrible it all was?

"I spent the rest of the night in a haze of sick fright and so tense that I could not make a single movement naturally. I was in such fear that any desire for action that came to me might be prompted by the Influence that I knew was at work on me. And outside of the barrier that ghastly thing went round and round, grabbing and grabbing in the air at me. Twice more was the body of the dead cat molested. The second time I heard every bone in its body scrunch and crack. And all the time the horrible wind was blowing upon me from the corner of the room to the left of the bed.

"Then, just as the first touch of dawn came into the sky the unnatural wind ceased in a single moment and I could see no sign of the hand. The dawn came slowly and presently the wan light filled all the room and made the pale glare of the Electric Pentacle look more unearthly. Yet it was not until the day had fully come that I made any attempt to leave the barrier, for I did not know but that there was some method abroad in the sudden stopping of that wind to entice me from the pentacles.

"At last, when the dawn was strong and bright, I took one last look round and ran for the door. I got it unlocked in a nervous, clumsy fashion; then locked it hurriedly and went to my bedroom where I lay on the bed and tried to steady my nerves. Peters came presently with the coffee and when I had drunk it I told him I meant to have a sleep, as I had been up all night. He took the tray and went out quietly, and after I had locked my door I turned in properly and at last got to sleep.

"I woke about midday and after some lunch went

up to the Grey Room. I switched off the current from the Pentacle, which I had left on in my hurry; also, I removed the body of the cat. You can understand, I did not want anyone to see the poor brute.

"After that I made a very careful search of the corner where the bedclothes had been thrown. I made several holes through the woodwork and probed, but found nothing. Then it occurred to me to try with my instrument under the skirting. I did so and heard my wire ring on metal. I turned the hook-end of the probe that way and fished for the thing. At the second go I got it. It was a small object and I took it to the window. I found it to be a curious ring made of some greyish metal. The curious thing about it was that it was made in the form of a pentagon; that is, the same shape as the inside of the magic pentacle, but without the 'mounts' which form the points of the defensive star. It was free from all chasing or engraving.

"You will understand that I was excited when I tell you that I felt sure I held in my hand the famous Luck Ring of the Anderson family which, indeed, was of all things the most intimately connected with the history of the haunting. This ring had been handed on from father to son through generations, and always—in obedience to some ancient family tradition—each son had to promise never to wear the ring. The ring, I may say, was brought home by one of the Crusaders under very peculiar circumstances, but the story is too long to go into here.

"It appears that young Sir Hulbert, an ancestor of Anderson's, made a bet one evening, in drink, you know, that he would wear the ring that night. He did so, and in the morning his wife and child were found strangled in the bed in the very room in which I stood. Many people, it would seem, thought young Sir Hulbert was guilty of having done the thing in drunken anger and he, in an attempt to prove his innocence, slept a second night in the room. He also was strangled.

"Since then no one has spent a night in the Grey

Room until I did so. The ring had been lost so long that its very existence had become almost a myth, and it was most extraordinary to stand there with the actual thing in my hand, as you can understand.

"It was whilst I stood there looking at the ring that I got an idea. Supposing that it were, in a way, a doorway—you see what I mean? A sort of gap in the world-hedge, if I may so phrase my idea. It was a queer thought, I know, and possibly was not my own, but one of those mental nudgings from the Outside.

"You see, the wind had come from that part of the room where the ring lay. I pondered the thought a lot. Then the shape—the inside of a pentacle. It had no 'mounts,' and without mounts, as the Sigsand MS. has it:—'Thee mownts wych are thee Five Hills of safetie. To lack is to gyve pow'r to thee daemon; and surlie to fayvor thee Evill Thynge.' You see, the very shape of the ring was significant. I determined to test it.

"I unmade my pentacle, for it must be 'made' afresh *and around* the one to be protected. Then I went out and locked the door, after which I left the house to get certain matters, for neither 'yarbs nor fyre nor water' must be used a second time. I returned about seven-thirty and as soon as the things I had brought had been carried up to the Grey Room I dismissed Peters for the night, just as I had done the evening before. When he had gone downstairs I let myself into the room and locked and sealed the door. I went to the place in the centre of the room where all the stuff had been packed and set to work with all my speed to construct a barrier about me and the ring.

"I do not remember whether I explained to you, but I had reasoned that if the ring were in any way a 'medium of admission,' and it were enclosed with me in the Electric Pentacle it would be, to express it loosely, insulated. Do you see? The Force which had visible expression as a Hand would have to stay beyond the Barrier which separates the Ab from the

Normal, for the 'gateway' would be removed from accessibility.

"As I was saying, I worked with all my speed to get the barrier completed about me and the ring for it was already later than I cared to be in that room 'unprotected.' Also, I had a feeling that there would be a vast effort made that night to regain the use of the ring. For I had the strongest conviction that the ring was a necessity to materialisation. You will see whether I was right.

"I completed the barriers in about an hour and you can imagine something of the relief I felt when I saw the pale glare of the Electric Pentacle once more all about me. From then onwards, for about two hours, I sat quietly facing the corner from which the wind came.

"About eleven o'clock I had a queer knowledge that something was near to me, yet nothing happened for a whole hour after that. Then suddenly I felt the cold, queer wind begin to blow upon me. To my astonishment it seemed now to come from behind me and I shipped round with a hideous quake of fear. The wind met me in the face. It was flowing up from the floor close to me. I stared in a sickening maze of new frights. What on earth had I done now! The ring was there, close beside me, where I had put it. Suddenly, as I stared, bewildered, I was aware that there was something queer about the ring—funny shadowy movements and convolutions. I looked at them stupidly. And then, abruptly, I knew that the wind was blowing up at me from the ring. A queer indistinct smoke became visible to me, seeming to pour upwards through the ring and mix with the moving shadows. Suddenly I realised that I was in more than any mortal danger, for the convoluting shadows about the ring were taking shape and the death-hand was forming *within* the Pentacle. My goodness, do you realise it? I had brought the 'gateway' into the pentacles and the brute was coming through—pouring into the material world, as gas might pour out from the mouth of a pipe.

"I should think that I knelt for a couple of moments in a sort of stunned fright. Then with a mad, awkward movement I snatched at the ring, intending to hurl it out of the Pentacle. Yet, it eluded me as though some invisible, living thing jerked it hither and thither. At last I gripped it, but in the same instant it was torn from my grasp with incredible and brutal force. A great black shadow covered it and rose into the air and came at me. I saw that it was the Hand, vast and nearly perfect in form. I gave one crazy yell and jumped over the Pentacle and the ring of burning candles and ran despairingly for the door. I fumbled idiotically and ineffectually with the key, and all the time I stared, with the fear that was like insanity, toward the Barriers. The hand was plunging towards me; yet, even as it had been unable to pass into the pentacle when the ring was without; so, now that the ring was within it had no power to pass out. The monster was chained, as surely as any beast would be, were chains rivetted upon it.

"Even then, in that moment, I got a flash of this knowledge, but I was too utterly shaken with fright to reason and the instant I managed to get the key turned I sprang into the passage and slammed the door with a crash. I locked it and got to my room, somehow; for I was trembling so that I could hardly stand, as you can imagine. I locked myself in and managed to get the candle lit; then I lay down on the bed and kept quiet for an hour or two, and so I grew steadier.

"I got a little sleep later, but woke when Peters brought my coffee. When I had drunk it I felt altogether better and took the old man along with me whilst I had a look into the Grey Room. I opened the door and peeped in. The candles were still burning wan against the daylight and behind them was the pale, glowing star of the Electric Pentacle. And there in the middle was the ring—the gateway of the monster, lying demure and ordinary.

"Nothing in the room was touched and I knew that

the brute had never managed to cross the Pentacles. Then I went out and locked the door.

"After a further sleep of some hours I left the house. I returned in the afternoon in a cab. I had with me an oxy-hydrogen jet and two cylinders, containing the gases. I carried the things to the Grey Room and there, in the centre of the Electric Pentacle, I erected the little furnace. Five minutes later the Luck Ring, once the 'luck' but now the 'bane' of the Anderson family, was no more than a little splash of hot metal."

Carnacki felt in his pocket and pulled out something wrapped in tissue paper. He passed it to me. I opened it and found a small circle of greyish metal something like lead, only harder and rather brighter.

"Well," I asked, at length, after examining it and handing it round to the others, "did that stop the haunting?"

Carnacki nodded. "Yes," he said. "I slept three nights in the Grey Room before I left. Old Peters nearly fainted when he knew that I meant to, but by the third night he seemed to realise that the house was just safe and ordinary. And you know, I believe in his heart he hardly approved."

Carnacki stood up and began to shake hands. "Out you go!" he said, genially.

And, presently, we went pondering to our various homes.

A GOOD JUDGE OF CHARACTER

Susan Dunlap

SUSAN DUNLAP has written three series of mystery novels, each one featuring a different type of detective, from homicide detective Jill Smith, to utility meter reader Veejay Haskell, to forensic pathologist turned private detective Kiernan O'Shaughnessy. She also served as the president of Sisters in Crime for 1990–91. She also writes excellent short stories, as evidenced here.

Have you ever had the urge to do something suicidal? Walking past an eighth-story window, you stop and look out, your gaze drawn down to the street far below. Suddenly the pull is almost irresistible and you have to brace your hands against the ledge to keep yourself from jumping.

Or you're stopped in your car at a railway crossing at night. The train whistle cuts the dark, it vibrates your flesh. You can feel it in the hollow of your stomach. The white light on the train races at you, taunting: *Can you beat me?* Your foot hits the gas pedal; the car surges forward, smashes through the wooden barrier, jolts over the tracks just in front of the train. The engine roars behind you, a gust of air batters the back of your neck as you crash through the far barricade.

And when the engine actually does race by, horn blasting against your ears, you can hardly believe you haven't moved at all. You sit there, shaking all over, wondering how close you really came to killing yourself.

That type of thing happened to me not long ago. And yet now it seems ages ago. It was in the third week of what was to be a six-week stay in a sleepy beach town near San Luis Obispo. After a hectic year as director of the convention bureau in San Francisco, forced to be pleasant to the head of every professional association, brotherhood, sisterhood, political party, or union that might possibly be wooed to convene in the City, I'd needed to be someplace where no one knew me. Director was one of those jobs whose reward is a lot of show and responsibility rather than much pay. The thrill of being in the public eye had faded. The stress had mounted and I'd made snap decisions, taken chances, acquired things I never would have considered at a more normal time. And my lover, Jeff—one of those new and questionable acquisitions—and his demands had only made the pressure worse. Even he—especially he—had agreed I had to get away.

There in the beach town nothing much happened. My biggest decisions each day were whether to wear a one- or two-piece bathing suit, and when to turn over on my towel and sun my other side.

I was walking along the sand as I did at the tail end of most afternoons. The beach was crowded during the days, with radios clashing, volleyball nets strung up, and teams shrieking and groaning, halfhearted body surfers riding too small waves. But as soon as the first shadow of fog climbed over the horizon the beach emptied. That was my favorite time, when I could pretend the beach was all mine. With five hundred thousand dollars, I'd say to myself, I could buy a retreat with a secluded beach that no one would walk on but me.

The beach was wide there; the palm trees grew close to the walkway. I liked to amble between the trees and the water and pretend the wooden walkway and the road beyond didn't exist. The day had been hot, but now fingers of fog inched their way in from the Pacific, tentatively caressing the sky like a hand in the dark, like a new lover. I'd put a yellow flowered shirt and cutoffs over my bathing suit. My skin prickled against the rough fabric, and I felt, as you do at those times, icy but with shots of fire cutting through. My feet were bare, my hands empty. A couple of dollar bills in my pocket rubbed the point of my hipbone.

It was almost dusk, the light too dim for a family to be taking pictures.

I don't know why I even looked over and noticed that family. What momentarily caught my eye was one of those clear plastic name tags with the red and gold ribbons we use at the convention bureau. The smallest child was wearing it in the middle of his T-shirt; it covered half of his chest. I was only a few feet away from the low cement wall that separates the beach from the walkway. The camera sat on top of the wall. The father, a short, ripply-fleshed man in blue-and-white bathing trunks and a white short-sleeved shirt hanging open, a man in his mid-forties, had set the camera timer and was walking stiffly back to the others. I remember this part very clearly. The two small boys, maybe three and six, were yelling at him to hurry. "Ten seconds, ten seconds! Come on, Daddy!" The older one was wearing a San Francisco 49ers cap. A teenage girl stood, weight on one leg, arms crossed in exaggerated boredom. Divorced father, weekend family, I remember thinking.

The father threw himself on the ground in front of the boys and grinned at the camera. The smile stopped at his upper lip, and his eyes had a tight, wary look that was out of place in this quiet beach town. The effect was jarring. I can still see that stiff grin painted on for the camera.

And that's when life shifted, like the train whistle daring me. My scalp quivered. Suddenly everything was crisper; the dusk sun shone noon-strong off the sand. I started to run, pushing back the sand with the

balls of my feet. My steps were light, my gait fluid. I
picked up speed, veered right toward the family. The
camera sparkled. I scooped it up and didn't even
break pace. I pushed off the cement base of the wall
with my right foot and ran faster, striding like a wild
horse, full out down the beach beyond the line of
palms.

The family's shouts burst up behind me. *They* were
the train, the thousands of tons of steel bearing down
on me. My bare feet dug hard into the sand. The roar
of their voices shifted, the kids' mixing like the clack
of wheels on the track, the father's—loud, grating—
cutting through the evening breeze, like the train horn
shrieking in my ears.

"Hey," he yelled, "you drop that Spectra!"

I didn't look back. My head throbbed. I pressed my
feet harder against the sand as I ran past the empty
lifeguard chair. I looked up, knowing it was after
hours now, but still half expecting to see the guard's
blond hair creeping out from under his billed cap.

And that's when life shifted back again. The
throbbing of my head evened out; my eyes seemed to
refocus. My steps were leaden, my breath short. I
glanced down at the camera. No sun hit it now. It was
a Polaroid. My fingers were pressed white against its
surface. The picture was pushing out between them,
scratching my skin. *What was I doing with this thing?*
I asked myself in horror. *What had possessed me to
steal it?*

I should have just stopped and handed it back to
the man, fallen all over myself apologizing, told him
that my mother was dying, or my husband leaving me,
or made up some tale. I knew that then. But I
couldn't. Suppose he recognized me.

He was no more than twenty feet behind me, panting between his shouts of "Thief. I'm going to get
you. Thief! I know cops all over the state. That's an
expensive camera. You're dead, unless you drop it."

I ran on. My shins ached, the insides of my knees
burned, and each new breath seared my lungs.

"I'll get you for this! I don't forget."

What I did then was the worst of all possible moves. I lobbed the camera over my head, high in the air. The picture came free in my hand. I looked back, just long enough to see the camera fall, neck strap sailing behind it. It came down, right through his hands and smashed into the hard sand. His face flushed; he looked humiliated. He glanced up in time to see that I had seen.

He skidded to a stop. I kept running. I was panting so hard I could barely hear his shout. "I know what you look like. In an hour every cop in the state'll have your description." His voice was gravelly but the rage was clear. It didn't fit with the image of the wary man I'd first seen.

I was gasping, my throat and lungs yanking in the air. I wasn't a runner, and my legs felt like cement, the sand like quicksand.

He could still see me, I was sure, when I came to the street that led to my motel. I ran on, but I knew he wasn't following anymore and the adrenaline from that danger was just about used up. I was moving barely faster than a walk.

At the next corner I looked back. I couldn't see him. But I could still feel the ache of fear in my ribs. I hadn't been thinking at all when I grabbed the camera. Now I was running eight tracks of thought at once: reconstructing that moment, asking myself what had possessed me, figuring the way to the motel, picturing him at the motel, picturing the town cops there, and interspersing it all with remembrances of that cold rage on his face, and single-frame shots of my dire future. I was a good judge of character—that skill had saved me more than once. At lightning speed I'd judged this man, and I'd been eons off on him. That frightened me. If you can't judge people, you're dead. I would never had suspected he'd have so violent a reaction.

It wasn't till I got to the motel that I noticed the picture crumpled in my hand. A new wave of panic chilled me. The last thing I needed was to be found with the evidence of my crime right in my hand. I could see the headlines—CONVENTION BUREAU DIRECTOR IS THIEF! That would be it for me! I started to toss the photo in the nearest trash can, but couldn't resist stretching it out for a look. There were nothing but lines and shadows with clumps of dark where the family would have been. You wouldn't even have realized they were people.

Still shaking, I dropped it in the trash. But I wasn't going to escape so easily. It would be simple for him to find me in this small beach town. There were only a few motels here. Exhorting myself to move faster, I trudged to my room. When I opened the door, the phone was ringing. Automatically, I picked it up. "Hello?" I could hear someone at the other end, then the phone clicked dead. Shaking harder, I stood staring at it. Slowly, I put it down. How could he have traced me so soon?

The phone rang again, but I didn't touch it. I threw my clothes into the back of my car, paid for the room, and headed out of town, slowly, careful not to do anything that would draw the police. Maybe he didn't know police all over the state, but just maybe he did. Maybe he hadn't been the hang-up call either.

I stopped for gas near San Jose. I hadn't eaten since lunch and it was nearly 10:00 P.M. now, but the idea of eating seemed as alien as shoving Styrofoam into my throat. I drank a Coke for the sugar and caffeine and drove on, still shaking with fear. You were overreacting about the phone call, I told myself. There's no proof it was him. He's not coming after you. But I couldn't make myself believe that.

When I had left San Francisco, Jeff and I agreed we'd have no contact at all for six weeks—a sort of trial separation, he'd said laughingly. He'd make do with a photo of me he'd cut out of the paper. The plan was the sensible thing to do, we'd agreed on that. Then at the end of that time we'd go to Mazatlán. It galled me to be the one to break our covenant. It had taken us ages to work everything out, and now as I headed toward the city, I wasn't at all sure Jeff would be glad to see me.

Thick streams of fog blew down the streets in the city. A hundred feet ahead everything was whited out. I had the windshield wipers on. I passed Jeff's apartment, the lower floor of a Victorian. His light was on. I let out a long breath, and felt myself safe, even though I knew coming to his place was another panicky run from danger, as illogical a reaction to stress as grabbing the camera.

"What are you doing here?" was his curt greeting. It didn't encourage me to tell him about stealing the camera, and that a man with police connections was after me.

"I needed a change. It's just for a day or two."

"We agreed you wouldn't come here." He stepped back and let me in. "Where are you parked?"

"Next block." His was an iffy neighborhood, with lots of auto heists and cops making rounds. "I didn't leave anything in plain sight in the car."

He shrugged, clearly uncomforted. "You can stay tonight, but you have to leave tomorrow."

"Jeff—"

"No. We made this agreement for a reason. Don't blow it all on a whim."

I started to protest, but I'd been as much a party to the covenant as he. I sank down on the bed, still wired from the day and the drive. Patting a spot next to me, I grinned and said, "I could sleep on the couch."

Jeff plopped down and ran a hand down my thigh. "Since you are here, we might as well make the best use of the time." His kiss was gentler than his words. It reminded me why I kept him around.

"You know," I said at some point during the night, "I may just be encouraging you because you're so good in bed. You're really not my type."

"What is your type?" he asked, clearly not put off.

"Well, not auditors." I grinned. "Auditing isn't very exciting."

It was too dark to see his expression, but I knew

from the shift of his head and the tiny snort that he was smiling, too. "My sentiments exactly. If you saw me in my dark auditor's suit, heading into Creston's Hardware or Minton's Jewelry, you'd be even more convinced. But don't you worry, I won't even pack it for Mazatlán."

But in the morning there was no cheery talk of Mexico. As Jeff pointed out it was better that I left before rush hour. And in the light of morning, my escapade with the camera seemed more ridiculous than alarming. Chances were that by now I was nothing more than a bizarre story for the camera owner to tell at dinner.

He was vacationing with his kids; he probably only got them a couple weeks a year, he wasn't likely to ruin that time chasing after me.

Jeff was in the shower when I left—not a very positive indicator for our relationship. I took his blue carry-on bag and headed out to my clothes-strewn car trunk. Auditors understand the importance of keeping your things orderly and where you can find them. It was just 7:03 when I got to my car. There was a ticket on the window! Panic shot through me. Meter maids don't work at night. This ticket had been written by a patrol officer! Impeding a driveway, it said. Shaking, I looked at the front bumper. It was a couple inches past the edge of the driveway—normal for San Francisco. Patrol officers don't spend their nights flashing lights on the edges of driveways, not unless they're called specially, or they are looking for something, or someone. *I know cops all over the state!*

So much for being no more than a dinner story. The man was after me, and he knew where to find me! No longer could I wrap myself in illusions of safety. It was the last thing I wanted to do, but there was no avoiding it: I had to go back and make amends. If I offered a sincere apology, told him I felt like a fool—which I certainly did—and said I'd pay for repairs or replacement, surely he'd forgive me, and call off his cop friends.

Shaking harder, I started my car. Rush hour had already begun. I avoided the freeway entrances, afraid to sit stopped in traffic on display to the world. Instead I wound through South San Francisco and caught 101 nearer to the airport. Why had he only had my car ticketed? Why hadn't he just sent the police to Jeff's apartment and had them drag me out? It wasn't till I was on the freeway that I thought maybe he didn't know about Jeff; he might have gotten my license number from the beach motel and had his police buddies look out for it. In which case the highway patrol would still be watching for me.

I pulled off the freeway at the next exit and drove south through the peninsula towns. He couldn't have friends in every police department in every suburban town.

The drive took forever. I must have stopped at fifty red lights before I got to San Jose. My head throbbed; my teeth hurt from biting back the urge to yell at the fools who didn't signal, the double-parkers, the mothers moseying along at twenty miles per hour. By the time I hit the open farmland around Monterey, the air seemed to become thicker. It pressed in on my lungs, weighed down my arms, made every move an effort, like I'd never stopped running on the beach.

Somewhere this side of San Luis I did think that maybe the hang-up call at the motel was no more than a wrong number and maybe some San Francisco neurotic had had it with people blocking his driveway and called the police. The thoughts were momentarily comforting, but I didn't believe in coincidence. And I certainly wasn't about to go back to my beach motel for another night and let him take me unawares. I had to have my wits about me when I saw him. I stopped in a Motel 6, transposed two of my license-plate letters on the registration form, and made myself walk to the restaurant across the street and order a hamburger I couldn't eat.

I didn't bother to set the alarm. No need. By eight the next morning I was up, showered, and checked out. At nine I was on the beach watching for the camera man and his kids. I paced along the sand, all the way south to where the pampas grass grew, back north past the spot where I'd seen him, and on to the waterbreak, and then back again, all the time practicing my apology. God, I hated being in this position, cringing, ready to grovel. Beaten.

By six in the evening I was sunburned and exhausted. He hadn't shown up. Had he taken the kids to the mountains for a day or two? Would he be on the beach tomorrow? Maybe. But I knew I couldn't go on as haphazardly as I was. Stealing the camera had been stupid, and this method of hunting the owner showed not much more sense.

I was tempted to give up, get in my car, drive south to Mazatlán. My reservations about Jeff didn't seem so important compared with this threat. Get away from the camera man, part of me insisted. Keep out of his sight. But I felt too uneasy about him. He'd reacted so violently that I couldn't be sure he'd ever let go. And if, as I was coming to believe, he really did know cops all over, he could hound me till he found something; we all have secrets. I wouldn't be hard to find. In a job like director of the convention bureau everyone in the city knew me. Maybe the camera man had recognized me. If I didn't deal with this guy now, I'd be looking over my shoulder forever. Cringing, beaten. And, I had to admit, there was the issue of having misjudged him. I'd always been a good judge of character. It frightened me to think I was losing it.

What to do? I could check at all the motels. There were only five or six. But my description of him and his kids could have fit any number of families. He could be at any motel, eat at any restaurant, be on the beach, or out sailing, or playing miniature golf.

But there was only one photography shop in town, a family operation with cameras, processing, picture frames, and postcards. I'd stopped there for postcards last week. Or that was my excuse. There were two or three points in my stay that I'd gotten lonely enough to pay fifty cents for an excuse to talk to someone.

The Polaroid camera I'd grabbed was expensive, or so the man had said. Surely he would have taken it in to see how costly was the damage. If he'd left it, I'd have an address.

Feeling in control for the first time in a week, I checked into a different motel, walked to a Mexican café—my favorite here—and had a man-sized meal.

The next morning it took me twenty minutes of small talk with the camera-store owner to discover that my harasser had refused to leave his camera, but not before the store owner had written up the repair slip. The name on it was Lawrence Leavenworth, the address: 36 Seaview Street, Eden Valley.

It hadn't occurred to me that Lawrence Leavenworth wouldn't be at a motel here in town. I didn't even know where Eden Valley was. Thirty miles inland, the store owner told me, with a scornful smile. He hadn't liked Lawrence Leavenworth—acted like a pushy tourist, he said. The impression I got from him was that staying in Eden Valley was an appropriate punishment for ungracious behavior to shopkeepers.

I sat in my car a few minutes, trying to figure which of the facts I had about Leavenworth was worth anything. Could Leavenworth be a San Francisco cop? But if he were a cop he'd be here on vacation and he'd be staying at the beach. If you get your kids a couple weeks a year, you want those to be special, and Eden Valley sounded anything but. That made me even more uneasy. Maybe I'd be better off looking over my shoulder forever rather than walking into a place I had no clue about.

The thirty-mile drive was along a winding two-lane road, with few turnoffs and lots of spots where it would be easy to run someone off into the underbrush below.

Eden Valley was an anachronism for this part of California, a tiny town that seemed to have no purpose, on the road to nowhere, with no beach, no mountains, no rivers or movie sets. It would have been at home in the San Joaquin Valley, or in the middle of Kansas. Five streets ran east-west. Inaptly named Seaview Street was the last of them.

Number 36 was a single-story Victorian with dust-scraped white paint. I pulled up across the street. The hot sun prickled my arms. On sunny days like this I had sat out on a plastic-stringed deck chair on the cement walkway in front of my motel door each morning, drinking a cup of the pale coffee from the Mr. Coffee in the motel office. It had pleased me then to not read a newspaper, not plan the day's activities, not have any commitments at all, just to think of Jeff making his rounds to one small business after another till he did the books at Minton's once more. He'd done Minton's the day before I'd left. After he finished there the next time, he'd be in a deck chair south of Mazatlán.

Leavenworth's little boys' cycles—one tricycle, one small bike with training wheels—lay in the burned grass of the front yard, clearly where they'd dropped them last night. I found myself surprised. The Lawrence Leavenworth I'd seen was Mr. Uptight. *His* sons would put their bicycles in the garage and wait for him to lock the door.

The door to the house opened. A small boy in a fresh red and tan SF 49ers cap scooted out, grabbed the bicycle, and pulled it toward the sidewalk.

"Take care of your cap, Larry. You want it to still be nice when Daddy comes back."

"Ahh, Mom!" little Larry grumbled. He was nearly in front of me when he climbed awkwardly onto the bike. He was a sturdy, fleshy child, the image of his father. He didn't have that conventioneer's wary look that had "graced" his father's face. Not yet, anyway, but he looked like a child who could throw a tantrum. He lurched once then pressed hard on the pedal and moved more quickly, though still cautiously down the sidewalk.

His mother brushed her long blond hair off her

forehead. In the sunlight her smooth skin glistened. She had wide-spaced blue eyes, pouty mouth, and leaned one hip against the doorjamb. She was the "teenager" I'd taken to be Leavenworth's daughter. I'd misjudged her, too! I really was losing it. Sweat coated my face; my hands were clammy against the steering wheel. I hadn't been like this in San Francisco. I hadn't! I'd walked confidently on dark, deserted Market Street at 2:00 A.M., seen men lurking by the door, and knew I could handle them. I'd been a good judge of character when it counted.

But I hadn't had a decent look at this woman on the beach. If I'd had a chance to study her then, I wouldn't have made a mistake. It had been her bored-teenager stance more than anything that I had noticed. I was still okay! Now in the morning light, of course, I could see that she was older. But early twenties at the outside, hardly old enough to have a cycling son. She was wearing pale jeans with the knees ripped. Her feet were bare. And on her toenails was bright violet polish. All in all she looked like the type of California beach girl whose husband was more likely to be selling speed than nabbing speeders. No wonder I'd thought she was a teenager.

She stepped back inside the house. I didn't even try to follow her. I was too sweaty and nervous and confused. Nothing was right here. I'd been so far off base on Leavenworth I couldn't hang on to anything as "fact."

I drove slowly around the block till I spotted little Larry in his 49ers cap. Hopping out in time to intercept him, I said, "Larry, where do you live?"

"Thirty-six Seaview Street," he rattled off, blond hair bouncing above his eyes. Then suddenly he realized how close he was to me. He stood on the brakes. The metal screeched. The bike was a couple sizes too big for him, the bar too high. He lurched to the right. I caught him and held on while he yanked his leg over the bar.

"Did your daddy give you the bike?"

"He mailed it for my birthday. He goes away."

In a fit of inspiration I asked him, "What school do you go to?"

"Eden Valley. I don't know you. I'm not supposed to talk to strangers about Daddy."

I wanted to ask more, but I didn't dare chance headlines screaming: CONVENTION BUREAU DIRECTOR ATTEMPTS KIDNAP! THIEVING DIRECTOR STEALS CHILD!!! I got back in the car before the child had remounted the too-big bike.

As I drove the winding road back to the beach I tried to view Leavenworth afresh. He didn't live in San Francisco, he lived here—with a wife young enough to be his daughter, with a six-year-old whose birthday he wasn't home for. The bicycle looked pretty new; that birthday couldn't have been more than a month or so ago. He'd come home sometime after that and brought the boy a billed cap that said "SF 49ers" and given the younger one his convention tag.

It pleased me to conclude that Leavenworth wasn't what he seemed—not just an outraged father. But perhaps a man who's hiding something. I smiled. A man with a secret isn't so likely to be contacting the cops.

Freed from the panic that had driven me for days, I treated myself to dinner at the Ocean Side Hotel, where I could watch the sun set over the Pacific. The clouds were green and pink and golden yellow at dusk. I ordered one of those rum drinks with the paper umbrella, and sat watching the sun drop and pondering the rest of my stay here, lying safely on the beach, practicing my Spanish.

I was supposed to be relaxing, but my stomach was still queasy. And as I had my second drink I recognized the nagging doubt that was still clutching me. How could I, a good judge of character, not have suspected him? Was I losing it? That scared me more than he had. The man had threatened me. He'd bluffed and almost beaten me. Almost.

I ordered grilled swordfish steak and pondered

Leavenworth and whatever he might be hiding. Everything had shifted again; I wasn't cringing anymore. Now the possibility of his secret began to have the same irresistible pull as the oncoming train.

Leavenworth and Eden Valley didn't fit. The family lived there. But he *sent* his son a bicycle. He wouldn't have done that if he had been away from home for a short time. No, that was the action of a man gone a lot. A father gone so much he can't recall what size bicycle his child needs.

Wherever Leavenworth was the rest of the time was just where I wanted to confront him. I smiled. An apology wouldn't be necessary to a man with a guilty secret. For the first time I felt like my old self, back at the convention bureau, the director.

I gobbled down a few bites of fish, called for the bill, and was out of town in half an hour. It was after midnight when I got back to San Francisco. Pages of newsprint blew down Market Street, the occasional trolley moved along the tracks, its light emphasizing its empty seats. The only life to be seen was a cop in a patrol car and a street person sleeping in the doorway of the building I'd come out of just a month ago. It had seemed much warmer then, but that was 2:00 A.M. instead of midnight and I was weighed down.

As I had a month ago, I parked my car a block off Market. But this time I passed Minton's and headed straight for the convention bureau. I'd kept a key, just in case. The watchman must have been on rounds. Once inside I made my way up the stairs and into the office unseen.

The convention bureau wouldn't have a list of individuals in every profession or trade, but if there was a state, national, or international fraternity that could be wooed to assemble in San Francisco hotels, the address would be here. If they had assembled here, there would be a booking list and a group photo. And I was betting that Leavenworth had picked up the convention badge he'd given his younger son while he was out of town missing the other's birthday. A convention badge isn't something you hang on to. You only bring it home if you're coming right from the convention.

I opened the Bureau door, went to the files. I'd been gone for three and a half weeks. To be safe I decided to cover the last two months. I picked up the schedule for May and groaned silently. May was one of our most popular months. The city is warm then, the skies a clear California blue, and the problem was not luring groups but finding enough hotel space. I checked the rosters for Pharmacists, Philatists, Freight Forwarders, Fruit Growers, Root Growers, and eighty-seven other groups. It took me two hours, kneeling behind the desk, beaming a flashlight on the lists, terrified all along that even with those precautions the night watchman would spot something amiss, or that the batteries would give out. All that and I found not one Leavenworth among the attendees of any of the ninety-two conventions. Could the photo-store man have misread his name?

Each of the convention groups sent us an official group photo. I could look for him. I snorted at the monumental ludicrousness of that scheme. Ninety-two group photos, the head of each conventioneer an eighth of an inch tall!

Defeated, I turned off the flashlight and slumped back against the desk drawers. In the dark the cable car bell outside clanged menacingly; police sirens rose and fell but never stopped. When I had worked here, I never noticed the sirens, but they must have been shrieking then, too. I just hadn't thought about them then. No reason why I would have.

But when I stole his camera, Lawrence Leavenworth (or whatever his real name was) came up with his police threat right away. It wasn't the generic threat: I'll call the cops. It was *I'm going to get you. I know cops all over the state,* the threat of a man who really did have some connection with the cops.

Two-thirty-seven A.M. My eyes were barely focusing. I turned on the flashlight and checked through the list of organizations again, this time for ones that had some law enforcement connection. I was in luck! There were only three: The California Court Reporters, the National Bailiffs' Association, and the National Association of Juvenile Court Justices. I scanned the rosters and was almost relieved to find no Lawrence Leavenworth. Not just relieved, but excited. I could feel the train barreling down the track, challenging me. Lawrence Leavenworth's secret was real!

I walked to the pile of group photos on the back table. It was in the Juvenile Court Justices' Association picture that I found him.

It took a magnifying glass to make out Leavenworth's face. But he was there all right, smiling that fake smile. A shiver ran down my back. How awful would it be to see that face across the bench at you when you were in the dock?

Still, a judge—that pleased me a lot—a man in a very visible position. I knew what that felt like from my time as director. I knew the pitfalls. I could almost hear the train whistle, feel its pull. A judge with an alias. A judge who is away from home so much he can't remember how big his son is.

But without Leavenworth's real name I was not a whit closer to finding him. In fact I was worse off. I didn't know any more about him except that the guy was a judge, so he really did have friends in the police and on the bench, and he'd have no trouble convincing the cops to put out an all-points bulletin for me.

Sticking the roster of juvenile judges under my shirt, I made my way down the steps and back outside. Had I known how easy this building was to break into, I would have been a lot more nervous when I'd worked late alone.

Going through the roster, particularly when I didn't know what I was looking for, was going to be a long and tedious task. I couldn't sit in a lighted car without drawing the police. Even twenty-four-hour coffee shops made me wary. But years in the convention bu-

reau had taught me the one place you can sit at any
hour: the airport.

A little over an hour later I paid for a burger and
coffee and settled in the United area with the roster.

Joseph Acker, Professional Building, 55 Bellingham
Drive, Cincinnati, OH.

Mary E. Allen, 907 West Loma Linda, Ste. 107, San
Diego, CA.

It wasn't till I got to Richard Prescetti, 8 East Sev-
enth Street, Leavenworth, KS, that I felt a tickle of
reward.

Leavenworth, *Kansas. Lawrence Leavenworth.* Business address in Leavenworth. Where would his home
be? I called information in *Lawrence* Kansas and
found that yes, a Richard Prescetti did have a phone
there.

The next flight to Kansas City left at 7:00 A.M. I
tossed my clothes in the front and slept a couple hours
in the back of my car, then changed clothes. It would
be hot in Kansas this time of year, but I didn't want
beach clothes, not for this. I pushed Jeff's carry-on
aside and pulled out one suitcase from the trunk, but
it had winter clothes. The next had jackets and acces-
sories. But the third had a black striped business suit
that would do just fine. Tucked in among the socks
was a small gray cloth bag with a big "M" on it. I
stuck it in my purse.

The plane touched down in Kansas City at 11:03. I
checked the luggage at the airport. By ten after I was
looking up Prescetti in the phone book. His office address—his chambers?—were in Leavenworth and his
residence in Lawrence.

I called his office. A woman, doubtless his secretary,
announced he wouldn't be back till Monday. He'd
been at the convention out in California.

Was he still out there? I couldn't stand it. I started
to dial his home and caught myself just before the
phone rang. No. If he was there, I didn't plan to take
the chance of tipping him off.

I wanted to see his face when I arrived at his door.

Even with a map it took me a while to find it. The house was a brick ranch type that could have been in any upper-middle-class suburb. The grass had been mowed short, but it was still green. The shrubs had been trimmed. A Cadillac stood in the driveway. This was certainly nothing like his wife's place at the beach.

I walked up and rang the bell.

But it wasn't he who opened the door. It was a woman in her late thirties, in shorts and a striped blouse. She had flour on her hands. "Sorry," she said, "I'm just in the middle of—"

"Mrs. Prescetti?"

"Yes?"

I smiled. "Is Richard at home?"

"Yes?"

"He's expecting me. My name's Valley, Ellen Valley." I smiled and hoped that smile didn't look too satisfied at my little play on names.

She shrugged, as if he'd forgotten to tell her things before. "He's still asleep. He got in real late from his convention last night."

"I don't want to disturb him," I said with a straight face.

"He's not a late sleeper anytime. I think I hear him stirring already. I'll just go let him know you're here. Why don't you come in and wait?"

"Thanks." She was a nice woman. She deserved better than a bigamist for a husband. I followed her in and settled on the sofa. In her absence I took the gray cloth bag I'd had wadded up in my purse and stuffed it under the sofa. The big "M" stenciled on it particularly pleased me. A fishbowl of quarters sat on the end table by the door. I amused myself trying to guess how many. Scooping out a handful I counted sixteen, so there had to be . . .

Footsteps on the stairs startled me. I stood up, jammed the quarters in my pocket, and walked to the bottom of the stairs. "You remember me from the beach, Mr. Leavenworth."

Clearly, he did. His ripply face paled and it was a

moment before he croaked out, "My name isn't Leavenworth."

"And mine isn't Ellen Valley. Or Eden Valley, either."

"I don't know what—"

"And you don't own a Polaroid Spectra. Come on, Larry," I said with delicious sarcasm.

He glanced nervously up toward the kitchen, checking whether his wife, *this* wife, was in hearing distance. He lowered his voice, "Okay, let's cut the crap. How much do you want for the picture?"

It took me a moment to recall the Polaroid shoving out that overexposed picture I'd crumpled and tossed out. I smiled. So that was what Leavenworth was worried about, the picture of him and his other family! I should have realized the significance of the photograph sooner: Leavenworth and his other family.

I'd learned the hard way that it's dangerous to be photographed unawares, particularly if you're emptying Minton's safe. If you put your mind to it when you're going over a business's financial records, you can collect a lot of miscellaneous information. You get some from the records themselves, some from conversations, and the rest by just keeping your eyes open, or so Jeff said. Jeff had given me the door keys, alarm code, the safe's combination, but he must have forgotten about the surveillance camera. While he was in Los Angeles creating an alibi I had been making photographic history slinking out of the jeweler's, cash bag in hand.

"How much?" Leavenworth demanded. The man was condescending. A judge dealing with a thief! I glared up at that ripply face, the lips pressed so hard they bunched the skin at the corners.

Bargaining from a position of power was fun. Whatever the judge came up with would be gravy. I didn't *need* his money.

Leavenworth-Prescetti began to tap his finger. *Tap tap tap,* the judge calling for order.

It would have been the decent thing to tell his wives about each other. But I am a good judge of character, and I realized then that "doing the decent thing" was no longer part of my character.

Prescetti's finger tapped more insistently.

How often is an excess of money a problem, I asked myself? Prescetti already supported two women, why not add a third? It wouldn't take long to detour by his bank for a down payment. I'd get just enough to make him uncomfortable.

I had judged Prescetti correctly, all right. That pleased me. Like the men waiting outside Minton's jewelry store the night I took the money Jeff had known would be in the safe. I knew they were just street people, not undercover cops. I had been a good judge of character—of everyone but Jeff. An auditor is a meticulous type—not a person who sets up a robbery and "forgets" there's a camera above the safe. And when the story broke in the papers, the blurry picture that accompanied it was of me. Nothing connected Jeff to me; he'd seen to that.

And nothing did now. Jeff's blue carry-on bag, the one he kept the money in, is a common make.

Nothing connects me to Minton's anymore either. After all, I was supposedly in the beach town when the robbery occurred. On the other hand, Richard Prescetti has doubtless made a lot of unexplained trips to California, and his convention was in the city around that time.

I made one call before boarding my plane. The police in Kansas should have found the gray cotton bag from Minton's safe in Prescetti's living room by now. I wonder which he'll have harder time explaining, his connection to the theft or the bigamy.

I won't be going back to the beach town, or to Mazatlán. I think Barcelona is more my style. But I'll have to be careful. These thefts have to be the last potentially suicidal things I do, because I can't always count on racing across the tracks before the train hits me.

THE ANGEL OF
THE LORD

Melville Davisson Post

MEVILLE DAVISSON POST (1869–1930) was a successful lawyer who turned to writing. He first gained fame with his three books of crime stories about Randolph Mason, a lawyer who used his knowledge to help criminals evade justice. Later, he combined elements of both the mystery and fantasy genres in the tales of Uncle Abner, a highly religious man who battled evil wherever it could be found, but primarily in the Virginia backwoods.

I always thought my father took a long chance, but somebody had to take it and certainly I was the one least likely to be suspected. It was a wild country. There were no banks. We had to pay for the cattle, and somebody had to carry the money. My father and my uncle were always being watched. My father was right, I think.

"Abner," he said, "I'm going to send Martin. No one will ever suppose that we would trust this money to a child."

My uncle drummed on the table and rapped his heels on the floor. He was a bachelor, stern and silent. But he could talk . . . and when he did, he began at the beginning and you heard him through; and what he said—well, he stood behind it.

"To stop Martin," my father went on, "would be only to lose the money; but to stop you would be to get somebody killed."

I knew what my father meant. He meant that no one would undertake to rob Abner until after he had shot him to death.

I ought to say a word about my Uncle Abner. He was one of those austere, deeply religious men who were the product of the Reformation. He always carried a Bible in his pocket, and he read it where he pleased. Once the crowd at Roy's Tavern tried to make sport of him when he got his book out by the fire; but they never tried it again. When the fight was over Abner paid Roy eighteen silver dollars for the broken chairs and the table—and he was the only man in the tavern who could ride a horse. Abner belonged to the church militant, and his God was a war lord.

So that is how they came to send me. The money was in greenbacks in packages. They wrapped it up in newspaper and put it into a pair of saddle-bags, and I set out. I was about nine years old. No, it was not as bad as you think. I could ride a horse all day when I was nine years old—most any kind of a horse. I was tough as whit'-leather, and I knew the country I was going into. You must not picture a little boy rolling a hoop in the park.

It was an afternoon in early autumn. The clay roads froze in the night; they thawed out in the day and they were a bit sticky. I was to stop at Roy's Tavern, south of the river, and go on in the morning. Now and then I passed some cattle driver, but no one overtook me on the road until almost sundown; then I heard a horse behind me and a man came up. I knew him. He was a cattleman named Dix. He had once been a shipper, but he had come in for a good deal of bad luck. His partner, Alkire, had absconded with a big sum of money due the grazers. This had ruined Dix; he had given up his land, which wasn't very much, to the grazers. After that he had gone over the mountain to his people, got together a pretty big sum of money and bought a large tract of grazing land. Foreign claimants had sued him in the courts on some old title, and he had lost the whole tract and the money that he had paid for it. He had married a remote cousin of ours, and he had always lived on her lands, adjoining those of my Uncle Abner.

Dix seemed surprised to see me on the road.

"So it's you, Martin," he said; "I thought Abner would be going into the upcountry."

One gets to be a pretty cunning youngster, even at this age, and I told no one what I was about.

"Father wants the cattle over the river to run a month," I returned easily, "and I'm going up there to give his orders to the grazers."

He looked me over, then he rapped the saddlebags with his knuckles. "You carry a good deal of baggage, my lad."

I laughed. "Horse feed," I said. "You know my father! A horse must be fed at dinner time, but a man can go till he gets it."

One was always glad of any company on the road, and we fell into an idle talk. Dix said he was going out into the Ten Mile country; and I have always thought that was, in fact, his intention. The road turned south about a mile our side of the tavern. I never liked Dix; he was of an apologetic manner, with a cunning, irresolute face.

A little later a man passed us at a gallop. He was a drover named Marks, who lived beyond my Uncle Abner, and he was riding hard to get in before night. He hailed us, but he did not stop; we got a shower of mud and Dix cursed him. I have never seen a more evil face. I suppose it was because Dix usually had a grin about his mouth, and when that sort of face gets twisted there's nothing like it.

After that he was silent. He rode with his head down and his fingers plucking at his jaw, like a man in some perplexity. At the crossroads he stopped and sat for some time in the saddle, looking before him. I left him there, but at the bridge he overtook me. He said he had concluded to get some supper and go on after that.

Roy's Tavern consisted of a single big room, with a loft above it for sleeping quarters. A narrow covered way connected this room with the house in which Roy and his family lived. We used to hang our saddles on wooden pegs in this covered way. I have seen that wall so hung with saddles that you could not find a place for another stirrup. But tonight Dix and I were alone in the tavern. He looked cunningly at me when I took the saddle-bags with me into the big room and when I went with them up the ladder into the loft. But he said nothing—in fact, he had scarcely spoken. It was cold; the road had begun to freeze when we got in. Roy had lighted a big fire. I left Dix before it. I did not take off my clothes, because Roy's beds were mattresses of wheat straw covered with heifer skins— good enough for summer but pretty cold on such a night, even with the heavy, hand-woven coverlet in big white and black checks.

I put the saddle-bags under my head and lay down. I went at once to sleep, but I suddenly awaked. I thought there was a candle in the loft, but it was a gleam of light from the fire below, shining through a crack in the floor. I lay and watched it, the coverlet pulled up to my chin. Then I began to wonder why the fire burned so brightly. Dix ought to be on his way some time, and it was a custom for the last man to rake out the fire. There was not a sound. The light streamed steadily through the crack.

Presently it occurred to me that Dix had forgotten the fire and that I ought to go down and rake it out. Roy always warned us about the fire when he went to bed. I got up, wrapped the great coverlet around me, went over to the gleam of light and looked down through the crack in the floor. I had to lie out at full length to get my eye against the board. The hickory logs had turned to great embers and glowed like a furnace of red coals.

Before this fire stood Dix. He was holding out his hands and turning himself about as though he were cold to the marrow; but with all that chill upon him, when the man's face came into the light I saw it covered with a sprinkling of sweat.

I shall carry the memory of that face. The grin was there at the mouth, but it was pulled about; the eyelids were drawn in; the teeth were clamped together. I have seen a dog poisoned with strychnine look like that.

I lay there and watched the thing. It was as though something potent and evil dwelling within the man were in travail to re-form his face upon its image. You cannot realize how the devilish labor held me—the face worked as though it were some plastic stuff, and the sweat oozed through. And all the time the man was cold; and he was crowding into the fire and turning himself about and putting out his hands. And it was as though the heat would no more enter in and warm him than it will enter in and warm the ice.

It seemed to scorch him and leave him cold—and he was fearfully and desperately cold! I could smell the singe of the fire on him, but it had no power against this diabolic chill. I began myself to shiver, although I had the heavy coverlet wrapped around me.

The thing was a fascinating horror; I seemed to be looking down into the chamber of some abominable maternity. The room was filled with the steady red light of the fire. Not a shadow moved in it. And there was silence. The man had taken off his boots and he twisted before the fire without a sound. It was like the shuddering tales of possession or transformation by a drug. I thought the man would burn himself to death. His clothes smoked. How could he be so cold?

Then, finally, the thing was over! I did not see it for his face was in the fire. But suddenly he grew composed and stepped back into the room. I tell you I was afraid to look! I do not know what thing I expected to see there, but I did not think it would be Dix.

Well, it was Dix; but not the Dix that any of us knew. There was a certain apology, a certain indecision, a certain servility in that other Dix, and these things showed about his face. But there was none of these weaknesses in this man.

His face had been pulled into planes of firmness and decision; the slack in his features had been taken up; the furtive moving of the eye was gone. He stood now squarely on his feet and he was full of courage. But I was afraid of him as I have never been afraid of any human creature in this world! Something that had been servile in him, that had skulked behind disguises, that had worn the habiliments of subterfuge, had now come forth; and it had molded the features of the man to its abominable courage.

Presently he began to move swiftly about the room. He looked out at the window and he listened at the door; then he went softly into the covered way. I thought he was going on his journey; but then he could not be going with his boots there beside the fire. In a moment he returned with a saddle blanket in his hand and came softly across the room to the ladder.

Then I understood the thing that he intended, and I was motionless with fear. I tried to get up, but I could not. I could only lie there with my eye strained to the crack in the floor. His foot was on the ladder, and I could already feel his hand on my throat and that blanket on my face, and the suffocation of death in me, when far away on the hard road I heard a horse!

He heard it, too, for he stopped on the ladder and turned his evil face about toward the door. The horse was on the long hill beyond the bridge, and he was coming as though the devil rode in his saddle. It was a hard, dark night. The frozen road was like flint; I could hear the iron of the shoes ring. Whoever rode that horse rode for his life or for something more than his life, or he was mad. I heard the horse strike the bridge and thunder across it. And all the while Dix hung there on the ladder by his hands and listened. Now he sprang softly down, pulled on his boots and stood up before the fire, his face—this new face—gleaming with its evil courage. The next moment the horse stopped.

I could hear him plunge under the bit, his iron shoes ripping the frozen road; then the door leaped back and my Uncle Abner was in the room. I was so glad that my heart almost choked me and for a moment I could hardly see—everything was in a sort of mist.

Abner swept the room in a glance, then he stopped.

"Thank God!" he said; "I'm in time." And he drew his hand down over his face with the fingers hard and close as though he pulled something away.

"In time for what?" said Dix.

Abner looked him over. And I could see the muscles of his big shoulders stiffen as he looked. And again he looked him over. Then he spoke and his voice was strange.

"Dix," he said, "is it you?"

"Who would it be but me?" said Dix.

"It might be the devil," said Abner. "Do you know what your face looks like?"

"No matter what it looks like!" said Dix.

"And so," said Abner, "we have got courage with this new face."

Dix threw up his head.

"Now, look here, Abner," he said, "I've had about enough of your big manner. You ride a horse to death and you come plunging in here; what the devil's wrong with you?"

"There's nothing wrong with me," replied Abner, and his voice was low. "But there's something damnably wrong with you, Dix."

"The devil take you," said Dix, and I saw him measure Abner with his eye. It was not fear that held him back; fear was gone out of the creature; I think it was a kind of prudence.

Abner's eyes kindled, but his voice remained low and steady.

"Those are big words," he said.

"Well," cried Dix, "get out of the door then and let me pass!"

"Not just yet," said Abner; "I have something to say to you."

"Say it then," cried Dix, "and get out of the door."

"Why hurry?" said Abner. "It's a long time until daylight, and I have a good deal to say."

"You'll not say it to me," said Dix. "I've got a trip to make tonight; get out of the door."

Abner did not move. "You've got a longer trip to make tonight than you think, Dix," he said; "but you're going to hear what I have to say before you set out on it."

I saw Dix rise on his toes and I knew what he wished for. He wished for a weapon; and he wished for the bulk of bone and muscle that would have a chance against Abner. But he had neither the one nor the other. And he stood there on his toes and began to curse—low, vicious, withering oaths, that were like the swish of a knife.

Abner was looking at the man with a curious interest.

"It is strange," he said, as though speaking to himself, "but it explains the thing. While one is the servant of neither, one has the courage of neither; but when he finally makes his choice he gets what his master has to give him."

Then he spoke to Dix.

"Sit down!" he said; and it was in that deep, level voice that Abner used when he was standing close behind his words. Every man in the hills knew that voice; one had only a moment to decide after he heard it. Dix knew that, and yet for one instant he hung there on his toes, his eyes shimmering like a weasel's, his mouth twisting. He was not afraid! If he had had the ghost of a chance against Abner he would have taken it. But he knew he had not, and with an oath he threw the saddle blanket into a corner and sat down by the fire.

Abner came away from the door then. He took off his great coat. He put a log on the fire, and he sat down across the hearth from Dix. The new hickory sprang crackling into flames. For a good while there was silence; the two men sat at either end of the hearth without a word. Abner seemed to have fallen into a study of the man before him. Finally he spoke:

"Dix," he said, "do you believe in the providence of God?"

Dix flung up his head.

"Abner," he cried, "if you are going to talk nonsense I promise you upon my oath that I will not stay to listen."

Abner did not at once reply. He seemed to begin now at another point.

"Dix," he said, "you've had a good deal of bad luck. . . . Perhaps you wish it put that way."

"Now, Abner," he cried, "you speak the truth; I have had hell's luck."

"Hell's luck you have had," replied Abner. "It is a good word. I accept it. Your partner disappeared with all the money of the grazers on the other side of the river; you lost the land in your lawsuit; and you are tonight without a dollar. That was a big tract of land to lose. Where did you get so great a sum of money?"

"I have told you a hundred times," replied Dix. "I got it from my people over the mountains. You know where I got it."

"Yes," said Abner. "I know where you got it, Dix. And I know another thing. But first I want to show you this," and he took a little penknife out of his pocket. "And I want to tell you that I believe in the providence of God, Dix."

"I don't care a fiddler's damn what you believe in," said Dix.

"But you do care what I know," replied Abner.

"What do you know?" said Dix.

"I know where your partner is," replied Abner.

I was uncertain about what Dix was going to do, but finally he answered with a sneer.

"Then you know something that nobody else knows."

"Yes," replied Abner, "there is another man who knows."

"Who?" said Dix.

"You," said Abner.

Dix leaned over in his chair and looked at Abner closely.

"Abner," he cried, "you are talking nonsense. Nobody knows where Alkire is. If I knew I'd go after him."

"Dix," Abner answered, and it was again in that deep, level voice, "if I had got here five minutes later you would have gone after him. I can promise you that, Dix.

"Now, listen! I was in the upcountry when I got your word about the partnership; and I was on my way back when at Big Run I broke a stirrup-leather. I had no knife and I went into the store and bought this one; then the storekeeper told me that Alkire had gone to see you. I didn't want to interfere with him and I turned back. . . . So I did not become your partner. And so I did not disappear. . . . What was it that prevented? The broken stirrup-leather? The knife? In old times, Dix, men were so blind that God had to open their eyes before they could see His angel in the way before them. . . . They are still blind, but they ought not to be that blind. . . . Well, on the night that Alkire disappeared I met him on his way to your house. It was out there at the bridge. He had broken a stirrup-leather and he was trying to fasten it with a nail. He asked me if I had a knife, and I gave him this one. It was beginning to rain and I went on, leaving him there in the road with the knife in his hand."

Abner paused; the muscles of his great iron jaw contracted.

"God forgive me," he said; "it was His angel again! I never saw Alkire after that."

"Nobody ever saw him after that," said Dix. "He got out of the hills that night."

"No," replied Abner; "it was not in the night when Alkire started on his journey; it was in the day."

"Abner," said Dix, "you talk like a fool. If Alkire had traveled the road in the day somebody would have seen him."

"Nobody could see him on the road he traveled," replied Abner.

"What road?" said Dix.

"Dix," replied Abner, "you will learn that soon enough."

Abner looked hard at the man.

"You saw Alkire when he started on his journey," he continued; "but did you see who it was that went with him?"

"Nobody went with him," replied Dix; "Alkire rode alone."

"Not alone," said Abner; "there was another."

"I didn't see him," said Dix.

"And yet," continued Abner, "you made Alkire go with him."

I saw cunning enter Dix's face. He was puzzled, but he thought Abner off the scent.

"And I made Alkire go with somebody, did I? Well, who was it? Did you see him?"

"Nobody ever saw him."

"He must be a stranger."

"No," replied Abner, "he rode the hills before we came into them."

"Indeed!" said Dix. "And what kind of a horse did he ride?"

"White!" said Abner.

Dix got some inkling of what Abner meant now, and his face grew livid.

"What are you driving at?" he cried. "You sit here beating around the bush. If you know anything, say it out; let's hear it. What is it?"

Abner put out his big sinewy hand as though to thrust Dix back into his chair.

Alkire would be in it in his bloody shirt. Do I give the answer?"

"You do not," replied Abner.

"No!" cried Dix. "Your sodded plot no grave, and Alkire not within it waiting for the trump of Gabriel! Why, man, where are your little damned conclusions?"

"Dix," said Abner, "you do not deceive me in the least; Alkire is not sleeping in a grave."

"Then in the air," sneered Dix, "with the smell of sulphur?"

"Nor in the air," said Abner.

"Then consumed with fire, like the priests of Baal?"

"Nor with fire," said Abner.

Dix had got back the quiet of his face; this banter had put him where he was when Abner entered. "This is all fools' talk," he said; "if I had killed Alkire, what could I have done with the body? And the horse! What could I have done with the horse? Remember, no man has ever seen Alkire's horse any more than he has seen Alkire—and for the reason that Alkire rode him out of the hills that night. Now, look here, Abner, you have asked me a good many questions. I will ask you one. Among your little conclusions do you find that I did this thing alone or with the aid of others?"

"Dix," replied Abner, "I will answer that upon my own belief you had no accomplice."

"Then," said Dix, "how could I have carried off the horse? Alkire I might carry; but his horse weighed thirteen hundred pounds!"

"Dix," said Abner, "no man helped you do this thing; but there were men who helped you to conceal it."

"And now," cried Dix, "the man is going mad! Who could I trust with such work, I ask you? Have I a renter that would not tell it when he moved on to another's land, or when he got a quart of cider in him? Where are the men who helped me?"

"Dix," said Abner, "they have been dead these fifty years."

I heard Dix laugh then, and his evil face lighted as though a candle were behind it. And, in truth, I thought he had got Abner silenced.

"In the name of Heaven!" he cried. "With such proofs it is a wonder that you did not have me hanged."

"And hanged you should have been," said Abner.

"Well," cried Dix, "go and tell the sheriff, and mind you lay before him those little, neat conclusions: How from a horse track and the place where a calf was butchered you have reasoned on Alkire's murder, and to conceal the body and the horse you have reasoned on the aid of men who were rotting in their graves when I was born; and see how he will receive you!"

Abner gave no attention to the man's flippant speech. He got his great silver watch out of his pocket, pressed the stem and looked. Then he spoke in his deep, even voice.

"Dix," he said, "it is nearly midnight; in an hour you must be on your journey, and I have something more to say. Listen! I knew this thing had been done the previous day because it had rained on the night that I met Alkire, and the earth of this ant heap had been disturbed after that. Moreover, this earth had been frozen, and that showed a night had passed since it had been placed there. And I knew the rider of that horse was Alkire because, beside the path near the severed twigs lay my knife, where it had fallen from his hand. This much I learned in some fifteen minutes; the rest took somewhat longer.

"I followed the track of the horse until it stopped in the little valley below. It was easy to follow while the horse ran, because the sod was torn; but when it ceased to run there was no track that I could follow. There was a little stream threading the valley, and I began at the wood and came slowly up to see if I could find where the horse had crossed. Finally I found a horse track and there was also a man's track, which meant that you had caught the horse and were leading it away. But where?

"On the rising ground above there was an old orchard where there had once been a house. The work about that house had been done a hundred years. It was rotted down now. You had opened this orchard into the pasture. I rode all over the face of this hill and finally I entered this orchard. There was a great, flat, moss-covered stone lying a few steps from where the house had stood. As I looked I noticed that the moss growing from it into the earth had been broken along the edges of the stone, and then I noticed that for a few feet about the stone the ground had been resodded. I got down and lifted up some of this new sod. Under it the earth had been soaked with that . . . red paint.

"It was clever of you, Dix, to resod the ground; that took only a little time and it effectually concealed the place where you had killed the horse; but it was foolish of you to forget that the broken moss around the edges of the great flat stone could not be mended."

"Abner!" cried Dix. "Stop!" And I saw that spray of sweat, and his face working like kneaded bread, and the shiver of that abominable chill on him.

Abner was silent for a moment and then he went on, but from another quarter.

"Twice," said Abner, "the Angel of the Lord stood before me and I did not know it; but the third time I knew it. It is not in the cry of the wind, nor in the voice of many waters that His presence is made known to us. That man in Israel had only the sign that the beast under him would not go on. Twice I had as good a sign, and tonight, when Marks broke a stirrup-leather before my house and called me to the door and asked me for a knife to mend it, I saw and I came!"

The log that Abner had thrown on was burned down, and the fire was again a mass of embers; the room was filled with that dull red light. Dix had got on to his feet, and he stood now twisting before the fire, his hands reaching out to it, and that cold creeping in his bones, and the smell of the fire on him.

Abner rose. And when he spoke his voice was like a thing that has dimensions and weight.

"Dix," he said, "you robbed the grazers; you shot Alkire out of his saddle; and a child you would have murdered!"

And I saw the sleeve of Abner's coat begin to move, then it stopped. He stood staring at something against the wall. I looked to see what the thing was, but I did not see it. Abner was looking beyond the wall, as though it had been moved away.

And all the time Dix had been shaking with that hellish cold, and twisting on the hearth and crowding into the fire. Then he fell back, and he was the Dix I knew—his face was slack; his eye was furtive; and he was full of terror.

It was his weak whine that awakened Abner. He put up his hand and brought the fingers hard down over his face, and then he looked at this new creature, cringing and beset with fears.

"Dix," he said, "Alkire was a just man; he sleeps as peacefully in that abandoned well under his horse as he would sleep in the churchyard. My hand has been held back; you may go. Vengeance is mine, I will repay, saith the Lord."

"But where shall I go, Abner?" the creature wailed; "I have no money and I am cold."

Abner took out his leather wallet and flung it toward the door.

"There is money," he said, "a hundred dollars—and there is my coat. Go! But if I find you in the hills tomorrow, or if I ever find you, I warn you in the name of the living God that I will stamp you out of life!"

I saw the loathsome thing writhe into Abner's coat and seize the wallet and slip out through the door; and a moment later I heard a horse. And I crept back on to Roy's heifer skin.

When I came down at daylight my Uncle Abner was reading by the fire.

FALLING BOY

David Dean

DAVID DEAN served with the 82nd Airborne Division and is currently a police sergeant in New Jersey. His writing career began in 1989, when his first story was published in *Ellery Queen's Mystery Magazine*. Since then, a number of stories have appeared in *EQMM*, as well as several anthologies. Dean is married and has three children.

The small, single-engine Cessna thrummed and shuddered as it coursed its way through the autumn night, buffeted occasionally by unseen turbulence. The tired young man in the cockpit was concentrating on the instrument panel, glancing up and out the windscreen only when the monotony became too great and he needed to rest his eyes and ease the tension in his back. He would only allow this for a few moments, aware of the disorientation that would quickly seize any pilot flying in these conditions of poor visibility. With the earth invisible below and no horizon in the distance, spatial delusions, like harpies, hovered beguilingly at the edge of consciousness. With no earth below and no sky above, were you right-side up, or upside down?

Snatches of grey cloud raced by the windows as if

torn from the greater whole and flung away. The young man, staring straight ahead now, felt as if he had entered a tunnel, the stratus clouds fleeing the vortex that he was hurtling into.

Little by little, it occurred to him that the wraithlike moisture was not escaping past him in a horizontal plane, he was driving up into it. Naturally, he began to adjust, bringing the nose of his aircraft down. Yet nothing seemed to change, the cloud cover continued to stream downward past him, therefore he must still be ascending!

Beads of sweat formed on his upper lip. It seemed impossible to stop his climb, so he pressed harder against the wheel. Outside, a whining sound began faintly to reach his ears. A small voice said, "Look down. Look down now!"

With an effort so great he felt his neck muscles creak with strain, he forced himself away from the mesmerizing windscreen and checked his instruments. Airspeed ... gaining. Horizon indicator ... horizon indicator! He was nosing over into a dive! Vertical speed was increasing!

With forced control, he eased the wheel back, correcting the plane's attitude and inadvertently raising his head as he did so. The whining sound had vanished. The night world still rushed past his cockpit. *I was never climbing to begin with,* he thought with a chill.

Down, boy! he commanded himself. Scan the instruments, damn you. There's nothing out there to see, anyway.

But, there was.

Something had flashed, small and white, out to his left, at almost the same attitude. Oh my God, he pleaded, don't let it be another aircraft. I've got enough on my plate now, without playing Dodgem. He could call the nearest airfield and ask if they had it on their radar. He had the right of way here.

It was too late. Out of the corner of his eye, he saw it coming. At right angles to his aircraft, it rushed for him as if in joyous greeting and resolved itself into something coherent. Instinctively, he began to descend, desperately hoping to avoid collision. The instrument panel completely forgotten now, he gaped in horror, white-faced through the tiny window.

It came on, tumbling and falling through the night. He could see it clearly now, little arms and legs thrashing and the plump body spinning. Occasionally the face would flash into view, the eyes seeking him, but then it was spun away. His amazement was so great that he only partially registered the phenomenon of an object falling sideways and not down, and he began unconsciously to wingover to his left. A can of soda began to roll across the floor towards him.

With a soft thud, the boy struck the cockpit and stayed, his face pressed against the glass, his sleepy almond-shaped eyes slowly roaming the interior—"Jesus Christ!" the young pilot screamed. He was incapable of any further action or thought.

Meanwhile, the boy continued his perusal, seemingly oblivious to his plight. His pudgy, short-fingered hands grabbed at the window as his thick lips, curved in a lazy smile, smeared the glass. He appeared fascinated with the instrument panel, gleeful. The pilot couldn't see how he was holding on. He was just there!

At that moment, the boy found the pilot's eyes, cowering in the dark of the cabin, and his heavy, moon-shaped face lit up. He pounded on the cabin door with obvious excitement and pointed at the young man, his small mouth working in silence. The pilot saw the door handle begin to turn and lunged for it, feeling the calm, heated air of the cabin already rushing out into the turbulent atmosphere with a gasp; he seized the door and forced it shut again, shouting and cursing incoherently now. When he looked up again the boy was gone.

"Help me! Help me!" he cried aloud as his plane continued its erratic and spiraling descent through the clouds, seeking the earth on its own.

*   *   *

The psychologist sat in the grey cubicle that was his office and awaited his next patient. The day's paper, its headlines screaming of fresh horrors, lay half-heartedly folded next to his chair. Murders, rapes, and kidnappings heralded each day in a fresh parade. How many of the perpetrators of these atrocities, he pondered, had sat across from him in his tiny office over the years?

Were they insane at the time of the act, or did they understand the difference between right and wrong? That was all the court wished to know. Distressingly, the majority had been perfectly lucid when they killed or tortured.

He sighed aloud at the memory of fifteen-year-old murderers, parents who had smothered their infants, and old women who poisoned their decrepit lodgers for their social security checks. He no longer found humor in *Arsenic and Old Lace*.

As he attempted to clean his thick glasses with an old and not-so-clean handkerchief, he admitted to himself some interest in this new referral nonetheless. Here was something different and unbloodied. Possibly a true psychological puzzle.

He had been requested by a local FAA official to do a workup on the young man waiting in his reception area, with the understanding that the patient would pick up the expense. The FAA was simply affording the young man the opportunity to clear himself and regain his aviation license, which had been temporarily suspended pending investigation.

Absently brushing some dandruff from his shoulder, the psychologist flipped through the reports that had been made available to him. The papers gave the young pilot's name as Ernest Thorvald, white male, twenty-four years of age, a college graduate, and a pilot for six years. Urinalysis and blood samples taken within hours of his "incident" had shown no traces of narcotics or alcohol use. A full and lengthy physical conducted over several days had shown him to be free of any disease or organic problems that might affect his judgment or performance. That left the mind. That shrouded and shifting landscape that resisted microscopes and X-rays, yet affected its host far more profoundly than any physical stimuli.

The psychologist leaned forward and spoke into his desk intercom and then quickly stubbed out his cigarette, fanning the smoke with his small hands as he did so. As a final concession to the patient's comfort, he tilted his overflowing ashtray into the wastebasket next to his desk, spilling several butts onto the floor for his efforts. He looked up to see the young man standing nervously in his doorway.

Thorvald was tall and slender and stood with an athlete's easy grace, in spite of his fidgeting. The little man behind the desk could clearly see that he was troubled. His plain, youthful face was pale, the cheeks hollowed. The eyes were red-rimmed and puffy, a painful suffering evident in their nervous travels. A poster boy for college recruitment in his better days, the psychologist thought with a little subjective envy. He himself had graduated college at seventeen and been derided for his small stature, dark complexion, and love of opera. A nerd. Yet now he must help someone who years ago, had they been contemporaries, would probably have made him the butt of cruel dormitory humor.

He pushed his plump body away from his cluttered desk and stood to his full five-foot, five-inch height and indicated the chair opposite. Apprehensively, Thorvald folded himself into the proffered seat. He felt like a high-schooler summoned to the principal's office. The small man across from him intimidated him in spite of his size. He had glimpsed the nameplate on the desk and was not comforted by his foreign-sounding name, Anthony Valerian. Plus, he stank of cigarette smoke, the whole room did, and his clothes looked as if they had never seen an iron. This is a psychologist, he thought angrily. This weirdo is supposed to help me?

Valerian said nothing for a few moments, watching

the workings of Thorvald's face. Subtle, he's not, Valerian mused. Clearly, he does not want to be here. And
yet there is a certain sensitivity to his face. Maybe not
just a jock.

"So, Mr. Thorvald, you've had a problem recently,"
he began without preamble. He often found going
straight at a problem the best method; he eschewed
smarmy introductions and reassurances. Most patients
were too intelligent or neurotic to be lulled by them
in any case. He also knew, from long experience, that
there was no immediate need for them to like the man
who was probing into their thoughts and feelings.
Trust and confidence were things that he would have
to earn along the way.

Thorvald pulled himself upright in his chair and
clasped his hands tightly together. "Yes, I guess so—
a problem."

Valerian said nothing. The silence went on into the
uncomfortable zone.

"An unauthorized landing," Thorvald quietly resumed. "On a closed airfield," he clarified with just a
touch of indignation creeping in. The silence returned.

"Is that bad?" Valerian asked evenly.

Thorvald looked directly at him now, trying to as-
sess whether this earthbound gnome was pulling his
leg or really did not appreciate the gravity of his violation and its subsequent consequences. He couldn't decide, so he answered in what he hoped were the same
bland tones.

"Yes, it's bad. I'm looking at permanent revocation
of my aviator's license. I think that's pretty damn
bad," he finished on a rising note. Control yourself,
he thought.

"Why is it bad?" Valerian asked with exasperating
naivete.

"What?" exploded out of Thorvald before he could
call it back. Was this guy a simpleton, or what? "It's
my living. I need that license in order to fly airplanes,
which happens to be how I make my living. I would

have thought that would be obvious, even to a non-flyer!" He threw in the last for good measure.

"No, no, Mr. Thorvald. You misunderstand me. Why is an unauthorized landing on an abandoned airfield a bad thing? What's the harm?"

Now Thorvald felt like a jerk. He was reacting like a self-centered child. "It's dangerous. Not only to the pilot and his crew and passengers—though I was flying alone at the time—but also to other aircraft in the area. You see, you're supposed to stick with a flight plan and observe certain air traffic control rules along the way."

Valerian could see that he was warming to his subject and nodded to encourage him to go on.

"When you enter an air traffic control zone, they give you altitude and air-speed instructions in order to lessen the chance of midair collisions. They watch the big picture on radar and know better than you could what's out there." He couldn't tell if the little man was understanding him or not. He felt like a grade-school teacher with a bored class.

"So, when you suddenly go sliding off-screen with no explanation, they've got to scramble. They've got to get any other aircraft out of the area, because they don't know what you're doing or where you're going.

"As far as landing at a closed airfield, well, anything or anyone could've been on that strip. I could've plowed into an old fuel truck or a carload of kids sitting out there drinking beer. As it turned out, I got lucky. It's an airfield that hasn't been closed long and was in pretty good shape. What's even luckier is that I'd flown that field before, a number of times actually, and remembered the layout real well. Which was good, because it was darker than hell out there." He finished quietly, rubbing his eyelids with his fingertips as if to massage away the memories of that night.

Well, thought Valerian, very good. He's not in denial of the event, at least. He seems to accept responsibility for his actions. That's a lot more than I usually

get the first time out. This might not be so hard. Now
for why.

"Um, yes, I see, I guess you were lucky, then." He
paused. Thorvald knew what was coming and was preparing himself, beginning to tense around the mouth.
"What made it necessary to change your flight plan,
Mr. Thorvald?"

Thorvald was looking away now, the classic body
language of the liar. After a moment, he turned and
faced Valerian, looking him directly in the eyes for
the first time. *Here we go, his first lie.* Valerian
groaned inwardly.

"I just blacked out, I guess." Thorvald's gaze slid
away to his left. Like a dog, Valerian thought.

"Have you ever experienced such a thing before?"
The psychologist already knew he hadn't, having read
his medical history.

"No, not that I remember."

"Never in school? Or when you were a child?" Valerian persisted.

"No, never," Thorvald answered more firmly.

"Perhaps your parents might remember. Your
mother. Would you mind if I called her?" It could be
very risky bringing up a patient's parents. However,
Thorvald was not here for long-term therapy, only an
evaluation, and Valerian didn't have time for such
niceties.

"No! I mean, yes! I would mind. I'm telling you
I've never had a blackout!"

Valerian guessed that he had told his mother the
truth. They often did.

"Exactly, Mr. Thorvald. You have never experienced blackouts."

Thorvald felt cornered, confused. Was this guy calling him a liar or agreeing with him?

"Mr. Thorvald, blackouts, if they are not organic in
nature, and your medical records show no sign of this,
are usually brought about as a result of great stress.
Now, given that you are an experienced pilot and were
piloting an aircraft that according to your instructor's

evaluations you were very comfortable with, and the weather conditions were challenging but not overly demanding of someone of your experience and training, where was the stress? This episode—was it prior to the flight or during?"

"Episode?" Thorvald spluttered, leaning forward, then back, then forward again. "I'm not sure what you mean."

"Event, Mr. Thorvald. The event that brought about your blackout." The pilot glanced up suspiciously at his heavy emphasis. "As you have pointed out, you have no history of blackouts and for the moment that rules out a long-standing psychosis, which leaves us with the present, or at least, the very recent past.

"Understand that the details of our conversation will remain confidential! The only issue the FAA board is concerned with is your fitness to fly again. Something you wish for as well, I think. Naturally, you must be forthcoming or my report will simply read, 'No conclusions possible.' Whenever you are ready, Mr. Thorvald."

You cagey little bastard, Thorvald thought. You've got me. With a deep, slow exhalation, he began.

When he finished, dry-mouthed and exhausted, nothing happened. No white-coated attendants rushed in to bind him. The little man, Valerian, remained hunched over in his chair staring at the desk top, either lost in thought or totally uninterested. During the telling of his fantastic and, even to himself, unbelievable story, Valerian had shown no reaction. Only occasionally, he would jot something down on a piece of scrap paper and then return to his reverie.

Outside, in the hallway, two people walked by the closed door of the office in subdued conversation. One of them laughed softly at some shared joke. Valerian looked up.

"Did anything strike you as unusual about the boy?" he asked softly.

Thorvald stared at him for a moment, trying to

grasp his meaning. "You mean besides the fact that he was clinging to the outside of my plane as I was racing home in a storm?" He laughed aloud at the absurdity of the question. "I thought that was unusual enough at the time!" He couldn't stop laughing now. The tension was gushing from him in gales.

"What I mean," Valerian continued unperturbed, "is that you actually gave a very good description of the boy. Forget for a moment the circumstances. What impression did he make on you?"

Thorvald's laughter began to subside little by little. He focused on the memory of the face pressed against the rain-drenched windscreen. Yes, there was something. The drooling smile, the thick-lidded, oddly shaped eyes.

"I think," he began hesitantly, "I think he may have been retarded or something."

"Yes," Valerian murmured. "Perhaps he was." He continued to stare thoughtfully at Thorvald. "Mr. Thorvald, do you know this boy?"

For reasons he could not understand, this question alarmed him terribly. He felt anxiety, like ants, crawling and running over his body. "Know him? How could I know him? He's not real! Even I know that! And if you don't, chief, maybe you and I should switch seats."

Valerian leaned sideways and reached for something on the floor, grunting with the effort. When he came up, he had a wad of newspapers clutched in his hand and began to smooth them out on his desk. He spun one of the newspapers around and pushed it in front of Thorvald. His finger rested on a grainy photo of a boy about ten years of age. "Do you know this boy?" Valerian asked him.

Thorvald didn't answer; he slumped forward in his seat, unconscious, his face pressed against that of the boy in the picture.

Valerian spoke quietly into the pay phone in the diner, not wishing to be overheard. "I believe I have a young man who may be of some help in the Edison kidnapping." He waited for a reply from Captain Masterson of the prosecutor's office before continuing. Masterson and he had been thrown together a number of times over the years and had achieved something of a relationship. He knew what Masterson would ask next.

"Anthony, is this young man a patient of yours?"

Valerian understood the implications of the question immediately and had anticipated Masterson's concern. If a trial resulted from information obtained through the therapy, the defense would seize on the ethical violation of patient confidentiality and the whole case would be torpedoed. But there was a young boy missing. A boy with a serious handicap. How long would his captors tolerate the demands this put on them? Or had they planned to tolerate them at all? The clock was ticking.

"Yes," he answered. "He is a patient, a referral for evaluation, actually, but he has expressed a willingness to meet with you. Naturally, I do not intend to reveal what was said in our session. I'm not sure it would be of help, in any case."

There was a significant pause. "Then what can he do for us?"

"I'm not sure."

"Anthony." Masterson's impatience was beginning to show. "Is he a suspect?"

"Again, I'm not sure," Valerian answered truthfully.

Masterson had agreed to the meeting nonetheless, acknowledging inwardly that they had precious little to go on in this case and hadn't the luxury to be choosy. A difficult and sometimes capricious retarded boy had been kidnapped from a prominent local couple. The heir apparent to an aviation empire started by his father, dead now for several years.

His mother, a society girl from old and dwindling money, had married new money in the person of Franklin Edison, thirty years her senior. Brilliant but grasping, bullying, and crude, he had amassed a considerable fortune in his time, saving marriage for his old age. He had sired but one offspring, hopefully christened "Thomas."

Now Thomas was gone. Taken without apparent force from his own bedroom. That in itself was puzzling. Tommy was known to be a handful when angered or frightened. It was hard to picture him going quietly. Of course, they, whoever "they" were, could have been prepared. Ether, gags, and even suffocation could not be ruled out. Even so, it was hard to accept. The bed was hardly mussed. It was as if he had simply risen in the night and floated out his open window. No telltale ladder had been left behind in this kidnapping. His mother claimed the window had been closed when she had last looked in on him.

Had it not been for the computer-generated note left on the bed, there would have been doubts about an abduction at all. The note itself was useless. It might as well have been beamed down from Mars. It was virtually impossible to narrow down its source to any computer or printer, and naturally there were no fingerprints.

The note had simply read, "We have taken the boy. You will hear from us." No demands, rules, or threats. Just a conspicuous "us." Masterson wondered about that. Intended to mislead, or an inadvertent slip?

That was three days ago and there had been no follow-up as of yet. There had been dozens of letters from various psychos and psychics, all claiming revealed knowledge or involvement, and even a bogus ransom note demanding a cool million in cash. All had been easily run down, including the high-school gang that had demanded the money, but none had furthered the investigation one iota.

Not that there weren't suspects. Masterson had two. The mother, Catherine, and her second husband, Roger Scrope. Obvious, really, but not a shred of evidence to connect them with the crime. They had opportunity, means, and motive. A powerful motive, in Masterson's experience. Gain.

Only Tommy stood between them and Edison's aviation empire. In a move typical of the irascible Edison, he had left his retarded son his entire estate. His pining young wife became de facto regent for the young heir but stood to gain nothing directly as long as he lived. Masterson had learned through the rumor mill that this was possibly due to various indiscretions committed by the youthful bride. Especially with Edison's senior executive, Roger Scrope.

Tellingly, the widow was married to the ambitious Scrope just a year later. There was something positively medieval about the whole arrangement, and now the heir apparent had vanished like Richard the Third's princely nephews, leaving the kingdom up for grabs. Masterson had no doubt that once Tommy was found dead, or was legally declared so, the courts would settle the fortune on the mother and, indirectly, on her slightly sinister husband.

Yet, Masterson admitted, this was all speculation. Masterson had met and interviewed both of the Scropes extensively and each had provided the other with an alibi. They were asleep in the same bed the night of the abduction. They had heard nothing and seen nothing and slept through the night undisturbed.

More than that, Masterson doubted that Catherine could have participated in such a scheme. In spite of her reserved, brittle manner, it was obvious that she was racked with grief and terror for her son. It had not escaped Masterson that during Tommy's young life, she had never attempted to hide him in spite of the embarrassment his condition must have created among her society friends. She had often been seen in his company at air shows and local events.

There was one troubling point in her vouchsafing of Scrope, however. She admitted that since her remarriage she slept very soundly and often relied on her husband to wake her when Tommy called for her in the night.

Even so, it was difficult to believe that Scrope could lure the volatile Tommy away in the dead of night. It was well attested that Tommy had little liking for his stepfather, often having tantrums and other less pleasant episodes when forced to be in his company. In fact, when the family had to travel, mother and son traveled separately from the husband, in order to avoid these displays.

Masterson's next step would be to place the couple on the polygraph but he dreaded to do so. In the public's eye it would cast them as prime suspects and the press would make the most of it. The result would be a political firestorm that the prosecutor's office was ill-equipped to weather, especially if they came off clean. They were, after all, extremely powerful citizens and there was no evidence that they were anything but grieving victims.

The office phone rang. It was the receptionist announcing that Captain Masterson's appointments were waiting in the interview room. Masterson hung up, straightened her pantyhose, and walked dispiritedly down the corridor to meet them.

Thorvald sat up quickly from his slouch and felt his face coloring when Masterson introduced herself. It had never occurred to him that "Captain" Masterson would be a female. Especially an attractive, if older one. She must be in her late thirties, he figured, judging by the worry lines around her eyes. Her legs, however, were those of a schoolgirl, long and shapely. She must take pride in them, he thought, as the skirt of her rather severe business suit was just a tad shorter than it needed to be. He was embarrassed by his own reaction, in spite of himself, and relieved that she seemed to take no notice.

Valerian had simply nodded in greeting and returned to studying the top of the table at which they were all seated. Thorvald thought he seemed uncomfortable, as if he were the one in the hot seat. Inwardly, he rued agreeing to meet with Masterson and couldn't imagine what he had to offer her investigation.

"Well, Mr. Thorvald," Masterson opened. "I understand that you have some information about the Edison kidnapping that might be of use to us. Is that so?"

Thorvald looked up at her cool, appraising eyes and began to flush again. "Well, um, you see, I had this . . ." He glanced desperately at Valerian, who was now engrossed in studying his shoes. "I was flying back from Memphis when . . . oh hell! I don't know! I saw something and the good shrink here thinks it might mean something. I really don't know what you two expect from me. I was tired. It was raining.

"You tell me!" He pointed at Valerian. "You're the head doctor!" Masterson's gaze shifted to Valerian. "Anthony? Care to enlighten me a little?"

Valerian roused himself and turned in his chair like a schoolboy facing his teacher. His small hands were clasped together on the tabletop. "It seems Mr. Thorvald had an hallucination, I needn't go into the details of it, that featured the missing boy. What struck me as potentially important about it was that during the experience, and for several days after, he did not recognize the boy as someone he knew. Someone he had been in contact with on many occasions. Memorable occasions, I would think. In fact, a very memorable boy.

"It came out during our session that Mr. Thorvald was employed by the boy's family as a pilot and often flew the mother and child on their trips and escorted them about once they arrived. He is one of the few adult males that the boy appeared to take a genuine liking to. His being a pilot no doubt helped in this, the boy being enamored of planes and flying in general."

Valerian paused, letting the facts sink in. "The night Mr. Thorvald was flying and experienced his 'episode' was the same night the Edison boy was abducted."

Now there was a very long pause. Masterson blinked. "Yes, I see . . . I think. You're insinuating that Mr. Thorvald had some inside knowledge of the abduction plans?"

"Wait a minute! I don't know—" Thorvald started, the color draining from his face.

"No," Valerian interrupted. "I don't mean that, exactly. I believe that Mr. Thorvald, subconsciously, perhaps, may possess some insight into the situation that could be useful in your inquiries." He finished without looking up at either of them.

Masterson stared at him for a while as silence settled on the room. She was unsure of the little man's reasoning, yet based on their past associations, wanted to trust him. To what end, she didn't know. If Valerian thought Thorvald was involved, then he was treading thin ice professionally, but she could have that checked out easily enough. Thorvald was in the air the night it happened and undoubtedly would be remembered by airport personnel. His unauthorized landing had made a minor stir, which only served to clinch his alibi.

But what about the hallucination? Was Valerian hinting at a guilty conscience? She could have her office confirm Thorvald's movements, but what was she to do with him in the meantime? Being an investigator, she hated vagueness.

"Anthony, I'm at a loss here. What exactly is it that you want me to do?"

For the first time during their meeting he turned and faced her directly. "I'd like to suggest that we visit Mr. and Mrs. Scrope at their home." He paused a beat. "All of us."

Masterson glanced over to Thorvald, who looked as if he wished he was anywhere but there. "Would that be agreeable to you, Mr. Thorvald?" she asked.

"Yeah, I guess," he answered reluctantly. "Though I still don't see what you people want from me."

"No," she concurred. "I'm not too sure myself." She glanced significantly at Valerian. "However, I don't see what harm could come of a little visit."

She rose from her chair. "Shall we?"

*   *   *

The Edison estate was a rambling, mock-medieval affair built of grey stone and occupying sprawling, well-tended grounds. Though charming at a distance, at close quarters it presented a rather somber facade, inadvertently achieving an effect shared with its genuine counterparts in Europe. The steep, slated roof gave it a brooding, secretive countenance that Masterson felt matched its new occupant, the usurper Scrope, very well. As she brought the car to a crunching halt in the smoothly raked drive, she thought that at least this would be interesting. The lack of movement in this case had made her restless and combative.

They were greeted at the door by Yolanda, a pretty German au pair whom Masterson had met previously. Too pretty, Masterson thought. Either Catherine was very confident or Scrope was used to getting his way. As a woman, she didn't like the looks of it.

"Gut afternoon, Captain." She smiled through her thick accent. "Haben ze an appointment?"

"Nein, fräulein," Masterson replied breezily. She knew the girl could speak English perfectly when she wanted to. "Haben ze badge. Now run and fetch your master and mistress. It's a little cool to be kept waiting on the stoop."

Yolanda hesitated, annoyance beginning to cloud her smooth face, then thought better of it and ushered them in. Without another word, or taking their coats, she turned pertly on her heel and walked briskly down the hallway, her tight skirt clearly delineating the movements beneath. Masterson turned to the two men with her and noted, with some annoyance, that both had come to attention in the presence of the lovely Yolanda and were raptly following her sinuous exit.

"Anthony," she snapped. "You might want to take a handkerchief to that drool on your chin."

He actually began to dig in his rear pocket and caught himself. Blushing, he turned to study some eminently forgettable artwork hanging nearby.

"Men are so easy," she murmured aloud.

Scrope startled them all, appearing suddenly and
hailing Masterson too loudly. "Bridgid!" he called out.
He had made a point of finding out her first name
shortly after their initial meeting. "Come in, come in."
He was waving them into his office/study. He breathed
good whiskey on her as he forced her to squeeze past
him in the doorway. He stepped aside for the men.
She thought she detected a puzzled, worried look on
his face as he took them in.

"Ernest," he greeted the young man. "What brings
you here? She hasn't got you under arrest, has she?"
Masterson thought he sounded almost hopeful.

"No, sir," he began nervously. "They seem to
think—"

Masterson smoothly cut him off. "We think, since
Mr. Thorvald knew, um, knows Tommy so well and
spent a good deal of time with him, that maybe he can
help us. Point out something we might have missed."
Sounds good, she thought.

"And who's this?" Scrope asked, nodding at
Valerian.

"This is Mr. Anthony Valerian, a professional col-
league of mine. I asked him to assist me," she lied.

As they took seats in the overstuffed armchairs of
the study, Masterson asked after Mrs. Scrope. Roger
was still eyeing the other two men, a bit uneasily,
she thought.

"Eh? Mrs. . . . Catherine? Much as you'd think.
She's taking it damn hard. Lying down now, I expect.
The doctor's got her on some pretty strong sedatives.
Her only child, you know," he added by way of expla-
nation to the men present.

As if it would be any different if she had a dozen,
thought Masterson. This reptile doesn't have an ounce
of feeling for the missing boy or his suffering mother.
She also mentally noted that he had yet to ask about
the progress of the investigation. Most victims didn't
let you get through the doorway before they asked.

Scrope returned his attention to her. "You don't
need to question her anymore, do you?"

"I would like to talk to her, yes."

"Listen, Bridgid, we've done all we can to cooperate, now what I'd like to see—"

He didn't get to finish because at that moment his wife stumbled into the room. "Any news, Ms. Masterson? Have you found him?"

Masterson was shocked. Just three days before Mrs. Scrope had still worn the facade of class and wealth. Not so now. The deterioration was marked. Her hair was ludicrously askew, all the more so because it retained the phantom of its former coiffure. Her face, naked of makeup, was ashen and dry, revealing a woman who was plain, bordering on ugly. The eyes were sunken and dark, whites showing all around. Masterson hardly recognized her. She leaned against an end table for support, wobbling as she clutched a damp handkerchief to her chest.

She seemed slowly to comprehend the effect she had created and made a visible effort to compose herself. Masterson caught Scrope looking at his wife with obvious distaste. The woman's eyes sought Masterson's and managed to hold. "My baby?" she pleaded.

Masterson was on her feet and guiding the wretched woman to a chair. "No news yet, Mrs. Scrope. We just stopped by to follow up on a few things. I know it's a bad time, but really, time is our enemy in situations like these. You understand, don't you?"

"Yes," she whispered, her voice hoarse and faint. "I do."

"Mrs. Scrope, you remember Ernest Thorvald, of course." Masterson nodded in the direction of the uneasy young pilot.

The other woman turned in his direction, puzzlement, then delight rippling across her features. "Ernest!" she cried. "I'm so glad you've come. Tommy was always so glad to see you. It's so thoughtful of you to come by."

Thorvald was virtually squirming with discomfort, his sense of participating in a subterfuge causing a blush to climb his cheeks. He managed to stammer, "The captain, that is Ms. Masterson, thought I should ... well, since I know Tommy, that maybe I could help ... or something," he finished lamely.

Tommy's mother took no notice. "Yes! Yes, of course! That's very clever of the captain."

It was Masterson's turn to blush. She glanced at Valerian, who continued silently to study the Scropes.

Mrs. Scrope rushed on, "You know Tommy as well as anyone. He admired you so much!" She had risen unsteadily from her chair, her eyes bright with excitement. "You talked about boy things with him, didn't you? When I was dozing on our trips? I'm sure I heard you, though I tried not to eavesdrop."

Everyone present was frozen with embarrassment, knowing that such a conversation with Tommy was highly unlikely.

"Catherine, you'd best go lie down," Scrope barked. "I'll send Yolanda round."

She plowed on. "Tommy would confide in you, wouldn't he? About boy things. About hiding places and such?" Tears of hope had begun to slide down her drawn cheeks. She turned toward the doorway, as if to begin the search immediately, her movements now charged with energy. Yolanda had appeared, blocking her path, looking composed and capable, her former perkiness gone as if it had never existed.

Scrope struggled to his feet and shouted, "That's enough!" He spun on Masterson. "You happy now? You people clear out of here! Thorvald, you come see me first thing in the morning at the office," he added ominously.

"Roger, no!" Catherine wailed. "They've come to help, don't you see? They've brought Ernest along. He'll know where Tommy's hiding! He'll find him!"

"Like hell he will," Scrope growled. "He can't find the goddamn airport, for Christ's sake!"

Thorvald sprang to his feet, fists clenched. "You son of a bitch."

Masterson stepped between them and placed one

hand on Thorvald's chest. With the other she gently encircled his thumb, preparing for a straight-wrist take-down. If the one hand didn't work, she was prepared to use the other.

"Take it easy. That's enough now," she murmured, looking directly into Thorvald's eyes. It took a moment for the pressure against her palm to relax and she watched as the pupils began to contract. She knew then he would be okay. She disentangled her hand. "Come on, maybe we'd better get out of here."

"Perhaps first we could take a look at his bedroom?" It was Valerian, who had remained silent throughout and was even now seated, hands folded in his lap, looking small and myopic. He had directed his question to Mrs. Scrope.

"Oh yes," she breathed. "Please, let's look."

Scrope fixed his gaze on Valerian for the first time, his face clearly registering his contempt. "And who the hell are you?"

"Mr. Scrope," Masterson interceded smoothly, "maybe it wouldn't hurt for us to have another look in the boy's room. After all, Thorvald just might notice something we've missed. He did spend quite a bit of time with the boy.

"And I think it would calm your wife to see us making some kind of effort, don't you think?" she added quietly.

He looked as if he thought nothing of the kind, and was about to say so, but his wife had seized Valerian and was escorting him towards the hall. The unhappy Thorvald trailed morosely behind like a forgotten chaperone. Yolanda was left sulking.

"Well, I'll be damned," Scrope muttered. "It seems it doesn't matter what I think. You run along with your little friends now, Bridgid, and have your look. But I just hope it's been worth it to you 'cause I'm gonna have your job over this. You've gotten nowhere with this investigation and now you're grasping at straws."

"I don't think you'd want it," she replied evenly.

"The job. You have to deal with too many people like yourself. It can be very unpleasant and not a little depressing." With that she smiled, turned on her heel, and went to join the others, wondering how she was going to explain her actions to the prosecutor. She prayed Valerian knew what he was doing.

She found the room much as she remembered it, large and oblong, with leaded windows overlooking an ill-kept garden. Only now the bed was made and the windows closed. She noted a trace of fingerprint powder on the sill and thought how difficult the damn stuff was to get rid of.

Every conceivable surface was cluttered with the objects of Tommy's great, if limited, passion. Airplanes. Toy planes clustered on every shelf and nightstand. Paintings and photographs lined the walls. Picture books of aircraft spilled from his bookshelves and desk. Even his quilt was stitched with them and the curtains framing his windows were an airplane print. Finally, in a crowning achievement, dozens of scale models dangled by invisible wires, festooning the very air in Tommy's room.

Tommy had made no distinction between the civil and the military, but suspended them all in the crowded skies above his bed. Everything from the Wright Brothers' first effort to the space shuttle was represented. To complete the effect, the ceiling was painted a sky-blue and laced with puffy white clouds.

At the far end of the room, Catherine Scrope was chatting loudly and gaily to Valerian, her plumpish and distracted escort, pointing out each model as evidence of her Tommy's incipient, if undiscovered, intelligence. Masterson smiled as Valerian dutifully nodded. Catherine could not have been more delighted at his responses. For the moment she was happy again, playing hostess to this odd assortment of visitors who seemed to care about her boy. For the moment Tommy's room was a source of joy and pride to her and the terrors of its vacancy were held at bay.

Thorvald had been forgotten for the moment and was left standing over the missing boy's bed. Upon seeing Masterson, he glanced furtively in the direction of Mrs. Scrope and her owlish partner and then hissed under his breath, "Great goin', Captain. Just great! Now I'm not only suspended, I'm unemployed as well."

He certainly hasn't benefited from his relationship with Valerian and me, Masterson thought grimly, and began to ponder what strings she could pull to help him out. But Thorvald wasn't finished.

"I want out of here. There's nothing we can do to help this poor woman. In fact, we've probably done more harm than good by coming here. She thinks Tommy and I shared some kind of secrets! I could hardly understand him when he talked, which wasn't very damn much. Mostly he just showed me his newest models when I'd come around to pick up him and his mom. Sometimes he'd even punch me when she wasn't looking."

Masterson couldn't hide her smile. Thorvald sounded just like an aggrieved older brother complaining of a roughneck younger sibling. She wondered if he knew that combative behavior was sometimes an expression of love. At least, when she thought about her own boys, she certainly hoped so. It wasn't hard to see why Tommy might have loved this young man. Especially when you considered Scrope as the alternative.

Out of the corner of her eye she saw Valerian waving them over.

"Mr. Thorvald," Valerian began. "Perhaps you could tell us which of these aircraft"—he waved vaguely at the ceiling—"would have been Tommy's favorite?"

Catherine Scrope smiled confidently at the young man, obviously sure that he would have the answer. Thorvald hardly missed a beat.

"The B-seventeen. Definitely. He was always wanting me to unhook it from the ceiling so he could show it to me. He had it hanging right over his bed." He pointed helpfully at the ceiling but a filament with nothing on the end twisted slowly in the air currents of the room like an unbaited fishing line. Thorvald's gaze darted from plane to plane, always coming back to the empty line. "I'm sure it was here. He especially liked that one because his dad, Mr. Edison, had one in mothballs stored out at the old . . ." Thorvald's face went slack for a moment and he seemed to lose his train of thought. "The old airfield. The one I landed at that night."

"I see," Valerian replied. "Maybe we should take a ride out there?"

It took several minutes for Masterson to realize that she was looking at a crime scene. Once she had placed it together in her mind, replayed it for discrepancies and continuity, she believed she knew what had happened here.

Standing next to her in the dimly lit interior of the old bomber's fuselage, Thorvald thought he heard a sharp intake of breath and glanced fearfully at the woman next to him. She continued to stare down into the plastic bowl that projected from the plane's underside. The belly-gunner's turret.

In his hand he held the severed end of a length of hose that snaked its way into the turret and ended in an ancient, high-altitude oxygen mask, its deflated, insectlike face staring emptily back at them like the discarded carapace of some giant species of locust. It shifted a little, as if it had a life of its own, animated by the inadvertent movement of his arm. As it did so, it crept forward, partially covering the crushed remains of a plastic miniature of the aircraft whose belly they stood in. It reminded him of an octopus settling over a wounded fish.

Masterson looked at Thorvald, who had visibly paled at finding these traces of the missing boy's passage. He was swaying and she thought he might faint.

She reached over and gently removed the tubing

from his grasp and spoke in a whisper. "Let's step out of here now. Try not to touch anything else on your way out."

He numbly obeyed and led the way to the ladder. It had taken less than twenty minutes to drive to the airfield from the Scrope home. The lock on the double-gated, chain-link fence had yielded easily to the key reluctantly supplied by Scrope himself. Masterson was sure he had been on the verge of demanding she produce a search warrant when some warning device went off in his head, reminding him that victims, innocent victims, do not obstruct the police in a search for their children. Even stepchildren. Masterson had greatly enjoyed the alarmed expression on Scrope's face when she announced their intention to visit the airfield.

On their way out the door, almost as an afterthought, she asked Scrope who else had keys to the airfield. "The caretaker," he spat. "Among others. How the hell should I know?"

Catherine had cheerfully corrected him. "Oh, no, Roger," she chirped, her mood buoyed with hope. "You dismissed him several weeks ago, don't you remember? And then changed the locks in case he tried to come back and damage anything. There's no one on the grounds anymore. You're the only one with keys, dear."

Scrope's face was ashen as Masterson eased the door closed.

On the drive over, Masterson made several calls from her car phone as she let Thorvald drive the route he knew so well. The first whispered, cryptic conversation was with her sergeant, whom she had given the task of verifying Thorvald's alibi prior to leaving the office.

It was much as she'd thought. Assisting officers of the Nashville P.D. had confirmed his filing of a flight plan during the time in question and several of the airport's female employees remembered his face from the grainy, black and white photo published in the

local paper—an embarrassing commemoration of his
inexplicable change of landing sites.

The second call was to the detective she had assigned to keep the Scrope home under surveillance.
"If he leaves the house, follow him—discreetly. Don't
put a stop on him unless I say so. Anything unusual,
call me. Anything."

She hung up and glanced back uneasily at Valerian
and Catherine Scrope in the rear seat. She needn't
have worried about being overheard. Catherine was
chatting with the taciturn Valerian like a schoolgirl on
her first double date, undeterred by her escort's lack
of social skills. Masterson couldn't help but smile at
the unlikely pairing.

The corrugated metal doors of the antiquated aircraft hangar had presented more of a problem than
the gates. The lock had yielded easily enough, but it
had taken Thorvald several moments to get the heavy
doors to separate and roll open on their rusty,
dented tracks.

The cavernous interior was gloomy and echoed
slightly with their steps on the cracked concrete flooring. Above, a weak, greenish daylight filtered in
through tinted fiberglass, giving everything a murky,
underwater look.

The great warbird bristled with armament—a mechanical revenant of an era of heroes and just causes.
Twin guns thrust forward defiantly from turrets located at its belly, top, and tail. An additional two were
mounted at the front in stationary positions. Masterson glanced quizzically at Thorvald.

"All the firing pins and bolts have been removed,"
he offered.

Behind them Catherine Scrope called out,
"Tommy?" She took a few halting steps toward the
ancient World War II bomber, but Masterson, suddenly afraid of what she might find inside, forestalled her.

She took Catherine gently by the elbow. "Why

don't you wait with Mr. Valerian while I take a look around? All right? It won't take but a moment."

"The gunner's turrets were Tommy's favorite," Thorvald said when Valerian had taken Catherine's hand and led her out into the sun. "He liked them so much that his dad, Mr. Edison, had their motors hooked up to the power in the hangar."

Masterson gave no sign of having heard him. Her face was pressed to the gunner's port beneath the plane.

"So now you can operate them. That was Tommy's favorite thing. He would sit inside for hours with an old oxygen mask on and spin the turret around. All you've got to do is press on the foot pedals." He finished awkwardly, oppressed by the silence that surrounded them.

Masterson turned toward him, a smudge of dust on her cheek. "There's something in there. Can we get inside?"

It was debris, obscure and dimly seen through the scratched and scarred plastic of the belly-gunner's turret, that drew them into the fuselage. Inside, threading their way cautiously through a hanging garden of wires and cracked tubing, they were greeted by the smell of old leather and moldering canvas.

Peering into the belly turret with the aid of her penlight, Masterson could now make out clearly what she had noticed from outside. Evidence that Tommy had been here. Over her shoulder, she heard Thorvald murmur, "That's Tommy's model."

But it was the high-altitude mask that had her attention. One of the straps that secured it to the wearer's face was broken, recently if she was any judge. The rubber tubing that led from the mouthpiece snaked its way up and out of the turret. She followed its course with the light, turning to her left. It ended, severed, within a few feet of a fire extinguisher mounted to the inner wall of the aircraft. The remaining half dangled from the ceiling.

On hands and knees, she crept to the extinguisher,

playing the light across its metal surface. "CO_2," she whispered. She noted the splayed end of the oxygen tube and compared it to the slightly flared nozzle of the extinguisher. A hot anger began to flush her cheeks. She knew what had been done here.

She walked back to the turret and stared down, an ugly picture forming in her mind. She saw a young boy, seated and strapped into the gunner's harness, high-altitude mask in place for added realism, grasping the handles of the neutered .50 cals., ready for action. She saw him pressing furiously on the control pedals, spinning first this way, then that, to counter the enemy threat, busily blasting away at a sky swarming with enemy fighters. Oblivious to any distractions but the mission at hand. A happy and excited boy.

A boy awakened in the middle of the night and promised an unexpected treat. An adventure. A trip to the old airfield and its wonderful bomber. She saw the bargain of his cooperation and silence sealed with the treasured model that spun lazily over his bed. Always just beyond his reach.

She also saw a man. A man smiling down at the tiny warrior happily ensconced in the gunner's turret beneath him. She saw him unstrap a fire extinguisher from the wall of the aircraft and carry it closer to the edge of the turret, being careful so as not to tug on the boy's mask and gain his attention. She saw the man sever the tubing and carefully fit it over the nozzle of the extinguisher.

She watched. Still smiling, the man leans over the rim of the turret and looks down at the boy. The boy, beginning to notice the lack of air, looks back at him, eyes widening in panic. His small hands begin to pluck frantically at the carefully tightened straps. But the man is quicker. He pulls the safety pin on the extinguisher and squeezes the release handle. A rush of freezing gas pushes its way through the tubing and into the boy's straining lungs. His struggles are fierce, but brief.

She sees the man disengage the tube and return the

extinguisher, pin intact, to its wall mount. Then calmly detach the tubing and remove the boy's mask. Straining because of the acute angle, he lifts the boy's inert body out and carries it away to dispose of it. He fails to remember the scale model of the B-17 crushed beneath the boy's body in his final struggles.

Turning to leave, Masterson sees Thorvald, puzzled and shaken, studying the cut tubing. She takes it from him and says something. She isn't sure what.

Leaving Thorvald to guard the hangar, Masterson made a series of calls from her car phone. The first was to the assistant prosecutor assigned to the case. She wanted an immediate search warrant for the Edison estate and all vehicles garaged there. If Tommy's body had been transported from the airfield, it was probably in the trunk of a car. Fibers from his clothing would likely be found there.

She wanted included in the warrant all clothing worn by Roger Scrope. If and when they found Tommy, fibers adhering to his body could place Scrope at the scene. Lastly, she wanted a thorough search conducted for any sedatives, prescription or otherwise, that might be concealed in the house. Catherine's statement that since her marriage to Scrope she slept soundly had taken on an ominous meaning.

Oh yes, she almost forgot. Fingerprints. She wanted both Scrope and the German woman printed for comparison to any latents they might find in the aircraft. He might be able to explain most of them away legitimately as part of his proprietorship, she thought, but the fire extinguisher and the model aircraft would be tough. Still, it was all circumstantial, and she knew it. She didn't even have a body or the slightest clue where to look for it.

Her second call was to her sergeant. She needed him to get the evidence van and its crew mobilized and on its way ASAP and to make arrangements with the sheriff's office for a body dog. If Tommy had been buried nearby and in a shallow grave, and remember-

ing Scrope's lean but flabby physique she'd bet that
was the case, then the dog had a reasonable chance
of finding him. To shore up their chances, she also
asked that the sergeant coordinate with the state police for a chopper and an infrared scope. The heat
generated by decomposition often produced red spots
or "readings" against a cooler landscape. It could, at
least, produce targets for the dog to check out.

Masterson sat back in her seat and surveyed the
scene. Thorvald still stood at the hangar door, nervously shifting from one foot to the other. Valerian
and Catherine Scrope had found a seat on a grassy
knoll nearby and seemed to be enjoying the sun. Occasionally, Valerian would glance in Masterson's direction with a quizzical expression. Perceptive, as always,
he knew something was up.

In a short while, she thought, this tranquil scene
would erupt with activity. Vehicles, searchers, dogs,
evidence men, and helicopters would descend on them
like an invading army. She decided to send the others
back in her car. Once Catherine realized that it was a
body that was being looked for, she would be incon-
solable. Masterson knew she would not have time to
deal with that.

While she still had a few minutes and the privacy
of her car, she mulled over the situation. Without a
body and autopsy results her case was circumstantial
at best. She felt her confidence and energy drifting
away but then an idea, small at first, but insistent and
pugnacious, began to force its way into her consciousness. Climbing its way up from some darker part of
her, it seized her imagination and demanded action.
It challenged her to set aside such things as physical
evidence and logic and come to grips with the enemy.
If you have no strengths, it whispered, then probe for
your opponent's weaknesses. She reached for the
phone and dialed Scrope's number.

Yolanda answered on the second ring. "Scrope residence." Her voice was low and husky, with only the
trace of an accent.

"Ah, Yolanda," Masterson purred. "This is Captain Masterson. I'm calling from the airfield. Is your boss available?"

There was a pause. Masterson pictured Scrope shaking his head vigorously.

"No, *Miss* Masterson, I'm afraid he's engaged with business at the moment."

Bridgid didn't miss the catty dig. "Well, look over your shoulder and tell him that it is very important. Then hand him the phone."

There was a hiss of breath: Yolanda was not happy. Masterson heard the receiver clatter onto a hard surface. A few moments later it was snatched up by Scrope.

"Yes?" he nearly shouted. Nerves, she thought.

She summoned up all her bravado. "Roger," she began, letting the use of his first name sink in. "I've some important news for you."

"By God, I should hope so, after all the upset you've caused around here. Where's my wife?"

Somewhere along the line, she heard the faint click of an extension being lifted.

"Yolanda? Is that you? Good. Stay on the line. This affects you, too."

Scrope burst in, "There's no one else on the line! What are you getting at?"

Masterson continued without answering his concerns. "We've come across several items of evidence in the hangar containing the old B-seventeen. With some physical evidence to work with now, naturally we wish to begin eliminating suspects—and family or household members."

"What . . ." Scrope sounded as if he was choking. "What kind of evidence have you found?" His tone was very reasonable now. A concerned stepfather.

Masterson ignored him. "Yolanda, is your hair naturally blond, or does it come from a bottle?"

The question was so unexpected that she forgot herself. "What? I am natural. What do you mean?"

Gotcha! Masterson crowed to herself.

"Yes, of course you are. It's just that we'll have to have some hair samples from you to compare to some we found at the airfield. Not to worry, the ones we have looked bleached ... I think. Besides, you've never had reason to go out there with Tommy, have you? At least, I don't remember you mentioning it in your statements."

This time there was no answer, just a long pause followed by the quiet click of the extension receiver being replaced.

Scrope stepped into the silence. "Where's this leading, Captain?" He had restored her rank. "I can vouch for Yolanda."

"Even at the time of night that Tommy was taken from his bed? I don't think so, Roger. You were asleep then, remember? In any case, I'm not singling her out. I'll have to have prints from you both, as well as fiber samples from your clothes. It shouldn't take long. We can do it all right in your home."

"You suspect me, don't you?" Scrope hissed into the phone, fear and stress burning off his thin veneer. "You suspect I had something to do with Tommy's death—"

"Death? I thought we were investigating a kidnapping."

She heard a chair scrape across hardwood flooring.

"Just relax, Roger. My team will take about thirty minutes getting there."

She disconnected and immediately dialed another number. The investigator surveilling the Scrope home answered. "Yeah, boss."

"Stan, in about ten minutes, I think, you'll see both Scrope and Yolanda leave the house in a hurry. Don't let 'em. Detain them both and separate them. I think she'll want to help us out with this thing. I've got a search warrant and team headed your way. Call me as soon as anything breaks, and remember, keep them apart!"

"Right-o, boss. I'm on it."

*   *   *

The call came just as the evidence van was pulling up to the hangar. "Masterson here."

"Well, boss, you were wrong. They came out in five, not ten minutes. I thought the house was on fire!"

"Anything, Stan?" Her temples were beginning to throb.

"Other than her spillin' her guts and claiming Scrope coerced her into the scheme? Nah, nothing much."

"Stan, you son of a—"

"Oh yeah, there was something else. She says she's willing to cooperate and testify against Scrope if we'll offer her a deal. She's pretty smart, huh? How long she been in this country?"

Masterson felt a sense of euphoria coming over her. "Give the big man a call and see what he's willing to go for. Remind him she's a foreigner. He'll have some calls to make."

The sight of Catherine Scrope reminded her of reality. "Stan," she whispered unnecessarily. "Can she lead us to the body?"

There was a heavy sigh on the other end. "Yeah, that too. She says they planted him out by the runway."

Masterson's euphoria completely vanished.

It was after midnight and the medical examiner's van had borne its small cargo into the darkness before Masterson had a chance to speak privately with Valerian. She had sent Thorvald and Catherine Scrope away shortly after the arrival of the evidence team with no explanation of her planned activities. Now it would be her sad duty to meet with the wretched woman and break the news of her son's death and her husband's involvement. Her comrades' congratulations only served to make her feel jaded and cynical.

She turned and looked for a moment at Valerian, who stood silently staring at the invisible horizon, floodlights from the adjacent excavations making his glasses opaque, his mood unreadable.

"Anthony," she began quietly, "there's something that doesn't quite add up in all this."

He did not turn and face her or give any indication that he had heard.

"It's about Thorvald," she resumed. "When you first brought him to me, I thought you were taking a big chance. I figured you suspected he had some involvement or inside knowledge of what had happened to Tommy and that that knowledge, that guilt, was what had caused the episode. I thought you were playing it close to the wire professionally by bringing a patient that you knew wanted to talk. But it didn't turn out that way. He really knew nothing."

A moisture-laden breeze drifted across them, causing them to draw closer together in the shadows of the arc lights. At the edge of the field, the same wind moved sighing through the pines and disappeared.

"So why, Anthony?" She was straining to see his face in the darkness. "Why did Thorvald land at this field? What did he see up there? If it was guilt, I could understand it. Anthony?"

When he began to speak, it was so softly that she had to bend down to hear him, though each word was distinct, as if he had thought on his reply for a long time. "Bridgid, when I brought Thorvald to your office, it wasn't because I believed he had guilty knowledge. Quite the contrary. If I had suspected that, ethically, I would have been prohibited from doing so.

"No, I knew he was telling the truth during our session. I've been in this business for twenty-five years. If anything, he was more bewildered than I was. I brought him to you because he seemed to have some connection to the case. I couldn't understand what myself. Yet I couldn't discount the coincidence of his episode with the disappearance of that poor boy. I had no idea if he had anything of value to offer you. As it was, he led us to this airfield. He had some connection to the boy. Or, more likely, the boy to him."

"Anthony, how—"

"I've no idea how." He removed his glasses and began to polish them absently with his tie. "I've spent most of my life studying the mind and its workings, yet I confess I know nothing about the movements of the soul."

They both turned, each with their separate thoughts, and stared down at the tiny empty grave.

THE EXISTENTIAL MAN

Lee Killough

LEE KILLOUGH has blended the science fiction and mystery genres together with extremely satisfying results, as evidenced by the novels *Deadly Silents*, *Spider's Play*, and *Dragon's Teeth*, all involving crimes on high-technology planets. She is no less successful at combining the mystery genre with the supernatural, as evidenced by her short stories, some of which have collected in the book *Aventine*. Born in Kansas, she works as a radiologic technologist, and currently lives in Manhattan.

The gun muzzle gaped like a cave before the con- demned man's eyes. He screamed silently behind his gag ... furious, terrified, disbelieving. *I can't really be about to die.* He struggled to breathe through his smashed nose. *I can't end here, not like this!* In the mud of a riverbank, trussed like an animal for slaughter. Someone would see them. A full moon shone overhead, for god's sake! Help had to come in time to save him!

He kicked at his executioner, but his legs, cramped from hours in the car trunk waiting for dark, jerked without control. The killer cocked his gun.

Terror and fury blazed to incandescence. The condemned man glared over his gag at the shadowed face. *No! I refuse to die! And I sure as hell won't let you get away with what you've done, you fucking bastard! Somehow, some way, I'll find a way to—*

Ripping pain cut off the thought.

Sergeant David Amaro shaded his camera lens from the glare of July sunlight off the river. Sweat trickled down his neck. What the hell had possessed him to volunteer for this floater call? Granted, it could be worse. At least the sodden body sprawled on the riverbank did not smell.

David focused the lens for closeups of the shattered, exposed bone where a face had been, then on the large hole in the forehead. "Do you mind repeating your story once more, Mr. Ballard?"

The fisherman sighed. "My hook snagged off my hat and the current carried it into this backwater. When I waded in after it I saw—his face just under the water." The fisherman paused. "Why dump him where the river's so shallow?"

David shrugged. "Intelligence isn't a prerequisite for crime. Thank you. We won't keep you any longer."

The fisherman hesitated, glancing from David to the coroner and ambulance attendants, obviously reluctant to give up the thrill of his part in a police investigation, before picking up his tackle box and trudging away.

David watched him pass the uniformed officers securing the crime scene perimeter, then turned back to the river. *Had* the killer dumped the body in shallow water? The woods marking the normal water level stood five or six feet back from this year's shoreline.

"How long has he been dead, Doc?"

Dr. Miles Jacobs peeled open the shirt to expose the chest. "Hard to say. The fish have done a job on all the exposed flesh so he's been in the water a while. Also notice he's mummified. I expect I'll find a lot of him gone to adipocere. Until the autopsy, my best guess is one to five years."

The skin under the shirt looked dark and leathery. One to five years ... but it could be even longer. David remembered reading of adipocere, fatty tissues changed chemically to waxy material, preserving bodies for decades. "Do you suppose we can get fingerprints?"

Jacobs examined the clenched fists, cut loose from the wire binding the wrists to a concrete block. "Maybe. I'll see at the autopsy tomorrow." He stepped back. "If you'll finish we'll pack him up and be on our way."

David pulled on a pair of surgical gloves from the crime scene kit and reached for the nearest pocket of the dead man's trousers. But as he touched the fabric, a storm of emotions blasted him ... furious anger, bowel-loosening terror, driving urgency. *Get him!* a voiceless cry screamed in his head. *Burn the fucking scum who did this to me!*

"Amaro? What's wrong?"

David glanced up to see Jacobs eyeing him in concern. He ducked back over the body. "Nothing. Just a lunch hamburger versus the heat." No way would he mention the voice and have everyone accuse him of going wacko again.

The pockets contained nothing. The hands bore no watch or rings. Stepping back, David stripped off the gloves and scrubbed his hands on his thighs. But the voice continued in his head.

It raged on even with the body hauled away in a black plastic bag, and while he and the uniformed officers assisting in the crime scene investigation searched the area. They turned up trash and tracks, but none appeared more than a few months old, and all more related to fishing and canoeing than murder.

About what David expected. He had a better chance of winning the lottery than finding any relevant physical evidence of the murder after all the time and weather since—

The thought choked off in a new wave of terror. The scene blurred to a double exposure, the river running simultaneously sunlit and sheened with moon-light. Terrible chill gripped him ... followed by an explosion in his head.

"Sergeant Amaro?"

The uniforms stared at him. David fought panic. Could he be going psycho again? He forced a grin. "I've had a vision. Of air-conditioning. Let's pack it in."

Back at the Law Enforcement Center across the alley from the county courthouse, David nodded to a deputy coming out of the Sheriff's Office then pushed through the door into the detectives' squadroom on the PD side of the corridor.

He dropped into his desk chair and pressed the heels of his hands against his eyes, willing the voice to shut up. With all the victims deserving righteous wrath—high school kids killed by cocaine and crack, the Chaffin girl's strangulation, still unsolved after two years—why did this one affect him so much more? The manner of death suggested an execution, a falling out of thieves.

"You all right, Dave?"

David made himself raise his brows at Lieutenant Christopher. "I'm fine."

His lanky commander rested a hip on the edge of the desk. "You look a bit like you did when ..."

No need to finish. David knew what he meant.

Memory told David he kissed Jan goodbye that Tuesday two years ago and drove straight to head-quarters. Except he walked in on Wednesday morning.

Fellow officers testified he had come in Tuesday, but left again to investigate crack and cocaine appearing in the area, and never came back. They found his car in the high school parking lot. Several students remembered talking to him. But what happened after that? He returned with a nightmare but no sign of physical injury, clean-shaven and neatly dressed—just stripped of possessions as well as memory ... gun, ID, handcuffs, keys, even his watch and wedding ring. Investigation failed to trace him, and the shrinks to recover his memory.

He rolled a report form into the typewriter. "I'm feeling the heat is all. Do you want to know about the body?"

Christopher eyed him, then nodded.

David consulted his notebook. "Dead over a year. Male, black hair, about five-eleven, mid-thirties, average weight. Possibly Hispanic. Complexion . . . hard to tell. Not exactly a unique description; it stretches to fit even me. Shot through the forehead with a large caliber weapon, maybe a .45."

"What's your game plan?"

He shrugged. "See if the autopsy gives us anything useful. Check missing persons reports. Run his prints through NCIC. Contact informants about criminal disputes over the past several years. The regular routine."

But David knew he lied. The anger of the dead man beating him made this one anything but routine.

He fled down a long, dark tunnel. Heavy breath snarled behind him. Terror kept David from looking back at what pursued him, but every instinct screamed against letting it catch him.

Ahead glowed the end of the tunnel. The golden light there promised sanctuary and peace. David struggled toward it, breath scorching his throat.

Figures moved in the light ahead. David fought for breath to call. "Help!"

The figures turned. The breathing behind rasped louder with every step.

"*Please* help me!"

Why did they always just stand there!

The terror behind blasted him with fetid, suffocating breath. Claws closed on his shoulder. Bitter cold and white-hot heat spread out through his body from their touch. He screamed, fighting the grip. But as always the claws bit deeper, pulling him back . . . turning him. And as the terror came into view . . .

He woke thrashing.

Jan threw her arms around him. "David! It's all

right! You've had a nightmare, but it's over now and you're safe."

He buried his head against her breasts, drinking in her familiar scent, the silk of her skin, clutching at the security of her reality. "I love you."

Her cheek rubbed the top of his head. "What was it about?"

"I don't know." The truth could only worry her. "It's the kind you can't remember."

Presently she went back to sleep, but David could not make himself close his eyes again. He lay awake the rest of the night, cold with remembered terror.

In daylight, the nightmare faded beneath the routine of investigation as David combed through missing persons records. Even a rat pack member must have people who cared enough to miss him. To be thorough, he went back ten years, and checked not only his department's records but those of the Sheriff's Office and the MPs at neighboring Fort Carey. Eight men fit his dead man's description.

By noon he sat at his desk going through the eight missing persons reports. At the desk back-to-back with his, Bill Purviance snarled over a file of his own.

David raised his brows. "Your drug case not going well?"

Purviance grimaced. "I can't get a hold on this Stacey kid."

David sympathized. "I never could, either."

"He's like Teflon!" Purviance slapped the folder closed.

"He smells every plant, undercover officer, and wire a mile away. I'd try sweating the supplier's name out of him, but he'd just laugh at me. And then the supplier will find another dealer and we'll be back to fucking square one. How's your floater?"

"I'm trying to identify him." Anger swirled around David. He felt the pile of flesh and bone fuming at the hospital where it waited for today's autopsy. David gritted his teeth. *Back off! I'm doing what I can.* After waiting so long to have his death discovered, John Doe could wait a few more days for retribution.

But the demand for immediate action nagged at David until he scooped together the photographs of his possibles and headed for the door.

Most of his informants rose late. Only a handful held day jobs. Like Arlie Rudd at the European Motors garage. "Do you know any of these faces?"

Arlie wiped his hands on a shop rag before picking up the photos. "You think one might be the dude in the river?" He flipped through the stack. Twice he paused, giving David hope, but when he handed the photos back, he shook his head. "Sorry, man. None of them rings a bell."

"Maybe you can think of someone who might not be reported missing because of what he was into and with whom?"

Arlie picked up a socket wrench and leaned back under the hood of an MG GB. "I haven't heard of anything recent."

"This wouldn't be recent. It could be anytime up to five to ten years ago."

Arlie hooted. "Ten years! Man, you're talking ancient history. No one remembers that far back!"

"The killer might. You listen around, like at that midnight chop shop of yours, and see if finding this body has made anyone nervous."

Two other informants he found had no better information. Neither heard of any executions. Neither recognized the missing men as linked to criminal activity that might be fatal.

David headed for Jacobs' office at the hospital.

The pathologist relaxed in his desk chair, still in scrub clothes. "We had a time unclenching the fingers but here are your prints."

"Yes!" David snatched up the card Jacobs shoved across the desk. The squares designated for the thumbprints showed only smudges, but the fingertips produced discernable ridge patterns ... all ulnar loops except for a tented arch on the right index finger. With luck he would have an ID by tomorrow. "What else can you tell me?"

The pathologist sucked on an empty pipe. "He died of a bullet fired through his frontal bone and exiting through the occipital bone. No surprises there. He also sustained multiple facial fractures ... a broken nose several hours before dying then malar and maxillary fractures post mortera. The fracture lines indicate several blows with something broad and flat."

Such as a concrete block? David's stomach lurched at the image of the killer pounding identity out of the dead face. "Any change in your estimate of the time of death?"

Jacobs shook his head. "Sorry."

So much for that. "What about distinguishing details?"

"He didn't smoke." Air hissed through the empty pipe. "X-rays show retained lower wisdom teeth, very few fillings, and old healed fractures of the distal right radius and ulna and left second and third metacarpals."

The dead man broke a hand? Driving back to headquarters, David rubbed his own left hand, slammed in a car door by an angry motorist, and grimaced in displeasure. Just what he needed, shared trauma to give the dead man added hold over him.

At headquarters he wired the prints to the FBI's National Criminal Information Center, then began calling relatives of the missing men to ask about habits and medical histories. Had their husband ... brother ... father ... son ever broken his right arm and left hand? Did the missing man smoke? Would they please give him the name of their dentist?

The questions eliminated most of the men. They had the wrong number of wisdom teeth, and either they had never broken a bone or they broke different ones than the dead man. The three names left remained mostly because of unknown dental and fracture histories.

The watch ended without word from NCIC on the fingerprints.

*   *   *

The tunnel seemed darker than ever . . . colder, longer. David ran harder than ever, straining toward the light. Yet the horror behind gained just as fast. Its claws closed on his shoulder, and from beyond the excruciating cold and heat came the voice he associated with the dead man. *No you don't! First you have to nail that murdering bastard.*

The claws dragged David around.

He woke drenched and shaking but, this time, without screaming. Jan slept undisturbed against him.

He sat up and stared into the darkness. Now the dead man had joined the horror. Or . . . *had* he just joined? One to five years ago put the death within the time frame of David's lost day. Did the events connect? Did that account for the dead man's effect on him?

Which suggested a more disturbing question. Had his vision at the river been something seen through the dead man's eyes or . . . his own?

He had been hunting the drug supplier whose junk killed three kids, working the case with righteous wrath. In the darkness, David hugged his knees, his gut knotting. Had he caught up with the scum and lost control? According to the shrink, amnesia resulted from an experience so traumatic that the mind rejected all memory of it. Violating his cherished belief in law and due process could fall into that category.

He leaned his head on his knees. What had he done that missing day?

The report on the dead man's prints came back from NCIC shortly before noon. David snatched the telex from the secretary and read it with fingers crossed. But the charm failed. The FBI had no match in their criminal files. He slam-dunked the telex in his wastebasket. This damned case refused to give him a break!

He fired a telex back to Washington requesting that the prints be checked against the civilian files, then shoved on his sunglasses and headed for the parking lot. It appeared he must make his own break.

First stop ... Rusty Ubel at the Easy-Cash pawn shop on the road west out of town.

Opening the door brought a welcoming wave of cool air and a two-tone chime. At the sound, carroty hair and a pair of eyes appeared above the rear edge of a display case. "Sergeant Amaro. I heard you were looking for me yesterday."

David nodded. "I need to know if any of these men look familiar." He held out the three photos.

A short arm reached up from behind the display case for them. "Ah. The body in—"

Screaming brakes interrupted him. David raced for the door. On Fort Carey Boulevard outside, a driver swore at a boy on a skateboard.

From under the arm David used to hold the door open, Rusty sniffed. "Crazy kids."

Agreed, David reflected, remembering his own skateboarding days. He and his friends not only darted through traffic, they caught tows on passing cars and trucks. It took a broken arm to convince him of the stupidity of that ...

The thought stumbled. That break had been in his right arm ... the distal end of the radius and ulna. The same place the dead man broke his.

A chill slid down his spine. First the similarity of hand fractures, now this one. What were the odds of him sharing not only physical description but medical history with a victim? And dental history. He, too, retained just his lower wisdom teeth. Still, it had to be coincidence. What else could it be?

David turned his hands palm up. Fingerprints would prove the coincidence. When he got back to headquarters he would—

The thought remained unfinished. The sunlight at the open door highlighted the ridges of his fingers enough to see the general pattern. David's breath stuck in his chest. The highlighting showed ulnar loops on finger after finger ... except for the tented arch on the right index finger.

"Sergeant! What's wrong?"

The nightmare tunnel stretched before him. Fiery-cold claws clamped on his shoulder. The pain sapped all his strength, destroying resistance to the pull. Inexorably, he turned, and saw . . . a man standing over him on the riverbank, silhouetted against the moonlit sky. A gun muzzle pressed against his forehead. He glared up at the silhouette, fury raging in him. *Somehow I'll get you.* Then the night disappeared in excruciating noise and pain.

David bolted for his car and gunned it out of the parking space. *No!* He could not be the dead man! He breathed; his heart beat; he bled when he nicked himself shaving. How existential could life be? *I think therefore, I am?*

Yet the voice of the shrink two years ago murmured over his denials. He lost a day. Amnesia resulted from the need to forget some trauma. What trauma could be greater than his own violent death?

A blaring horn jerked his attention back to driving. He braked in mid-turn to avoid an oncoming car. After it passed, he saw why he turned, and grinned. Yes! The high school parking lot, the last place he had been seen his missing day. Tracking himself would prove that riverbank had nothing to do with him.

In the parking lot he sat on the hood of the parked car, concentrating, willing himself to remember. But his mind remained blank. Over and over, however, his gaze wandered to the sandstone wall on the north side of the parking lot, separating the campus from Memorial Cemetery.

That seemed little to go on. Still, what else did he have? David trotted across to the wall and vaulted it.

Standing in the cemetery felt . . . familiar. Encouraged, he started forward between the headstones, trying not to think, just move.

To his surprise, his feet took him to the gutted old bell tower in the middle of the cemetery. He stared at it. Why come here? Connie Chaffin had not been his case.

Then, why did he think of her? Because her strangled body had been found here?

She was running one time and saw them.

Someone said that to him, said it the day he vanished. A girl's voice. Who? Of course ... Kim Harris,
one of Connie's girlfriends. He had been asking, about
Brad Stacey and the Harris girl started talking about
Connie. *"She saw Brad with someone."*

Saw him where? David looked around. Connie, a
star of the girls' track team, ran every noon, often in
the cemetery. Her failure to show up for afternoon
classes started the search which ended at the bell
tower. Did she see a meeting here?

She also ran along Bandit Creek, he remembered
hearing. The stream had cut a ravine behind the high
school and cemetery and on north through a residential area.

David slid down the side of the ravine and leaped
the stream to the path on the far side, worn hard and
even by the track team and local joggers. In his head
his conversation with the Harris girl replayed as
though it had never been lost.

"When did she tell you about seeing Brad?" he
asked.

"That morning—you know, the day she—" Tears
cut off the sentence.

Had someone overheard? Did that conversation
doom Connie?

That day David had followed the creek path, just
as he did now ... looking for places Connie could
have seen Stacey and his supplier.

Passing the boundary of the cemetery and into the
residential area, cold grabbed David's guts. His heart
hammered. The trees arching together over the ravine
reminded him of his nightmare tunnel. Balconies and
windows of the Westminster Apartment complex
looked down from beyond the trees on the eastern
rim. Did Connie see Stacey up there? Or maybe
around one of the houses along the western side?
Steps led from the ravine to most of the back yards.

Steps. Memory clicked. He had climbed steps. Stone steps. To . . . somewhere with bright flowers. He studied the houses. Several had stone steps, but only one a greenhouse. Sight of it brought a wave of fury and terror.

He savored the emotions with satisfaction. So, the horror began up there. He leaned against a tree and let memory flow.

Answering his tap on the glass had been a grey-haired man who carried himself with military erectness. Being this close to Fort Carey, a number of officers retired here.

David showed his ID. "May I talk to you, Captain?"

The firm chin lifted. "It's Major . . . Major Charles Burris, retired."

Behind the major, flowers in riotous colors filled the greenhouse. "Those are beautiful," David said.

The stiff shoulders relaxed. "Aren't they. I did some advisory work in Central America after my formal retirement and fell in love with the jungle flora. So I brought back seeds and cuttings."

Advisory work? Mercenary, he meant. It conjured up an interesting image . . . the major in camouflage fatigues and face paint pausing on a jungle march to admire flowers. David moved down the long benches. "They must take a lot of work." Which would keep him in the greenhouse for long periods.

"Hours every day." Burris raised an eyebrow. "But I'm sure you're not here to talk about flowers."

"True. You have a good view of people on the ravine path from here."

"The joggers and dog walkers? Yes." The major nodded.

"Do you remember ever seeing Connie Chaffin?"

The major's face went grave. "The girl strangled last week? That was so . . . senseless. Yes, I saw her often. But not that day she was killed, as I told the detective who talked to me. Do you have a new lead on her death?"

An intensity in his tone had caught David's ear. He

eyed the major more closely. "You know how these things go—check and recheck everything." He paused. "Have you seen a boy, tall, over six feet, very thin, white-blond hair? He would probably have been in street clothes, not running gear."

Burris had pursed his lips. "Offhand, no, I don't remember a boy like that. Sorry."

But the major's pupils dilated during the description of Stacey, and dilated again while denying seeing him. Every cop instinct in David snapped to attention. Liar, that dilatation screamed. What if Burris brought more than flower seeds back from Central America? The man deserved checking. "Well, thank you for your time." He turned to leave.

Just as a tall, thin, white-blond boy bounded through the door. "Major, that Harris bitch told—" He stopped short, staring at David.

Two thoughts collided in David. *Jackpot!* and *Oh, shit!* Movement flashed at the edge of his vision. He ducked too late. Burris smashed a flowerpot square in his face. David's nose flattened in blinding agony that paralyzed him long enough for the other two to pin, disarm, and tie him. They emptied his pockets and stripped off his watch and wedding ring, then carried him into the garage adjoining the greenhouse and dumped him in the trunk of the major's car.

The major slammed the trunk closed. "Now, what was it you were about to tell me, Brad?"

David missed the answer, but he guessed that Stacey told Burris about Kim Harris talking to their prisoner. Burris's crisp voice came back, ". . . so she won't mention her conversations with the girl and cop to anyone else, but without leaving any marks on her."

Leaning against the tree beneath the major's greenhouse, David understood why no one tracked him past the high school. Fear kept Kim Harris from repeating what she told him.

So, now he had his day back . . . and had identified the dead man. He could no longer deny what he was. At least acceptance ended the fear. But not the hatred of his killer. What to do about Burris? He lacked proof the major killed Connie Chaffin, and he could hardly arrest the man for murdering David Amaro, despite the fingerprint evidence. Thought of nailing Burris on drug charges did not satisfy him at all. David wanted the major for murder, for his and Connie's and the kids who OD'd on the major's drugs. He wanted Burris revealed to the world as scum, wanted him blackened, reviled, hated, and, most of all, dead.

And he knew just how to do that. David bared his teeth. It bypassed due process, but what the hell did a dead man care about due process?

A great sense of freedom filled him. Humming, David mounted the steps to the yard next to Burris and showed his ID to the woman who answered his rap on the back door.

"May I please use your phone?"

When she showed him to an extension in the kitchen, he looked up Burris in the phone book and punched in the number.

"Hello?"

The major's crisp voice sent a shaft of fury through David. He did not bother hiding the anger in his voice, just whispered to keep the residents of the house from hearing. "Major, I know all about your drug business. Meet me in your greenhouse in two minutes if you don't want me talking to the police." David jiggled the switch hook and punched the Law Enforcement Center's number. "Kate, this is David Amaro," he told the dispatcher who answered. "I've learned that Connie Chaffin saw the Stacey kid's drug supplier. So the supplier killed her. He's a retired army major named Charles Burris. He also murdered my guy in the river. Send backup to 610 Franklin Drive."

He left the house, vaulted the fence into Burris's backyard, and opened the greenhouse door. Stepping over the threshold brought a shiver of remembered terror . . . quickly replaced by grim anticipation of vengeance.

Inside, the major stood silhouetted against the glow

of ultraviolet lights over the tables. "I don't know who the hell you are or what drug business you're talking about, but I won't tolerate being threatened."

David felt stunned. Burris did not *recognize* him? He hurled his badge case at the major. "The name is David Amaro, you bastard! Maybe you can forget a man whose head you've blown off, but I sure as hell haven't forgotten you! And your ass is mine, slimeball."

Burris opened the badge case. Now he remembered. David saw it in his face. But Burris remained composed. He tossed back the ID and shoved his hands in the rear pockets of his jeans. "You're raving. If I killed you, how do you come to be standing there? You surely don't expect me to believe you're a ghost." His right hand came back into sight ... holding a .45 that must have been stuck in the back of his waistband.

"Instead, I believe you're a trespasser who makes me fear for my life."

Fierce joy blazed in David. *Gotcha!* "You damned well should fear for your life." He drew his own gun.

As the .45 flashed fire, David reminded himself: *You're only as real as you believe. The bullet can't hurt you.* Sure enough, he felt no pain, though the wound spurted blood. Behind him, a section of the greenhouse wall shattered.

Grinning, David stalked toward Burris. "You're wasting ammunition, Major. You can't kill me again."

Burris tried, firing repeatedly. Amid splintering glass and spraying blood, David continued forging forward.

Burris's eyes went wild and white. "Fall, damn you!" He backed away—still firing.

Before the major emptied the clip, David forced him against the garage wall and shoved the gun upward so the barrel pointed back toward Burris himself. The next shot, by now fired in convulsive desperation, entered the major's throat and exploded out the top of his head.

As the major collapsed, David heard the whoop of an approaching siren. Relief filled him. Good. He could leave everything else to the police.

It made a hell of a report to write. Officers arriving to back up Amaro met an hysterical neighbor with a story of hearing gunfire and running to her kitchen window to see her neighbor in his greenhouse firing bullet after bullet into a detective who had used her phone just minutes before. They found only the major's body in the greenhouse, however . . . amid a scene that belonged in a slaughterhouse, with blood splashed and smeared and pooled everywhere. Except for a bloody pile of clothing, Sergeant Amaro had disappeared. Lab tests showed most of the blood to be Amaro's type, and the bloody fingerprints on the edges of the tables matched his. The gun, however, bore only Burris's prints.

"What do you think happened?" the investigating officer asked Lieutenant Christopher. "Where is Amaro's body? He couldn't have walked away after losing that much blood."

Christopher had no suggestions, especially after NCIC's report on the fingerprints of the dead man in the river. They found a match in their civilian section . . . a law enforcement officer named David Douglas Amaro.

After comparing the dead man's prints to those in the greenhouse and Amaro's personnel file, Christopher showed it all to the chief. "What do you think about this? What should we do?"

The chief studied the prints for a long time, then returned the personnel file to Christopher. "I think we tell the press that an officer who solved the Chaffin murder has probably paid for it with his life, with his body being removed by some accomplice the neighbor didn't see. As soon as possible we'll make sure Amaro's family receives his pension. We bury the file on the river body. The rest . . ." He tore the NCIC telex into confetti. "The rest we forget."

THE MIDNIGHT EL

Robert Weinberg

ROBERT WEINBERG has spent the last thirty-five years ensuring that the thousands of pulp stories printed in the first half of the century remain in print today. In his spare time he writes in all genres of fiction, recently appearing in the anthology *Dark Love*. He is currently finishing the last of a trilogy of novels for White Wolf where the main character is an occult detective similar to Sidney Taine.

Cold and alone, Sidney Taine waited for the Midnight El. Collar pulled up close around his neck, he shivered as the frigid Chicago wind attacked his exposed skin. Not even the usual drunks haunted the outdoor subway platforms on nights like these. With temperatures hovering only a few degrees above zero, the stiff breeze off Lake Michigan plunged the wind chill factor to twenty below. Fall asleep outside in the darkness and you never woke up.

Taine hated the cold. Though he had lived in Chicago for more than a year, he had yet to adjust to the winter weather. Originally from San Francisco, he delighted his hometown friends when he groused that he never realized what the phrase "chilled to the bone" meant until he moved to the Windy City.

Six feet four inches tall, weighing a bit more than two hundred and thirty pounds, Taine resembled a professional football player. Yet he moved with the grace of a stalking tiger and, for his size, was incredibly light on his feet. A sly grin and dark, piercing eyes gave him a sardonic, slightly mysterious air. An image he strived hard to cultivate.

Like his father and grandfather before him, Taine worked as a private investigator. Though he had opened his office in Chicago only fourteen months ago, he was already well known throughout the city. Dubbed by one of the major urban newspapers as "The New-Age Detective," Taine used both conventional techniques and occult means to solve his cases. While his unusual methods caused a few raised eyebrows, no one mocked his success rate. Specializing in missing-person investigations, Taine rarely failed to locate his quarry. He had his doubts, though, about tonight's assignment.

Before leaving his office this evening, Taine had mixed, then drunk, an elixir with astonishing properties. According to the famous grimoire, *The Key of Solomon,* the potion enabled the user to see the spirits of the dead. Its effects only lasted till dawn. Which was more than enough time for Taine. If he failed tonight, there would be no second chance.

The detective glanced down at his watch for the hundredth time. The glowing hands indicated five minutes to twelve. According to local legends, it was nearly the hour for the Midnight El to start its run.

No one knew how or when the stories began. A dozen specialists in urban folklore supplied the detective with an equal number of fabled origins. One and all, they were of the opinion that the tales dated back to the first decades of the century, when the subway first debuted in Chicago.

A few old-timers, mostly retired railway conductors and engineers, claimed the Midnight El continued an even older tradition—the Phantom Train, sometimes called the Death's Head Locomotive. Despite the disagreements, several elements remained constant in all the accounts. The Midnight El hit the tracks exactly at the stroke of twelve. Its passengers consisted of those who had died that day in Chicago. The train traversed the entire city, starting at the station closest to the most deaths of the day, and working its way along from there.

Knowing that fact, Taine waited on a far south side platform. Earlier in the day, twelve people had died in a flash fire only blocks from this location. There was little question that this would be the subway's first stop.

Slowly, the seconds ticked past. A harsh west wind wailed off the lake, like some dread banshee warning Taine of his peril. With it came the doleful chiming of a distant church bell striking the hour. Midnight—the end of one day, start of another.

The huge train came hurtling along the track rumbling like distant thunder. Emerging ghostlike out of thin air, dark and forbidding, blacker than the night, it lumbered into the station. Lights flashed red and yellow as it slowed to a stop. Taine caught a hurried vision inside a half-dozen cars as they rumbled past. Pale, vacant, *dead* faces stared out into the night. Riders from another city, or another day, he wasn't sure which, and he had no desire to know. Young and old, black and white, men and women, all hungering for a glimpse of life.

Hissing loudly, double doors swung open on each car. A huge, shadowy figure clad in a conductor's uniform emerged from midway along the train. In his right hand he held a massive silver pocket watch, hooked by a glittering chain to his vest. Impatiently, he stood there, waiting for new arrivals.

The conductor's gaze swept the station, rested on Taine for a moment, then continued by. The ghost train and all its passengers were invisible to mortal eyes. There was no way for him to know that the man on the platform could actually see him. Nor suspect what Taine planned to do.

Once he had been a ferryman. The ancient Greeks knew him as Charon. To the Egyptians, he had been Anubis, the Opener of the Way. A hundred other cultures named him a hundred different ways. But always his task remained the same—transporting the newly dead to their final destination.

They came with the wind. Not there, then suddenly there. Each one stopped to face the conductor for an instant before being allowed to pass. The breath froze in Taine's throat as he watched them file by. Those who had died that day.

His hands clenched into fists when he sighted three pajama-clad black children. The detective recognized the trio immediately. Today's newspapers had been filled with all the grisly details of that sudden tenement fire that had resulted in their deaths. None of them had been over six years old.

Wordlessly, the last of the three turned. Lonely, mournful eyes stared deep into Taine's for an instant. The detective remained motionless. If he reacted now, it might warn the conductor. An instant passed, and then the child and all the other passengers were gone. Disappeared into the Midnight El.

The conductor stepped back into the doorway. Raising one hand, he signaled to some unseen engineer to continue. Seeing his chance, Taine acted.

Moving incredibly fast for a man his size, the detective darted at, then around, the astonished doorman. Before the shadowy figure could react, Taine was past him and into the subway. Ignoring the restless dead on all sides, the detective headed for the front of the car.

"Come back here," demanded the conductor, swinging aboard. Behind him, the doors thudded shut. An instant later, the car jerked forward as the engine came to life. Outside scenery blurred as the train gained speed. The floor shook with a gentle, rocking motion. The Midnight El was off to its next stop.

Taine relaxed, letting his pursuer catch up to him. Surprise had enabled him to board the ghostly train. Getting off might not prove so easy.

"You do not belong on the Midnight El, Mr. Taine," said the conductor. He spoke calmly, without any trace of accent. Listening closely, Taine caught the barest hint of amusement in the phantom's voice. "At least, not yet. Your time is not for years and years."

"You know my name, and the instant of my death?" asked Taine, not the least bit intimidated by the imposing bulk of the other. Surrounded by shadows, the ticket taker towered over Taine by a head. His face, though human, appeared cut from weathered marble. Only his black, black eyes burned with life.

"Of course," answered the conductor. His body swayed gracefully with every motion of the subway car. "Past, present, future mean nothing to me. One look at a man is all I need to review his entire life history, from the moment of his birth to the last breath he takes. It's part of my job, supervising the Midnight El."

"For what employer?" asked Taine, casually.

"Someday you'll learn the answer," replied the conductor, with a chuckle. "But it won't matter much then."

The phantom reached into his vest pocket and pulled out the silver pocket watch. "Thirteen minutes to the next stop. This train, unlike most, always runs on time. You shall exit there, Mr. Taine."

"And if I choose not to," said Taine.

The conductor frowned. "You must. I cannot harm you. Such action is strictly forbidden under the terms of my contract. However, I appeal to your sense of compassion. A living presence on this train upsets the other passengers. Think of the pain you are inflicting on them."

Darkness gathered around the railroad man. He no longer looked so human. His black coal eyes burned into Taine's with inhuman intensity. "Leave them to their rest, Mr. Taine. You do not belong here."

"Nor does one other," replied the detective.

The conductor sighed, his rock-hard features softening in sorrow. "I should have guessed. You came searching for Maria Hernandez. Why?"

"Her husband hired me. He read about my services in the newspapers. I'm the final resort for those who refuse to give up hope.

"Victor told me what little he knew. My knowledge of the occult filled in the blanks. Combined together, the facts led me here."

"All trails end at the Midnight El," declared the conductor solemnly. "Though I'm surprised that you realized that."

"After examining the information, it was the only possible solution," said Taine. "Maria disappeared three nights ago. She vanished without a trace from an isolated underground subway platform exactly at midnight. No one else recognized the significance of the time.

"The police admitted they were completely baffled. The ticket seller remembered Maria taking the escalator down to the station a few minutes before twelve. A transit patrolman spoke to her afterward. He remembered looking up at the clock and noting the lateness of the hour. But when he looked around, the woman was no longer there. Somehow, she disappeared in the blink of an eye. Searching the tunnels for her body turned up nothing."

Taine paused. "Victor Hernandez considered me his last and only chance. I promised him I would do my best. I never mentioned the Midnight El."

"My thanks to you for that," said the conductor, nodding his understanding. "Suicides cause me the greatest pain. Especially those who sacrifice themselves to join the one they love."

"She meant a great deal to him," said Taine. "They were only married a few months. It seemed quite unfair."

"The world is unfair, Mr. Taine," said the conductor, shrugging his massive shoulders. "Or so I have been told by many of my passengers. Again and again, for centuries beyond imagining."

"She wasn't dead," said Taine. "If I don't belong here, then neither does she."

The conductor grimaced, his black eyes narrowing. He looked down at his great silver watch and shook his head. "There's not enough time to explain," he said. "Our schedule is too tight for long talks. Please understand my position."

"The Greeks considered Charon the most honorable of the gods," said Taine, sensing his host's inner conflict. "Of course, that was thousands of years ago."

"Spare me the dramatics," said the conductor. A bitter smile crossed his lips. He nodded to himself, as if making an important decision. Slowly, ever so slowly, he twisted the stem on the top of his watch.

All motion ceased. The subway car no longer shook with motion. Outside, the blurred features of the city solidified into grotesque, odd shapes, faintly resembling the Chicago skyline.

Taine grunted in surprise. "You can stop time?"

"For a little while," said the conductor. "Don't forget, the Midnight El visits every station in the city and suburbs within the space of a single night. On a hot summer night in a violent city like this, we often need extra minutes for all the passengers. Thus my watch. Twisting a little more produces a timeless state."

"The scenery?" asked Taine, not wanting to waste his questions, but compelled to ask by the alienness of the landscape.

"All things exist in time as well as space," said the conductor. "Take away that fourth dimension and the other three seem twisted."

The phantom turned and beckoned with his other hand. "Maria Hernandez. Attend me."

A short, slender woman in her early twenties pushed her way forward through the ranks of the dead. Long brown hair, knotted in a single thick braid, dropped down her back almost to her waist. Wide, questioning eyes looked at the detective. Unlike all the others on the train, a spark of color still touched

Maria's cheeks. And her chest rose and fell with her every breath.

"Tell Mr. Taine how you missed the subway two weeks ago," said the conductor. He glanced over at Taine, almost as if checking to make sure the detective was paying attention.

"There was a shortage in one of the drawers at closing time," began Maria Hernandez, her voice calm, controlled. "My superior asked me to do a crosscheck. It was merely a mathematical error, but it took nearly twenty minutes to find. By then, I was ten minutes late for my train."

She hesitated, as if remembering something particularly painful. "I was in a hurry to get home. It was our six-month anniversary. When I left that morning for the bank, my husband, Victor, promised me a big surprise when I returned. I loved surprises."

"Yes, I know," said the conductor, his voice gentle. "He bought you tickets to the theater. But that is incidental to the story. Please continue."

"Usually, I have to wait a few minutes for my train," said Maria. "Not that night. It arrived exactly on schedule. When I reached the el platform, the conductor was signaling to close the doors. The next subway wasn't for thirty minutes. So, I ran."

Again, she paused. "I would have made it, too, if it wasn't for my right heel." She looked down at her shoes. "It caught in a crack in the cement. Wedged there so tight I couldn't pull my foot loose. By the time I wrenched free, the train had already left."

"Two weeks ago," said Taine, comprehension dawning. "The day of the big subway crash in the Loop."

"Correct," said the conductor. "Four minutes after Mrs. Hernandez missed her train, it crashed headlong into another, stalled on the tracks ahead. Fourteen people died when several of the cars sandwiched together. *Fifteen* should have perished."

"Fate," said Taine.

"She was destined to die," replied the conductor,

as if explaining the obvious. "It was woven in the threads. A mistake was made somewhere. Her heel should have missed that crack. There was probably a knot in the twine. I assure you her name was on my passenger list. Maria was scheduled to ride the Midnight El."

"So, when she didn't, you decided to correct that mistake on your own," said Taine, his temper rising. Mrs. Hernandez stood silent, as if frozen in place. Her story told, the conductor ignored her. "I thought a living person on board disturbed the dead?"

"With effort, the rules can be bent," said the conductor. He sighed. "It grows so boring here, Taine. You cannot imagine how terribly boring. I desired company, someone to talk to. Someone alive, someone with feelings, emotions. The dead no longer care about anything. They are so dull.

"The Three Sisters had to unravel a whole section of the cloth. They needed to weave a new destiny for Mrs. Hernandez to cover up their mistake. Meanwhile, Maria should have been dead but was still alive. Her spirit belonged to neither plane of existence. It took no great effort to bring her on the train as a passenger. And here she will remain, for all eternity, neither living nor dead but in a state between the two. Immortal, undying, unchanging—exactly like me. Forever."

Taine's fist clenched in anger. "Who gave you the power to decide her fate. That's not your job. You're only the ferryman, nothing more. She doesn't belong here. I won't allow you to do this."

"Your opinion means nothing to me, Mr. Taine," said the conductor, his features hardening. His left hand rested on the stem of the pocket watch. "There is nothing you can do to stop me."

"Like hell," said the detective, and leaped forward.

A big, powerfully built man, he moved with astonishing speed. Once tonight he had caught the conductor by surprise. This time, he did not.

The phantom's left hand shot out and caught Taine by the throat. Without effort, he raised the detective into the air, so that the man's feet dangled inches off the floor.

"I am not fooled so easily a second time," he declared.

Taine flailed wildly with both hands at the conductor. Not one of his punches connected. Desperately the detective lashed out one foot, hitting the other in the chest. The phantom didn't even flinch. He hardly seemed to notice Taine's struggles.

"In my youth," said the conductor, "I wrestled with Atlas and Hercules. Your efforts pale before theirs, Mr. Taine."

The conductor's attention focused entirely on the detective. Neither man nor spirit noticed Mrs. Hernandez cautiously reaching for the silver pocket watch the trainman held negligently in his other hand. Not until she suddenly grabbed it away.

"What!" bellowed the conductor, dropping Taine and whirling about. "You . . . you . . ."

"Just because I obeyed your commands," said Mrs. Hernandez, "didn't mean that I no longer possessed a will of my own. I was waiting for the right opportunity." She gestured with her head at the crowds of the dead all around them. "I'm not like them. I'm alive."

She held the pocket watch tightly, one hand on the stem. "If you try to take this away, I'll break it. Don't make me do that."

Taine, his throat and neck burning with pain, staggered to Mrs. Hernandez's side. "Let us go. Otherwise, we'll remain here forever, frozen in time."

"Nonsense," said the conductor. "I told you the rules can only be bent so far. Sooner or later, the strain would become too great and snap this train back to the real world."

"But if Maria breaks your watch," said Taine, "what then? You admitted needing its powers. Think of the problems maintaining your schedule without it."

"True enough," admitted the conductor. He paused for a moment, as if in thought. "Listen, I am willing to offer this compromise. Maria cannot leave this train without my permission. The Fates will not spin her a new destiny as long as she remains on the El. Return the watch to me and I'll give her a chance to return to her husband. And resume her life on Earth."

"A chance?" said the detective, suspiciously. "What exactly do you mean by that?"

"A gamble, a bet, *a wager,* Mr. Taine," said the conductor. "Relieve my boredom. Ask me a question, any question. If I cannot answer, you and Mrs. Hernandez go free. If I guess correctly, then both of you remain here for all eternity—not dead but no longer among the living—on the Midnight El. It will take a great deal of effort, but I can manage. Take it or leave it. I refuse to bend any further."

"Both of us?" said Taine. "You raised the stakes. And what about disturbing the dead? A little while ago you were anxious for me to leave."

"As I stated before, the rules can be bent. After all, I am the ferryman. And," continued Charon, the faintest trace of a smile on his lips, "what better way to sharpen your wits, Mr. Taine, than to put your own future at peril?"

"But," said the detective, "according to your earlier remarks, there's nothing in the world you don't know."

"There is only one omniscient presence," said the conductor. "Man or spirit, we are mere reflections of his glory. Still," he added, almost in afterthought, "the universe holds few mysteries for me."

Shadows gathered around the phantom. He extended one huge hand. "Make your decision. Now. Before I change my mind." His eyes burned like two flaming coals. "No tricks, either. An answer must exist for your question."

"Give him the watch," Taine said to Maria Hernandez.

"Then you agree?" asked the conductor.

"I agree," replied the detective, calmly.

Chuckling, the conductor twisted the stem of his great silver watch. Immediately, the scenery shifted and the subway car started shaking. They were back in the real world.

"We arrive at the next station in a few minutes," Charon announced smugly. "You have until then to frame your question, Mr. Taine."

Maria Hernandez gasped, raising her hands to her face. "But ... but ... that's cheating."

"Not true," said the conductor. "I promised no specific length of time for our challenge." He glanced down at his watch. "Your time is ticking by quickly. Better think fast."

Taine took a deep breath. Not all questions depended on facts for their answer. He prayed that the ferryman would not renege on their bargain once he realized his mistake. "You trapped yourself," said the detective. "I'm ready now."

"You are?" said the conductor, frowning. He sounded surprised.

"Of course," said Taine. "Are you prepared to accept defeat?"

"Impossible," replied the conductor, bewildered. "I know the answer to every question."

"Then tell me," said Taine, "the answer to the question raised when I first boarded the train. When is the exact moment of my death."

"You will perish ..." began the conductor, then stopped. He stood silent, mouth open in astonishment. Slowly, the fire left his eyes. The phantom shook his head in dismay. "Caught by my own words."

Not exactly sure what the conductor meant, Maria Hernandez directed her attention to Taine. "I don't understand. Caught? How?"

"The conductor bragged earlier that he knew the date of my death," said Taine. "If he answers correctly, then he wins our bet."

"And," continued Maria, comprehension dawning, "by the terms of the agreement, you must remain on the Midnight El forever."

"Thus making his prediction false," finished Taine, "since I cannot die when he predicts. On the other hand, if he says that I will never die, then he does not know the date of my death. Which means he cannot answer the question. So, whatever he says, I am the winner. The bet is ours."

With a sigh, the conductor pocketed his watch. "You would have made good company, Mr. Taine." Metal screeched on metal as the Midnight El pulled into the next station. "This is your stop. Farewell."

They were outside. Alone. On a deserted subway station. With a cold wind blowing, but neither of them noticed.

Tears filled Maria Hernandez's eyes. "Are we free? Really free?"

Taine nodded, his thoughts drifting. Already, he searched for an explanation for Maria's disappearance that would satisfy both the police and her husband.

"As free as any man or woman can be," he answered somberly. "In the end, we all have a date to keep with the Midnight El."

THE CARDULA
DETECTIVE AGENCY

Jack Ritchie

JACK RITCHIE (1922–1983) has had his work re-
printed in *Best Mystery Detective Stories* more than
any other writer. He won an Edgar for his tale "The
Absence of Emily." That, along with over five hundred more stories, makes up a body of work, mostly
detective fiction, that is sometimes humorous, sometimes serious. Ritchie never published a novel, pre-
ferring instead to work exclusively within the short
story genre.

I yawned, rubbed the stubble of my beard, and reflected once again what a boring and basically awkward process it was for me to shave myself every evening. Jamos—my man—had done the task for me until
two months ago, when I had had to let him go. I
simply could not afford to feed him any longer.

I climbed out of bed and went to the dark windows.
It was raining heavily. Certainly no weather for flying.

I plugged in my electric razor and went to work. I
was becoming a bit more skilled at the job. Actually,
of course, putting a straight part in my hair was much
more difficult. When I finished shaving, I slipped out
of my pajamas and showered.

I moved on to the closet and surveyed my two remaining suits. Top quality, certainly, but both had seen better days. I sincerely hoped that some night soon I might replenish my wardrobe with something new, possibly even other than black.

I finished dressing and donned my black raincoat. I checked to make certain that I carried my tobacco pouch. There was no telling where circumstances might force me to spend the day.

Outside my apartment building, I raised my umbrella and began walking toward my office, slightly more than a mile away.

The rain slackened to a light drizzle as I proceeded down Wisconsin Avenue, crossed the bridge, and turned into the alley shortcut I usually take when I find it necessary to walk.

I had almost reached the opposite street—East Wells—when someone leaped upon me from behind, hooking his arm under my chin.

Clearly I was being mugged.

I reached back, grasped his collar, and flipped him head over heels some twenty feet into the side of a brick wall, from which point he dropped to the alley surface and remained still.

But apparently he was not alone. Another and larger figure sprang from a building recess and threw an overhand right which caught me squarely on the jaw. I distinctly heard several phalanges of his fist fracture and he yelped with surprise at the injury.

I then lifted him high overhead and sent him crashing across the alley to join his inert companion.

I brushed off my raincoat, picked up my umbrella, and continued on to my office. Really, I thought, this was outrageous. It was no longer safe for an innocent pedestrian to walk the streets or alleys at night.

When I reached my office, I found a young woman, probably in her late twenties, waiting at my office door.

She seemed a bit startled when she first saw me, but then most people are. She looked at the keys in my hand. "Do you work for the Cardula Detective Agency?"

I smiled sparingly. "I *am* the Cardula Detective Agency." I unlocked the door and we entered my one-room office.

She sat down, produced a silver case, and offered me a cigarette.

"No, thank you," I said. "I don't smoke."

She lit her cigarette. "My name is Olivia Hampton. I phoned about an hour ago. A recording said that your office hours are from 8 P.M. to 4 A.M.?"

I nodded. "They vary according to the solstices."

"It's my Uncle Hector," she said. "Someone shot at him while he was dressing for dinner. The bullet went through his bedroom window and missed him by inches."

"Hm," I said thoughtfully. "Since you came to me, I gather that you did not go to the police."

"We regard the incident as a family matter. All of the logical suspects are relatives. Except for Uncle Custis Clay Finnegan. I mean, he's a relative, but not one of the suspects, because he has millions of his own."

"Why does anyone want your Uncle Hector dead?"

"Because he's going to change his will tomorrow morning when he sees his lawyer. He called us into the study and told us that he was cutting all of us out of his will."

"Why would he want to do that?"

"He said he just read a book and now he doesn't believe in individuals inheriting wealth. He's going to give his money to various charities."

"How much money does he have?"

"The last time he mentioned the subject, I think he said three million."

"Aha, and you want me to find out who's trying to kill him?"

"If you can, of course. But the main idea is for you to see that Uncle Hector is still alive when he sees his lawyer at nine tomorrow morning. After that, there won't be any motive for any of us to kill him because we'll be out of the will anyway."

I drummed my fingers for a moment or two. "I'm afraid I can guarantee his safety only until approximately 6 A.M. tomorrow. After that I have another commitment."

She thought about that. "Well, it's better than nothing, I suppose. I don't imagine I could get anybody else at this time of the night." She got up. "I think we'd better get going right away. If anyone's going to murder Uncle Hector, it's got to happen tonight. I have a car and chauffeur waiting downstairs."

As we approached a Volkswagen minibus, the driver's door burst open and a small uniformed chauffeur hopped out. He rushed forward and kissed the back of my hand.

It was Janos.

"Count," he breathed fervently. "It is so wonderful to see you again."

Olivia smiled. "It was Janos who recommended that I come to you. Did he call you Count?"

I shrugged. "That was yesterday and today is today."

"His highness has fallen on bad times," Janos said, "through no fault of his own."

I sighed. "At one time the subject of money never disturbed my mind. I had extensive holdings in Cuba, the Belgian Congo, Lebanon, Angola, and Bangla Desh. What wasn't confiscated or nationalized was destroyed."

Janos slid back the side door of the minibus. "In the old country the people's government has made his castle a state shrine. Busloads of school children and tourists stop there every day, and the grounds are sprinkled with souvenir and food stands. The entire lower east gallery has been converted to public restrooms."

As Olivia and I rode in the back of the minibus, she gave me some background on the members of Uncle Hector's household. There was Cousin Albert, whose right arm was three inches longer than his left, and Cousin Maggie, who liked red port, and Cousin Wendy, who wrote the kindest rejection slips, and Cousin Fairbault, who detested crustaceans.

After some twenty miles of freeway travel, we took an off-ramp and continued on a two-lane road into the countryside, where only an occasional farmyard light broke the darkness.

It began to rain heavily again. Lightning flashed across the sky and thunder rolled—truly a splendid evening.

It was nearly ten-thirty when we turned in at a pair of gateposts and followed the graveled and bumpy driveway through a cordon of grotesque, bare-branched trees. In the revelation of another bolt of lightning, I saw ahead the looming monster of a Victorian mansion. Here and there a light gleamed from behind pulled drapes.

Janos stopped the Volkswagen and Olivia and I rushed up the wide steps to the shelter of the porch. She opened a huge door and we stepped into the large, dimly lit vestibule.

I heard a muffled crash from somewhere deep inside the house followed almost instantly by a brief series of splinterings. Strange, I thought, it sounded exactly like a bowling alley.

"I'll introduce you all around," Olivia said. "And we might just as well start with Albert." She led me through a passageway and then down a flight of stairs to high-ceilinged cellars.

I looked about as we proceeded. Stone walls, stone floors, roomy, damp, musty-smelling, grimed by a century of dampened dust.

I heard the crashing noise again, this time much closer.

Olivia opened a door and we stepped into the bright lights of an elongated room containing a two-lane bowling alley.

A gangly man in his thirties, concentrating intensely, stood poised to bowl. He took a five-step approach and delivered the ball smoothly with a flawless follow-through. The ball hit the pins solidly and he had a strike.

The automatic pin-spotter scooped up the pins and returned the ball.

"Albert," Olivia said, "this is Mr. Cardula. He's a private detective and he's spending the night with us to see that Uncle Hector doesn't get killed."

Albert shook hands, but he seemed eager to get back to his bowling.

I glanced at his score sheet. He had a string of seven strikes. I nodded approvingly. "What is your average?"

He brightened. "I have 257 over the last one thousand games."

Was he pulling my leg? A 257 *average*? I smiled slightly. "Magnificent bowling."

He agreed. "I practice ten hours a day. I would make it more, but that's about all the bowling the human body can take."

I glanced down. Yes, his right arm did seem to be several inches longer than his left.

"When I'm not bowling," Albert said, "I do all of the maintenance work down here. I can even take the pin-spotters apart and put them back together blindfolded." He smiled. "I have 983 perfect games so far."

983 perfect games? Oh, come now, I thought.

But he nodded earnestly. "And the alleys aren't grooved or anything like that. They could pass inspection anytime by the American Bowling Congress."

When we left him, Olivia said, "Albert's father was something of a local bowling celebrity in his hometown. He and Albert's mother were killed in an automobile accident when Albert was ten. He spent six years in an orphanage before Uncle Hector heard about him and got him out. But by then ..." She sighed. "Uncle Hector had the alleys built because bowling seemed to be the only thing that interested Albert."

I followed her through an archway. "Albert

shouldn't have to brood about being cut out of the will. If what he says about his bowling is true, he is the greatest bowler this world has ever seen or is likely to. He would sweep any tournament he entered, and what with endorsements and such, he could easily become a millionaire in a relatively short time."

Olivia shook her head. "No. Albert has never left these grounds since the day he came here. He doesn't want to see any other part of the world, no matter what it has to offer."

She led me to another door and switched on a light.

I found myself gazing upon bushel baskets and boxes of apples, potatoes, beets, rutabagas, squashes, and bins of sand which I surmised contained carrots and other root vegetables. One side of the room was totally shelved and occupied by an array of glass jars containing preserved tomatoes, green and wax beans, and dozens of other fruits and vegetables. Two large top-loading freezers stood at one end of the room.

"Cousin Fairbault does all of this himself," Olivia said. "The seeding, the cultivating, the harvesting. Then he cans and freezes and preserves. He's converted the carriage house into a barn and he raises all our beef, and pork, and chickens. He also makes sausages and hams and even cheeses."

She closed the door. "Fairbault was a Navy pilot. He got shot down and was washed ashore onto a tiny uninhabited island not more than an acre in size. It had three palm trees and all kinds of miscellaneous vegetation, but none of it edible. He couldn't even fish, because he had nothing to fish with. But there were spider crabs and slugs and all kinds of things that crawled and scuttled and came out mostly at night. Fairbault was on that island for seven years before he was rescued—he was down to eighty pounds. He spent another five years in an asylum where he tried to hoard food under his mattress."

We took the stairs up. "When Fairbault first came here, he kept that room locked at all times. We had to ask his permission whenever we wanted anything for the kitchen and he would watch over us while we got it. But he's been here eleven years now and he trusts us so much that he leaves the room unlocked and we are free to take anything we want at any time, just as long as we don't waste it."

We returned to the first floor and entered a large, well-ordered kitchen. In one corner, a heavyset woman in her fifties sat at a table working at a jigsaw puzzle. A half-empty bottle of red wine and a glass were at her elbow.

Olivia introduced me to Cousin Maggie. "She does the cooking for us and she's really the best cook in the world."

Maggie beamed. "I try to do the best I can and I don't touch a drop until seven. Are you hungry, Mr. Cardula? Could I fix you a snack?"

"No, thank you," I said. "I had something last week."

She blinked. "Last week?"

I cleared my throat. "I mean I have taken nourishment lately enough not to be hungry. How do you feel about your Uncle Hector changing his will and leaving all of you out?"

Maggie shrugged. "Well, it's his money and I wasn't really counting on any part of it, even assuming that I would outlive him." Her eyes clouded with worry. "Just as long as I have my job here. That's all that really counts."

We left Maggie to her jigsaw puzzle and bottle and proceeded to the second floor.

"You employ a *cousin* to do the cooking?" I asked.

"Maggie likes to be useful."

"Why is she worried about the possibility of losing her job here? If she's as good a cook as you claim, she shouldn't have any difficulty getting another job."

"Unfortunately, whenever she worked anywhere else, she began drinking as soon as she woke up in the morning and kept it up as long as she was able to stand, or sit. She was continually getting fired without references and was in quite desperate straits when Uncle Hector found her."

Olivia stopped at an open doorway.

I looked into an abundantly furnished room. A plump balding man sat comfortably ensconced in a deep easy chair, puffing a large curved pipe and engrossed in a book whose jacket read *Secrets with Broccoli*.

Olivia introduced me to Fairbault.

He offered me wine, but I declined.

He held his own glass to the light. "Six years in the cask. I call it Fairbault 71. Because of the climate here, I am forced to concentrate on the northern grapes. Not nearly as ideal for wine as the sweet California varieties, but one must make do."

I glanced at the bookshelves. All of the volumes seemed concerned with vegetable and fruit gardening and animal husbandry. One entire shelf contained what was very likely eleven years of an organic gardening magazine. "Do you do any greenhousing?" I asked.

He shook his head. "No. Greenhousing would expand the season to twelve months a year and too much is too much. Besides, half of the fun of gardening is to store and stock and preserve during the winter months and read gardening magazines and make plans for the spring."

We left Fairbault and continued down the corridor. We turned a corner and found a somewhat hefty and firm-hawed lady in her forties, nearly supine in a window seat, her face deathly white with perhaps a a few touches of green. A cigar, one inch smoked, dangled from her somewhat limp square hand.

Olivia sighed. "Why don't you give up trying to smoke cigars, Wendy? You know you just can't do it."

Cousin Wendy opened her eyes. "One of these damn days I'll find the right brand."

"Cousin Wendy is the founder and editor of the Trempleau County Poetry Review. It has one hundred and ten subscribers from all over the country and one hundred and nine of them are also contributors."

Cousin Wendy nodded. "Believe me, it makes for a twelve-hour day. Last month I had to plow through 800 manuscripts before I could make up the November issue. But I suppose nobody really appreciates all the work I put in and the correspondence and the free constructive criticism."

"Now, Wendy," Olivia said, "you know that every one of your readers is absolutely *depending* on you to sift and winnow, to separate the wheat from the chaff." She turned to me. "Cousin Wendy is not only an editor, but she is also a top poetry person."

Cousin Wendy shrugged modestly. "I try to keep my hand in when I have the time."

When we left her, I said, "Trempleau County? Isn't that about three hundred miles north?"

"Yes. That's where Cousin Wendy used to live. She was a waitress in a roadside cafe and wrote poetry on the side. Then one day a trucker came on a batch of her poems and started reading them out loud to the customers. So she crushed his skull with a counter stool. She was still in prison when Uncle Hector heard about her and he vouched for her at the parole hearing."

"Just one moment," I said. "Are you telling me that all of these people are really blood relatives of Uncle Hector?"

Olivia sighed and smiled faintly. "Well, to tell the truth, none of us really is. But we like to think of ourselves as cousins because it's warmer."

We went downstairs this time.

"Uncle Custis is our houseguest about once every six months or so," Olivia said. "He came here after supper tonight and Uncle Hector insisted that none of us breathes a word about the murder attempt on his life. He doesn't want Uncle Custis to worry. So I'll just tell Uncle Custis that you are also a houseguest."

We found Uncles Hector and Custis at a pool table in the game room.

Uncle Hector, a short man with soft white hair, had good nature stamped into his face.

Uncle Custis, on the other hand, was tall and gimlet-eyed. He regarded me sourly. "A houseguest? Or are you another one of those damn cousins Hector digs up now and then?"

"How much has Uncle Custis won from you so far this evening?" Olivia asked.

Uncle Hector shrugged. "Fifteen dollars."

"Uncle Custis is quite a pool player," Olivia said. "Eight ball is his favorite game."

"Eight ball?" I said. "Is that anything like billiards? I remember in my student years at the university I played the game a number of times."

Uncle Custis eyed me pityingly for a moment. Then he allowed himself an economical smile and explained to me the simple rules of eight ball. "Would you care to try your hand at it? I like to make things a little more interesting. How does five dollars a game strike you?"

I lost the first game, and the second.

Uncle Custis consulted his watch. "I'm just about ready for bed. What do you say about a final game? Let's make it for fifty dollars?"

I agreed and then proceeded to win that game with the utmost skill and dispatch.

Uncle Custis watched as I bank shot the eight ball into the side pocket and then glared. "I've been hustled. I *know* when I've been hustled." He flung five tens onto the table and stormed out of the room.

Uncle Hector regarded me with approval. "Damn, I've been wanting to do that for years."

I turned to business. "Sir, if you don't mind my saying so, wouldn't it have been wiser to change your will secretly and *then* inform your household that it had been disinherited? Do you realize how many people who boldly and blatantly announce that they are going to change their wills the first thing in the morning never get to see the sun rise?" I winced slightly at the last two words.

"Nonsense," Uncle Hector said. "Ninety-nine percent of will changers survive to see their lawyers the next morning. The one percent who are murdered get all of the publicity and give the entire process a bad name." He glanced at the wall clock. "Well, I suppose it's bedtime for all of us too. I understand that you are going to keep watch outside of my bedroom door tonight?"

"No," I said firmly. "I will be inside your bedroom. I do not intend to allow you out of my sight for one moment."

We said goodnight to Olivia and went upstairs.

Hector's bedroom was quite as large as my entire apartment and contained a huge canopy bed and a capacious fireplace.

While Hector changed to pajamas, I searched the room thoroughly. I then went to the windows and checked to make certain that they were all securely locked. I drew the drapes and sat down.

I frowned. There was something wrong here. Something I should have seen, but didn't. My eyes went over the room again, but I simply couldn't put my finger on it.

Hector sat on the bed and took off his slippers. "There's really no need for you to stay up all night. Why not lie down on that couch? I could get you a pillow and some blankets."

"No, thank you," I said. I went to the bookshelves, found a volume on hematology, and sat down.

Hector climbed into bed and closed his eyes. After five minutes he turned restlessly. He repeated the turnings at fairly regular intervals. Finally he sighed and sat up. "I simply can't go to sleep without my regular glass of warm milk and tonight I completely forgot about it. You wouldn't care to slip down to the kitchen and see if Maggie is still up? If she isn't, could you put a glass of milk into a saucepan and heat it slowly? Short of boiling, you know. And then add a teaspoon of sugar and a few dashes of cinnamon?"

"I'm sorry," I said. "But I am not leaving this room."

He thought it over. "Then I think I'll just hop down there myself."

"Very well," I said, "but I will accompany you. And we will make certain that the milk is taken from a fresh sealed bottle."

Hector scratched the back of his neck. "Forget it. It's too far to the kitchen anyway." He brightened. "There's a liquor cabinet over there. Why don't you help yourself to something? There's nothing like a good snort or two for relaxation."

"I do not intend to relax," I said. "And besides, I do not drink. At least not liquor."

Hector sank back onto his pillow and closed his eyes.

The hours passed. It was somewhat after five in the morning when I suddenly realized what it was that I should have seen earlier, but didn't.

I looked in Hector's direction. Was he really asleep or was he faking it?

I allowed five minutes to pass, then yawned and let my eyelids droop and finally close, except for a calculated millimeter or two. I began breathing heavily and allowed the book to slip from my hands to the carpeted floor.

Uncle Hector's eyes opened and he watched me intently for perhaps three minutes. Then he slipped quietly out of bed and tiptoed over to a bureau. He opened a drawer and removed a Finnish-stye hunting knife.

I tensed a bit, but he crept past me to the door and disappeared into the hall.

I rose and followed him.

As he threaded through the halls, he looked back frequently, but I kept myself confined to the darkness of the high ceiling.

He paused before a door, slowly turned its knob, and crept inside. I silently swooped into the room myself.

The room was very much like the one he had left. It too was graced by a canopy bed and upon it lay Uncle Custis, gently snoring.

Hector approached the bed and raised the dagger high into the air.

I quickly sprang forward, grasped his wrist, and removed the knife from his grip. He was startled at my appearance and action, but he made no exclamation. He merely closed his eyes for a moment.

On the bed, Uncle Custis continued his snoring without interruption.

I moved to one of the windows and pushed aside the drape for a moment. It was still raining heavily and the lightning periodically fractured the dark sky. Exhilarating.

I let the drapes fall back into position, motioned to Hector, and we went back into the hall.

On our way back to his room, Uncle Hector glanced at the ceiling now and then. "You know, I could have sworn I caught just a glimpse of something flying up there a little while ago."

Once inside his room, I said, "Aha, the old bedroom-switch ploy."

He portrayed innocence. "What old bedroom-switch ploy?"

"When I first came into this room and searched it, I should have seen something, but it was not there. If it *had* been there, I would certainly have noticed it immediately. It took me a bit of time to realize it was not there, but once I did, I suspected that there was mischief afoot and that you were probably at the root of it."

"What are you talking about?"

"Olivia came to me because someone took a shot at you through your bedroom window." I pointed in the direction of the windows. "Neither one of those has a bullet hole in it."

He thought fiercely and then smiled. "I forgot to mention that the window was open at the time."

"Good try," I acknowledged. "But then how do you

explain the fact that one of the windows in the room Custis now occupies *does* have a bullet hole in it?"

He resumed thinking, but I cut the effort short. "You faked that attempt on your life and this evening you probably told Custis that his regular guest room was being painted, or something of the sort, and he should take your bedroom instead."

"Why would I do that?"

"Because you intended to murder Custis and make it appear as though the crime had occurred by *accident*. Someone in the house, thinking that you still occupied your own bed, sneaked into the room, and in the darkness mistook Uncle Custis for you, and stabbed him to death."

Hector evaded my eyes and said nothing.

"Why?" I asked. "Why were you trying to murder Custis?"

He finally sighed. "Money, of course."

"But you've got millions."

"I *had* millions. Good solid investments in Angola, Lebanon, Bangla Desh ..." He shrugged. "Today I am almost dead broke."

Now his eyes met mine. "You have seen and talked to the people who inhabit this house?"

I nodded.

"Then you know that they have all been severely wounded by the world we live in. If they had to return to it, they would break completely. And I really couldn't allow that to happen. So I decided that the only way I could get enough money to keep this household going was to kill Custis. Basically he's a mean bastard anyway and wouldn't be missed by anyone. And we really *are* cousins, you know. Custis has no visible heirs other than me, so if he should die, I would certainly get first crack at his estate. You don't suppose you could let me have the knife again so I could finish ..."

"No," I said firmly.

And yet I could sympathize with Uncle Hector. He

had a duty and a responsibility to the members of the household.

Hector needed and deserved help. I sighed. All right. I would do the job for him. Not tonight or in this house, of course. But some evening a week or two from now when Custis walked a city street I would leap upon him, snap his neck, and remove his wallet. The crime would be put down in the police records as a fatal mugging.

I put my hand on Hector's shoulder. "I absolutely insist that you put the idea of murdering Custis completely out of your mind. I have the strongest premonition that your fortune will change dramatically within a week or two."

Hector seemed ready to wait. "To tell you the truth, I'm a little relieved that I didn't go through with it tonight."

I glanced at my watch. It was that time again.

I went to the window and pulled aside the drapes. Still raining. A bad night for fliers. I turned to Hector. "You don't suppose that Janos could drive me back to the city?"

"Of course. His room is on the third floor, right next to the bust of Edgar Allan Poe."

I went up to the third floor and woke Janos with my request.

He yawned and consulted his alarm clock. "I'm sorry, your highness, but in wet weather like this, water condenses in the distributor of our Volkswagen. By the time I got everything apart and wiped dry and put together and the engine perhaps started, we would never be able to make it to the city in time. And the minibus is the only vehicle we have."

Damn, I thought, that leaves me no alternative but getting wet. If I leave right now I might have time for a hot footbath when I get to my apartment.

"Why don't you stay here?" Janos said. "There's a nice roomy place in the cellar. I could fix up an army cot. I am certain that nobody would disturb you down there."

We carried what we needed downstairs to a large chamber in the cellar. Janos unfolded the cot and put a mattress on top of it. "Your tobacco pouch, sir?"

I handed it to him. "It isn't necessary to sprinkle the stuff all over the mattress anymore, Janos. I discovered that simply putting the full pouch under the pillow will suffice. I suppose it is the spirit of the thing rather than the letter that counts."

Janos finished putting on the sheets, the pillowcases, and the blankets. "Have a nice sleep, sir."

When he was gone, I slipped into the pajamas and lay down. Really a most spacious chamber. Beautiful vaulting at the doorway. The aroma of damp, stagnant air. I could almost imagine what the place would look like if I brought in a few choice items of furnishings from my apartment.

I sighed. But it was not to be. This was a strange household, but it was really expecting too much of its occupants to accept me.

I thought I heard a noise in the passageway outside.

I put on my slippers and hid in the shadows near the archway.

Olivia passed by outside. She wore a dressing gown, slippers, and from the turban-like creation on her head, I guessed that she had her hair in curlers.

She opened a door at the end of the passageway.

I saw a room elegant with draped antique spiderwebs and in the center of it, on a marble pedestal, stood a magnificent, comfortable-looking sarcoph—

Olivia entered the room and closed the door behind her. After a few moments, I distinctly heard the creak of a lid rising. And then lowering.

I smiled and went back to my cot.

I don't care what tradition demands, I always sleep on my left side.

THE CHRONOLOGY
PROTECTION CASE

Paul Levinson

PAUL LEVINSON, Ph.D., is the author of three novels,
Mind at Large (1988), *Electronic Chronicles* (1992),
and *Learning Cyberspace* (1995) as well as more
than one hundred fifty articles on the philosophy of
technology. His science fiction has appeared in *Analog*, *Amazing*, and *Xanadu 3*. Levinson is the president of Connected Education, Inc., an education
organization that offers academic credit courses
learned entirely through on-line conferencing.

Carl put the call through just as I was packing up for the day. "She says she's some kind of physicist," he said, and although I rarely took calls from the public, I jumped on this one.

"Dr. D'Amato?" she asked.

"Yes?"

"I saw you on television last week—on that cable talk show. You said you had a passion for physics." Her voice had a breathy elegance.

"True," I said. Forensic science was my profession, but cutting edge physics was my love. Too bad there wasn't a way to nab rapist murderers with spectral traces. "And you're a physicist?" I asked.

215

"Oh yes, sorry," she said. "I should introduce myself. I'm Lauren Goldring. Do you know my work?"

"Ahm . . ." The name did sound familiar. I ran through the Rolodex in my head, though these days my computer was becoming more reliable than my brain. "Yes!" I snapped my fingers. "You had an article in *Scientific American* last month about some Hubble data."

"That's right," she said, and I could hear her relax just a bit. "Look, I'm calling you about my husband—he's disappeared. I haven't heard from him in two days."

"Oh," I said. "Well that's really not my department. I can connect you to—"

"No, please," she said. "It's not what you think. I'm sure his disappearance has something to do with his work. He's a physicist, too."

Forty minutes later I was in my car on my way to her house, when I should have been home with a pizza and the cat. No contest: a physicist in distress always wins.

Her Bronxville address wasn't too far from mine in Yonkers.

"Dr. D'Amato?" She opened the door.

I nodded. "Phil."

"Thank you so much for coming," she said, and ushered me in. Her eyes looked red, like she suffered from allergies or had been crying. But few people have allergies in March.

The house had a quiet appealing beauty. As did she.

"I know the usual expectations in these things," she said. "He has another woman, we've been fighting. And I'm sure that most women whose vanished husbands *have* been having affairs are quick to profess their certainty that that's not what's going on in *their* cases."

I smiled. "OK, I'm willing to start with the assumption that your case is different. Tell me how."

"Would you like a drink, some wine?" She walked over to a cabinet, must've been turn of the century.

"Just ginger ale, if you have it," I said, leaning back in the plush Morris chair she'd shown me into.

She returned with the ginger ale, and some sort of sparkling water for herself. "Well, as I told you on the phone, Ian and I are physicists—"

"Is his last name Goldring, like yours?"

Lauren nodded. "And, well, I'm sure this has something to do with his project."

"You two don't do the same work?" I asked.

"No," she said. "My area's the cosmos at large—big bang theory, blackholes in space, the big picture. Ian's was, is, on the other end of the spectrum. Literally. His area's quantum mechanics." She started to sob.

"It's OK," I said. I got up and put my hand on her shoulder. Quantum mechanics could be frustrating, I know, but not *that* bad.

"No," she said. It isn't OK. Why am I using the past tense for Ian?"

"You think some harm's come to him?"

"I don't know," her lips quivered. She did know, or thought she knew.

"And you feel this has something to do with his work with tiny particles? Was he exposed to dangerous radiation?"

"No," she said. "That's not it. He was working on something called quantum signaling. He always told me everything about his work—and I told him everything about mine—we had that kind of relationship. And then a few months ago, he suddenly got silent. At first I thought maybe he *was* having an affair—"

And the thought popped into my head: if I had a woman with your class, an affair with someone else would be the last thing on my mind.

"But then I realized it was deeper than that. It was something, something that frightened him, in his work. Something that I think he wanted to shield me from."

"I'm pretty much of an amiable amateur when it comes to quantum mechanics," I said, "but I know something about it. Suppose you tell me all you know about Ian's work, and why it could be dangerous."

* * *

What I, in fact, fully grasped about quantum mechanics I could write on a postcard to my sister in Boston and it would likely fit. It had to do with light and particles so small that they were often indistinguishable in their behavior, and prone to paradox at every turn. A particularly vexing aspect that even Einstein and his colleagues tried to tackle in the 1930s involved two particles that at first collided and then traveled at sublight speeds in opposite directions: would observation of one have an instantaneous effect on the other? Did the two particles, having once collided, now exist ever after in some sort of mysterious relationship or field, a bond between them so potent that just to measure one was to influence the other, regardless of how far away? Einstein wondered about this in a thought experiment. Did interaction of subatomic particles tie their futures together forever, even if one stayed on Earth and the other wound up beyond Pluto? Real experiments in the 1960s and after suggested that's just what was happening, at least in local areas, and this supported Heisenberg's and Bohr's classic "Copenhagen" interpretation that quantum mechanics was some kind of mind-over-matter deal—that just looking at a quantum or tiny particle, maybe even thinking about it, could affect not only it but related particles. Einstein would've preferred to find another cause—non-mental—for such phenomena. But that could lead to an interpretation of quantum mechanics as faster-than-light action—the particle on Earth somehow sent an instant signal to the particle in space—which of course ran counter to Einstein's relativity theories.

Well, I guess that would fill more than your average postcard. The truth is, blood and semen and DNA evidence were a lot easier to make sense of than quantum mechanics, which was one reason that kind of esoteric science was just a hobby with me. Of course, one way that QM had it over forensics is that it rarely had to do with dead bodies. But Lauren Goldring was wanting to tell me that maybe it did in at least one case, her husband's.

"Ian was part of a small group of physicists working to demonstrate that QM was evidence of faster-than-light travel, time travel, maybe both," she said.

"Not a product of the mind?" I asked.

"No," she said, "not as in the traditional interpretation."

"But doesn't faster-than-light travel contradict Einstein?" I asked.

"Not necessarily," Lauren said. "It seems to contradict the simplest interpretations, but there may be some loopholes."

"Go on," I said.

"Well, there's a lot of disagreement even among the small group of people Ian was working with. Some think the data supports both faster-than-light *and* time travel. Others are sure that time travel is impossible even though—"

"You're not saying that you think some crazy envious scientist killed him?" I asked.

"No," Lauren said. "It's much deeper than that."

A favorite phrase of hers. "I don't understand," I said.

"Well, Stephen Hawking, for one, says that although the equations suggest that time travel might be possible on the quantum level, the Universe wouldn't let this happen. . . ." She paused and looked at me. "You've heard about Hawking's work in this area?"

"I know about Hawking in general," I said. "I'm not that much of an amateur. But not about his work in time travel."

"You're very unusual for a forensic scientist," she said, with an admiring edge I very much liked. "Anyway, Hawking thinks that whatever quantum mechanics may permit, the Universe just won't allow time travel—because the level of paradox time travel would create would just unravel the whole Universe."

"You mean like if I could get a message back to

JFK that he would be killed, and he believed me and acted upon that information and didn't go to Dallas and wasn't killed, this would create a world in which I would grow up with no knowledge that JFK had ever been killed, which would mean I would have no motive to send the message that saved JFK, but if I didn't send that message then JFK would be killed—"

"That's it," Lauren said. "Except on the quantum level you might achieve that paradox by sending back information just a few seconds in time—say, in the form of a command that would shut down the generating circuit and prevent the information from being sent in the first place—"

"I see," I said.

"And, well, because things like that, if they could happen, if they happened all the time, would lead to a constantly remade, inside-out, self-effacing universe. Hawking promulgated his 'Chronology Protection Conjecture'—the Universe protects the existing time line, whatever the theoretical possibilities of time travel."

"How does your husband fit into this?" I asked.

"He was working on a device, an experiment, to disprove Hawking's conjecture," she said. "He was trying to create a local wormhole with temporal effects."

"And you think he somehow disappeared into this?" Jeez, this was beginning to sound like a bad episode of "Star Trek." But she seemed rational, everything she'd outlined made sense, and something in her manner continued to compel my attention.

"I don't know," she looked like she was close to tears again.

"All right," I said. "Here's what I think we should do. I'm going to call in Ian's disappearance to a friend in the department. He's a precinct captain, and he'll take this seriously. He'll contact all the airports, get Ian's picture out to cops on the beat—"

"But I don't think—"

"I know," I said. "You've got a gut feeling that

something more profound is going on. And maybe you're right. But we've got to cover all the bases."

"OK," she said quietly, and I noticed that her lips were quivering again.

"Will you be all right tonight? I'll be back to you tomorrow morning." I took her hand.

"I guess so," she said huskily, and squeezed my hand.

I didn't feel like letting go, but I did.

The news the next morning was terrible. I don't care what the shrinks say: flat-out confirmed death is always worse than ambiguous unresolved disappearance.

I couldn't bring myself to just call her on the phone. I drove to her home, hoping she was in.

She opened the door. I tried to keep a calm face, but I'm not that good an actor.

She understood immediately. "Oh no!" she cried out. She staggered and collapsed in my arms. "Please no."

"I'm sorry," I said, and touched her hair. I felt like kissing her forehead, but didn't. I hardly knew her, yet I felt very close to her, a part of her world. "They found him a few hours ago near Columbia University. Looks like another stupid, senseless, goddamned random drive-by shooting. That's the kind of world we live in." I didn't know whether this would in any way lessen her pain. At least his death had nothing to do with his work.

"No, not random," she said, sobbing. "Not random."

"OK," I said, "you need to rest, I'm going to call someone over here to give you a sedative. I'll stay with you till then."

The medic was over in fifteen minutes. He gave her a shot, and she was asleep a few minutes later. "Not random. Not random," she mumbled.

I called the Captain, and asked if he could send a uniform over to stay with Lauren for the afternoon. He wasn't happy—his people were overworked, like everyone—but he owed me. Many's the time I'd saved his butt with some piece of evidence I'd uncovered in the back of an orifice.

I dropped by the autopsy. Nothing unusual there. Three bullets from a cheap punk's gun, one shattered the heart, did all the damage, Ian Goldring's dead. No sign of radiation damage, no strange chemistry in the body. No possible connection that I could see to anything Lauren had told me. Still, the coroner was a friend, I explained to him that the victim was the husband of a friend, and asked if he could run any and every conceivable test at his disposal to determine if there was anything different about this corpse. He said sure. I knew he wouldn't find anything, though.

I went back to my office. I thought of calling Lauren and telling her about the autopsy, but she'd be better off if I let her rest. I was tired of looking at dead bodies. I turned on my computer and looked at its screen instead. I was on a few physics lists on the Internet. I logged on and did some reading about Hawking and his chronology protection conjecture.

"Lady physicist on the phone for you again," Carl called out. It was late afternoon already. I logged off and rubbed my eyes.

"Hi," Lauren said.

"You OK?" I asked.

"Yeah," she said. "I just got off the phone with one of the other researchers in Ian's group, and I think I've got part of this figured out." She sounded less tentative than yesterday—like she was indeed more on top of what was actually going on, or thought she was—but more worried.

I started to tell her, as gently as I could, about the autopsy.

"Doesn't matter," she interrupted me. "I mean, I don't think the *way* that Ian was killed has any relevance to this. It's the fact that he *was* killed that counts—the reason he was killed."

The reason—everyone wants reasons in this irrational society. Science in the laboratory deals with reason. In the outside world, you're lucky if you can find a reason. "I know it's painful," I said. "But Ian's death had no reason—his killer was likely just a high-flying kid with a gun. Happens all the time. Ian was just in the wrong place. A random victim in the murder lottery."

"No, not random," Lauren said.

She'd said the same thing this morning. I could hear her starting to sob again.

"Look, Phil," she continued. "I really think I'm close to understanding this. I'm going to make a few more calls. I, uh, we hardly know each other, but I feel good talking this out with you. Our conversation last night helped me a lot. Can I call you back in an hour? Or maybe—I don't know, if you're not busy tonight—could you come over again?"

She didn't have to ask twice. "I'll see you at seven. I'll also bring some food in case you're hungry—you have to eat."

I knew even before I drove up that something was wrong. I guess my eyes, after all these years of looking around crime scenes, are especially sensitive to the weak flicker of police lights on the evening sky at a distance. The flicker still turns my stomach.

"What's going on here?" I got out of my car, Chinese food in hand, and asked the uniform.

"Who the hell are you?" he replied.

I fumbled for my ID.

"He's OK," Janny Murphy, the uniform who'd come to stay with Lauren in the afternoon, walked over. "He's forensics."

The food dropped from my hand when I saw the expression on her face. Brown moo-shoo pork juice dribbled down the driveway.

"It's crazy," Janny said. "Doc says it's less than one in ten thousand. Some rare allergy to the shot the medic gave her. It wasn't his fault. It somehow brings out an asthma attack hours later. Fifty percent fatality."

"And Lauren—Dr. Goldring—was in the unlucky part of the curve."

Janny nodded.

"I don't believe this," I said, shaking my head.

"I know," Janny said. "Helluva coincidence. Physicist and his wife, also a physicist, both dying like that."

"Maybe it's not a coincidence," I said.

"What do you mean?" Janny said.

"I don't know what I mean," I said. "Is Lauren—is the body—still here? I'd like to have a look at her."

"Help yourself," Janny gestured inside the house.

I can't say Lauren looked at peace in death. I could almost still see her lips quivering, straining to tell me something, though they were as sealed as the deadest night now. I had an urge to kiss her face. I'd known her all of two days, wanted as many times to kiss her. Now I never would.

I was aware of Janny standing beside me.

"I'm going home now," I said.

"Sure," Janny said. "The captain says he'd like to talk to you tomorrow morning. Just to wrap this whole mess up. Bad karma."

Yeah, karma, like in Fritz Capra's *Tao of Physics*. Like in two entities crossing each other's paths and then never more touching each other's destinies. Like me and this soul with the soft, still lips. Except I had no power to influence Lauren, to make things better for her any more. And the truth is, I hadn't done much for her when she was alive.

I was awake all night. I logged on to a few more fringy physics lists with my computer and did more reading. Finally it was light outside. I thought about calling Stephen Hawking. He was where? California? Cambridge, England? I wasn't sure. I knew he'd be able to talk to me if I could reach him—I'd seen a video of him talking through a special device—but he'd probably think I was crazy when I told him what I had to say. So I called Jack Donovan instead. He was another friend who owed me. I had lots of friends

like that in the city. Jack was a science reporter for
Newsday, and I'd come through for him with off-the-
record background on murder investigations in my
bailiwick lots of times. I hoped he'd come through for
me now. I was starting to get worried. He had lots of
connections in the field—he could talk to scientists
who'd shy away from me, my being in the department
and all.

It was seven in the morning. I expected to get his
answering machine, but I got him. I told him my story.

"OK," he said. "Why don't you go see the captain
at the precinct, and then come over to see me? I'll do
some checking around in the meantime."

I did what Jack said. I kept strictly to the facts with
the captain—no suppositions, no chronological or any
other protection schemes—and he took it all in with
his customary frown. "Damn shame," he muttered.
"Nice lady like that. They oughta take that sedative
off the market. Damn drug companies are too
greedy."

"Right," I said.

"You look exhausted," he said. "You oughta take
the rest of the day off."

"More or less what I had in mind," I said, and left
for Jack's.

I thought *my* office was high-tech, but Jack's Hemp-
stead newsroom looked like something well into the
next century. Computer screens everywhere you
looked, sounds of modems chirping on and off like
the patter of tiny raindrops.

Jack looked concerned. "You're not going to like
this," he said.

"What else is new?" I said. "Try me."

"Well, you were right about my having better entrée
to these physicists than you. I did a lot of checking,"
Jack said. "There were six people working actively in
conjunction with Ian on this project. A few more, of
course, if you take into account the usual complement
of graduate student assistants. But outside of that, the

project was sealed up pretty tightly—not by the government or any agency, but by the researchers themselves. Sometimes they do that when the research gets really flaky—like they don't want anyone to know what they're really doing until they're sure they have a reliable effect. You wouldn't believe some of the wild things people have been getting into in the past few years—especially the physicists—now that they have the Internet to yammer at each other."

"I'm tired, Jack. Please get to the point."

"Well, four of the seven—that includes Ian Goldring—are now dead. One had a heart attack—the day after his doctor told him his cholesterol was in the bottom 10 percent. I guess that's not so strange. Another fell off his roof—he was cleaning out his gutters—and severed his carotid artery on a sharp piece of flagstone that was sticking up on his walk. He bled to death before anyone found him. Another was struck by a car—DOA. And then there's Ian. I could write a story on this even without your conjecture—"

"Please don't," I said.

"It's a weird situation, all right. Four of seven dying like that—and also Goldring's wife."

"How are the spouses of the other fatalities?" I asked.

"All OK," Jack said. "But none are physicists. None knew anything at all about their husbands' work—all of the dead were men. Lauren Goldring is the only one who had any idea what her husband was up to."

"She wasn't sure," I said. "But I think she figured it out just before she died."

"Maybe they all picked up some virus at a conference they attended—something which threw off their sense of balance, caused their heart rate to speed up," Sam Abrahmson, Jack's editor, strolled by and jumped in. Clearly he'd been listening on the periphery of our conversation. "That could explain the two accidents and the heart attack," he added. "Maybe even the sedative death."

"But not the drive-by shooting of Goldring," I said.

THE CHRONOLOGY PROTECTION CASE   227

"No," Abrahmson admitted. "But it could be an interesting story anyway. Think about it," he said to Jack and strolled away.

I looked at Jack. "Please, I'm begging you. If I'm right—"

"It's likely something completely different," Jack said. "Some completely different hidden variable."

Hidden variables. I'd been reading about them all night. "What about the other three? Have you been able to get in touch with them?" I asked.

"Nope," Jack said. "Hays and Strauss refused to talk to me about it. Both had their secretaries tell me they were aware of some of the deaths, had decided not to do any more work on the local wormhole project, had no plans to publish what they'd already done, didn't want to talk to me about it or hear from me again. Each claimed to be involved now in something completely different."

"Does that sound to you like the usual behavior of research scientists?" I asked.

"No," Jack said. "The ones I know eat up publicity, and they'd hang on to a project like this for decades, like a dog worrying a bone."

I nodded. "And the third physicist?"

"Fenwick? She's in a small plane somewhere in the outback of Australia. I couldn't reach her at all."

"Call me immediately if you hear the plane crashes," I said. I really meant "when" not "if," but I didn't want Jack to think I was even more far gone than I was. "Please try to hold off on any story for now," I said and made to leave.

"I'll do what I can," Jack said. "Try to get some rest. I think there's something going on here all right, but not what you think."

The drive back to Westchester was harrowing. Two cars nearly sideswiped me, and one big-ass truck stopped so suddenly in front of me that I had all I could do to swerve out of crashing into it and becoming an instant Long Island Expressway pancake.

Let's say the QM time-travel people were right. Particles are able to influence each other traveling away from each other at huge distances, because they're actually traveling back in time to an earlier position when they were in immediate physical contact. So time travel on the quantum mechanical level is possible—technically.

But let's say Hawking was also right. The Universe can't allow time travel—for to do so would unravel its very being. So it protects itself from dissemination of information backwards in time.

That wouldn't be so crazy. People are saying the Universe can be considered one huge organism—a Gaia writ large. Makes sense then, that this organism, like all other organisms, would have tendencies to act on behalf of its own survival—would act to prevent its dissolution via time travel.

But how would such protection express itself? A physicist figures out a way of creating a local wormhole that can send some information back in time—back to his earlier self and equipment—in some non-blatantly paradoxical way. It doesn't shut off the circuit that sent it. So this information is in fact sent and in fact received—by the scientist. But the Universe can't allow that information transfer to stand. So what happens?

Hawking says the Universe's first line of defense is to create energy disturbances severe enough at the mouths of the wormhole to destroy it and its time-channeling ability. OK. But let's say the physicist is smart or lucky enough to create a wormhole that can withstand these self-disruptive forces? What does the Universe do then?

Maybe it makes the scientist forget this information. Maybe causes a minor stroke in the scientist's brain. Maybe causes the equipment to irreparably break down. Maybe the lucky physicist is really unlucky. Maybe this already happened lots of times.

But what happens when a group of scientists around the world who achieve this time travel transfer reach a critical mass—a mass that will soon publish its findings, and make them known, irrevocably, to the world?

Jeez!—I jammed the heel of my hand into my car horn and swerved. The damn Volkswagen driver must be drunk out of his mind—

So what happens when this group of scientists gets information from its own future? Has proof of time travel, information that can't be? The Universe regulates itself, polices its time-line, in a more drastic way. All existence is equilibrium—a stronger threat to existence evokes a stronger reaction. A freak fatal accident. A sudden massive heart attack. Another no-motive, drive-by shooting that the Universe already dishes out to all too many people in this hapless world of ours. Except in this case, the Universe's motive is quite clear and strong: it must protect its chronology, conserve its current existence.

Maybe this already happened too. How many physicists on the cutting edges of this science died too young in recent years? Jeez, here was a story for Jack all right.

But why Lauren? Why did she have to die?

Maybe because the Universe's protection level went beyond just those who received illicit future information. Maybe it extended to those who understood just what it was doing, just—

"Whamp! Something big had smashed into the rear of my car, and I was skidding way out of control towards the edge of the Throgs Neck Bridge, towards where some workers had removed the barriers to fix some corrosion or something. I was strangely calm, above it all. I told myself to go easy on the brakes, but my leg clamped down anyway and my speed increased. I wrenched my wheel around, but all that did was spin me into a backward skid off the bridge. My car sailed way the hell out over the black-and-blue Long Island Sound.

The way down took a long time. They'd say I was overwrought, overtired, that I lost control. But I knew

the truth, knew exactly why this was happening. I
knew too much, just like Lauren.

Or maybe there was a way out, a weird little corner
of my brain piped up.

Maybe I didn't know the truth. Maybe I was wrong.

Maybe if I could convince myself of that, the Universe wouldn't have to protect itself from me. Maybe
it would give me a second chance.

My car hit the water.

I was still alive.

I was a pretty fair swimmer.

If only I could force myself never to think of certain
things, maybe I had a shot.

Maybe the deaths of the physicists were coincidental
after all. . . .

I lost consciousness thinking no, I couldn't just forget what I already knew so well. . . . How could I will
myself not to think of that very thing I was trying to
will myself not to think about . . . that blared in my
mind now like a broken car horn. . . . But if I died,
what I knew wouldn't matter anymore. . . .

I awoke fighting sheets . . . of water. No, these were
too white. Maybe hospital sheets. Yeah, white hospital
sheets. They smelled like that too.

I opened my eyes. Hospital rooms were hell—I
knew better than most the truth of that—but this was
just a hospital room. I was sure of that. I was alive.

And I remembered everything. With a spasm that
both energized and frightened me, I realized that I
recalled everything I'd been thinking about the Universe and its protective clutch. . . .

But I was still alive.

So maybe my reasoning was not completely right.

"Dr. D'Amato," a female voice, soft but very much
in command, said to me. "Good to see you awake."

"Good to *be* awake, Nurse, ah, Johnson." I squinted
at her name tag, then her face. "Uhm, what's my situation? How long have I been here?"

She looked at the chart next to my bed. "Just a day

and a half," she said. "They fished you out of the
Sound. You were suffering from shock. Here," she
gave me a cup of water. "Now that you're awake, you
can take these orally." She gave me three pills, and
turned off the intravenous that I'd just realized was
attached to me. She disconnected the tubing from
my vein.

I held the pills in my hand. I thought about the
Universe again. I envisioned it, rightly or wrongly, as
a personal antagonist now. Let's say I was right about
the reach of its chronology protection after all? Let's
say it had spared me in the water, because I was on
the verge of willing myself to forget? Let's say it had
allowed me to get medicine and nutrition intrave-
nously, while I was unconscious, because while I was
unconscious I posed no threat? But let's say now that
I was awake, and remembered, it would—

"Dr. D'Amato. Are you falling back asleep on
me?" She smiled. "Come on now, be a good boy and
take your pills."

They burned in my palm. Maybe they were poison.
Maybe something I had a lethal allergy to. Like
Lauren. "No," I said. "I'm OK, now, really. I don't
need them." I put the pills on the table, and swung
my legs out of bed.

"I don't believe this," Johnson said. "It's true—you
doctors make the worst god-awful patients. You just
stay put now—hear me?" She gave me a look of exas-
peration and stalked out the door, likely to get the
resident on duty, or, who knew, security.

I looked around for my clothes. They were on a
chair, a dried out crumpled mess. They stank of oil
and saltwater. At least my wallet was still inside my
jacket pocket, money damp but intact. Good to see
there was still some honesty left in this town.

I dressed quickly and opened the door. The corridor
was clear. Goddamn it, I could leave if I wanted to. I
was a patient, not a prisoner.

At least insofar as the hospital was concerned. As
for the larger realm of being, I couldn't say any more.

*   *   *

I took a cab straight home.

The most important new piece of evidence—to this whole case, as well as to me personally—was that I was alive. This meant that my assessment of the Universe's vindictiveness was missing something. Or maybe the Universe was just a less effective assassin of forensic scientists than quantum physicists and their knowing wives.

I called Jack to see if there was anything new.

"Oh, just a second please," the *Newsday* receptionist said. I didn't like the tone of her voice.

"Hello, can I help you?" This was a man's voice, but not Jack's. He sounded familiar but I couldn't place him.

"Yes, I'm Dr. Phil D'Amato of NYPD Forensics calling Jack Donovan."

Silence. Then, "Hello, Phil. I'm Sam Abrahmson. You still in the hospital?"

Right. Abrahmson. That was the voice. "No. I'm out. Where's Jack?"

Abrahmson cleared his throat. "He was killed with Dave Strauss this morning. He'd talked Strauss into going public with this, Strauss supported your story. He'd picked Strauss up at his summer cottage in Ellenville—Strauss had been hiding out there—and was driving him back to the city. They got blown off a small bridge. Freak accident."

"No freakin' accident," I said. "You know that as well as I do." Another particle who'd danced this sick quantum twist with me. Another particle dead. But this one was completely my fault—I'd brought Jack into this.

"I don't know what I know," Abrahmson said. "Except that at this point the story's on hold. Until we find out more."

I was glad to hear he sounded scared. "That's a good idea," I said. "I'll be back to you."

"Take care of yourself," Abrahmson said. "God knows what that subatomic radiation can do to the body and mind. Or maybe it's all just coincidence. God only knows. Take care of yourself."

"Right." Subatomic radiation. Abrahmson's latest culprit. First it was a virus, now it was radiation. I'd said the same stupid thing to Lauren, hadn't I? People like to latch on to something they know when faced with something they don't know—especially something that kills some physicists here, a reporter there, who knew who else? But radiation had nothing to do with this. Stopping it would take a lot more than lead shields.

I tracked down Richard Hays. I was beginning to get a further inkling of what might be going on, and I needed to talk it out with one of the principals. One of the last remaining principals. It could save both our lives.

I used my NYPD clout to intimidate enough secretaries and assistants to get directly through to him.

"Look, I don't care if you're the bleeding head of the FBI," he said. He was British. "I'm going to talk to you about this just once, now, and then never again."

"Thank you, Doctor. So please tell me what you think is happening here. Then I'll tell you what I know, or think I know."

"What's happening is this," Hays said. "I was working on a project with my colleagues. That's true. But I came to realize the project was a dead-end—that the phenomena we were investigating weren't real. So I ceased my involvement in that research. I have no intention of ever picking up that research again—of ever publishing about it, or even talking about it, except to indicate that it was a waste of time. I'd strongly advise you to do the same."

I had no idea how he talked ordinarily, but his words on the phone sounded like each had been chosen with the utmost care. "Why do I feel like you're reading from a script, Dr. Hays?"

"I assure you everything I'm saying is real. As you

no doubt already have evidence of yourself," Hays said.

"Now you look," I raised my voice. "You can't just sweep this under the rug. If the Universe *is* at work here in some way, you think you can just avoid it by pretending you don't know about it? The Universe would know about your pretense too—it's after all still part of the Universe. And word of this will get out anyway—someone will sooner or later publish something. If you want to live, you've got to face this, find out what's really happening here, and—"

"I believe you are seriously mistaken, my friend. And that, I'm afraid, concludes our interview, now and forever." He hung up.

I held on to the disconnected phone, which beeped like a seal, for a long time. I realized that the left side of my body hurt, from my chest up through my shoulder and down my arm. The pain had come on, I thought, at the end of my futile lecture to Hays. Right when I'd talked about publishing. Maybe publishing was the key—maybe talk about dissemination of this information, as opposed to just thinking about it, is what triggered the Universe's backlash. But I was also sure I was right in what I'd said to Hays about the need to confront this, about not running away. . . .

I put the phone back in its receiver and lay down. I was bone tired. Maybe I was getting a heart attack, maybe I wasn't. Maybe I was still in shock from my dip in the Sound. I couldn't fight this all on my own much longer.

The phone rang. I fumbled with the receiver. How long had I been sleeping? "Hello?"

"Dr. D'Amato?" a female voice, maybe Lauren's, maybe Nurse Johnson's. No, someone else.

"Yes?"

"I'm Jennifer Fenwick."

Fenwick, Fenwick—yes, Jennifer Fenwick, the last quantum physicist on this project. I'd wheedled her number from Abrahmson's secretary and left a message for her in Australia—the girl at the hotel wasn't sure if she'd already left. "Dr. Fenwick, I'm glad you called. I, uhm, had some ideas I wanted to talk to you about—regarding the quantum signaling project." I wasn't sure how much she knew, and didn't want to scare her off.

She laughed, oddly. "Well, I'm wide open for ideas. I'll take help wherever I can get it. I'm the only damn person left alive from our research group."

"Only person?" So she knew—apparently more than I.

I looked at the clock. It was tomorrow morning already—I'd slept right through the afternoon and night. Good thing I'd called my office and gotten the week off, the absurd part of me that kept track of such trivia noted.

"Richard Hays committed suicide last night," Fenwick's voice cracked. "He left a note saying he couldn't pull it off any longer—couldn't surmount the paradox of deliberately not thinking of something—couldn't overcome his lifelong urge as a scientist to tell the world what he'd discovered. He'd prepared a paper for publication—begged his wife to have it published posthumously if he didn't make it. I spoke to her this morning. I told her to destroy it. And the note too. Fortunately for her, she had no idea what the paper was about. She's a simple woman—Richard didn't marry her for her brains."

"I see," I said slowly. "Where are you now?"

"I'm in New York," she said. "I wanted to come home—I didn't want to die in Australia."

"Look, you're still alive," I said. "That means you've still got a chance. How about meeting me for lunch"—I looked at the clock again—"in about an hour. The Trattoria II Bambino on 12th Street in the Village is good. As far as I know, no one there has died from the food as yet." How I could bring myself to make a crack like that at a time like this, I didn't know.

"OK," Fenwick said.

*   *   *

She was waiting for me when I arrived. On the way
down, I'd fantasized that she'd look just like Lauren.
But in fact she looked a little older and wiser. And
even more frightened.

"All right," I said after we'd ordered and gotten rid
of the waiter. "Here's what I have in mind. You tell
me as a physicist where this might not add up. First,
everyone who's attempted to publish something about
your work has died."

Jennifer nodded. "I spoke to Lauren Goldring the
afternoon she died. She told me she was going to
the press."

I sighed. "I didn't know that—but it supports my
point. In fact, the two times I even toyed with going
public about this, I had fleeting interviews with death.
The first time in the water, the second with some sort
of preheart attack, I'm sure."

Jennifer nodded again. "Same for me. Wheeler
wrote about cosmic censorship. Maybe he was on to
the same thing as Hawking."

"All right, so what does that tell us?" I said. "Even
thinking about publishing this is dangerous. But apparently it's not a capital offense—knowing about this
is in itself not fatal. We're still alive. It's as if the
Universe allows private, crackpot knowledge in this
area—'cause no one takes crackpots seriously, even
scientific ones. It's the danger of public dissemination
that draws the response—the threat of an objectively
acceptedly scientific theory. Our private knowledge
isn't the real problem here. Communication is. The
definite intention to publish. That's what kills you.
Yeah, cosmic censorship is a good way of putting it."

"OK," Jennifer said.

"OK," I said. "But it's also clear that we can't just
ignore this—can't expect to suppress it in our minds.
Not having any particular plan to publish won't be
enough to save us—not in the long run. Sooner or
later after a dark silent night we'd get the urge to
shout it out. It's human nature. It's inside of us. Hays's

suicide proves it—his note spells it out. You can't just not think of something. You can't just will an idea into oblivion. It's self-defeating. It makes you want to get up on the rooftop and scream it to the world even more—like a repressed love."

"Agreed," Jennifer said. "So what do we do, then?"

"Well, we can't go public with this story, and we can't will ourselves to forget it. But maybe there's a third way. Here's what I was thinking. I can tell you—in strict confidence—that we sometimes do this in forensics." I lowered my voice. "Let's say we have someone who was killed in a certain way, but we don't want the murderer to know that we know how the murder took place. We just deliberately at first publicity interpret the evidence in a different way—after all, there's usually more than one trauma that can result in a given fatal injury to a body—more than one plausible explanation of how someone was killed. Slipped and hit your head on a rock, or someone hit you on the head with a rock—sometimes there's not much difference between the results of the two."

"The Universe is murderous; all right, I can see that, but I don't see how what you're saying would work in our situation," Jennifer said.

"Well, you tell me," I said. "Your group thinks it built a wormhole that allows signaling through time. But couldn't you find another phenomenon to attribute those effects to? After all, we only have time travel on the brain because of H. G. Wells and his literary offspring. Let's say Wells had never written *The Time Machine*? Let's say science fiction had taken a different turn? Then your group would likely have come up with another explanation for your findings. And you can do this now anyway!" I took a sip of wine and realized I felt pretty good. "You can publish an article on your work, and attribute your findings to something other than time travel. Indicate they're some sort of other physical effect. Come up with the equivalent of a false phlogiston theory, an attractive bogus conception for this tiny sliver of subatomic phenomena, to account for the time travel effects. The truth is, few if any serious scientists actually believe that time travel is possible anyway, right? Most think it's just science fiction, nothing else. Who would have reason to suspect a time travel effect here unless you specifically called attention to it?"

Jennifer considered. "The graduate research assistants worked only on the data acquisition level. Only the project principals, the seven of us," she caught her breath, winced—"only the seven of us knew this was about time travel. No one else. Ours were supposedly the best minds in this area. Lot of good it did us."

"I know," I tried to be as reassuring as I could. "But then without that time travel label, all you've got is another of a hundred little experiments in this area per year—jeez, I checked the literature, there are a lot more than that—and your study would likely get lost in the wash. That should shut the Universe up. That should keep it safe from time travel—send the scientific community off on the wrong track, in a different direction—maybe not send them off in any direction at all. Could you do that?"

Jennifer sipped her wine slowly. Her glass was shaking. Her lips clung to the rim. She was no doubt thinking that her life depended on what she decided to do now. She was probably right. Mine too.

"Exotic matter is what makes the effect possible," she said at last. "Exotic matter keeps the wormhole open long enough. No one knows much about how it works—in fact, as far as I know, our group created this kind of exotic matter, in which weak forces are suspended, for the first time in our project. I guess I could make a case that a peculiar property of this exotic matter is that it creates effects that mimic time travel in artificial wormholes—I could make a persuasive argument that we didn't really see time travel through that wormhole at all, what we have instead is a reversal of processes to earlier stages when they come in contact with our exotic matter, no signaling from the future. You know—we thought the glass was half full, but it was really half empty."

"No," I said. "That's still not going far enough. You've got to be more daring in your deception—come up with something that doesn't invoke time travel at all, even in the negative. Publishing a paper with results that are explicitly said not to demonstrate time travel is akin to someone the police never heard of coming into the station and saying he didn't do it—that only arouses our suspicion. I'm sorry to be so blunt, Jennifer. But you've got to do more. Can't you come up with some effects of exotic matter that have nothing to do with time travel at all?"

She drained her wine glass and put it down, neither half full nor half empty. Completely empty. "This goes against everything in my life and training as a scientist," she said. "I'm supposed to pursue the truth, wherever it takes me."

"Right," I said. "And how much truth will you be able to pursue when you're like Hays and Strauss and the others?"

"Einstein said the Universe wasn't malicious," she said. "This is unbelievable."

"Maybe Einstein was saying the glass was half empty when he knew it was half full. Maybe he knew just what he was doing—knew which side his bread was buttered—maybe he wanted to live past middle age."

"God Almighty!" She slammed her hand on the table. Glasses rattled. "Couldn't I just swear before you and the Universe never to publish anything about this? Wouldn't that be enough?"

"Maybe, maybe not," I said. "From the Universe's point of view, your publishing a paper that explicitly attributes the effects to something other than time travel seems much safer—to you as well as the Universe. Let's say you change your mind, years from now, and try to publish a paper that says you succeeded with time travel after all. You'd already be on record in the literature as attributing those effects to something else—you'd be much less likely to be believed then. Safer for the Universe. Safer for you. A paper with a false lead is not only our best bet now, it's an insurance policy for our future."

Jennifer nodded, very slowly. "I guess I could come up with something—some phenomenon unrelated to time travel—unsuggestive of it. The connection of quantum effects to human thought has always had great appeal, and even though I personally never saw much more than wishful thinking in that direction."

"That's better," I said quietly.

"But how can we be sure no one else will want to look into these effects?" Jennifer asked.

I shrugged. "Guarantees of anything are beyond us in this situation. The best we can hope for are probabilities—that's how the QM realm operates anyway, isn't it—likelihoods of our success, statistics in favor of our survival. As for your effects, well, effects don't have much impact outside of a supportive context of theory. Psalm 51 says 'Cleanse me with hyssop and I shall be clean'—the penicillin mold was first identified on a piece of decayed hyssop by a Swedish chemist—but none of this led to antibiotics until spores from a mold landed in Fleming's petrie dish, and he placed them in the right scientific perspective. Scientists thought they had evidence of spontaneous generation of maggots in old meat, until they learned how maggots make love. Astronomers saw lots of evidence for a luminiferous ether, until Michelson-Morley decisively proved that wrong. You're working on the cutting edge of physics with your wormholes. No one knows what to expect—you said it yourself—yours were the best minds in this area. *You* can create the context. No one's left to contradict you. Let's face it, if you word your paper properly, it will likely go unnoticed. But if not, it will point people in the wrong direction—and once pointed that way, away from time travel, the world could take years, decades, longer, to look at time travel as a real scientific possibility again. The history of science is filled with wrong glittering paths, tenaciously taken and defended. That's the path of life for us. I'm not happy about it, but there it is."

Our food arrived. Jennifer looked away from me, and down at her veal.

I hadn't completely won her over yet. But she'd stopped objecting. I understood how she felt. To theoretical scientists, pursuit of truth was sometimes more important than life itself. Maybe that's why I went into flesh-and-blood forensics. I pushed on. "The truth is, we've all been getting along quite well without time travel anyway—it could wreak far more havoc in everyone's lives than nuclear weapons ever did. The Universe may not be wrong here."

She looked up at me.

"It's all up to you now," I said. "I'm not a physicist. I can't pull this off. I can take care of the general media, but not the scientific journals." I thought about Abrahmson at *Newsday*. He hadn't a clue which way was up in this thing. He'd just as soon believe this nightmare was all coincidence—the ever popular placeholder for things people didn't want to understand. I could easily pitch it to him in that way.

She gave me a weak smile. "OK, I'll try it. I'll write the article with the mental spin on the exotic effects. *Physics Review D* was given some general info that we were doing something on exotic matter, and is waiting for our report. It'll have maximum impact on other physicists there. The human mind in control of matter will be catnip for a lot of them anyway."

"Good," I smiled back. I knew she meant it. I knew because I suddenly felt very hungry, and dug into my own veal with a zest I hadn't felt for anything in a while. It tasted great.

Two particles of humanity had connected again. Maybe this time the relationship would go somewhere.

It occurred to me, as I took Jennifer's hand and squeezed it with relief, that maybe this was just what the Universe had wanted all along.

As they say in the Department, an ongoing string of deaths is a poor way to keep a secret.

CHILDREN OF UBASTI

Seabury Quinn

SEABURY QUINN (1889–1969) wrote almost exclusively for *Weird Tales,* and his most famous creation, the psychic sleuth Jules Grandin, appeared there an astonishing ninety-three times, encountering all kinds of supernatural phenomena. Quinn was born in Washington, D.C., received a law degree from the National University in 1910, taught medical jurisprudence, and served in World War I. He wrote over five hundred short stories during his career.

Jules de Grandin regarded the big red-headed man entering the breakfast room with a quick, affectionate smile. "Is it truly thou, *mon sergent?*" he asked. "I have joy in this meeting!"

Detective Sergeant Jeremiah Costello grinned somewhat ruefully as he seated himself and accepted a cup of steaming, well-creamed coffee. "It's me, all right, sir," he admitted, "an' in a peck o' trouble, as I usually am when I come botherin' you an' Dr. Trowbridge at your breakfast."

"Ah, I am glad—I mean I grieve—no, *pardieu,* I mean I sorrow at your trouble, but rejoice at your

242

visit!" the little Frenchman returned. "What is it causes you unhappiness?"

The big Irishman emptied his cup at a gigantic gulp and wrinkled his forehead like a puzzled mastiff. "I dunno," he confessed. "Maybe it's not a case at all, an' then again, maybe it is. Have you been readin' the newspaper accounts of the accident that kilt young Tom Cableson last night?"

De Grandin spread a bit of butter on his broiled weakfish and watched it dissolve. "You refer to the mishap which occurred on the Albemarle Pike—the unfortunate young man who died when he collided with a tree and thrust his face through his windshield?"

"That's what they say, sir."

"Eh? 'They say'? Who are they?"

"The coroner's jury, when they returned a verdict of death by misadventure. Strictly speaking, it wasn't any of my business, but bein' on the homicide squad I thought I'd just drop round to the morgue and have a look at the body, an' when I'd seen it I came over here hot-foot."

"And what was it you saw that roused your suspicions, *mon vieux?*"

"Well, sir, I've seen lots of bodies of folks killed in motor accidents, but never one quite like young Cableson's. The only wound on him was a big, jagged gash in the throat—just one, d'ye mind—an' some funny-lookin' scratches on his neck—" He paused apologetically, as if debating the wisdom of continuing.

"*Cordieu,* is it a game of patience we play here?" de Grandin demanded testily. "Get on with thy story, great stupid one, or I must twist your neck!"

I laughed outright at this threat of the sparrow to chastise the turkey cock, and even Costello's gravity gave way to a grin, but he sobered quickly as he answered. "Well, sir, I did part of me hitch in China, you know, and once one of our men was picked up by some bandits. When we finally came to him we found they'd hung him up like a steer for th' slaugh-

ter—cut his throat an' left him danglin' by th' heels
from a tree-limb. There wasn't a tin-cupful o' blood
left in his pore carcass.

"That's th' way young Cableson looked to me—all
empty-like, if you get what I mean."

"*Parfaitement.* And—"

"Yes, sir, I was comin' to that. I went round to th'
police garage where his car was, and looked it over
most partic'lar. That's th' funny part o' th' joke, but
I didn't see nothin' to laugh at. There wasn't half a
pint o' blood spilled on that car, not on th' hood nor
instrument board, nor upholstery, an th' windshield
which was supposed to have ripped his throat open
when he crashed through it, that was clean as th' palm
o' my hand, too. Besides that, sir—did ye ever see a
man that had been mauled by a big cat?"

"A cat? How do you mean—"

"Lions an' tigers, an' th' like o' that, sir. Once in
th' Chinese upcountry I seen th' body of a woman
who'd been kilt by a tiger, one o' them big blue beasts
they have there. There was something about young
Cableson that reminded me of—"

"*Mort d'un rat rouge,* do you say so? This poor
one's injuries were like those of that Chinese
woman?"

"Pre-*cise*-ly, sir. That's why I'm here. You see, I
figured if he had died natural-like, as th' result o' that
accident, his car should 'a' been wringin' wet with
blood, an' his clothes drippin' with it. But, like I was
sayin'—"

"*Parbleu,* you *have* said it!" de Grandin exclaimed
almost delightedly. "Come, let us go at once." He
swallowed the remaining morsel of his fish, drained
his coffee cup and rose. "This case, he has the smell
of herring on him, *mon sergent.*

"Await me, if you please," he called from the hall
as he thrust his arms into his topcoat sleeves. "I shall
return in ample time for Madame Heacoat's *soirée,*
my friend, but at present I am burnt with curiosity to

see this poor, unfortunate young man who died of a cut throat, yet bled no blood. *A bientôt.*"

A little after 8 o'clock that night he came into my bedroom, resplendent in full evening dress. "Consider me, Friend Trowbridge," he commanded. "Behold and admire. Am I not superb, magnificent? Shall I not be the pride of all the ladies and the despair of the men?" He pirouetted like a dancer for my admiration.

To do him justice, he was a sight to command a second look. About his neck hung the insigne of the Legion of Honor; a row of miniature medals including the French and Belgian war crosses, the *Médaille Militaire* and the Italian Medal for Valor decorated the left breast of his faultless evening coat; his little wheat-blond mustache was waxed to needle sharpness and his sleek blond hair was brushed and brilliantined until it fitted flat against his shapely little head like a skullcap.

"Humpf," I commented, "if you behave as well as you look I suppose you'll not disgrace me."

"*O, la, la!*" He grinned delightedly as he patted the gardenia in his lapel with gentle, approving fingers. "Come, let us go. I would arrive at Madame Heacoat's before all the punch is drunk, if you please." He flung his long, military-cut evening cape about him with the air of a comic-opera conspirator, picked up his lustrous top hat and silver-headed ebony cane and strode debonairly toward the door.

"Just a moment," I called as the desk 'phone gave a short chattering ring.

"Hullo, Trowbridge, Donovan speaking," came a heavy voice across the wire as I picked up the instrument. "Can you bring that funny little Parisian friend of yours over to City Hospital tonight? I've got a brand new variety of nut in the psychopathic ward— a young girl sane as you or I—well, anyhow, apparently as sane as you, except for an odd fixation. I think she'd interest de Grandin—"

"Sorry," I denied. "We're just going to a shindig at

Mrs. Heacoat's. It'll be a frightful bore, most likely, but they're valuable patients, and—"

"Aw, rats," Dr. Donovan interrupted. "If I had as much money as you I'd tell all the tea-pourin' old ladies to go fry an egg. Come on over. This nut is *good,* I tell you. Put your Frenchman on the 'phone, maybe he'll listen to reason, even if you won't."

"*Hélas,* but I am desolated!" the Frenchman declared as Donovan delivered his invitation. "At present Friend Trowbridge and I go to make the great whoopee at Madame Heacoat's. Later in the evening, if you please, we shall avail ourselves of your hospitality. You have whiskey there, yes? *Bon.* Anon, my friend, we shall discuss it and the young woman with the *idée fixe.*"

Mrs. Heacoat's was the first formal affair of the autumn, and most of the élite of our little city were present, the men still showing the floridness of golf course and mountain trail, sun-tan, painfully acquired at fashionable beaches, lying in velvet veneer on the women's arms and shoulders.

Famous lion-huntress that she was, Mrs. Heacoat had managed to impound a considerable array of exotic notables for her home-town guests to gape at, and I noted with amusement how her large, pale eyes lit up with elation at sight of Jules de Grandin. The little Frenchman, quick to understand the situation, played his rôle artistically. "Madame," he bent above our hostess's plump hand with more than usual ceremony, "believe me, I am deeply flattered by the honor you have conferred on me."

What would have been a simper in anyone less distinguished than Mrs. Watson Heacoat spread over the much massaged and carefully lifted features of Harrisonville's social arbiter. "So sweet of you to come, Dr. de Grandin. Do you know Monsieur Arif? Arif Pasha, Dr. Jules de Grandin—Dr. Trowbridge."

The slender, sallow-skinned young man whom she presented had the small regular features, sleek black hair and dark, slumbrous eyes typical of a night club band leader, or a waiter in a fashionable café. He bowed jerkily from the hips in continental fashion and murmured a polite greeting in stilted English. "You, I take it, are a stranger like myself in strange company?" he asked de Grandin as we moved aside for a trio of newcomers.

Further conversation developed he was attached to the Turkish consulate in New York, that he had met Mrs. Heacoat in England the previous summer, and that he would be exceedingly glad when he might bid his hostess good night.

"*Tiens,* they stare so, these Americans," he complained. "Now, in London or Paris—"

"Monsoor and Modom Bera!" announced the butler, his impressive full-throated English voice cutting through the staccato of chatter as the booming of the surf sounds through the strains of a seaside resort band.

We turned casually to view the newcomers, then kept our eyes at gaze; they were easily the most interesting people in the room. Madame Bera walked a half-pace before her husband, tall, exquisite, exotic as an orchid blooming in a New England garden. Tawny hair combed close to a small head framed a broad white brow, and under fine dark-brown brows looked out the most remarkable eyes I had ever seen. Widely separated, their roundness gave them an illusion of immensity which seemed to diminish her face, and their color was a baffling shade of greenish amber, contrasting oddly with her leonine hair and warm, maize-tan complexion. From cheek to cheek her face was wide, tapering to a pointed chin, and her nostrils flared slightly, like those of an alert feline scenting hidden danger. Her evening dress, cut rather higher than the prevailing mode, encased her large, supple figure with glove-tightness from breast to waist, then flared outward to an uneven hem that almost swept the floor. Beneath the edge of her sand-colored chiffon gown her feet, in sandals of gold kid, appeared absurdly small for her height as she crossed the room with a lithe, easy stride that seemed positively pantherine in its effortless grace.

Older by a score of years than his consort, Monsieur Bera yet had something of the same feline ease of movement that characterized her. Like hers, his face was wide from cheek to cheek, pointed at the chin and with unusually wide nostrils. Unlike his wife's, his eyes were rather long than round, inclined to be oblique, and half closed, as if to shade them from the glitter of the electric lights. Fast-thinning gray hair was combed back from his brow in an effort to conceal his spreading bald spot, and his wide mouth was adorned by a waxed mustache of the kind affected by Prussian officers in pre-Nazi days. Through the lens of a rimless monocle fixed in his right eye he seemed to view the assemblage with a sardonic contempt.

"Ye Allah!" the young Turk who stood between de Grandin and me sank his fingers into our elbows. *"Bism'allah ar-rahman ar-rahim!* Do you see them? They look as if they were of *that people!"*

"Eh, you say what?" whispered Jules de Grandin sharply.

"It is no matter, sir; you would not understand."

"Pardonnez-moi, Monsieur, I understand you very well, indeed. Some little time ago I had to go to Tunis to make investigation of a threatened uprising of the tribesmen. Disguised as a *Père Blanc*—and other things—I mingled with the natives. It was vile—I had to shave off my mustaches!—but it was instructive. I learned much. I learned, by example, of the djinn that haunt the ruins of Carthage, and of the strange ones who reside in tombs; a weird and dreadful folk without a name—at any rate, without a name which can be mentioned."

Arif Pasha looked at Jules de Grandin fearfully. "You have seen them?" he asked in a low breath.

"I have heard much of them, and their stigmata has been described to me. Come, let us seek an introduction to *la belle* Bera."

"Allah forbid," the young Turk denied, walking hastily away.

The lady proved gracious as she was beautiful. Viewed closely, her strange eyes were stranger still, for they had a trick of contracting their pupils in the light, bringing out the full beauty of their fine irises, and expanding in shadow till they seemed black as night. Too, I noted when she smiled her slow wide smile, all four canine teeth seemed over-prominent and sharp. This, perhaps, accounted for the startling contrast between her crimson lips and her perfect dentition. Her hands were unusual, too. Small and fine they were, with supple slender fingers but unusually wide palms, and the nails, shaped to a point and brightly varnished, curved oddly downward over the fingertips; had they been longer or less carefully tended they would have suggested talons. Her voice was a rich heavy contralto, and when she spoke slow hesitant English there was an odd purring undertone beneath her words.

The odd characteristics which seemed somehow exotically attractive in his wife were intensified in Monsieur Bera. The over-prominent teeth which lent a kind of piquant charm to her smile were a deformity in his thin-lipped mouth; the overhanging nails that made her long fingers seem longer still were definitely clawlike on his hands, and the odd trick of contracting and expanding his pupils in changing lights gave his narrow eyes a furtive look unpleasantly reminiscent of the eyes of a dope-fiend or a cruel, treacherous cat.

"Madam, I am interested," de Grandin admitted with the frankness only he could employ without seeming discourteous. "Your name intrigues me. It is not French, yet I heard you introduced as Monsieur and Madame—"

The lady smiled languidly, showing pearly teeth and crimson lips effectively. "We are Tunisians," she answered. "Both my husband and I come from North Africa."

"Ah, then I am indeed fortunate," he smiled delightedly. "Is it by some great fortune you reside in this city? If so I should greatly esteem permission to call—"

I heard no summons, but Madame Bera evidently did, for with another smile and friendly nod she left us to join Mrs. Heacoat.

"Beard of a small blue man!" de Grandin grinned wryly as we rejoined the young Turk, "it seems that Jules de Grandin loses his appeal for the sex. Was ever the chilled shoulder more effectively presented than by *la charmante* Bera?

"Come, *mes amis,*" he linked his hands through our elbows and drew us toward the farther room, "women may smile, or women may frown, but champagne punch is always pleasant to the taste."

We sampled several kinds of punch and sandwiches and small sweet cakes, then made our adieux to our hostess. Outside, as Arif Pasha was about to enter his taxi, de Grandin tapped him lightly on the shoulder. "If we should hear more of them, I can find you, my friend?" he asked cryptically.

The young Turk nodded. "I shall be ready if you call," he promised.

"Would you guys like a spot o' proletarian whiskey to take the taste of all that champagne out o' your mouths?" asked Dr. Donovan as we joined him in his office at the hospital.

"A thousand thanks," de Grandin answered. "Champagne is good, but whiskey, as your saying puts it so drolly, hits the spot. By all means, let us indulge.

"You are not drinking?" he asked as Donovan poured a generous portion for him, and a like one for me.

"Nope, not on duty. Might give some o' my nuts bad ideas," the other grinned. "However, bottoms up, you fellers, then let's take a gander at my newest curio.

"It was nearly this morning, half-past 4 or so, when a state constabulary patrol found her wandering around the woods west of Mooreston with nothing but a nightdress on. They questioned her, but could get nowhere. Most of the time she didn't speak at all, and when she did it was only to slobber some sort o' meaningless gibberish. According to Hoyle they should have taken her to the State Hospital for observation, but they're pretty full over there, and prefer to handle only regularly committed cases, so the troopers brought her here and turned her over to the city police.

"Frankly, the case has my goat. Familiar with dementia praecox, are you, Doctor?" he turned questioningly to de Grandin.

"Quite," the Frenchman answered. "I have seen many poor ones suffering from it. Usually it occurs between the ages of fifteen and thirty-five, though most cases I have observed were in the early thirties. Wherever I have seen it the disease was characterized by states of excitement accompanied by delusions of aural or visual type. Most patients believed they were persecuted, or had been through some harrowing experience—occasionally they posed, gesticulated and grimaced."

"Just so," agreed Donovan. "You've got it down pat, Doctor. I thought I had, too, but I'm not so sure now. What would be your diagnosis if a patient displayed every sign of ataxic aphasia, couldn't utter a single intelligent word, then fell into a stupor lasting eight hours or so and woke up with a case of the horrors? This girl's about twenty-three, and absolutely perfect physically. What's more, her reflexes are all right—knee-jerks normal, very sensitive to pain, and all that, but—" He looked inquiringly at de Grandin.

"From your statement I should suggest dementia praecox. It is well known that such dements frequently fall into comatose sleeps in which they suffer nightmares, and on awaking are so mentally confused they cannot distinguish between the phantoms of their dreams and their waking surroundings."

"Precisely. Well, I had a talk with this child and

heard her story, then gave her a big dose of codeine
in milk. She slept three hours and woke up seemingly
as normal as you or I, but I'm damned if she didn't
repeat the same story, chapter and verse, that she gave
me when she first came out of her stupor. I'd say she's
sane as a judge if it weren't for this delusion she per-
sists in. Want to come up now and have a look at
her?"

Donovan's patient lay on the neat white-iron hospital cot, staring with wide frightened eyes at the little
observation-grille in the unlocked door of her cell.
Even the conventional high-necked, long-sleeve mus-
lin bedgown furnished by the hospital could not hide
her frail prettiness. With her pale smooth skin, light
short hair and big violet eyes in which lay a look of
perpetual terror, she was like a little frightened child,
and a wave of sympathy swept over me as we entered
her room. That de Grandin felt the same I could tell
by the kindly smile he gave her as he drew a chair to
her bedside and seated himself. He took her thin blue-
veined hand in his and patted it gently before placing
his fingers on her pulse.

"I've brought a couple of gentlemen to see you,
Annie," Dr. Donovan announced as the little Frenchman gazed intently at the tiny gold watch strapped to
the underside of his wrist, comparing its sweep-second
hand with the girl's pulsation. "Dr. de Grandin is a
famous French detective as well as a physician; he'll
be glad to hear your story; maybe he can do something
about it."

A tortured look swept across the girl's thin face as
he finished. "You think I'm crazy," she accused, half
rising from her pillow. "I know you do, and you've
brought these men here to examine me so you can
put me in a madhouse for always. Oh, it's dreadful—
I'm not insane, I tell you; I'm as sane as you are, if
you'd only listen—"

"Now, Annie, don't excite yourself," Donovan
soothed. "You know *I* wouldn't do anything like that;
I'm your friend—"

"My name's not Annie, and you're *not* my friend. Nobody is. You think I'm crazy—all you doctors think everyone who gets into your clutches must be crazy, and you'll send me to a madhouse, and I'll really *go* crazy there!"

"Now, Annie—"

"My name's not Annie, I tell you. Why do you keep calling me that?"

Donovan cast a quick wink at me, then turned a serious face to the girl. "I thought your name was Annie. I must have been mistaken. What is it?"

"I've told you it's Trula, Trula Petersen. I used to live in Paterson, but lost my place there and couldn't get anything to do, so I came to Harrisonville looking for work, and—"

"Very good, Friend Donovan," de Grandin announced, relinquishing the girl's wrist, but retaining her fingers in his, "when first this young lady came here she could not tell her name. Now she can. *Bon,* we make the progress. Her heart action is strong and good. I think perhaps we shall make much more progress. Now, Mademoiselle," he gave the girl one of his quick friendly smiles, "if you will be so good as to detail your adventures from the start we shall listen with the close attention. Believe me, we are friends, and nothing you say shall be taken as a proof of madness."

The girl's smile was a pitiful, small echo of his own. "I do believe you, sir," she returned, "and I'll tell you everything, for I know I can trust you."

"When the Clareborne Silk Mills closed down in Paterson I lost my place as timekeeper. Most of the other mills were laying off employees, and there wasn't much chance of another situation there. I'm an orphan with no relatives, and I had to get some sort of work at once, for I didn't have more than fifty dollars in bank. After trying several places with no luck I came to Harrisonville where nobody knew me and registered at a domestic servants' agency. It was better to be a housemaid than starve, I thought.

"The very day I registered a Mrs. d'Afrique came looking for a maid, and picked two other girls and me as possibilities. She looked us all over, asked a lot of questions about our families, where we were born, and that sort of thing, then chose me because she said she preferred a maid without relatives or friends, who wouldn't be wanting to run out every evening. Her car was waiting outside, and I had no baggage except my suitcase, so I went along with her."

"U'm?" de Grandin murmured. "And she did take you where?"

"I don't know."

"*Hein?* How do you say?"

"I don't know, sir. It was a big foreign car with a closed body, and she had me sit in the tonneau with her instead of up front with the chauffeur. When we'd started I noticed for the first time that the windows were of frosted glass, and I couldn't see where we went. We must have gone a long way, though, for the car seemed traveling very fast, and there were no traffic stops. When we finally stopped we were under a porte-cochère, and we entered the house directly from the car, so I couldn't get any idea of surroundings."

"*Dites!* Surely, in the days that followed you could look about?"

A look of terror flared in the girl's eyes and her pale lips writhed in a grimace of fear. "The days that followed!" she repeated in a thin scream; "it's the days that followed that brought me *here!*"

"Ah? Do you say so?"

"*Now* we're gettin' it!" Donovan whispered in my ear with a low chuckle. "Go ahead and ask her, de Grandin; you tell him, Annie. This is goin' to be good."

His voice was too low for de Grandin and the girl to catch his words, but his tone and laugh were obvious. "Oh!" the patient wailed, wrenching her hand from de Grandin's and putting it to her eyes. "Oh, how cruel! You're all making fun of me!"

"Be silent, *imbécile,*" de Grandin turned on Donovan savagely. "*Parbleu,* cleaning the roadways would be more fitting work for you than treating the infirm of mind! Do not attend him, Mademoiselle." He repossessed himself of the girl's hand and smoothed it gently. "Proceed with your narrative. I shall listen, and perhaps believe."

For a moment the little patient shook as with an ague, and I could see her grip on his fingers tighten. "Please, *please* believe me, Doctor," she begged. "It's really the truth I'm telling. They wanted—they wanted to—"

"Did they so, *pardieu?*" de Grandin replied. "Very good, Mademoiselle, you escaped them. No one shall hurt you now, nor shall you be persecuted. Jules de Grandin promises it. Now to proceed."

"I was frightened," she confessed, "terribly frightened from the moment I got into the car with Mrs. d'Afrique and realized I couldn't look out. I thought of screaming and trying to jump out, but I was out of work and hungry; besides, she was a big woman and could have overpowered me without trouble.

"When we got to the house I was still more terrified, and Mrs. d'Afrique seemed to notice it, for she smiled and took me by the arm. Her hands were strong as a man's—stronger!—and when I tried to draw away she held me tighter and sort of chuckled deep down in her throat—like a big cat purring when it's caught a mouse. She half led, half shoved me down a long hall that was almost bare of furniture, through a door and down a flight of steps that led to the basement. Next thing I knew she'd pushed me bodily into a little room no bigger than this, and locked the door.

"The door was solid planking, and the only window was a little barred opening almost at the ceiling, which I couldn't reach to look through, even when I pushed the bed over and stood on it.

"I don't know how long I was in that place. At first I thought the window let outdoors, but the light seemed the same strength all the time, so I suppose it really looked out into the main basement and what

I thought weak sunlight was really reflected from an electric bulb somewhere. At any rate, I determined to fight for my freedom the first chance I had, for I'd read stories of white slavers who kidnaped girls, and I was sure I'd fallen into the hands of some such gang. If I only had!

"How they timed it I don't know, but they never opened that door except when I was sleeping. I'd lie awake for hours, pretending to be asleep, so that someone would open the door and give me a chance to die fighting; but nothing ever happened. Then the moment I grew so tired I really fell asleep the door would be opened, my soiled dishes taken out and a fresh supply of food brought in. They didn't starve me, I'll say that. There was always some sort of meat—veal or young pork, I thought—and bread and vegetables and a big vacuum bottle of coffee and another of chilled milk. If I hadn't been so terribly frightened I might have enjoyed it, for I'd been hungry for a long time.

"One night I woke up with a start. At least, I suppose it was night, though there was really no way of telling. There were voices outside my door, the first I'd heard since I came there. 'Please, please let me go,' a girl was pleading sobbingly. 'I've never done anything to you, and I'll do anything—*anything* you ask if you'll only let me go!'

"Whoever it was she spoke to answered in a soft, gentle, purring sort of voice, 'Do not be afraid, we seek only to have a little sport with you; then you are free.'

"It was a man's voice, I could tell that, and I could hear the girl sobbing and pleading in terror till he took her upstairs and closed the basement door.

"I didn't know what to think. Till then I'd thought I was the only prisoner in the house, now I knew there was at least one more. 'What were they doing to her— what would they do to me when my turn came?' I kept asking myself. I'd read about the white-slave stockades of Chicago where young girls were 'broken in' by professional rapists, and when I heard the sound of several people running back and forth in the room right above me I went absolutely sick with terror. It seemed to me that several people were running about in tennis shoes or bare feet, and then there was a scream, then more running, and more screams. Then everything was still, so still that I could hear my heart beating as I lay there. I kept listening for them to bring her back; but they never did. At last I fell asleep."

De Grandin tweaked the waxed ends of his little blond mustache. "This Madame d'Afrique, what did she look like, *ma pauvre?*"

"She was a big woman—tall, that is, sir, with lots of blond hair and queer-looking brown-green eyes and odd, long nails that turned down over her finger-tips, like claws. She—"

"Name of an intoxicated pig, they are undoubtedly one and the same! Why did I not recognize it at once?" de Grandin exclaimed. "Say on, my child. Tell all; I wait with interest."

The girl swallowed convulsively and gave her other hand into his keeping. "Hold me, Doctor, hold me tight," she begged. "I'm afraid; terribly afraid, even now.

"I knew something dreadful was going to happen when he finally came for me, but I hadn't thought how terrible it would be. I was sound asleep when I felt someone shaking me by the shoulder and heard a voice say, 'Get up. We're going to let you go—if you can.'

"I tried to ask questions, to get him to wait till I put on some clothes, but he fairly dragged me, just as I was, from the bed. When I got upstairs I found myself in a big bare room brightly lighted by a ceiling chandelier, and with only a few articles of furniture in it—one or two big chairs, several small footstools, and a big couch set diagonally across one corner. It was night. I could see the rain beating on the window and hear the wind blowing. In the sudden unaccustomed light I saw a tall old man with scant white hair and a big white mustache held me by the shoulder. He wore a sort of short bathrobe of some dark-colored cloth and his feet were bare. Then I saw the woman, Mrs. d'Afrique. She was in a sort of short nightgown that reached only to her knees, and like the man she, too, was barefooted. The man shoved me into the middle of the room, and all the time the woman stood there smiling and eyeing me hungrily.

" 'My wife and I sometimes play a little game with our guests,' the old man told me. 'We turn out the lights and enjoy a little romp of rag. If the guest can get away in the darkness she is free to go; if she can not—' He stopped and smiled at me—the cruelest smile I've ever seen.

" 'Wh—what happens if she can not?' I faltered.

"He put his hand out and stroked my bare arm. 'Very nice,' he murmured, 'nice and tender, eh?' The woman nodded and licked her red lips with the tip of her red tongue, while her queer green eyes seemed positively shining as she looked at me.

" 'If the guest can not get away,' the man answered with a dreadful low laugh, then he looked at the woman again. 'You have eaten well since you came here,' he went on, apparently forgetting what he'd started to say. 'How did you like the meat we served?'

"I nodded. I didn't know what to say. Then: 'Why, it was very nice,' I whispered, fearing to anger him if I kept silent.

" 'Ye-es, very nice,' he agreed with another laugh. 'Very nice, indeed. That meat, dear, tender young lady—that meat was the guests who couldn't get away!'"

"I closed my eyes and thought hard. This couldn't be true, I told myself. This was just some dreadful dream. They might be going to maul and beat me—even kill me, perhaps—to satisfy their sadistic lust, but to kill and *eat* me—no, such things just couldn't happen in New Jersey today!

"It was a lucky thing for me I'd closed my eyes, for while I stood there swaying with nauseated horror I heard a faint click. Instantly I opened my eyes to find the light had been shut off and I was standing alone in the center of the great room."

"How'd you know you were alone if the light had been shut off?" demanded Donovan. "You say the room was pitch-dark."

The girl never turned her head. Her terrified eyes remained steadily, pleadingly, on de Grandin's face as she whispered:

"By their eyes!"

"The woman stood at one end of the room, the man had moved to the other, though I'd heard no sound, and in the darkness I could see their eyes, like the phosphorescent orbs of wild jungle-beasts at night.

"The steady, green-gleaming eyes came slowly nearer and nearer, sometimes moving in a straight line, sometimes circling in the darkness, but never turning from me for an instant. I was being stalked like a mouse by hungry cats—the creatures could see in the dark!

"I said a moment ago it was fortunate for me I'd closed my eyes. That's all that saved me. If they'd been open when the lights went out I'd have been completely blinded by the sudden darkness, but as it was, when I opened them the room was just a little lighter than the absolute darkness of closed eyes. The result was I could see their bodies like moving blotches of shadow slightly heavier than that of the rest of the room, and could even make out the shapes of some of the furniture. I could distinguish the dull-gray of the rain-washed window, too.

"As I turned in terror from one creeping shadow-thing to the other the woman let out a low, dreadful cry like the gradually-growing miaul of a hunting cat, only deeper and louder. The man answered it, and it seemed there was an undertone of terrible, half-human laughter in the horrible catawaul.

"It seemed to me that all the forces of hell were let loose in that great dark room. I heard myself screaming, praying, shrieking curses and obscenities I'd never realized I even knew, and answering me came the wild, inhuman screeches of the green-eyed things that haunted me.

"Scarcely knowing what I did I snatched up a heavy footstool and hurled it at the nearer pair of eyes. They say a woman can't throw straight, but my shot took effect. I saw the blurred outline of a body double up with an agonized howl and go crashing to the floor, where it flopped and contorted like a fish jerked from the water.

"With a shrill, ear-splitting scream the other form dashed at me, and I dropped to my knees just in time to avoid a thrashing blow it aimed at me—I felt my nightdress rip to tatters as the long sharp nails slashed through it.

"I rolled over and over across the floor with that she-devil leaping and springing after me. I snatched another hassock as I rolled, and flung it behind me. It tripped her, and for a moment she went to her knees, but her short dress offered no hindrance to her movement, and she was up and after me, howling and screaming like a beast, in another second.

"I'd managed to roll near the window, and as I came in contact with another stool I grasped it and hurled it with all my might at the panes. They shattered outward with a crash, and I dived through the opening. The ground was scarcely six feet below, and the rain had softened it so it broke my fall almost like a mattress. An instant after I'd landed on the rain-soaked lawn I was on my feet and running as no woman ever ran before."

"Yes, and then—?" de Grandin prompted.

The girl shook her slim, muslin-clad shoulders and shuddered in the ague of a nervous chill. "That's all there is to tell, sir," she stated simply. "The next thing I knew I was in this bed and Dr. Donovan was asking me about myself."

*   *   *

"That's letter-perfect," Donovan commented. "Exactly the way she told it twice before. What's your verdict, gentlemen?"

I shook my head pityingly. It was all too sadly evident the poor girl had been through some terrifying experience and that her nerves were badly shaken, but her story was so preposterous—clearly this was a case of delusional insanity. "I'm afraid," I began, and got no farther, for de Grandin's sharp comment forestalled me.

"The verdict, *mon cher* Donovan? What can it be but that she speaks the truth? But certainly, of course!"

"You mean—" I began, and once again he shut me off.

"By damnit, I mean that the beauteous Madame Bera and her so detestably ugly spouse have overreached themselves. There is no doubt that they and the d'Afriques are one and the same couple. Why should they not choose that name as *nom de ruse;* are they not from Tunis, and is Tunis not in Africa? But yes."

"Holy smoke!" gasped Donovan. "D'ye mean you actually *believe* this bunk?"

"*Mais certainement,*" de Grandin answered. "So firmly do I believe it I am willing to stand sponsor for this young lady immediately if you will release her on parole to accompany Friend Trowbridge and me."

"Well, I'm a monkey's uncle, I sure am," declared Dr. Donovan. "Maybe I should have another room swept out for you an' Trowbridge—" He sobered at the grim face de Grandin turned on him. "O.K. if that's the way you want it, de Grandin. It's your responsibility, you know. Want to go with these gentlemen, Annie?" He regarded the girl with a questioning smile.

"Yes! I'll go anywhere with him, he trusts me," she returned; then, as an afterthought, "And my name's not Annie."

"All right, Annie, get your clothes on," Donovan grinned back. "We'll be waitin' for you in the office."

As soon as we had reached the office de Grandin rushed to the telephone. "I would that you give this message to Sergeant Costello immediately he arrives," he called when his call to police headquarters had been put through. "Request that he obtain the address given by Monsieur and Madame d'Afrique when they went to secure domestic help from Osgood's Employment Agency, and that he ascertain, if possible, the names and addresses of all young women who entered their employ from the agency. Have him take steps to locate them at once, if he can.

"Très bon," he nodded as Trula Petersen made her appearance dressed in some makeshift odds and ends of clothing found for her by the nurses. "You are not *chic,* my little one, but in the morning we can get you other clothes, and meantime you will sleep more comfortably in an unbarred room. Yes, let us go."

A little after 4 o'clock next afternoon Costello called on us. "I got some o' th' dope you're wantin', Dr. de Grandin," he announced. "Th' de Africans hired four girls from Osgood's about a week part; but didn't seem to find any of 'em satisfactory. Kept comin' back for more."

"Ah? And these young women are now where, if you please?"

"None of 'em's been located as yet sir. It happens they was all strangers in town, at least, none of 'em had folks here, an' all was livin' in furnished rooms when they was hired. None of 'em's reported back to her roomin' house or applied to Osgood's for reëmployment. We'll look around a bit more, if you say so, but I doubt we'll find out much. They're mostly fly-by-nights, these girls, you know."

"I fear that what you say is literally true," de Grandin answered soberly. "They have flown by night, yes flown beyond all mortal calling, if my fears are as well grounded as I have reason to believe.

"And the address of Monsieur and Madame Ber— d'Afrique? Did you ascertain it from the agency?"

"Sure, we did. It's 762 Orient Boulevard."

"Good. I shall go there and—"

"Needn't be troublin' yourself, sir. I've been there already."

"*Ah bah;* I fear that you have spoiled it all. I did not wish them to suspect we knew. Now, I much fear—"

"You needn't; 762 Orient Boulevard's a vacant lot."

"Hell and ten thousand furies! Do you tell me so?"

"I sure do. But I got something solid for us to sink our teeth into. I think I've uncovered a lead on th' Cableson case."

"Indeed?"

"Well, it ain't much, but it's more'n we knew before. He wasn't alone when he died; least wise, he wasn't alone a few minutes before. I ran across a pair o' young fellers that saw him takin' a lady into his coupé on th' Albermarle Pike just a little way outside Mooreston late th' night before he was found dead with his car jammed up against a tree."

"*Chapeau d'un bouc vert,* is it so? Have you a description of the lady of mystery?"

"Kind of, yes, sir. She was big and blond, an' wrapped in some sort o' cloak, but didn't wear a hat. That's how they know she was a blonde, they saw her hair in th' light o' th' car's lamps."

The little Frenchman turned from the policeman to our guest. "My child," he told her, "the good God has been most kind to you. He has delivered those who harried you like a brute beast into the hands of Jules de Grandin."

"What are you going to do?" I asked, wondering.

"Do?" His waxed mustaches quivered like the whiskers of an irritable tom-cat. "Do? *Parbleu,* should one slap the face of Providence? *Mille nons.* Me, I shall serve them as they deserve, no less. May Satan fry me in a saucepan with a garnish of mushrooms if I do not so!"

A moment later he was thumbing through the telephone directory. "Ah, Madam Heacoat," he announced when the lady finally answered his call. "I am unhappy, I am miserable; I am altogether desolate. At your charming *soirée* I met the so delightful Monsieur and Madame Bera, and we discovered many friends in common. Of the goodness of their hearts they invited me to call, but *hélas* I have misplaced my memorandum of their address. Can you—ah, *merci bien; merci bien une mille fois*—a thousand thanks, Madame!

"My friends," he turned on us as he laid down the 'phone, "we have them in a snare. They are the clever ones, but Jules de Grandin is more clever. They dwell near Mooreston; their house abuts upon the Albermarle Pike. To find them will be a small task.

"Trowbridge, my old and rare, I pray you have the capable Nora McGinnis, that queen among cooks, prepare us a noble dinner this night. There is much to be done, and I would do it on a well-fed stomach. Meantime I shall call that Monsieur Arif and request his presence this evening. It was he who first roused my suspicions; he deserves to be here at the finish."

A little before dinner a special messenger from Ridgeway's Hardware Store arrived with a long parcel wrapped in corrugated paper which de Grandin seized and bore to his room. For half an hour or more he was engaged in some secret business there, emerging with a grin of satisfaction on his face as the gong sounded for the evening meal.

He took command at table, keeping up a running fire of conversation, most of it witty, all of it inconsequential. Stories of student days at the Sorbonne, droll tales of the War, anecdotes of travel in the far places of the world—anything but the slightest reference to the mystery of Monsieur and Madame Bera he rattled off like a wound-up gramophone.

Finally, when coffee was served in the drawing room, he lighted a cigar, stretched his slender patent-leather-shod feet to the blazing logs and regarded

Trula Petersen and me in turn with his quick, birdlike glance. "You trust me, *ma petite?*" he asked the girl.

"Oh, yes."

"*Très bon.* We shall put that trust to the test before long." He smiled whimsically, then:

"You have never hunted the tiger in India, one assumes?"

"Sir? No! I've never been anywhere except Norway where I was born, and this country, where I've lived since I was ten."

"Then it seems I must enlighten you. In India, when they would bring the stripèd one within gunshot, they tether a so small and helpless kid to a stake. The tiger scents a meal, approaches the small goat; the hunter, gun in hand, squeezes the trigger and—*voilà,* there is a tigerskin rug for some pretty lady's boudoir. It is all most simple."

"I—I don't think I understand, sir," the girl faltered, but there was a telltale widening of her eyes and a constriction of the muscles of her throat as she spoke.

"Very well. It seems I must explain in detail. Anon our good friend Arif Pasha comes, and with him comes the good Sergeant Costello. When all is ready you are to assume the same costume you wore when they brought you to the hospital, and over it you will put on warm wrappings. Thereafter Friend Trowbridge drives us to the house of Monsieur Bera, and you will descend, clad as you were when you fled. You will stagger across the lawn, calling pitifully for help. Unless I am much more mistaken than I think one or both of them will sally forth to see who cries for help in the night. Then—"

"O-o-o-oh, *no!*" the girl wailed in a stifled voice. "I couldn't! I wouldn't go there for all the money in the world—"

"It is no question of money, my small one. It is that you do it for the sake of humanity. Consider: Did you not tell me you woke one night to hear the odious Bera leading another girl to torture and death? Did not you thereafter hear the stamping of feet which fled and feet which pursued, and the agonized scream of one who was caught?"

The girl nodded dumbly.

"Suppose I tell you four girls were hired by these beast-people from the same agency whence you went into their service. That much we know; it is a matter of police record. It is also a matter of record that none of them, save you, was ever seen again. How many other unfortunate ones went the same sad road is a matter of conjecture, but unless you are willing to do this thing for me there is a chance that those we seek may escape. They may move to some other place and play their infernal games of hide-and-seek-in-the-dark with only the good God knows how many other poor ones.

"Attend me further, little pretty one: The night you escape by what was no less than a miracle a young man named Thomas Cableson—a youth of good family and position—young, attractive, in love; with everything to live for, drove his coupé through Mooreston along the Albemarle Pike. A short distance from Mooreston he was accosted by a woman—a big, blond woman *who sought for something in the roadside woods.*

"In the kindness of his heart he offered her a ride to Harrisonville. Next morning he was found dead in his motor. Apparently he had collided with a roadside tree, for his windshield was smashed to fragments, and through the broken glass his head protruded. But nowhere was there any blood. Neither on the car nor on his clothing was there any stain, yet he had bled to death. Also, I who am at once a physician and an observer of facts, examined his poor, severed throat. Such tears as marred his flesh might have been made by teeth, perhaps by claws; but by splintered glass, never. What happened in that young man's car we cannot know for certain, but we can surmise much. We can surmise, by example, that a thing that dotes on human flesh and blood had been thwarted of its prey and hunted for it in those roadside woods. We can surmise that when the young man, thinking her alone upon the highroad, offered her a ride, she saw an opportunity. Into his car she went, and when they were come to a lonely spot she set upon him. There was a sudden shrill, inhuman scream, the glare of beast-eyes in the dark, the stifling weight of a body hurled on unsuspecting shoulders, and the rending of shrinking flesh by bestial teeth and claws. The car is stopped, then started; it is run against a tree; a head, already almost severed from its body, is thrust through the broken windshield, and—the nameless horror which wears woman's shape returns to its den, its lips red from the feast, its gorge replenished."

"De Grandin!" I expostulated. "You're raving. Such things can't be!"

"Ha, can they not, *parbleu?*" he tweaked the ends of his diminutive mustache, gazing pensively at the fire a moment, then:

"Regard me, my friend. Listen, pay attention: Where, if you please, is Tunis?"

"In northwest Africa."

"*Précisément.* And Egypt is where, if you please?"

"In Africa, of course, but—"

"No buts, if you please. Both lie on the same dark continent, that darksome mother of dark mysteries whose veil no man has ever completely lifted. Now, regard me: in lower Egypt, near Zagazig, are the great ruins of Tell Besta. They mark the site of the ancient, wicked city of Bubastis, own sister of Sodom and Gomorrah of accursed memory. It was there, in the days of the third Rameses, thirteen hundred years before the birth of Christ, that men and women worshipped the cat-headed one, she who was called Ubasti, sometimes known as Bast. Yes. With phallic emblems and obscenities that would shock present-day Montmartre, they worshipped her. Today her temples lie in ruins, and only the hardest stones of her many monuments endure.

"But there are things much more enduring than granite and brass. The olden legends tell us of a race apart, a race descended from the loins of this cat-headed one of Bubastis, who shared her evil feline nature even though they wore the guise of women, or, less often, men.

"The fellaheen of Egypt are poor, wretchedly poor, and what the bare necessities of living do not snatch from them the tax-collector does; yet not for all the English gold that clinks and jingles at Shepard's Hotel in Cairo could one bribe a fella to venture into the ruins of Tell Besta after sunset. No, it is a fact; I myself have seen it.

"For why? Because, by blue, that cursèd spot is ghoul-haunted. Do not laugh; it is no laughing matter; it is so.

"The ancient gods are dust, and dust are all their worshippers, but their memories and their evil lives after them. The fellaheen will tell you of strange, terrible things which dwell amid the ruins of Bubastis; things formed like human creatures, but which are, as your own so magnificent Monsieur Poe has stated,

> " '. . . neither man nor woman,
> . . . neither brute nor human
> They are ghouls!'

"Yes, certainly. Like a man's or woman's, their faces are, so too are their bodies to some extent; but they see in the dark, like her from whom they are whelped, they wear long nails to seize their prey and have beast-teeth to tear it, and the flesh and blood of living men—or dead, if live be not available—they make their food and drink.

"Not only at Tell Besta are they found, for they are quick to multiply, and their numbers have spread. In the ruined tombs of all north Africa they make their lairs, awaiting the unwary traveler. Mostly they are nocturnal, but they have been known to spring on the lone voyager by day. The Arabs hate and fear them also, and speak of them by indirection. 'That people,' they call them, nor does one who has traveled in North Africa need ask a second time what the term connotes.

"Very well, then. When our friend Arif Pasha first showed fright, like a restive horse in the presence of hidden danger, at sight of those we know as Monsieur and Madame Bera, I was astonished. Such things might be in darker Africa, perhaps in Persia, or Asiatic Turkey, but in America—New Jersey—*non!*

"However, Jules de Grandin has the open mind. I made it a duty to meet this so strange couple, to observe their queer catlike eyes, to note the odd, clawlike nails of their hands, but most of all to watch their white, gleaming teeth and hear the soft, purring intonation of their words.

" 'These are queer folk, Jules de Grandin,' I say to me. 'They are not like others.'

"That very night we visited the City Hospital and listened to our little Trula tell her fearsome story. What she had to say of those who hired her and would have hunted her to death convinced me of much I should otherwise not have believed.

"Then came Sergeant Costello's report of the four girls hired by this Madame d'Afrique, whom we now know to be also Madame Bera—girls who went but did not return. Then comes the information of the strange woman who rode with the young Cableson the night he met his death.

" 'Jules de Grandin,' I tell me, 'your dear America, the place in which you have decided to remain, is invaded. The very neighborhood of good Friend Trowbridge's house, where you are to reside until you find yourself a house of your own, is peopled by strange night-seeing things.'

" 'It is, *hélas,* as you have said, Jules de Grandin,' I reply.

" 'Very well, then, Jules de Grandin,' I ask me, 'what are we to do about it?'

" '*Mordieu,*' I answer me, 'we shall exterminate the invaders. Of course.'

" '*Bravo,* it are agreed.'

"Now, all is prepared. Mademoiselle Trula, my little

pretty one, my small half orange, I need your help. Will you not do this thing for me?"

"I—I'm terribly afraid," the girl stammered, "but I—I'll do it, sir."

"Bravely spoken, my pigeon. Have no fear. Your guardian angel is with you. Jules de Grandin will also be there.

"Come. Let us make ready, the doorbell sounds."

Arif Pasha and Costello waited on the porch, and de Grandin gave a hand to each. "I haven't any more idea what th' pitch is than what th' King o' Siam had for breakfast this mornin'," Costello confessed with a grin when introductions had been made, "but I'm bankin' on you to pay off, Dr. de Grandin."

"I hope your confidence is not misplaced, my friend," the Frenchman answered. "I hope to show you that which killed the poor young Cableson before we're many hours older."

"What's that?" asked the detective. "Did you say 'that,' sir. Wasn't it a person, then? Sure, after all our bother, you're not goin' to tell me it was an accident after all?"

De Grandin shrugged. "Let us not quibble over pronouns, my old one. Wait till you have seen, then say if it be man or woman, beast or fiend from hell."

Led by de Grandin as ceremoniously as though he were escorting her to the dance floor, Trula Peterson ascended the stairs to don the ragged bedgown she wore the night she fled for life through the shattered window. She returned in a few moments, her pale childish face suffused with blushes as she sought to cover the inadequate attire by wrapping de Grandin's fur-lined overcoat more tightly about her slim form. Above the fleece-lined bedroom slippers on her feet I caught a glimpse of slender bare ankle, and mentally revolted against the Frenchman's penchant for realism which would send her virtually unclothed into the cold autumn night.

But there was no time to voice my protest, for de

Grandin followed close behind her with the corrugated cardboard carton he had received from Ridgeway's in his arms. "Behold, my friends," he ordered jubilantly displaying its contents—four magazine shotguns—"are these not lovely? *Pardieu,* with them we are equipped for any contingency!"

The guns were twelve-gauge models of the unsportsmanlike "pump" variety, and the barrels had been cut off with a hack-saw close to the wood, shortening them by almost half their length.

"What's th' armament for, sir?" inquired Costello, examining the weapon de Grandin handed him. "Is a riot we're goin' out to quell?"

The little Frenchman's only answer was a grin as he handed guns to Arif Pasha and me, retaining the fourth one for himself. "You will drive, Friend Trowbridge?" he asked.

Obediently, I slipped into a leather windbreaker and led the way to the garage. A minute later we were on the road to Mooreston.

He had evidently made a reconnaissance that afternoon, for he directed me unerringly to a large graystone structure on the outskirts of the suburb. On the north was the dense patch of second-growth pine through which the autumn wind soughed mournfully. To east and west lay fallow fields, evidently reservations awaiting the surveyor's stake and the enthusiastic cultivation of glib-tongued real estate salesmen. The house itself faced south on the Pike, on the farther side of which lay the grove of oak and chestnut into which Trula had escaped.

"Quiet, my friends, *pour l'amour d'un rat mort!*" de Grandin begged. "Stop the motor, Friend Trowbridge. *Attendez, mes braves. Allons au feu!*

"Now, my little lovely one!" With such courtesy as he might have shown in assisting a marchioness to shed her cloak, he lifted the overcoat from Trula Petersen's shivering shoulders, bent quickly and plucked the wool-lined slippers from her feet, then lifted her in his arms and bore her across the roadway intervening between us and the lawn, that gravel might not bruise her unshod soles. "Quick, toward the houses, *petite!*" he ordered. "Stagger, play the drunken one—cry out!"

The girl clung trembling to him a moment, but he shook her off and thrust her almost roughly toward the house.

There was no simulation in the terror she showed as she ran unsteadily across the front-burnt lawn, nor was the deadly fear that sounded in her wailing, thin-edged cry a matter of acting. "Help, help—please help me!" she screamed.

"Excellent; très excellent," applauded from his covert behind a rhododendron bush. "Make ready, *mes amis,* I damn think they come!"

A momentary flash of light showed on the dark background of the house as he spoke, and something a bare shade darker than the surrounding darkness detached itself from the building and sped with pitiless quickness toward the tottering, half-swooning girl.

Trula saw it even as we did, and wheeled in her tracks with a shriek of sheer mortal terror. "Save me, save me, it's he!" she cried wildly.

Half a dozen frenzied, flying steps she took, crashed blindly into a stunted cedar, and fell sprawling on the frosty grass.

A wild, triumphant yell, a noise half human, half bestial, came from her pursuer. With a single long leap it was on its quarry.

"Mordieu, Monsieur le Démon, we are well met!" de Grandin announced, rising from his ambush and leveling his sawed-off shotgun.

The leaping form seemed to pause in midair, to retrieve itself in the midst of its spring like a surprised cat. For an instant it turned its eyes on de Grandin, and they gleamed against the darkness like twin spheres of phosphorus. Next instant it pounced.

There was a sharp *click,* but no answering bellow of the gun. The cartridge had missed fire.

"Secours, Friend Trowbridge; *je suis perdu!"* the little Frenchman cried as he went down beneath an ava-

lanche of flailing arms and legs. And as he fought off his assailant I saw the flare of gleaming green eyes, the flash of cruel strong teeth, and heard the snarling beastlike growl of the thing tearing at his throat.

Nearer than the other two, I leaped to my friend's rescue, but as I moved a second shadowy form seemed to materialize from nothingness beside me, a battle-cry of feline rage shrilled deafeningly in my ears, and a clawing, screaming fury launched itself upon me.

I felt the tough oiled leather of my windbreaker rip to shreds beneath the scoring talons that struck at me, looked for an instant into round, infuriated phosphorescent eyes, then went down helpless under furious assault.

"There is no power nor might nor majesty save in Allah, the Merciful, the Compassionate!" Arif Pasha chanted close beside me. "In the glorious name of Allah I take refuge from Shaitan, the stoned and rejected!" A charge of BB shot sufficient to have felled a bear tore through the clawing thing above me, there was a sharp snapping of metal, and a second blaze of searing light as the riot gun roared again.

The ear-piercing scream of my assailant diminished to a growl, and the growl sank to a low, piteous moan as the form above me went limp, rolled from my chest and lay twitching on the frosted earth.

I fought unsteadily to my knees and went faint at the warm stickiness that smeared the front of my jerkin. No need to tell a doctor the feel of blood; he learns it soon enough in his grim trade.

Costello was battering with his gunstock at the infernal thing that clung to de Grandin, not daring to fire for fear of hitting the struggling Frenchman.

"Thanks, friend," the little fellow panted, wriggling from beneath his adversary and jumping nimbly to his feet. "Your help was very welcome, even though I had already slit his gizzard with this—" He raised the murderous double-edged hunting knife with which he had been systematically shashing his opponent from the moment they grappled.

"Good Lord o' Moses!" Costello gasped as de Grandin's flashlight played on the two forms quivering on the grass. " 'Tis Mr. an' Mrs. Bear! Who's 'a' thought swell folks like them would—"

"Folks? *Parbleu,* my friend, I damnation think you call them out of their proper name!" de Grandin interrupted sharply. "Look at this, if you please, and this, also!"

Savagely he tore the black-silk negligée in which the woman had been clothed, displaying her naked torso to his light. From clavicle to pubis the body was covered with coarse yellowish hair, and where the breasts should have been was scarcely a perceptible swelling. Instead, protruding through the woolly covering was a double row of mammillae, unhuman as the dugs of a multiparous beast.

"For the suckling of her whelps, had she borne any, which the good God forbid," he explained in a low voice. He turned the shot-riddled body over. Like the front, the back was encased in yellowish short hair, beginning just below the line of the scapulae and extending well down the thighs.

A quick examination of the male showed similar pelage, but in its case the hair was coarser, and an ugly dirty gray shade. Beneath the wool on its front side we found twin rows of rudimentary teats, the secondary sexual characteristics of a member of the multiparae.

"You see?" he asked simply.

"No, I'm damned if I do," I denied as the other held silence. "These are dreadful malformations, and their brains were probably as far from normal as their bodies, but—"

"Ah bah," he interrupted. "Here is no abnormality, my friend. These creatures are true to type. Have I not already rehearsed their history? From the tumuli of Africa they come, for there they were pursued with gun and dog like the beast-things they are. In this new land where their kind is unknown they did assume the garb and manners of man. With razor or depilatories

they stripped off the hair from their arms and legs, and other places where it would have been noticeable. Then they lived the life of the community—outwardly. Treasure from ravished tombs gave them much money; they had been educated like human beings in the schools conducted by well-meaning but thick-headed American missionaries, and all was prepared for their invasion. America is tolerant—too tolerant—of foreigners. More than due allowance is made for their strangeness by those who seek to make them feel at home, and unsuspected, unmolested, these vile ones plied their trade of death among us. Had the she-thing not capitulated to her appetite for blood when she slew young Cableson, they might have gone for years without the danger of suspicion. As it was"—he raised his shoulders in a shrug—"their inborn savageness and Jules de Grandin wrought their undoing. Yes, certainly; of course.

"Come, our work is finished. Let us go."

DEATH BY ECSTASY

Larry Niven

LARRY NIVEN has received the Hugo award four times for his short fiction, and a Hugo and Nebula award for his novel *Ringworld*. From his first story, "The Coldest Place," published in *If* in 1964, he has carved a wide niche for himself in the field of hard science fiction. Primarily working in his own universe called the Known Space, his fictional future involves mankind's first contact with aliens who are actually fully evolved humans, and the complications and triumphs that arise from this.

First came the routine request for a Breach of Privacy permit. A police officer took down the details and forwarded the request to a clerk, who saw that the tape reached the appropriate civic judge. The judge was reluctant, for privacy is a precious thing in a world of eighteen billion; but in the end he could find no reason to refuse. On November 2, 2123, he granted the permit.

The tenant's rent was two weeks in arrears. If the manager of Monica Apartments had asked for eviction he would have been refused. But Owen Jennison did not answer his doorbell or his room phone. Nobody could recall seeing him in many weeks. Apparently the manager only wanted to know that he was all right.

And so he was allowed to use his passkey, with an officer standing by.

And so they found the tenant of 1809.

And when they had looked in his wallet, they called me.

I was at my desk at ARM Headquarters, making useless notes and wishing it were lunchtime.

At this stage the Loren case was all correlate-and-wait. It involved an organlegging gang, apparently run by a single man, yet big enough to cover half the North American west coast. We had considerable data on the gang—methods of operation, centers of activity, a few former customers, even a tentative handful of names—but nothing that would give us an excuse to act. So it was a matter of shoving what we had into the computer, watching the few suspected associates of the ganglord Loren, and waiting for a break.

The months of waiting were ruining my sense of involvement.

My phone buzzed.

I put the pen down and said, "Gil Hamilton."

A small dark face regarded me with soft black eyes. "I am Detective-Inspector Julio Ordaz of the Los Angeles Police Department. Are you related to an Owen Jennison?"

"Owen? No, we're not related. Is he in trouble?"

"You do know him, then."

"Sure I know him. Is he here, on Earth?"

"It would seem so." Ordaz had no accent, but the lack of colloquialisms in his speech made him sound vaguely foreign. "We will need positive identification, Mr. Hamilton. Mr. Jennison's ident lists you as next of kin."

"That's funny. I—back up a minute. Is Owen dead?"

"Somebody is dead, Mr. Hamilton. He carried Mr. Jennison's ident in his wallet."

"Okay. Now, Owen Jennison was a citizen of the

Belt. This may have interworld complications. That makes it ARM's business. Where's the body?"

"We found him in an apartment rented under his own name. Monica Apartments, Lower Los Angeles, room 1809."

"Good. Don't move anything you haven't moved already. I'll be right over."

Monica Apartments was a nearly featureless concrete block, eighty stories tall, a thousand feet across the edges of its square base. Lines of small balconies gave the sides a sculptured look, above a forty-foot inset ledge that would keep tenants from dropping objects on pedestrians. A hundred buildings just like it made Lower Los Angeles look lumpy from the air.

Inside, a lobby done in anonymous modern. Lots of metal and plastic showing; lightweight, comfortable chairs without arms; big ashtrays; plenty of indirect lighting; a low ceiling; no wasted space. The whole room might have been stamped out with a die. It wasn't supposed to look small, but it did, and that warned you what the rooms would be like. You'd pay your rent by the cubic centimeter.

I found the manager's office, and the manager, a soft-looking man with watery blue eyes. His conservative paper suit, dark red, seemed chosen to render him invisible, as did the style of his brown hair, worn long and combed straight back without a part. "Nothing like this has ever happened here," he confided as he led me to the elevator banks. "Nothing. It would have been bad enough without his being a Belter, but *now*—" He cringed at the thought. "Newsmen. They'll *smother* us."

The elevator was coffin-sized, but with the handrails on the inside. It went up fast and smooth. I stepped out into a long, narrow hallway.

What would Owen have been doing in a place like this? Machinery lived here, not people.

Maybe it wasn't Owen. Ordaz had been reluctant to commit himself. Besides, there's no law against picking pockets. You couldn't enforce such a law on this crowded planet. Everyone on Earth was a pickpocket.

Sure. Someone had died carrying Owen's wallet.

I walked down the hallway to 1809.

It was Owen who sat grinning in the armchair. I took one good look at him, enough to be sure, and then I looked away and didn't look back. But the rest of it was even more unbelievable.

No Belter could have taken that apartment. I was born in Kansas; but even I felt the awful anonymous chill. It would have driven Owen bats.

"I don't believe it," I said.

"Did you know him well, Mr. Hamilton?"

"About as well as two men can know each other. He and I spent three years mining rocks in the main asteroid belt. You don't keep secrets under those conditions."

"Yet you didn't know he was on Earth."

"That's what I can't understand. Why the blazes didn't he phone me if he was in trouble?"

"You're an ARM," said Ordaz. "An operative in the United Nations Police."

He had a point. Owen was as honorable as any man I knew; but honor isn't the same in the Belt. Belters think flatlanders are all crooks. They don't understand that to a flatlander, picking pockets is a game of skill. Yet a Belter sees smuggling as the same kind of game, with no dishonesty involved. He balances the thirty percent tariff against possible confiscation of his cargo, and if the odds are right he gambles.

Owen could have been doing something that would look honest to him but not to me.

"He could have been in something sticky," I admitted. "But I can't see him killing himself over it. And . . . not here. He wouldn't have come here."

1809 was a living room and a bathroom and a closet. I'd glanced into the bathroom, knowing what I would find. It was the size of a comfortable shower stall. An adjustment panel outside the door would cause it to extrude various appurtenances in memory plastic, to become a washroom, a shower stall, a toilet, a dressing room, a steam cabinet. Luxurious in everything but size, as long as you pushed the right buttons.

The living room was more of the same. A King bed was invisible behind a wall. The kitchen alcove, with basin and oven and grill and toaster, would fold into another wall; the sofa, chairs, and tables would vanish into the floor. One tenant and three guests would make a crowded cocktail party, a cozy dinner gathering, a closed poker game. Card table, dinner table, coffee table were all there, surrounded by the appropriate chairs; but only one set at a time would emerge from the floor. There was no refrigerator, no freezer, no bar. If a tenant needed food or drink he phoned down, and the supermarket on the third floor would send it up.

The tenant of such an apartment had his comfort. But he owned nothing. There was room for him; there was none for his possessions. This was one of the inner apartments. An age ago there would have been an air shaft; but air shafts took up expensive room. The tenant didn't even have a window. He lived in a comfortable box.

Jut now the items extruded were the overstuffed reading armchair, two small side tables, a footstool, and the kitchen alcove. Owen Jennison sat grinning in the armchair. Naturally he grinned. Little more than dried skin covered the natural grin of his skull.

"It's a small room," said Ordaz, "but not too small. Millions of people live this way. In any case a Belter would hardly be a claustrophobe."

"No. Owen flew a singleship before he joined us. Three months at a stretch, in a cabin so small you couldn't stand up with the airlock closed. Not claustrophobia, but—" I swept my arm about the room. "What do you see that's his?"

Small as it was, the closet was nearly empty. A set of street clothes, a paper shirt, a pair of shoes, a small brown overnight case. All new. The few items in the bathroom medicine chest had been equally new and equally anonymous.

Ordaz said, "Well?"

"Belters are transients. They don't own much, but what they do own, they guard. Small possessions, relics, souvenirs. I can't believe he wouldn't have had *something*."

Ordaz lifted an eyebrow. "His space suit?"

"You think that's unlikely? It's not. The inside of his pressure suit is a Belter's home. Sometimes it's the only home he's got. He spends a fortune decorating it. If he loses his suit, he's not a Belter anymore.

"No, I don't insist he'd have brought his suit. But he'd have had *something*. His phial of Marsdust. The bit of nickel-iron they took out of his chest. Or, if he left all his souvenirs home, he'd have picked up things on Earth. But in this room—there's *nothing*."

"Perhaps," Ordaz suggested delicately, "he didn't notice his surroundings."

And somehow that brought it all home.

Owen Jennison sat grinning in a water-stained silk dressing gown. His space-darkened face lightened abruptly beneath his chin, giving way to normal suntan. His blond hair, too long, had been cut Earth style; no trace remained of the Belter strip cut he'd worn all his life. A month's growth of untended beard covered half his face. A small black cylinder protruded from the top of his head. An electric cord trailed from the top of the cylinder and ran to a wall socket.

The cylinder was a droud, a current addict's transformer.

I stepped closer to the corpse and bent to look. The droud was a standard make, but it had been altered. Your standard current addict's droud will pass only a trickle of current into the brain. Owen must have been getting ten times the usual charge, easily enough to damage his brain in a month's time.

I reached out and touched the droud with my imaginary hand.

Ordaz was standing quietly beside me, letting me make my examination without interruption. Naturally he had no way of knowing about my restricted psi powers.

With my imaginary fingertips I touched the droud in Owen's head, then ran them down to a tiny hole in his scalp, and further.

It was a standard surgical job. Owen could have had it done anywhere. A hole in his scalp, invisible under the hair, nearly impossible to find even if you knew what you were looking for. Even your best friends wouldn't know, unless they caught you with the droud plugged in. But the tiny hole marked a bigger plug set in the bone of the skull. I touched the ecstasy plug with my imaginary fingertips, then ran them down the hair-fine wire going deep into Owen's brain, down into the pleasure center.

No, the extra current hadn't killed him. What had killed Owen was his lack of will power. He had been unwilling to get up.

He had starved to death sitting in that chair. There were plastic squeezebottles all around his feet, and a couple still on the end tables. All empty. They must have been full a month ago. Owen hadn't died of thirst. He had died of starvation, and his death had been planned.

Owen my crewmate. Why hadn't he come to me? I'm half a Belter myself. Whatever his trouble, I'd have gotten him out somehow. A little smuggling— what of it? Why had he arranged to tell me only after it was over?

The apartment was so clean, so clean. You had to bend close to smell the death: the air conditioning whisked it all away.

He'd been very methodical. The kitchen was open so that a catheter could lead from Owen to the sink. He'd given himself enough water to last out the month; he'd paid his rent a month in advance. He'd cut the droud cord by hand, and he'd cut it short, deliberately tethering himself to a wall socket beyond reach of the kitchen.

A complex way to die, but rewarding in its way. A month of ecstasy, a month of the highest physical plea-sure man can attain. I could imagine him giggling every time he remembered he was starving to death. With food only a few footsteps away ... but he'd have to pull out the droud to reach it. Perhaps he post-poned the decision, and postponed it again ...

Owen and I and Homer Chandrasekhar, we had lived for three years in a cramped shell surrounded by vacuum. What was there to know about Owen Jen-nison that I hadn't known? Where was the weakness we didn't share? If Owen had done this, so could I. And I was afraid.

"Very neat," I whispered. "Belter neat."

"Typically Belter, would you say?"

"I would not. Belters don't commit suicide. Cer-tainly not this way. If a Belter had to go, he'd blow his ship's drive and die like a star. The neatness is typical. The result isn't."

"Well," said Ordaz. "Well." He was uncomfortable. The facts spoke for themselves, yet he was reluctant to call me a liar. He fell back on formality.

"Mr. Hamilton, do you identify this man as Owen Jennison?"

"It's him." He'd always been a touch overweight, yet I'd recognized him the moment I saw him. "But let's be sure." I pulled the dirty dressing gown back from Owen's shoulder. A near-perfect circle of scar tissue, eight inches across, spread over the left side of his chest. "See that?"

"We noticed it, yes. An old burn?"

"Owen's the only man I know who could show you a meteor scar on his skin. It blasted him in the shoul-der one day while he was outside the ship. Sprayed vaporized pressure-suit steel all over his skin. The doc pulled a tiny grain of nickel-iron from the center of the scar, just below the skin. Owen always carried that grain of nickel-iron. Always," I said, looking at Ordaz.

"We didn't find it."

"Okay."

"I'm sorry to put you through this, Mr. Hamilton. It was you who insisted we leave the body *in situ.*"

"Yes. Thank you."

Owen grinned at me from the reading chair. I felt the pain, in my throat and in the pit of my stomach. Once I had lost my right arm. Losing Owen felt the same way.

"I'd like to know more about this," I said. "Will you let me know the details as soon as you get them?"

"Of course. Through the ARM office?"

"Yes." This wasn't ARM business, despite what I'd told Ordaz; but ARM prestige would help. "I want to know why Owen died. Maybe he just cracked up ... culture shock or something. But if someone hounded him to death, I'll have his blood."

"Surely the administration of justice is better left to—" Ordaz stopped, confused. Did I speak as an ARM or as a citizen?

I left him wondering.

The lobby held a scattering of tenants, entering and leaving elevators or just sitting around. I stood outside the elevator for a moment, searching passing faces for the erosion of personality that must be there.

Mass-produced comfort. Room to sleep and eat and watch tridee, but no room to *be* anyone. Living here, one would own nothing. What kind of people would live like that? They should have looked all alike, moved in unison, like the string of images in a barber's mirrors.

Then I spotted wavy brown hair and a dark red paper suit. The manager? I had to get close before I was sure. His face was the face of a permanent stranger.

He saw me coming and smiled without enthusiasm. "Oh, hello, Mr. ... uh ... Did you find ..." He couldn't think of the right question.

"Yes," I said, answering it anyway. "But I'd like to

know some things. Owen Jennison lived here for six weeks, right?"

"Six weeks and two days, before we opened his room."

"Did he ever have visitors?"

The man's eyebrows went up. We'd drifted in the direction of his office, and I was close enough to read the name on the door: JASPER MILLER, *Manager*. "Of course not," he said. "Anyone would have noticed that something was wrong."

"You mean he took the room for the express purpose of dying? You saw him once, and never again?"

"I suppose he might ... no, wait." The manager thought deeply. "No. He registered on a Thursday. I noticed the Belter tan, of course. Then on Friday he went out. I happened to see him pass."

"Was that the day he got the droud? No, skip it, you wouldn't know that. Was it the last time you saw him go out?"

"Yes, it was."

"Then he could have had visitors late Thursday or early Friday."

The manager shook his head, very positively.

"Why not?"

"You see, Mr., uh ..."

"Hamilton."

"We have a holo camera on every floor, Mr. Hamilton. It takes a picture of each tenant the first time he goes to his room, and then never again. Privacy is one of the services a tenant buys with his room." The manager drew himself up a little as he said this. "For the same reason, the holo camera takes a picture of anyone who is *not* a tenant. The tenants are thus protected from unwarranted intrusions."

"And there were no visitors to any of the rooms on Owen's floor?"

"No, sir, there were not."

"Your tenants are a solitary bunch."

"Perhaps they are."

"I suppose a computer in the basement decides who is and is not a tenant."

"Of course."

"So for six weeks Owen Jennison sat alone in his room. In all that time he was totally ignored."

Miller tried to turn his voice cold, but he was too nervous. "We try to give our guests privacy. If Mr. Jennison had wanted help of any kind he had only to pick up the house phone. He could have called me, or the pharmacy, or the supermarket downstairs."

"Well, thank you, Mr. Miller. That's all I wanted to know. I wanted to know how Owen Jennison could wait six weeks to die while nobody noticed."

Miller swallowed. "He was dying all that time?"

"Yah."

"We had no way of knowing. How could we? I don't see how you can blame us."

"I don't either," I said, and brushed by. Miller had been close enough, so I had lashed out at him. Now I was ashamed. The man was perfectly right. Owen could have had help if he'd wanted it.

I stood outside, looking up at the jagged blue line of sky that showed between the tops of the buildings. A taxi floated into view, and I beeped my clicker at it, and it dropped.

I went back to ARM Headquarters. Not to work—I couldn't have done any work, not under the circumstances—but to talk to Julie.

Julie. A tall girl, pushing thirty, with green eyes and long hair streaked red and gold. And two wide brown forceps marks above her right knee; but they weren't showing now. I looked into her office, through the oneway glass, and watched her at work.

She sat in a contour couch, smoking. Her eyes were closed. Sometimes her brow would furrow as she concentrated. Sometimes she would snatch a glance at the clock, then close her eyes again.

I didn't interrupt her. I knew the importance of what she was doing.

Julie. She wasn't beautiful. Her eyes were a little too far apart, her chin too square, her mouth too wide. It didn't matter. Because Julie could read minds.

She was the ideal date. She was everything a man needed. A year ago, the day after the night I killed my first man, I had been in a terribly destructive mood. Somehow Julie had turned it into a mood of manic exhilaration. We'd run wild through a supervised anarchy park, running up an enormous bill. We'd hiked five miles without going anywhere, facing backward on a downtown slidewalk. At the end we'd been utterly fatigued, too tired to think ... But two weeks ago it had been a warm, cuddly, comfortable night. Two people happy with each other; no more than that. Julie was what you needed, anytime, anywhere.

Her male harem must have been the largest in history. To pick up on the thoughts of a male ARM, Julie had to be in love with him. Luckily there was room in her for a lot of love. She didn't demand that we be faithful. A good half of us were married. But there had to be love for each of Julie's men, or Julie couldn't protect him.

She was protecting us now. Each fifteen minutes, Julie was making contact with a specific ARM agent. Psi powers are notoriously undependable, but Julie was an exception. If we got in a hole, Julie was always there to get us out ... provided some idiot didn't interrupt her at work.

So I stood outside, waiting, with a cigarette in my imaginary hand.

The cigarette was for practice, to stretch the mental muscles. In its way my "hand" was as dependable as Julie's mind-touch, possibly because of its very limitations. Doubt your psi powers and they're gone. A rigidly defined third arm was more reasonable than some warlock ability to make objects move by wishing at them. I knew how an arm felt, and what it would do.

Why do I spend so much time lifting cigarettes? Well, it's the biggest weight I can lift without strain.

And there's another reason ... something taught me by Owen.

At ten minutes to fifteen Julie opened her eyes, rolled out of the contour couch, and came to the door. "Hi, Gil," she said sleepily. "Trouble?"

"Yah. A friend of mine just died. I thought you'd better know." I handed her a cup of coffee.

She nodded. We had a date tonight, and this would change its character. Knowing that, she probed lightly.

"Jesus!" she said, recoiling. "How ... how horrible. I'm terribly sorry, Gil. Date's off, right?"

"Unless you want to join the ceremonial drunk."

She shook her head vigorously. "I didn't know him. It wouldn't be proper. Besides, you'll be wallowing in your own memories, Gil. A lot of them will be private. I'd cramp your style if you knew I was there to probe. Now if Homer Chandrasekhar were here, it'd be different."

"I wish he were. He'll have to throw his own drunk. Maybe with some of Owen's girls, if they're around."

"You know what I feel," she said.

"Just what I do."

"I wish I could help."

"You always help." I glanced at the clock. "Your coffee break's about over."

"Slave driver." Julie took my earlobe between thumb and forefinger. "Do him proud," she said, and went back to her soundproof room.

She always helps. She doesn't even have to speak. Just knowing that Julie has read my thoughts, that someone understands ... that's enough.

All alone at three in the afternoon, I started my ceremonial drunk.

The ceremonial drunk is a young custom, not yet tied down by formality. There is no set duration. No specific toasts must be given. Those who participate must be close friends of the deceased, but there is no set number of participants.

I started at the Luau, a place of cool blue light and running water. Outside it was fifteen-thirty in the afternoon, but inside it was evening in the Hawaiian Islands of centuries ago. Already the place was half full. I picked a corner table with considerable elbow room and dialed for Luau grog. It came, cold, brown, and alcoholic, its straw tucked into a cone of ice.

There had been three of us at Cubes Forsythe's ceremonial drunk, one black Ceres night four years ago. A jolly group we were, too; Owen and me and the widow of our third crewman. Gwen Forsythe blamed us for her husband's death. I was just out of the hospital with a right arm that ended at the shoulder, and I blamed Cubes and Owen and myself, all at once. Even Owen had turned dour and introspective. We couldn't have picked a worse trio, or a worse night for it.

But custom called, and we were there. Then as now, I found myself probing my own personality for the wound that was a missing crewman, a missing friend. Introspecting.

Gilbert Hamilton. Born of flatlander parents, in April, 2093, in Topeka, Kansas. Born with two arms and no sign of wild talents.

Flatlander: a Belter term referring to Earthmen, and particularly to Earthmen who had never seen space. I'm not sure my parents ever looked at the stars. They managed the third largest farm in Kansas, ten square miles of arable land between two wide strips of city paralleling two strips of turnpike. We were city people, like all flatlanders, but when the crowds got to be too much for my brothers and me, we had vast stretches of land to be alone in. Ten square miles of playground, with nothing to hamper us but the crops and automachinery.

We looked at the stars, my brothers and I. You can't see stars from the city; the lights hide them. Even in the fields you couldn't see them around the lighted horizon. But straight overhead, they were there: black sky scattered with bright dots, and sometimes a flat white moon.

At twenty I gave up my UN citizenship to become a Belter. I wanted stars, and the Belt government

Larry Niven

holds title to most of the solar system. There are fabulous riches in the rocks, riches belonging to a scattered civilization of a few hundred thousand Belters; and I wanted my share of that, too.

It wasn't easy. I wouldn't be eligible for a singleship license for ten years. Meanwhile I would be working for others, and learning to avoid mistakes before they killed me. Half the flatlanders who join the Belt die in space before they can earn their licenses.

I mined tin on Mercury and exotic chemicals from Jupiter's atmosphere. I hauled ice from Saturn's rings and quicksilver from Europa. One year our pilot made a mistake pulling up to a new rock, and we damn near had to walk home. Cubes Forsythe was with us then. He managed to fix the com laser and aim it at Icarus to bring us help. Another time the mechanic who did the maintenance job on our ship forgot to replace an absorber, and we all got roaring drunk on the alcohol that built up in our breathing-air. The three of us caught the mechanic six months later. I hear he lived.

Most of the time I was part of a three-man crew. The members changed constantly. When Owen Jennison joined us he replaced a man who had finally earned his singleship license, and couldn't wait to start hunting rocks on his own. He was too eager. I learned later that he'd made one round trip and half of another.

Owen was my age, but more experienced, a Belter born and bred. His blue eyes and blond cockatoo's crest were startling against the dark of his Belter tan, the tan that ended so abruptly where his neck ring cut off the space-intense sunlight his helmet let through. He was permanently chubby, but in free fall it was as if he'd been born with wings. I took to copying his way of moving, much to Cubes' amusement.

I didn't make my own mistake until I was twenty-six.

We were using bombs to put a rock in a new orbit. A contract job. The technique is older than fusion drives, as old as early Belt colonization, and it's still cheaper and faster than using a ship's drive to tow the rock. You use industrial fusion bombs, small and clean, and you set them so that each explosion deepens the crater to channel the force of later blasts.

We'd set four blasts already, four white fireballs that swelled and faded as they rose. When the fifth blast went off we were hovering nearby on the other side of the rock.

The fifth blast shattered the rock.

Cubes had set the bomb. My own mistake was a shared one, because any of the three of us should have had the sense to take off right then. Instead, we watched, cursing, as valuable oxygen-bearing rock became near-valueless shards. We watched the shards spread slowly into a cloud . . . and while we watched, one fast-moving shard reached us. Moving too slowly to vaporize when it hit, it nonetheless sheared through a triple crystal-iron hull, slashed through my upper arm, and pinned Cubes Forsythe to a wall by his heart.

A couple of nudists came in. They stood blinking among the booths while their eyes adjusted to the blue twilight, then converged with glad cries on the group two tables over. I watched and listened with an eye and an ear, thinking how different flatlander nudists were from Belter nudists. These all looked alike. They all had muscles, they had no interesting scars, they carried their credit cards in identical shoulder pouches, and they all shaved the same areas.

. . . We always went nudist in the big bases. Most people did. It was a natural reaction to the pressure suits we wore day and night while out in the rocks. Get him into a shirtsleeve environment, and your normal Belter sneers at a shirt. But it's only for comfort. Give him a good reason and your Belter will don shirt and pants as quickly as the next guy.

But not Owen. After he got that meteor scar, I never saw him wear a shirt. Not just in the Ceres domes, but anywhere there was air to breathe. He just had to show that scar.

A cool blue mood settled on me, and I remembered ...

... Owen Jennison lounging on a corner of my hospital bed, telling me of the trip back. I couldn't remember anything after that rock had sheared through my arm.

I should have bled to death in seconds. Owen hadn't given me the chance. The wound was ragged; Owen had sliced it clean to the shoulder with one swipe of a com laser. Then he'd tied a length of fiberglass curtain over the flat surface and knotted it tight under my remaining armpit. He told me about putting me under two atmospheres of pure oxygen as a substitute for replacing the blood I'd lost. He told me how he'd reset the fusion drive for four gees to get me back in time. By rights we should have gone up in a cloud of starfire and glory.

"So there goes my reputation. The whole Belt knows how I rewired our drive. A lot of 'em figure if I'm stupid enough to risk my own life like that, I'd risk theirs too."

"So you're not safe to travel with."

"Just so. They're starting to call me four Gee Jennison."

"You think you've got problems? I can just see how it'll be when I get out of this bed. 'You do something stupid, Gil?' The hell of it is, it *was* stupid."

"So lie a little."

"Uh huh. Can we sell the ship?"

"Nope. Gwen inherited a third interest in it from Cubes. She won't sell."

"Then we're effectively broke."

"Except for the ship. We need another crewman."

"Correction. *You* need *two* crewmen. Unless you want to fly with a one-armed man. I can't afford a transplant."

Owen hadn't tried to offer me a loan. That would have been insulting, even if he'd had the money. "What's wrong with a prosthetic?"

"An iron arm? Sorry, no. I'm squeamish."

Owen had looked at me strangely, but all he'd said was, "Well, we'll wait a bit. Maybe you'll change your mind."

He hadn't pressured me. Not then, and not later, after I'd left the hospital and taken an apartment while I waited to get used to a missing arm. If he thought I would eventually settle for a prosthetic, he was mistaken.

Why? It's not a question I can answer. Others obviously feel differently; there are millions of people walking around with metal and plastic and silicone parts. Part man, part machine, and how do they themselves know which is the real person?

I'd rather be dead than part metal. Call it a quirk. Call it, even, the same quirk that makes my skin crawl when I find a place like Monica Apartments. A human being should be all human. He should have habits and possessions peculiarly his own, he should not try to look like or to behave like anyone but himself, and he should not be half robot.

So there I was, Gil the Arm, learning to eat with my left hand.

An amputee never entirely loses what he's lost. My missing fingers itched. I moved to keep from barking my missing elbow on sharp corners. I reached for things, then swore when they didn't come.

Owen had hung around, though his own emergency funds must have been running low. I hadn't offered to sell my third of the ship, and he hadn't asked.

There had been a girl. Now I'd forgotten her name. One night I was at her place waiting for her to get dressed—a dinner date—and I'd happened to see a nail file she'd left on a table. I'd picked it up. I'd almost tried to file my nails, but remembered in time. Irritated, I had tossed the file back on the table—and missed.

Like an idiot I'd tried to catch it with my right hand.

And I'd caught it.

I'd never suspected myself of having psychic powers. You have to be in the right frame of mind to use a psi power. But who had ever had a better opportunity than I did that night, with a whole section of brain tuned to the nerves and muscles of my right arm, and no right arm?

I'd held the nail file in my imaginary hand. I'd felt it, just as I'd felt my missing fingernails getting too long. I had run my thumb along the rough steel surface; I had turned the file in my fingers. Telekinesis for lift, esper for touch.

"That's it," Owen had said the next day. "That's all we need. One crewman, and you with your eldritch powers. You practice, see how strong you can get that lift. I'll go find a sucker."

"He'll have to settle for a sixth of net. Cubes' widow will want her share."

"Don't worry. I'll swing it."

"Don't worry!" I'd waved a pencil stub at him. Even in Ceres' gentle gravity, it was as much as I could lift—then. "You don't think TK and esper can make do for a real arm, do you?"

"It's better than a real arm. You'll see. You'll be able to reach through your suit with it without losing pressure. What Belter can do that?"

"Sure."

"What the hell do you want, Gil? Someone should give you your arm back? You can't have that. You lost it fair and square, through stupidity. Now it's your choice. Do you fly with an imaginary arm, or do you go back to Earth?"

"I can't go back. I don't have the fare."

"Well?"

"Okay, okay. Go find us a crewman. Someone I can impress with my imaginary arm."

I sucked meditatively on a second Luau grog. By now all the booths were full, and a second layer was forming around the bar. The voices made a continuous hypnotic roar. Cocktail hour had arrived.

... He'd swung it, all right. On the strength of my

imaginary arm, Owen had talked a kid named Homer Chandrasekhar into joining our crew.

He'd been right about my arm, too.

Others with similar senses can reach further, up to halfway around the world. My unfortunately literal imagination had restricted me to a psychic hand. But my esper fingertips were more sensitive, more dependable. I could lift more weight. Today, in Earth's gravity, I can lift a full shot glass.

I found I could reach through a cabin wall to feel for breaks in the circuits behind it. In vacuum I could brush dust from the outside of my faceplate. In port I did magic tricks.

I'd almost ceased to feel like a cripple. It was all due to Owen. In six months of mining I had paid off my hospital bills and earned my fare back to Earth, with a comfortable stake left over.

"Finagle's Black Humor!" Owen had exploded when I told him. "Of all places, why Earth?"

"Because if I can get my UN citizenship back, Earth will replace my arm. Free."

"Oh. That's true," he'd said dubiously.

The Belt had organ banks too, but they were always undersupplied. Belters didn't give things away. Neither did the Belt government. They kept the prices on transplants as high as they would go. Thus they dropped the demand to meet the supply, and kept taxes down to boot.

In the Belt I'd have to buy my own arm. And I didn't have the money. On Earth there was social security, and a vast supply of transplant material.

What Owen had said couldn't be done, I'd done. I'd found someone to hand me my arm back.

Sometimes I'd wondered if Owen held the choice against me. He'd never said anything, but Homer Chandrasekhar had spoken at length. A Belter would have earned his arm or done without. Never would he have accepted charity.

Was that why Owen hadn't tried to call me?

I shook my head. I didn't believe it.

The room continued to lurch after my head stopped shaking. I'd had enough for the moment. I finished my third grog and ordered dinner.

Dinner sobered me for the next lap. It was something of a shock to realize that I'd run through the entire lifespan of my friendship with Owen Jennison. I'd know him for three years, though it had seemed like half a lifetime. And it was. Half my six-year lifespan as a Belter.

I ordered coffee grog and watched the man pour it: hot, milky coffee laced with cinnamon and other spices, and high-proof rum poured in a stream of blue fire. This was one of the special drinks served by a human headwaiter, and it was the reason they kept him around. Phase two of the ceremonial drunk: blow half your fortune, in the grand manner.

But I called Ordaz before I touched the drink.

"Yes, Mr. Hamilton? I was just going home for dinner."

"I won't keep you long. Have you found out anything new?"

Ordaz took a closer look at my phone image. His disapproval was plain. "I see that you have been drinking. Perhaps you should go home now, and call me tomorrow."

I was shocked. "Don't you know *anything* about Belt customs?"

"I do not understand."

I explained the ceremonial drunk. "Look, Ordaz, if you know that little about the way a Belter thinks, then we'd better have a talk. Soon. Otherwise you're likely to miss something."

"You may be right. I can see you at noon, over lunch."

"Good. What have you got?"

"Considerable, but none of it is very helpful. Your friend landed on earth two months ago, arriving on the *Pillar of Fire,* operating out of Outback field, Australia. He was wearing a haircut in the style of Earth. From there—"

"That's funny. He'd have had to wait two months for his hair to grow out."

"That occurred even to me. I understand that a Belter commonly shaves his entire scalp, except for a strip two inches wide running from the nape of his neck forward."

"The strip cut, yah. It probably started when someone decided he'd live longer if his hair couldn't fall in his eyes during a tricky landing. But Owen could have let his hair grow out during a singleship mining trip. There'd be nobody to see."

"Still, it seems odd. Did you know that Mr. Jennison has a cousin on Earth? One Harvey Peele, who manages a chain of supermarkets."

"So I wasn't his next of kin, even on Earth."

"Mr. Jennison made no attempt to contact him."

"Anything else?"

"I've spoken to the man who sold Mr. Jennison his droud and plug. Kenneth Graham owns an office and operating room on Gayley in Near West Los Angeles. Graham claims that the droud was a standard type, that your friend must have altered it himself."

"Do you believe him?"

"For the present. His permits and his records are all in order. The droud was altered with a soldering iron, an amateur's tool."

"Uh huh."

"As far as the police are concerned, the case will probably be closed when we locate the tools Mr. Jennison used."

"Tell you what. I'll wire Homer Chandrasekhar tomorrow. Maybe he can find out things—why Owen landed without a strip haircut, why he came to Earth at all."

Ordaz shrugged with his eyebrows. He thanked me for my trouble and hung up.

The coffee grog was still hot. I gulped at it, savoring the sugary, bittery sting of it, trying to forget Owen

dead and remember him in life. He was always slightly
chubby, I remembered, but he never gained a pound
and he never lost a pound. He could move like a
whippet when he had to.

*And now he was terribly thin, and his death-grin was
ripe with obscene joy.*

I ordered another coffee grog. The waiter, a show-
man, made sure he had my attention before he lit the
heated rum, then poured it from a foot above the
glass. You can't drink that drink slowly. It slides down
too easily, and there's the added spur that if you wait
too long it might get cold. Rum and strong coffee.
Two of these and I'd be drunkenly alert for hours.

Midnight found me in the Mars Bar, running on
scotch and soda. In between I'd been barhopping.
Irish coffee at Bergin's, cold and smoking concoctions
at the Moon Pool, scotch and wild music at Beyond.
I couldn't get drunk, and I couldn't find the right
mood. There was a barrier to the picture I was trying
to rebuild.

It was the memory of the last Owen, grinning in an
armchair with a wire leading down into his brain.

I didn't know that Owen. I had never met the man,
and never would have wanted to. From bar to night-
club to restaurant I had run from the image, waiting
for the alcohol to break the barrier between present
and past.

So I sat at a corner table, surrounded by 3D panoramic views of an impossible Mars. Crystal towers
and long, straight blue canali, six-legged beasts and
beautiful, impossibly slender men and women, looked
out at me across never-never land. Would Owen have
found it sad or funny? He'd seen the real Mars, and
had not been impressed.

I had reached that stage where time becomes dis-
continuous, where gaps of seconds or minutes appear
between the events you can remember. Somewhere in
that period I found myself staring at a cigarette. I must
have just lighted it, because it was near its original

two-hundred-millimeter length. Maybe a waiter had snuck up behind me. There it was, at any rate, burning between my middle and index fingers.

I stared at the coal as the mood settled on me. I was calm, I was drifting, I was lost in time . . .

. . . We'd been two months in the rocks, our first trip out since the accident. Back we came to Ceres with a holdful of gold, fifty percent pure, guaranteed suitable for rustproof wiring and conductor plates. At nightfall we were ready to celebrate.

We walked along the city limits, with neon blinking and beckoning on the right, a melted rock cliff to the left, and stars blazing through the dome overhead. Homer Chandrasekhar was practically snorting. On this night his first trip out culminated in his first homecoming: and homecoming is the best part.

"We'll want to split up about midnight," he said. He didn't need to enlarge on that. Three men in company might conceivably be three singleship pilots, but chances are they're a ship's crew. They don't have their singleship licenses yet; they're too stupid or too inexperienced. If we wanted companions for the night—

"You haven't thought this through," Owen answered. I saw Homer's double take, then his quick look at where my shoulder ended, and I was ashamed. I didn't need my crewmates to hold my hand, and in this state I'd only slow them down.

Before I could open my mouth to protest, Owen went on. "Think it through. We've got a draw here that we'd be idiots to throw away. Gil, pick up a cigarette. No, not with your left hand—"

I was drunk, gloriously drunk and feeling immortal. The attenuated Martians seemed to move in the walls, the walls that seemed to be picture windows on a Mars that never was. For the first time that night, I raised my glass in toast.

"To Owen, from Gil the Arm. Thanks."

I transferred the cigarette to my imaginary hand.

By now you've got the idea I was holding it in my imaginary fingers. Most people have the same impression, but it isn't so. I held it clutched ignominiously in my fist. The coal couldn't burn me, of course, but it still felt like a lead ingot.

I rested my imaginary elbow on the table, and that seemed to make it easier—which is ridiculous, but it works. Truly, I'd expected my imaginary arm to disappear after I got the transplant. But I'd found I could dissociate from the new arm to hold small objects in my invisible hand, to feel tactile sensations in my invisible fingertips.

I'd earned the title Gil the Arm, that night in Ceres. It had started with a floating cigarette. Owen had been right. Everyone in the place eventually wound up staring at the floating cigarette smoked by the one-armed man. All I had to do was find the prettiest girl in the room with my peripheral vision, then catch her eye.

That night we had been the center of the biggest impromptu party ever thrown in Ceres Base. It wasn't planned that way at all. I'd used the cigarette trick three times, so that each of us would have a date. But the third girl already had an escort, and he was celebrating something; he'd sold some kind of patent to an Earth-based industrial firm. He was throwing money around like confetti. So we let him stay. I did tricks, reaching esper fingers into a closed box to tell what was inside, and by the time I finished all the tables had been pushed together and I was in the center, with Homer and Owen and three girls. Then we got to singing old songs, and the bartenders joined us, and suddenly everything was on the house.

Eventually about twenty of us wound up in the orbiting mansion of the first Speaker for the Belt Government. The goldskin cops had tried to bust us up earlier, and the First Speaker had behaved very rudely indeed, then compensated by inviting them to join us . . .

And that was why I used TK on so many cigarettes.

Across the width of the Mars Bar, a girl in a peach-colored dress sat studying me with her chin on her fist. I got up and went over.

My head felt fine. It was the first thing I checked when I woke up. Apparently I'd remembered to take a hangover pill.

A leg was hooked over my knee. It felt good, though the pressure had put my foot to sleep. Fragrant dark hair spilled beneath my nose. I didn't move. I didn't want her to know I was awake.

It's damned embarrassing when you wake up with a girl and can't remember her name.

Well, let's see. A peach dress neatly hung from a doorknob ... I remembered a whole lot of traveling last night. The girl at the Mars Bar. A puppet show. Music of all kinds. I'd talked about Owen, and she'd steered me away from that because it depressed her. Then—

Hah! Taffy. Last name forgotten.

"Morning," I said.

"Morning," she said. "Don't try to move, we're hooked together ..." In the sober morning light she was lovely. Long black hair, brown eyes, creamy un-tanned skin. To be lovely this early was a neat trick, and I told her so, and she smiled.

My lower leg was dead meat until it started to buzz with renewed circulation, and then I made faces until it calmed down. Taffy kept up a running chatter as we dressed. "That third hand is strange. I remember you holding me with two strong arms and stroking the back of my neck with the third. *Very* nice. It reminded me of a Fritz Leiber story."

"*The Wanderer*. The panther girl."

"Mm hmm. How many girls have you caught with that cigarette trick?"

"None as pretty as you."

"And how many girls have you told that to?"

"Can't remember. It always worked before. Maybe this time it's for real."

We exchanged grins.

A minute later I caught her frowning thoughtfully at the back of my neck. "Something wrong?"

"I was just thinking. You really crashed and burned last night. I hope you don't drink that much all the time."

"Why? You worried about me?"

She blushed, then nodded.

"I should have told you. In fact, I think I did, last night. I was on a ceremonial drunk. When a good friend dies it's obligatory to get smashed."

Taffy looked relieved. "I didn't mean to get—"

"Personal? Why not. You've the right. Anyway, I like—" *maternal types,* but I couldn't say that. "People who worry about me."

Taffy touched her hair with some kind of complex comb. A few strokes snapped her hair instantly into place. Static electricity?

"It was a good drunk," I said. "Owen would have been proud. And that's all the mourning I'll do. One drunk and—" I spread my hands. "Out."

"It's not a bad way to go," Taffy mused reflectively. "Current stimulus, I mean. I mean, if you've got to bow out—"

"Now drop that!" I don't know how I got so angry so fast. Ghoul-thin and grinning in a reading chair, Owen's corpse was suddenly vivid before me. I'd fought that image for too many hours. "Walking off a bridge is enough of a cop-out," I snarled. "Dying for a month while current burns out your brain is nothing less than sickening."

Taffy was hurt and bewildered. "But your friend did it, didn't he? You didn't make him sound like a weakling."

"Nuts," I heard myself say. "He didn't do it. He was—"

Just like that, I was sure. I must have realized it while I was drunk or sleeping. Of *course* he hadn't killed himself. *That* wasn't Owen. And current addiction wasn't Owen either.

"He was murdered," I said. "Sure he was. Why didn't I see it?" And I made a dive for the phone.

"Good morning, Mr. Hamilton." Detective-Inspector Ordaz looked very fresh and neat this morning. I was suddenly aware that I hadn't shaved. "I see you remembered to take your hangover pills."

"Right. Ordaz, has it occurred to you that Owen might have been murdered?"

"Naturally. But it isn't possible."

"I think it might be. Suppose he—"

"Mr. Hamilton."

"Yah?"

"We have an appointment for lunch. Shall we discuss it then? Meet me at Headquarters at twelve hundred."

"Okay. One thing you might take care of this morning. See if Owen registered for a nudist's license."

"Do you think he might have?"

"Yah. I'll tell you why at lunch."

"Very well."

"Don't hang up. You said you'd found the man who sold Owen his droud-and-plug. What was his name again?"

"Kenneth Graham."

"That's what I thought." I hung up.

Taffy touched my shoulder. "Do—do you really think he might have been—killed?"

"Yah. The whole setup depended on him not being able to—"

"No. Wait. I don't want to know about it."

I turned to look at her. She really didn't. The very subject of a stranger's death was making her sick to her stomach.

"Okay. Look, I'm a jerk not to at least offer you breakfast, but I've got to get on this right away. Can I call you a cab?"

When the cab came I dropped a ten-mark coin in the slot and helped her in. I got her address before it took off.

ARM Headquarters hummed with early morning

304   *Larry Niven*

activity. Hellos came my way, and I answered them without stopping to talk. Anything important would filter down to me eventually.

As I passed Julie's cubicle I glanced in. She was hard at work, limply settled in her contour couch, jotting notes with her eyes closed.

Kenneth Graham.

A hookup to the basement computer formed the greater part of my desk. Learning how to use it had taken me several months. I typed an order for coffee and donuts, then: INFORMATION RETRIEVAL. KENNETH GRAHAM. LIMITED LICENSE: SURGERY. GENERAL LICENSE: DIRECT CURRENT STIMULUS EQUIPMENT SALES. ADDRESS: NEAR WEST LOS ANGELES.

Tape chattered out of the slot, an instant response, loop after loop of it curling on my desk. I didn't need to read it to know I was right.

New technologies create new customs, new laws, new ethics, new crimes. About half the activity of the United Nations Police, the ARMs, dealt with control of a crime that hadn't existed a century ago. The crime of organ-legging was the result of thousands of years of medical progress, of millions of lives selflessly dedicated to the ideal of healing the sick. Progress had brought these ideals to reality, and, as usual, had created new problems.

1900 A.D. was the year Karl Landsteiner classified human blood into four types, giving patients their first real chance to survive a transfusion. The technology of transplants had grown with the growing of the twentieth century. Whole blood, dry bone, skin, live kidneys, live hearts could all be transferred from one body to another. Donors had saved tens of thousands of lives in that hundred years, by willing their bodies to medicine.

But the number of donors was limited, and not many died in such a way that anything of value could be saved.

The deluge had come something less than a hundred

years ago. One healthy donor (but of course there was no such animal) could save a dozen lives. Why, then, should a condemned murderer die to no purpose? First a few states, then most of the nations of the world had passed new laws. Criminals condemned to death must be executed in a hospital, with surgeons to save as much as could be saved for the organ banks.

The world's billions wanted to live, and the organ banks were life itself. A man could live forever as long as the doctors could shove spare parts into him faster than his own parts wore out. But they could do that only as long as the world's organ banks were stocked.

A hundred scattered movements to abolish the death penalty died silent, unpublicized deaths. Everybody gets sick sometimes.

And still there were shortages in the organ banks. Still patients died for the lack of parts to save them. The world's legislators had responded to steady pressure from the world's people. Death penalties were established for first, second, and third degree murder. For assault with a deadly weapon. Then for a multitude of crimes: rape, fraud, embezzlement, having children without a license, four or more counts of false advertising. For nearly a century the trend had been growing, as the world's voting citizens acted to protect their right to live forever.

Even now there weren't enough transplants. A woman with kidney trouble might wait a year for a transplant: one healthy kidney to last the rest of her life. A thirty-five-year-old heart patient must live with a sound but forty-year-old heart. One lung, part of a liver, prosthetics that wore out too fast or weighed too much or did too little ... there weren't enough criminals. Not surprisingly, the death penalty *was* a deterrent. People stopped committing crimes rather than face the donor room of a hospital.

For instant replacement of your ruined digestive system, for a *young* healthy heart, for a whole liver when you'd ruined yours with alcohol ... you had to go to an organlegger.

*   *   *

There are three aspects to the business of organlegging.

One is the business of kidnap-murder. It's risky. You can't fill an organ bank by waiting for volunteers. Executing condemned criminals is a government monopoly. So you go out and *get* your donors: on a crowded city slidewalk, in an air terminal, stranded on a freeway by a car with a busted capacitor . . . anywhere.

The selling end of the business is just as dangerous, because even a desperately sick man sometimes has a conscience. He'll buy his transplant, then go straight to the ARMs, curing his sickness and his conscience by turning in the whole gang. Thus the sales end is somewhat anonymous, but as there are few repeat sales, that hardly matters.

Third is the technical, medical aspect. Probably this is the safest part of the business. Your hospital is big, but you can put it anywhere. You wait for the donors, who arrive still alive; you ship out livers and glands and square feet of live skin, correctly labeled for rejection reactions.

It's not as easy as it sounds. You need doctors. Good ones.

That was where Loren came in. He had a monopoly.

Where did he get them? We were still trying to find out. Somehow, one man had discovered a foolproof way to recruit talented but dishonest doctors practically en masse. Was it really one man? All our sources said it was. And he had half the North American west coast in the palm of his hand.

Loren. No holographs, no fingerprints or retina prints, not even a description. All we had was that one name, and a few possible contacts.

One of these was Kenneth Graham.

The holograph was a good one. Probably it had been posed in a portrait shop. Kenneth Graham had a long Scottish face with a lantern jaw and a small, dour mouth. In the holo he was trying to smile and look dignified simultaneously. He only looked uncomfortable. His hair was sandy and close cut. Above his light gray eyes his eyebrows were so light as to be nearly invisible.

My breakfast arrived. I dunked a donut and bit it, and found out I was hungrier than I'd thought.

A string of holos had been reproduced on the computer tape. I ran through the others fairly quickly, eating with one hand and flipping the key with the other. Some were fuzzy; they had been taken by spy beams through the windows of Graham's shop. None of the prints were in any way incriminating. Not one showed Graham smiling.

He had been selling electrical joy for twelve years now.

A current addict has an advantage over his supplier. Electricity is cheap. With a drug, your supplier can always raise the price on you; but not with electricity. You see the ecstasy merchant once, when he sells you your operation and your droud, and never again. Nobody gets hooked by accident. There's an honesty to current addiction. The customer always knows just what he's getting into, and what it will do for him— and to him.

Still, you'd need a certain lack of empathy to make a living the way Kenneth Graham did. Else he'd have had to turn away his customers. Nobody becomes a current addict gradually. He decides all at once, and he buys the operation before he has ever tasted its joy. Each of Kenneth Graham's customers had reached his shop after deciding to drop out of the human race.

What a stream of the hopeless and the desperate must have passed through Graham's shop! How could they help but haunt his dreams? And if Kenneth Graham slept well at night, then—

Then, small wonder if he had turned organlegger.

He was in a good position for it. Despair is characteristic of the would-be current addict. The unknown, the unloved, the people nobody knew and nobody needed and nobody missed, these passed in a steady stream through Kenneth Graham's shop.

So a few didn't come out. Who'd notice?

I flipped quickly through the tape to find out who was in charge of watching Graham. Jackson Bera. I called down through the desk phone.

"Sure," said Bera, "we've had a spy beam on him about three weeks now. It's a waste of good salaried ARM agents. Maybe he's clean. Maybe he's been tipped somehow."

"Then why not stop watching him?"

Bera looked disgusted. "Because we've only been watching for three weeks. How many donors do you think he needs a year? Two. Read the reports. Gross profit on a single donor is over a million UN marks. Graham can afford to be careful who he picks."

"Yah."

"At that, he wasn't careful enough. At least two of his customers disappeared last year. Customers with families. That's what put us on him."

"So you could watch him for the next six months without a guarantee. He could be just waiting for the right guy to walk in."

"Sure. He has to write up a report on every customer. That gives him the right to ask personal questions. If the guy has relatives, Graham lets him walk out. Most people do have relatives, you know. Then again," Bera said disconsolately, "he could be clean. Sometimes a current addict disappears without help."

"How come I didn't see any holos of Graham at home? You can't be watching just his shop."

Jackson Bera scratched at his hair. Hair like black steel wool, worn long like a bushman's mop. "Sure we're watching his place, but we can't get a spy beam in there. It's an inside apartment. No windows. You know anything about spy beams?"

"Not much. I know they've been around awhile."

"They're as old as lasers. Oldest trick in the book is to put a mirror in the room you want to bug. Then you run a laser beam through a window, or even through heavy drapes, and bounce it off the mirror. When you pick it up it's been distorted by the vibrations in the glass. That gives you a perfect recording of anything that's been said in that room. But for pictures you need something a little more sophisticated."

"How sophisticated can we get?"

"We can put a spy beam in any room with a window. We can send one through some kinds of wall. Give us an optically flat surface and we can send one around corners."

"But you need an outside wall."

"Yup."

"What's Graham doing now?"

"Just a sec." Bera disappeared from view. "Someone just came in. Graham's talking to him. Want the picture?"

"Sure. Leave it on. I'll turn it off from here when I'm through with it."

The picture of Bera went dark. A moment later I was looking into a doctor's office. If I'd seen it cold I'd have thought it was run by a podiatrist. There was the comfortable tilt-back chair with the headrest and the footrest; the cabinet next to it with instruments lying on top, on a clean white cloth; the desk over in one corner. Kenneth Graham was talking to a homely, washed-out-looking girl.

I listened to Graham's would-be-fatherly reassurances and his glowing description of the magic of current addiction. When I couldn't take it any longer I turned the sound down. The girl took her place in the chair, and Graham placed something over her head.

The girl's homely face turned suddenly beautiful.

Happiness is beautiful, all by itself. A happy person is beautiful, per se. Suddenly and totally, the girl was full of joy and I realized that I hadn't known everything about droud sales. Apparently Graham had an inductor to put the current where he wanted it, without wires. He *could* show a customer what current addiction felt like, without first implanting the wires.

What a powerful argument that was!

Graham turned off the machine. It was as if he'd turned off the girl. She sat stunned for a moment, then reached frantically for her purse and started scrabbling inside.

I couldn't take anymore. I turned it off.

Small wonder if Graham had turned organlegger. He had to be totally without empathy just to sell his merchandise.

Even there, I thought, he'd had a head start.

So he was a little more callous than the rest of the world's billions. But not much. Every voter had a bit of the organlegger in him. In voting the death penalty for so many crimes, the law makers had only bent to pressure from the voters. There was a spreading lack of respect for life, the evil side of transplant technology. The good side was a longer life for everyone. One condemned criminal could save a dozen deserving lives. Who could complain about that?

We hadn't thought that way in the Belt. In the Belt survival was a virtue in itself, and life was a precious thing, spread so thin among the sterile rocks, hurtling in single units through all that killing emptiness between the worlds.

So I'd had to come to Earth for my transplant.

My request had been accepted two months after I landed. So quickly? Later I'd learned that the banks always have a surplus of certain items. Few people lose their arms these days. I had also learned, a year after the transplant had taken, that I was using an arm taken from a captured organlegger's storage bank.

That had been a shock. I'd hoped my arm had come from a depraved murderer, someone who'd shot fourteen nurses from a rooftop. Not at all. Some faceless, nameless victim had had the bad luck to encounter a ghoul, and I had benefited thereby.

Did I turn in my new arm in a fit of revulsion? No, surprising to say, I did not. But I had joined the ARMs, once the Amalgamation of Regional Militia, now the United Nations Police. Though I had stolen a dead man's arm, I would hunt the kin of those who had killed him.

The noble urgency of that resolve had been drowned in paperwork these last few years. Perhaps I was becoming callous, like the flatlanders—the *other* flatlanders around me, voting new death penalties year after year. *Income-tax evasion. Operating a flying vehicle on manual controls over a city.*

Was Kenneth Graham so much worse than they?

Sure he was. The bastard had put a wire in Owen Jennison's head.

I waited twenty minutes for Julie to come out. I could have sent her a memorandum, but there was plenty of time before noon, and too little time to get anything accomplished, and . . . I wanted to talk to her.

"Hi," she said. "Thanks," taking the coffee. "How went the ceremonial drunk? Oh, I *see*. Mmmmm. Very good. Almost poetic." Conversation with Julie has a way of taking shortcuts.

Poetic, right. I remembered how inspiration had struck like lightning through a mild high glow. Owen's floating cigarette lure. What better way to honor his memory than to use it to pick up a girl?

"Right," Julie agreed. "But there's something you may have missed. What's Taffy's last name?"

"I can't remember. She wrote it down on—"

"What does she do for a living?"

"How should I know?"

"What religion is she? Is she a pro or an anti? Where did she grow up?"

"Dammit—"

"Half an hour ago you were very complacently musing on how depersonalized all us flatlanders are except you. What's Taffy, a person or a foldout?" Julie stood with her hands on her hips, looking up at me like a short schoolteacher.

How many people is Julie? Some of us have never seen this Guardian aspect. She's frightening, the

Guardian. If it ever appeared on a date, the man she was with would be struck impotent forever.

It never does. When a reprimand is deserved, Julie delivers it in broad daylight. This serves to separate her functions, but it doesn't make it easier to take.

No use pretending it wasn't her business, either.

I'd come here to ask for Julie's protection. Let me turn unlovable to Julie, even a little bit unlovable, and as far as Julie was concerned I would have an unreadable mind. How, then, would she know when I was in trouble? How could she send help to rescue me from whatever? My private life *was* her business, her single, vastly important job.

"I *like* Taffy," I protested. "I didn't care who she was when we met. Now I like her, and I think she likes me. What do you want from a first date?"

"You know better. You can remember other dates when two of you talked all night on a couch, just from the joy of learning about each other." she mentioned three names, and I flushed. Julie knows the words that will turn you inside out in an instant. "Taffy is a person, not an episode, not a symbol of anything, not just a pleasant night. What's your judgment of her?"

I thought about it, standing there in the corridor. Funny: I've faced the Guardian Julie on other occasions, and it has never occurred to me to just walk out of the unpleasant situation. Later I think of that. At the time I just stand there, facing the Guardian/Judge/Teacher. I thought about Taffy . . .

"She's nice," I said. "*Not* depersonalized. Squeamish, even. She wouldn't make a good nurse. She'd want to help too much, and it would tear her apart when she couldn't. I'd say she was one of the vulnerable ones."

"Go on."

"I want to see her again, but I won't dare talk shop with her. In fact . . . I'd better not see her till this business of Owen is over. Loren might take an interest in her. Or . . . she might take an interest in me, and I might get hurt . . . have I missed anything?"

"I think so. You owe her a phone call. If you won't be dating her for a few days, call her and tell her so."

"Check." I spun on my heel, spun back. "Finagle's Jest! I almost forgot. The reason I came here—"

"I know, you want a time slot. Suppose I check on you at oh nine forty-five every morning?"

"That's a little early. When I get in deadly danger it's usually at night."

"I'm off at night. Oh nine forty-five is all I've got. I'm sorry, Gil, but it is. Shall I monitor you or not?"

"Sold. Nine forty-five."

"Good. Let me know if you get real proof Owen was murdered. I'll give you two slots. You'll be in a little more concrete danger then."

"Good."

"I love you. Yeep, I'm late." And she dodged back into the office, while I went to call Taffy.

Taffy wasn't home, of course, and I didn't know where she worked, or even what she did. Her phone offered to take a message. I gave my name and said I'd call back.

And then I sat there sweating for five minutes.

It was half an hour to noon. Here I was at my desk phone. I couldn't decently see any way to argue myself out of sending a message to Homer Chandrasekhar.

I didn't want to talk to him, then or ever. He'd chewed me out but good, last time I'd seen him. My free arm had cost me my Belter life, and it had cost me Homer's respect. I didn't want to talk to him, even on a one-way message, and I most particularly didn't want to have to tell him Owen was dead.

But someone had to tell him.

And maybe he could find out something.

And I'd put it off nearly a full day.

For five minutes I sweated, and then I called long distance and recorded a message and sent it off to Ceres. More accurately, I recorded six messages before I was satisfied. I don't want to talk about it.

I tried Taffy again; she might come home for lunch. Wrong.

I hung up wondering if Julie had been fair. What had we bargained for, Taffy and I, beyond a pleasant night? And we'd had that, and would have others, with luck.

But Julie would find it hard not to be fair. If she thought Taffy was the vulnerable type, she'd taken her information from my own mind.

Mixed feelings. You're a kid, and your mother has just laid down the law. But it *is* a law, something you can count on ... and she is paying attention to you ... and she *does* care ... when, for so many of those outside, nobody cares at all.

"Naturally I thought of murder," said Ordaz. "I always consider murder. When my sainted mother passed away after three years of the most tender care by my sister Maria Angela, I actually considered searching for evidence of needle holes about the head."

"Find any?"

Ordaz' face froze. He put down his beer and started to get up.

"Cool it," I said hurriedly. "No offense intended." He glared a moment, then sat down half mollified.

We'd picked an outdoor restaurant on the pedestrian level. On the other side of a hedge (a real live hedge, green and growing and everything) the shoppers were carried past in a steady one-way stream. Beyond them, a slidewalk carried a similar stream in the opposite direction. I had the dizzy feeling that it was we who were moving.

A waiter like a bell-bottomed chess pawn produced steaming dishes of chili size from its torso, put them precisely in front of us, and slid away on a cushion of air.

"Naturally I considered murder. Believe me. Mr. Hamilton, it does not hold up."

"I think I could make a pretty good case."

"You may try, of course. Better, I will start you on your way. First, we must assume that Kenneth Graham the happiness peddler did not sell a droud-and-plug to Owen Jennison. Rather, Owen Jennison was forced to undergo the operation. Graham's records, including the written permission to operate, were forged. All this we must assume, is it not so?"

"Right. And before you tell me Graham's escutcheon is unblemished, let me tell you that it isn't."

"Oh?"

"He's connected with an organlegging gang. That's classified information. We're watching him, and we don't want him tipped."

"That is news." Ordaz rubbed his jaw. "Organlegging. Well. What would Owen Jennison have to do with organlegging?"

"Owen's a Belter. The Belt's always drastically short of transplant materials."

"Yes, they import quantities of medical supplies from Earth. Not only organs in storage, but also drugs and prosthetics. So?"

"Owen ran a good many cargos past the goldskins in his day. He got caught a few times, but he's still way ahead of the government. He's on the records as a successful smuggler. If a big organlegger wanted to expand his market, he might very well send a feeler out to a Belter with a successful smuggling record."

"You never mentioned that Mr. Jennison was a smuggler."

"What for? All Belters are smugglers, if they think they can get away with it. To a Belter, smuggling isn't immoral. But an organlegger wouldn't know that. He'd think Owen was already a criminal."

"Do you think your friend—" Ordaz hesitated delicately.

"No, Owen wouldn't turn organlegger. But he might, he just *might* try to turn one in. The rewards for information leading to the capture and conviction of, et cetera, are substantial. If someone contracted Owen, Owen might very well have tried to trace the contact by himself.

"Now, the gang we're after covers half the west

coast of this continent. That's big. It's the Loren gang, the one Graham may be working for. Suppose Owen had a chance to meet Loren himself?"

"You think he might take it, do you?"

"I think he did. I think he let his hair grow out so he'd look like an Earthman, to convince Loren he wanted to look inconspicuous. I think he collected as much information as he could, then tried to get out with a whole skin. But he didn't make it.

"Did you find his application for a nudist license?"

"No. I saw your point there," said Ordaz. He leaned back, ignoring the food in front of him. "Mr. Jennison's tan was uniform except for the characteristic darkening of the face. I presume he was a practicing nudist in the Belt."

"Yah. We don't need licenses there. He'd have been one here, too, unless he was hiding something. Remember that scar. He never missed a chance to show it off."

"Could he really have thought to pass for a—" Ordaz hesitated—"flatlander?"

"With the Belter tan? No! He was overdoing it a little with the haircut. Maybe he thought Loren would underestimate him. But he wasn't advertising his presence, or he wouldn't have left his most personal possessions home."

"So he was dealing with organleggers, and they found him out before he could reach you. Yes, Mr. Hamilton, this is well thought out. But it won't work."

"Why not? I'm not trying to prove it's murder. Not yet. I'm just trying to show you that murder is at least as likely as suicide."

"But it's not, Mr. Hamilton."

I looked the question.

"Consider the details of the hypothetical murder. Owen Jennison is drugged, no doubt, and taken to the office of Kenneth Graham. There, an ecstasy plug is attached. A standard droud is fitted, and is then amateurishly altered with soldering tools. Already we see, on the part of the killer, a minute attention to details.

We see it again in Kenneth Graham's forged papers of permission to operate. They were impeccable.

"Owen Jennison is then taken back to his apartment. It would be his own, would it not? There would be little point in moving him to another. The cord from his droud is shortened, again in amateurish fashion. Mr. Jennison is tied up—"

"I wondered if you'd see that."

"But why should he not be tied up? He is tied up, and allowed to waken. Perhaps the arrangement is explained to him, perhaps not. That would be up to the killer. The killer then plugs Mr. Jennison into a wall. A current trickles through his brain, and Owen Jennison knows pure pleasure for the first time in his life.

"He is left tied up for, let us say, three hours. In the first few minutes he would be a hopeless addict, I think—"

"You must have known more current addicts than I have."

"Even I would not want to be pinned down. Your normal current addict is an addict after a few minutes. But then, your normal current addict asked to be made an addict, knowing what it would do to his life. Current addiction is symptomatic of despair. Your friend might have been able to fight free of a few minutes' exposure."

"So they kept him tied up for three hours. Then they cut the ropes." I felt sickened. Ordaz' ugly, ugly pictures matched mine in every detail.

"No more than three hours, by our hypothesis. They would not dare stay longer than a few hours. They would cut the ropes and leave Owen Jennison to starve to death. In the space of a month the evidence of his drugging would vanish, as would any abrasions left by ropes, lumps on his head, mercy needle punctures, and the like. A carefully detailed, well-thought-out plan, don't you agree?"

I told myself that Ordaz was not being ghoulish. He

was just doing his job. Still, it was difficult to answer objectively.

"It fits our picture of Loren. He's been very careful with us. He'd love carefully detailed, well-thought-out plans."

Ordaz leaned forward. "But don't you see? A carefully detailed plan is all wrong. There is a crucial flaw in it. Suppose Mr. Jennison pulls out the droud?"

"Could he do that? Would he?"

"Could he? Certainly. A simple tug of the fingers. The current wouldn't interfere with motor coordination. Would he?" Ordaz pulled meditatively at his beer. "I know a good deal about current addiction, but I don't know what it *feels* like, Mr. Hamilton. Your normal addict pulls his droud out as often as he inserts it, but your friend was getting ten times normal current. He might have pulled the droud out a dozen times, and instantly plugged it back each time. Yet Belters are supposed to be strong-willed men, very individualistic. Who knows whether, even after a week of addiction, your friend might not have pulled the droud loose, coiled the cord, slipped it in his pocket, and walked away scot free?

"There is the additional risk that someone might walk in on him—an automachinery serviceman, for instance. Or someone might notice that he had not bought any food in a month. A suicide would take that risk. Suicides routinely leave themselves a chance to change their minds. But a murderer?

"No. Even if the chance were one in a thousand, the man who created such a detailed plan would never have taken such a chance."

The sun burned hotly down on our shoulders. Ordaz suddenly remembered his lunch and began to eat.

I watched the world ride by beyond the hedge. Pedestrians stood in little conversational bunches; others peered into shop windows on the pedestrian strip, or glanced over the hedge to watch us eat. There were the few who pushed through the crowd with set expressions, impatient with the ten-mile-per-hour speed of the slidewalk.

"Maybe they *were* watching him. Maybe the room was bugged."

"We searched the room thoroughly," said Ordaz. "If there had been observational equipment, we would have found it."

"It could have been removed."

Ordaz shrugged.

I remembered the spy-eyes in Monica Apartments. Someone would have had to physically enter the room to carry a bug out. He could ruin it with the right signal, maybe, but it would surely leave traces.

And Owen had had an inside room. No spy-eyes.

"There's one thing you've left out," I said presently.

"And what would that be?"

"My name in Owen's wallet, listed as next of kin. He was directing my attention to the thing I was working on. The Loren gang."

"That is possible."

"You can't have it both ways."

Ordaz lowered his fork. "I *can* have it both ways, Mr. Hamilton. But you won't like it."

"I'm sure I won't."

"Let us incorporate your assumption. Mr. Jennison was contacted by an agent of Loren, the organlegger, who intended to sell transplant material to Belters. He accepted. The promise of riches was too much for him.

"A month later, something made him realize what a terrible thing he had done. He decided to die. He went to an ecstasy peddler and he had a wire put in his head. Later, before he plugged in the droud, he made one attempt to atone for his crime. He listed you as his next of kin, so that you might guess why he had died, and perhaps so that you could use that knowledge against Loren."

Ordaz looked at me across the table. "I see that you will never agree. I cannot help that. I can only read the evidence."

"Me too. But I knew Owen. He'd never have

worked for an organlegger, he'd never have killed himself, and if he had, he'd never have done it that way."

Ordaz didn't answer.

"What about fingerprints?"

"In the apartment? None."

"None but Owen's?"

"Even his were found only on the chairs and end tables. I curse the man who invented the cleaning robot. Every smooth surface in that apartment was cleaned exactly forty-four times during Mr. Jennison's tenancy." Ordaz went back to his chili size.

"Then try this. Assume for the moment that I'm right. Assume Owen was after Loren, and Loren got him. Owen knew he was doing something dangerous. He wouldn't have wanted me to get onto Loren before he was ready. He wanted the reward for himself. But he might have left me something, just in case.

"Something in a locker somewhere, an airport or spaceport locker. Evidence. Not under his own name, or mine either, because I'm a known ARM. But—"

"Some name you both know."

"Right. Like Homer Chandrasekhar. Or—got it. Cubes Forsythe. Owen would have thought that was apt. Cubes is dead."

"We will look. You must understand that it will not prove your case."

"Sure. Anything you find, Owen could have arranged in a fit of conscience. Screw that. Let me know what you get," I said, and stood up and left.

I rode the slidewalk, not caring where it was taking me. It would give me a chance to cool off.

Could Ordaz be right? Could he?

But the more I dug into Owen's death, the worse it made Owen look.

Therefore Ordaz was wrong.

Owen work for an organlegger? He'd rather have been a donor.

Owen getting his kicks from a wall socket? He never even watched tridee!

Owen kill himself? No. If so, not that way.

But even if I could have swallowed all that . . .

Owen Jennison, letting me know he'd worked with organleggers? Me, Gil the Arm Hamilton? Let *me* know *that*?

The slidewalk rolled along, past restaurants and shopping centers and churches and banks. Ten stories below, the hum of cars and scooters drifted faintly up from the vehicular level. The sky was a narrow, vivid slash of blue between black shadows of skyscraper.

Let *me* know *that*? Never.

But Ordaz' strangely inconsistent murderer was no better.

I thought of something even Ordaz had missed. Why would Loren dispose of Owen so elaborately? Owen need only disappear into the organ banks, never to bother Loren again.

The shops were thinning out now, and so were the crowds. The slidewalk narrowed, entered a residential area, and not a very good one. I'd let it carry me a long way. I looked around, trying to decide where I was.

And I was four blocks from Graham's place.

My subconscious had done me a dirty. I wanted to look at Kenneth Graham, face to face. The temptation to go on was nearly irresistible, but I fought it off and changed direction at the next disk.

A slidewalk intersection is a rotating disk, its rim tangent to four slidewalks and moving with the same speed. From the center you ride up an escalator and over the slidewalks to reach stationary walks along the buildings. I could have caught a cab at the center of the disk, but I still wanted to think, so I just rode halfway around the rim.

I could have walked into Graham's shop and gotten away with it. Maybe. I'd have looked hopeless and bored and hesitant, told Graham I wanted an ecstasy plug, worried loudly about what my wife and friends would say, then changed my mind at the last moment. He'd have let me walk out, knowing I'd be missed. Maybe.

But Loren had to know more about the ARMs than we knew about him. Some time or other, had Graham been shown a holo of yours truly? Let a known ARM walk into his shop, and Graham would panic. It wasn't worth the risk.

Then, dammit, what *could* I do?

Ordaz' inconsistent killer. If we assumed Owen was murdered, we couldn't get away from the other assumptions. The care, the nitpicking detail—and then Owen left alone to pull out the plug and walk away, or to be discovered by a persistent salesman or a burglar, or—

No. Ordaz' hypothetical killer, and mine, would have watched Owen like a hawk. For a month.

That did it. I stepped off at the next disk and got a taxi.

The taxi dropped me on the roof of Monica Apartments. I took an elevator to the lobby.

If the manager was surprised to see me, he didn't show it as he gestured me into his office. The office seemed much roomier than the lobby had, possibly because there were things to break the anonymous-modern decor: paintings on the wall, a small black worm track in the rug that must have been caused by a visitor's cigarette, a holo of Miller and his wife on the wide, nearly empty desk. He waited until I was settled, then leaned forward expectantly.

"I'm here on ARM business," I said, and passed him my ident.

He passed it back without checking it. "I presume it's the same business," he said without cordiality.

"Yah. I'm convinced Owen Jennison must have had visitors while he was here."

The manager smiled. "That's ridic—impossible."

"Nope, it's not. Your holo cameras take pictures of visitors, but they don't snap the tenants, do they?"

"Of course not."

"Then Owen could have been visited by any tenant in the building."

The manager looked shocked. "No, certainly not. Really, I don't see why you pursue this, Mr. Hamilton. If Mr. Jennison had been found in such a condition, it would have been reported!"

"I don't think so. Could he have been visited by any tenant in the building?"

"No. No. The cameras would have taken a picture of anyone from another floor."

"How about someone from the same floor?"

Reluctantly the manager bobbed his head. "Ye-es. As far as the holo cameras are concerned, that's possible. But—"

"Then I'd like to ask for pictures of any tenant who lived on the eighteenth floor during the last six weeks. Send them to the ARM Building, central L.A. Can do?"

"Of course. You'll have them within an hour."

"Good. Now, something else occurred to me. Suppose a man got out on the nineteenth floor and walked down to the eighteenth. He'd be holoed on the nineteenth, but not on the eighteenth, right?"

The manager smiled indulgently. "Mr. Hamilton, there are no stairs in this building."

"Just the elevators? Isn't that dangerous?"

"Not at all. There is a separate self-contained emergency power source for each of the elevators. It's common practice. After all, who would want to walk up eighty stories if the elevator failed?"

"Okay, fine. One last point. Could someone tamper with the computer? Could someone make it decide not to take a certain picture, for instance?"

"I ... am not an expert on how to tamper with computers, Mr. Hamilton. Why don't you go straight to the company? Caulfield Brains, Inc."

"Okay. What's your model?"

"Just a moment." He got up and leafed through a drawer in a filing cabinet. "EQ 144."

"Okay."

That was all I could do here, and I knew it . . . and still I didn't have the will to get up. There ought to be *something* . . .

Finally Miller cleared his throat. "Will that be all, sir?"

"Yes," I said. "No. Can I get into 1809?"

"I'll see if we've rented it yet."

"The police are through with it?"

"Certainly." He went back to the filing cabinet. "No, it's still available. I'll take you up. How long will you be?"

"I don't know. No more than half an hour. No need to come up."

"Very well." He handed me the key and waited for me to leave. I did.

The merest flicker of blue light caught my eye as I left the elevator. I would have thought it was my optic nerve, not in the real world, if I hadn't know about the holo cameras. Maybe it was. You don't need laser light to make a holograph, but it does get you clearer pictures.

Owen's room was a box. Everything was retracted. There was nothing but the bare walls. I had never seen anything so desolate, unless it was some asteroidal rock, too poor to mine, too badly placed to be worth a base.

The control panel was just beside the door. I turned on the lights, then touched the master button. Lines appeared, outlined in red and green and blue. A great square on one wall for the bed, most of another wall for the kitchen, various outlines across the floor. Very handy. You wouldn't want a guest to be standing on the table when you expanded it.

I'd come here to get the feel of the place, to encourage a hunch, to see if I'd missed anything. Translation: I was playing. Playing, I reached through the control panel to find the circuits. The printed circuitry was too small and too detailed to tell me anything, but I ran imaginary fingertips along a few wires and found that they looped straight to their action points, no detours. No sensors to the outside. You'd have to be in the room to know what was expanded, what retracted.

So a supposedly occupied room had had its bed retracted for six weeks. But you'd have to be in the room to know it.

I pushed buttons to expand the kitchen nook and the reading chair. The wall slid out eight feet; the floor humped itself and took form. I sat down in the chair, and the kitchen nook blocked my view of the door.

Nobody could have seen Owen from the hall.

If only someone had noticed that Owen wasn't ordering food. That might have saved him.

I thought of something else, and it made me look around for the air conditioner. There was a grill at floor level. I felt behind it with my imaginary hand. Some of these apartment air-conditioning units go on when the CO_2 level hits half a percent. This one was geared to temperature and manual control.

With the other kind, our careful killer could have tapped the air-conditioner current to find out if Owen was still alive and present. As it was, 1809 had behaved like an empty room for six weeks.

I flopped back in the reading chair.

If my hypothetical killer had watched Owen, he'd done it with a bug. Unless he'd actually lived on this floor for the four or five weeks it took Owen to die, there was no other way.

Okay, think about a bug. Make it small enough and nobody would find it except the cleaning robot, who would send it straight to the incinerator. You'd have to make it big, so the robot wouldn't get it. No worry about Owen finding it! And then, when you knew Owen was dead, you'd use the self-destruct.

But if you burned it to slag, you'd leave a burn hole somewhere. Ordaz would have found it. So. An asbestos pad? You'd want the self-destruct to leave something that the cleaning robot would sweep up.

And if you'll believe that you'll believe anything. It was too chancy. *Nobody* knows what a cleaning robot will decide is garbage. They're made stupid because it's cheaper. So they're programmed to leave large objects alone.

There had to be someone on this floor, either to watch Owen himself or to pick up the bug that did the watching. I was betting everything I had on a human watcher.

I'd come here mainly to give my intuition a chance. It wasn't working. Owen had spent six weeks in this chair, and for at least the last week he'd been dead. Yet I couldn't feel it with him. It was just a chair with two end tables. He had left nothing in the room, not even a restless ghost.

The call caught me halfway back to Headquarters.

"You were right," Ordaz told me over the wristphone. "We have found a locker at Death Valley Port registered to Cubes Forsythe. I am on my way there now. Will you join me?"

"I'll meet you there."

"Good. I am as eager as you to see what Owen Jennison left us."

I doubted that.

The Port was something more than two hundred thirty miles away, an hour at taxi speeds. It would be a big fare. I typed out a new address on the destination board, then called in at Headquarters. An ARM agent is fairly free; he doesn't have to justify every little move. There was no question of getting permission to go. At worst they might disallow the fare on my expense account.

"Oh, and there'll be a set of holos coming in from Monica Apartments," I told the man. "Have the computer check them against known organleggers and associates of Loren."

The taxi rose smoothly into the sky and headed east. I watched tridee and drank coffee until I ran out of coins for the dispenser.

If you go between November and May, when the climate is ideal, Death Valley can be a tourist's paradise. There is the Devil's Golf Course, with its fantastic ridges and pinnacles of salt; Zabriskie Point and its weird badlands topography; the old borax mining sites; and all kinds of strange, rare plants, adapted to the heat and the death-dry climate. Yes, Death Valley has many points of interest, and someday I was going to see them. So far all I'd seen was the spaceport. But the Port was impressive in its own way.

The landing field used to be part of a sizable inland sea. It is now a sea of salt. Alternating red and blue concentric circles mark the field for ships dropping from space, and a century's developments in chemical, fission, and fusion reaction motors have left blast pits striped like rainbows by esoteric, often radioactive salts. But mostly the field retains its ancient glare-white.

And out across the salt are ships of many sizes and many shapes. Vehicles and machinery dance attendance, and, if you're willing to wait, you may see a ship land. It's worth the wait.

The Port building, at the edge of the major salt flat, is a pastel green tower set in a wide patch of fluorescent orange concrete. No ship has ever landed on it—yet. The taxi dropped me at the entrance and moved away to join others of its kind. And I stood inhaling the dry, balmy air.

Four months of the year, Death Valley's climate is ideal. One August the Furnace Creek ranch recorded 134° Fahrenheit shade temperature.

A man behind a desk told me that Ordaz had arrived before me. I found him and another officer in a labyrinth of pay lockers, each big enough to hold two or three suitcases. The locker Ordaz had opened held only a lightweight plastic briefcase.

"He may have taken other lockers," he said.

"Probably not. Belters travel light. Have you tried to open it"

"Not yet. It is a combination lock. I thought perhaps . . ."

"Maybe." I squatted to look at it.

Funny: I felt no surprise at all. It was as if I'd known all along that Owen's suitcase would be there. And why not? He was bound to try to protect himself somehow. Through me, because I was already involved in the UN side of organlegging. By leaving something in a spaceport locker, because Loren couldn't find the right locker or get into it if he did, and because I would naturally connect Owen with spaceports. Under Cubes' name, because I'd be looking for that, and Loren wouldn't.

Hindsight is wonderful.

The lock had five digits. "He must have meant me to open it. Let's see . . ." and I moved the tumblers to 42217. April 22, 2117, the day Cubes died, stapled suddenly to a plastic partition.

The lock clicked open.

Ordaz went instantly for the manila folder. More slowly, I picked up two glass phials. One was tightly sealed against Earth's air, and half full of an incredibly fine dust. So fine was it that it slid about like oil inside the glass. The other phial held a blackened grain of nickel-iron, barely big enough to see.

Other things were in that case, but the prize was that folder. The story was in there . . . at least up to a point. Owen must have planned to add to it.

A message had been waiting for him in the Ceres mail dump when he returned from his last trip out. Owen must have laughed over parts of that message. Loren had taken the trouble to assemble a complete dossier of Owen's smuggling activities over the past eight years. Did he think he could ensure Owen's silence by threatening to turn the dossier over to the goldskins?

Maybe the dossier had given Owen the wrong idea. In any case, he'd decided to contact Loren and see what developed. Ordinarily he'd have sent me the entire message and let me try to track it down. I was the expert, after all. But Owen's last trip out had been a disaster.

His fusion drive had blown somewhere beyond Jupiter's orbit. No explanation. The safeties had blown his lifesystem capsule free of the explosion, barely. A rescue ship had returned him to Ceres. The fee had nearly broken him. He needed money. Loren may have known that, and counted on it.

The reward for information leading to Loren's capture would have bought him a new ship.

He'd landed at Outback Field, following Loren's instructions. From there, Loren's men had moved him about a good deal: to London, to Bombay, to Amberg, Germany. Owen's personal, written story ended in Amberg. How had he reached California? He had not had a chance to say.

But in between, he had learned a good deal. There were snatches of detail on Loren's organization. There was Loren's full plan for shipping illicit transplant materials to the Belt, and for finding and contacting customers. Owen had made suggestions there. Most of them sounded reasonable and would be unworkable in practice. Typically Owen. I could find no sign that he'd overplayed his hand.

But of course he hadn't known it when he did.

And there were holos, twenty-three of them, each a member of Loren's gang. Some of the pictures had markings on the back; others were blank. Owen had been unable to find out where each of them stood in the organization.

I leafed through them twice, wondering if one of them could be Loren himself. Owen had never known.

"It would seem you were right," said Ordaz. "He could not have collected such detail by accident. He must have planned from the beginning to betray the Loren gang."

"Just as I told you. And he was murdered for it."

"It seems he must have been. What motive could he have had for suicide?" Ordaz' round, calm face was doing its best to show anger. "I find I cannot believe in our inconsistent murderer either. You have ruined my digestion, Mr. Hamilton."

I told him my idea about other tenants on Owen's floor. He nodded. "Possibly, possibly. This is your department now. Organlegging is the business of the ARMS."

"Right." I closed the briefcase and hefted it. "Let's see what the computer can do with these. I'll send you photocopies of everything in here."

"You'll let me know about the other tenants?"

"Of course."

I walked into ARM Headquarters swinging that precious briefcase, feeling on top of the world. Owen had been murdered. He had died with honor, if not— oh, definitely not—with dignity. Even Ordaz knew it now.

Then Jackson Bera, snarling and panting, went by at a dead run.

"What's up?" I called after him. Maybe I wanted a chance to brag. I had twenty-three faces, twenty-three organleggers, in my briefcase.

Bera slid to a stop beside me. "Where *you* been?"

"Working. Honest. What's the hurry?"

"Remember that pleasure peddler we were watching?"

"Graham? Kenneth Graham?"

"That's the one. He's dead. We blew it." And Bera took off.

He'd reached the lab by the time I caught up with him.

Kenneth Graham's corpse was face up on the operating table. His long, lantern-jawed face was pale and slack, without expression; empty. Machinery was in place above and below his head.

"How you doing?" Bera demanded.

"Not good," the doctor answered. "Not your fault. You got him into the deepfreeze fast enough. It's just that the current—" he shrugged.

I shook Bera's shoulder. "What happened?"

Bera was panting a little from his run. "Something must have leaked. Graham tried to make a run for it. We got him at the airport."

"You could have waited. Put someone on the plane with him. Flooded the plane with TY-4."

"Remember the stink the last time we used TY-4 on civilians? Damn newscasters." Bera was shivering. I didn't blame him.

ARMs and organleggers play a funny kind of game. The organleggers have to turn their donors in alive, so they're always armed with hypo guns, firing slivers of crystalline anesthetic that melt instantly in the blood. We use the same weapon, for somewhat the same reason: a criminal has to be saved for trial, and then for the government hospitals. So no ARM ever expects to kill a man. There was a day I learned the truth. A small-time organlegger named Raphael Haine was trying to reach a call button in his own home. If he'd reached it all kinds of hell would have broken loose, Haine's men would have hypoed me, and I would have regained consciousness a piece at a time, in Haine's organ-storage tanks. So I strangled him.

The report was in the computer, but only three human beings knew about it. One was my immediate superior, Lucas Carner. The other was Julie. So far, he was the only man I'd ever killed.

And Graham was Bera's first killing.

"We got him at the airport," said Bera. "He was wearing a hat. I wish I'd noticed that, we might have moved faster. We started to close in on him with hypo guns. He turned and saw us. He reached under his hat, and then he fell."

"Killed himself?"

"Uh huh."

"How?"

"Look at his head."

I edged closer to the table, trying to stay out of the doctor's way. The doctor was going through the rou-

tine of trying to pull information from a dead brain
by induction. It wasn't going well.

There was a flat oblong box on top of Graham's
head. Black plastic, about half the size of a pack of
cards. I touched it and knew at once that it was
attached to Graham's skull.

"A droud. Not a standard type. Too big."

"Uh huh."

Liquid helium ran up my nerves. "There's a battery
in it."

"Right."

"I often wonder what the vintners buy, et cetera. A
cordless droud. Man, that's what *I* want for
Christmas."

Bera twitched all over. "Don't *say* that."

"Did you know he was a current addict?"

"No. We were afraid to bug his home. He might
have found it and been tipped. Take another look at
that thing."

The shape was wrong, I thought. The black plastic
case had been half melted.

"Heat," I mused. "Oh!"

"Uh huh. He blew the whole battery at once. Sent
the whole killing charge right through his brain, right
through the pleasure center of his brain. And, Jesus,
Gil, the thing I keep wondering is, what did it feel
like? Gil, what could it possibly have *felt* like?"

I thumped him across the shoulders in lieu of giving
him an intelligent answer. He'd be a long time wondering. And so would I.

Here was the man who had put the wire in Owen's
head. Had his death been momentary Hell, or all the
delights of paradise in one singing jolt? Hell, I hoped,
but I didn't believe it.

At least Kenneth Graham wasn't somewhere else in
the world, getting a new face and new retinas and new
fingertips from Loren's illicit organ banks.

"Nothing," said the doctor. "His brain's too badly
burned. There's just nothing there that isn't too scrambled to make sense."

"Keep trying," said Bera.

I left quietly. Maybe later I'd buy Bera a drink. He seemed to need it. Bera was one of those with empathy. I knew that he could almost feel that awful surge of ecstasy and defeat as Kenneth Graham left the world behind.

The holos from Monica Apartments had arrived hours ago. Miller had picked not only the tenants who had occupied the eighteenth floor during the past six weeks, but tenants from the nineteenth and seventeenth floors too. It seemed an embarrassment of riches. I toyed with the idea of someone from the nineteenth floor dropping over his balcony to the eighteenth, every day for five weeks. But 1809 hadn't had an outside wall, let alone a window, not to mention a balcony.

Had Miller played with the same idea? Nonsense. He didn't even know the problem. He'd just overkilled with the holos to show how cooperative he was.

None of the tenants during the period in question matched known or suspected Loren men.

I said a few appropriate words and went for coffee. Then I remembered the twenty-three possible Loren men in Owen's briefcase. I'd left them with a programer, since I wasn't quite sure how to get them into the computer myself. He ought to be finished by now.

I called down. He was.

I persuaded the computer to compare them with the holos from Monica Apartments.

Nothing. Nobody matched anybody.

I spent the next two hours writing up the Owen Jennison case. A programer would have to translate it for the machine. I wasn't that good yet.

We were back with Ordaz' inconsistent killer.

That, and a tangle of dead ends. Owen's death had bought us a handful of new pictures, pictures which might even be obsolete by now. Organleggers changed their faces at the drop of a hat. I finished the case outline, sent it down to a programer, and called Julie. I wouldn't need her protection now.

Julie had left for home.

I started to call Taffy, stopped with her number half dialed. There are times not to make a phone call. I needed to sulk; I needed a cave to be alone in. My expression would probably have broken a phone screen. Why inflict it on an innocent girl?

I left for home.

It was dark when I reached the street. I rode the pedestrian bridge across the slidewalks, waited for a taxi at the intersection disk. Presently one dropped, the white FREE sign blinking on its belly. I stepped in and deposited my credit card.

Owen had collected his holos from all over the Eurasian continent. Most of them, if not all, had been Loren's foreign agents. Why had I expected to find them in Los Angeles?

The taxi rose into the white night sky. City lights turned the cloud cover into a flat white dome. We penetrated the clouds, and stayed there. The taxi autopilot didn't care if I had a view or not.

. . . So what did I have now? Someone among dozens of tenants was a Loren man. That, or Ordaz' inconsistent killer, the careful one, had left Owen to die for five weeks, alone and unsupervised.

. . . Was the inconsistent killer so unbelievable?

He was, after all, my own hypothetical Loren. And Loren had committed murder, the ultimate crime. He'd murdered routinely, over and over, with fabulous profits. The ARMs hadn't been able to touch him. Wasn't it about time he started getting careless?

Like Graham. How long had Graham been selecting donors among his customers, choosing a few nonentities a year? And then, twice within a few months, he took clients who were missed. Careless.

Most criminals are not too bright. Loren had brains enough; but the men on his payroll would be about average. Loren would deal with the stupid ones, the ones who turned to crime because they didn't have enough sense to make it in real life.

If a man like Loren got careless, this was how it would happen. Unconsciously he would judge ARM intelligence by his own men. Seduced by an ingenious plan for murder, he might ignore the single loophole and go through with it. With Graham to advise him, he knew more about current addiction than we did; perhaps enough to trust the effects of current addiction on Owen.

Then Owen's killers had delivered him to his apartment and never seen him again. It was a small gamble Loren had taken, and it had paid off, this time.

Next time he'd grow more careless. One day we'd get him.

But not today.

The taxi settled out of the traffic pattern, touched down on the roof of my apartment building in the Hollywood Hills. I got out and moved toward the elevators.

An elevator opened. Someone stepped out.

Something warned me, something about the way he moved. I turned, quick-drawing from the shoulder. The taxi might have made good cover—if it hadn't been already rising. Other figures had stepped from the shadows.

I think I got a couple before something stung my cheek. Mercy-bullets, slivers of crystalline anesthetic melting in my bloodstream. My head spun, and the roof spun, and the centrifugal force dropped me limply to the roof. Shadows loomed above me, then receded to infinity.

Fingers on my scalp shocked me awake.

I woke standing upright, bound like a mummy in soft, swaddling bandages. I couldn't so much as twitch a muscle below my neck. By the time I knew that much it was too late. The man behind me had finished removing electrodes from my head and stepped into view, out of reach of my imaginary arm.

There was something of the bird about him. He was tall and slender, small-boned, and his triangular face reached a point at the chin. His wild, silken blond hair had withdrawn from his temples, leaving a sharp widow's peak. He wore impeccably tailored wool street shorts in orange and brown stripes. Smiling brightly, with his arms folded and his head cocked to one side, he stood waiting for me to speak.

And I recognized him. Owen had taken a holo of him, somewhere.

"Where am I?" I groaned, trying to sound groggy. "What time it it?"

"Time? It's already morning," said my captor. "As for where you are, I'll let you wonder."

Something about his manner . . . I took a guess and said, "Loren?"

Loren bowed, not overdoing it. "And you are Gilbert Hamilton of the United Nations Police. Gil the Arm."

Had he said Arm or ARM? I let it pass. "I seem to have slipped."

"You underestimated the reach of my own arm. You also underestimated my interest."

I had. It isn't much harder to capture an ARM than any other citizen, if you catch him off guard, and if you're willing to risk the men. In this case his risk had cost him nothing. Cops use hypo guns for the same reason organleggers do. The men I'd shot, if I'd hit anyone in those few seconds of battle, would have come around long ago. Loren must have set me up in these bandages, then left me under "russian sleep" until he was ready to talk to me.

The electrodes were the "russian sleep." One goes on each eyelid, one on the nape of the neck. A small current goes through the brain, putting you right to sleep. You get a full night's sleep in an hour. If it's not turned off you can sleep forever.

So this was Loren.

He stood watching me with his head cocked to one

side, birdlike, with his arms folded. One hand held a hypo gun, rather negligently, I thought.

What time was it? I didn't dare ask again, because Loren might guess something. But if I could stall him until 0945, Julie could send help ...

She could send help where?

Finagle in hysterics! Where was I? If I didn't know that, Julie wouldn't know either!

And Loren intended me for the organ banks. One crystalline sliver would knock me out without harming any of the delicate, infinitely various parts that made me Gil Hamilton. Then Loren's doctors would take me apart.

In government operating rooms they flash-burn the criminal's brain for later urn burial. God knows what Loren would do with my own brain. But the rest of me was young and healthy. Even considering Loren's overhead, I was worth more than a million UN marks on the hoof.

"Why me?" I asked. "It was me you wanted, not just any ARM. Why the interest in me?"

"It was you who were investigating the case of Owen Jennison. *Much* too thoroughly."

"Not thoroughly enough, dammit!"

Loren looked puzzled. "You really don't understand?"

"I really don't."

"I find that highly interesting," Loren mused. "Highly."

"All right, why am I still alive?"

"I was curious, Mr. Hamilton. I hoped you'd tell me about your imaginary arm."

So he'd said Arm, not ARM. I bluffed anyway. "My *what*?"

"No need for games, Mr. Hamilton. If I think I'm losing I'll use this." He wiggled the hypo gun. "You'll never wake up."

Damn! He knew. The only things I could move were my ears and my imaginary arm, and Loren knew all about it! I'd never be able to lure him into reach.

Provided he knew *all* about it.

I had to draw him out.

"Okay," I said, "but I'd like to know how you found out about it. A plant in the ARMs?"

Loren chuckled. "I wish it were so. No. We captured one of your men some months ago, quite by accident. When I realized what he was, I induced him to talk shop with me. He was able to tell me something about your remarkable arm. I hope you'll tell me more."

"Who was it?"

"Really, Mr. Hamil—"

"Who was it?"

"Do you really expect me to remember the name of every donor?"

Who had gone into Loren's organ banks? Stranger, acquaintance, friend? Does the manager of a slaughterhouse remember every slaughtered steer?

"So-called psychic powers interest me," said Loren. "I remembered you. And then, when I was on the verge of concluding an agreement with your Belter friend Jennison, I remembered something unusual about a crewman he had shipped with. They called you Gil the Arm, didn't they? Prophetic. In port your drinks came free if you could use your imaginary arm to drink them."

"Then damn you. You thought Owen was a plant, did you? Because of me! Me!"

"Breast beating will earn you nothing, Mr. Hamilton." Loren put steel in his voice. "Entertain me, Mr. Hamilton."

I'd been feeling around for anything that might release me from my upright prison. No such luck. I was wrapped like a mummy in bandages too strong to break. All I could feel with my imaginary hand were cloth bandages up to my neck, and a bracing rod along my back to hold me upright. Beneath the swathing I was naked.

"I'll show you my eldritch powers," I told Loren,

"if you'll loan me a cigarette." Maybe that would draw him close enough . . .

He knew something about my arm. He knew its reach. He put one single cigarette on the edge of a small table-on-wheels and slid it up to me. I picked it up and stuck it in my mouth and waited hopefully for him to come light it. "My mistake," he murmured; and he pulled the table back and repeated the whole thing with a lighted cigarette.

No luck. At least I'd gotten my smoke. I pitched the dead one as far as it would go: about two feet. I have to move slowly with my imaginary hand. Otherwise what I'm holding simply slips through my fingers.

Loren watched in fascination. A floating, disembodied cigarette, obeying my will! His eyes held traces of awe and horror. That was bad. Maybe the cigarette had been a mistake.

Some people see psi powers as akin to witchcraft, and psychic people as servants of Satan. If Loren feared me, then I was dead.

"Interesting," said Loren. "How far will it reach?"

He knew that. "As far as my real arm, of course."

"But why? Others can reach much further. Why not you?"

He was clear across the room, a good ten yards away, sprawled in an armchair. One hand held a drink, the other held the hypo gun. He was superbly relaxed. I wondered if I'd ever see him move from that comfortable chair, much less come within reach.

The room was small and bare, with the look of a basement. Loren's chair and a small portable bar were the only furnishings, unless there were others behind me.

A basement could be anywhere. Anywhere in Los Angeles, or out of it. If it was really morning, I could be anywhere on Earth by now.

"Sure," I said, "others can reach further than me. But they don't have my strength. It's an imaginary arm, sure enough, and my imagination won't make it ten feet long. Maybe someone could convince me it was, if he tried hard enough. But maybe he'd ruin what belief I have. Then I'd have two arms, just like everyone else. I'm better off ..." I let it trail away, because Loren was going to take all my damn arms anyway.

My cigarette was finished. I pitched it away.

"Want a drink?"

"Sure, if you've got a jigger glass. Otherwise I can't lift it."

He found me a shot glass and sent it to me on the edge of the rolling table. I was barely strong enough to pick it up. Loren's eyes never left me as I sipped and put it down.

The old cigarette lure. Last night I'd used it to pick up a girl. Now it was keeping me alive.

Did I really want to leave the world with something gripped tightly in my imaginary fists? Entertaining Loren. Holding his interest until—

Where was I? Where?

And suddenly I knew. "We're at Monica Apartments," I said. "Nowhere else."

"I knew you'd guess that eventually." Loren smiled. "But it's too late. I got to you in time."

"Don't be so damn complacent. It was my stupidity, not your luck. I should have *smelled* it. Owen would never have come here of his own choice. You ordered him here."

"And so I did. By then I already knew he was a traitor."

"So you sent him here to die. Who was it that checked on him every day to see he'd stayed put? Was it Miller, the manager? He has to be working for you. He's the one who took the holographs of you and your men out of the computer."

"He was the one," said Loren. "But it wasn't every day. I had a man watching Jennison every second, through a portable camera. We took it out after he was dead."

"And then waited a week. Nice touch." The wonder was that it had taken me so long. The atmosphere of the place . . . what kind of people would live in Monica Apartments? The faceless ones, the ones with no identity, the ones who would surely be missed by nobody. They would stay put in their apartments while Loren checked on them, to see that they really did have nobody to miss them. Those who qualified would disappear, and their papers and possessions with them, and their holos would vanish from the computer.

Loren said, "I tried to sell organs to the Belters, through your friend Jennison. I know he betrayed me, Hamilton. I want to know how badly."

"Badly enough." He'd guess that. "We've got detailed plans for setting up an organ-bank dispensary in the Belt. It wouldn't have worked anyway, Loren. Belters don't think that way."

"No pictures."

"No." I didn't want him changing his face.

"I was sure he'd left something," said Loren. "Otherwise we'd have made him a donor. Much simpler. More profitable, too. I needed the money, Hamilton. Do you know what it costs the organization to let a donor go?"

"A million or so. Why'd you do it?"

"He'd left something. There was no way to get at it. All we could do was try to keep the ARMs from looking for it."

"Ah." I had it then. "When anyone disappears without a trace, the first thing any idiot thinks of is organleggers."

"Naturally. So he couldn't just disappear, could he? The police would go to the ARMs, the file would go to you, and you'd start looking."

"For a spaceport locker."

"Oh?"

"Under the name of Cubes Forsythe."

"I knew that name," Loren said between his teeth. "I should have tried that. You know, after we had him hooked on current, we tried pulling the plug on him to get him to talk. It didn't work. He couldn't concentrate on anything but getting the droud back in his head. We looked high and low—"

"I'm going to kill you," I said, and meant every word.

Loren cocked his head, frowning. "On the contrary, Mr. Hamilton. Another cigarette?"

"Yah."

He sent it to me, lighted, on the rolling table. I picked it up, holding it a trifle ostentatiously. Maybe I could focus his attention on it—on his only way to find my imaginary hand.

Because if he kept his eyes on the cigarette, and I put it in my mouth at a crucial moment—I'd leave my hand free without his noticing.

What crucial moment? He was still in the armchair. I had to fight the urge to coax him closer. Any move in that direction would make him suspicious.

What time was it? And what was Julie doing? I thought of a night two weeks past. Remembered dinner on the balcony of the highest restaurant in Los Angeles, just a fraction less than a mile up. A carpet of neon that spread below us to touch the horizon in all directions. Maybe she'd pick it up . . .

She'd be checking on me at 0945.

"You must have made a remarkable spaceman," said Loren. "Think of being the only man in the solar system who can adjust a hull antenna without leaving the cabin."

"Antennas take a little more muscle than I've got." So he knew I could reach through things. If he'd seen that far—"I should have stayed," I told Loren. "I wish I were on a mining ship, right this minute. All I wanted at the time was two good arms."

"Pity. Now you have three. Did it occur to you that using psi powers against men was a form of cheating?"

"What?"

"Remember Raphael Haine?" Loren's voice had become uneven. He was angry, and holding it down with difficulty.

"Sure. Small-time organlegger in Australia."

"Raphael Haine was a friend of mine. I know he had you tied up at one point. Tell me, Mr. Hamilton: if your imaginary hand is as weak as you say, how did you untie the ropes?"

"I didn't. I couldn't have. Haine used handcuffs. I picked his pocket for the key ... with my imaginary hand, of course."

"You used psi powers against him. You had no right!"

Magic. Anyone who's not psychic himself feels the same way, just a little. A touch of dread, a touch of envy. Loren thought he could handle ARMs; he'd killed at least one of us. But to send warlocks against him was grossly unfair.

That was why he'd let me wake up. Loren wanted to gloat. How many men have captured a warlock?

"Don't be an idiot," I said. "I didn't volunteer to play your silly game, or Haine's either. *My* rules make you a wholesale murderer."

Loren got to his feet (what time was it?) and I suddenly realized my time was up. He was in a white rage. His silky blond hair seemed to stand on end.

I looked into the tiny needle hole in the hypo gun. There was nothing I could do. The reach of my TK was the reach of my fingers. I felt all the things I would never feel: the quart of Trastine in my blood to keep the water from freezing in my cells, the cold bath of half-frozen alcohol, the scalpels and the tiny, accurate surgical lasers. Most of all, the scalpels.

And my knowledge would die when they threw away my brain. I knew what Loren looked like. I knew about Monica Apartments, and who knew how many others of the same kind? I knew where to go to find all the loveliness in Death Valley, and someday I was going to go. What time was it? What time?

Loren had raised the hypo gun and was sighting down the stiff length of his arm. Obviously he thought he was at target practice. "It really is a pity," he said, and there was only the slightest tremor in his voice. "You should have stayed a spaceman."

What was he waiting for? "I can't cringe unless you loosen these bandages," I snapped, and I jabbed what was left of my cigarette at him for emphasis. It jerked out of my grip, and I reached and caught it and—

And stuck it in my left eye.

At another time I'd have examined the idea a little more closely. But I'd still have done it. Loren already thought of me as his property. As live skin and healthy kidneys and lengths of artery, as parts in Loren's organ banks, I was property worth a million UN marks. And I was destroying my eye! Organleggers are always hurting for eyes; anyone who wears glasses could use a new pair, and the organleggers themselves are constantly wanting to change retina prints.

What I hadn't anticipated was the pain. I'd read somewhere that there are no sensory nerves in the eyeball. Then it was my lids that hurt. Terribly!

But I only had to hold on for a moment.

Loren swore and came for me at a dead run. He knew how terribly weak was my imaginary arm. What could I do with it? He didn't know; he'd never known, though it stared him in the face. He ran at me and slapped at the cigarette, a full swing that half knocked my head off my neck and sent the now dead butt ricocheting off a wall. Panting, snarling, speechless with rage, he stood—within reach.

My eye closed like a small tormented fist.

I reached past Loren's gun, through his chest wall, and found his heart. And squeezed.

His eyes became very round, his mouth gaped wide, his larynx bobbed convulsively. There was time to fire the gun. Instead he clawed at his chest with a half-paralyzed arm. Twice he raked his fingernails across his chest, gaping upward for air that wouldn't come. He thought he was having a heart attack. Then his rolling eyes found my face.

My face. I was a one-eyed carnivore, snarling with the will to murder. I would have his life if I had to tear the heart out of his chest! How could he help but know?

He knew!

He fired at the floor, and fell.

I was sweating and shaking with reaction and disgust. The scars! He was all scars; I'd felt them going in. His heart was a transplant. And the rest of him—he'd looked about thirty from a distance, but this close it was impossible to tell. Parts were younger, parts older. How much of Loren was Loren? What parts had he taken from others? And none of the parts quite matched.

He must have been chronically ill, I thought. And the Board wouldn't give him the transplants he needed. And one day he'd seen the answer to all his problems ...

Loren wasn't moving. He wasn't breathing. I remembered the way his heart had jumped and wriggled in my imaginary hand, and then suddenly given up.

He was lying on his left arm, hiding his watch. I was all alone in an empty room, and I still didn't know what time it was.

I never found out. It was hours before Miller finally dared to interrupt his boss. He stuck his round, blank face around the door jamb, saw Loren sprawled at my feet, and darted back with a squeak. A minute later a hypo gun came around the jamb, followed by a watery blue eye. I felt the sting in my cheek.

"I checked you early," said Julie. She settled herself uncomfortably at the foot of the hospital bed. "Rather, you called me. When I came to work you weren't there, and I wondered why, and *wham*. It was bad, wasn't it?"

"Pretty bad," I said.

"I've never sensed anyone so scared."

"Well, don't tell anyone about it." I hit the switch to raise the bed to sitting position. "I've got an image to maintain."

My eye and the socket around it were bandaged and numb. There was no pain, but the numbness was obtrusive, a reminder of two dead men who had become part of me. One arm, one eye.

If Julie was feeling that with me, then small wonder if she was nervous. She was. She kept shifting and twisting on the bed.

"I kept wondering what time it was. What time was it?"

"About nine-ten." Julie shivered. "I thought I'd faint when that—that vague little man pointed his hypo gun around the corner. Oh, don't! Don't, Gil. It's *over*."

That close? Was it *that* close? "Look," I said, "you go back to work. I appreciate the sick call, but this isn't doing either of us any good. If we keep it up we'll both wind up in a state of permanent terror."

She nodded jerkily and got up.

"Thanks for coming. Thanks for saving my life too."

Julie smiled from the doorway. "Thanks for the orchids."

I hadn't ordered them yet. I flagged down a nurse and got her to tell me that I could leave tonight, after dinner, provided I went straight home to bed. She brought me a phone, and I used it to order the orchids.

Afterward I dropped the bed back and lay there awhile. It was nice being alive. I began to remember promises I had made, promises I might never have kept. Perhaps it was time to keep a few.

I called down to Surveillance and got Jackson Bera. After letting him drag from me the story of my heroism, I invited him up to the infirmary for a drink. His bottle, but I'd pay. He didn't like that part, but I bullied him into it.

I had dialed half of Taffy's number before, as I had last night, I changed my mind. My wrist phone was on the bedside table. No pictures.

" 'Lo."

"Taffy? This is Gil. Can you get a weekend free?"

"Sure. Starting Friday?"

"Good."

"Come for me at ten. Did you ever find out about your friend?"

"Yah. I was right. Organleggers killed him. It's over now, we got the guy in charge." I didn't mention the eye. By Friday the bandages would be off. "About that weekend. How would you like to see Death Valley?"

"You're kidding, right?"

"I'm kidding, wrong. Listen—"

"But it's hot! It's dry! It's as dead as the Moon! You did say Death Valley, didn't you?"

"It's not hot this month. Listen ..." And she did listen. She listened long enough to be convinced.

"I've been thinking," she said then. "If we're going to see a lot of each other, we'd better make a—a bargain. No shop talk. All right?"

"A good idea."

"The point is, I work in a hospital," said Taffy. "Surgery. To me, organic transplant material is just the tools of my trade, tools to use in healing. It took me a long time to get that way. I don't want to know where the stuff comes from, and I don't want to know anything about organleggers."

"Okay, we've got a covenant. See you at ten hundred Friday."

A doctor, I thought afterward. Well. The weekend was going to be a good one. Surprising people are always the ones most worth knowing.

Bera came in with a pint of J&B. "My treat," he said. "No use arguing, 'cause you can't reach your wallet anyway." And the fight was on.

SHORT STORY COLLECTIONS
FROM ROC [ROC]

☐ **SISTERS IN FANTASY Edited by Susan Shwartz and Martin H. Greenberg.** This collection gathers together fifteen all-original and thought-provoking stories by some of the most highly regarded women writing fiction today. From curses confronted and paths not followed to women gifted with magic as ancient as the earth itself, these powerful tales provide insight into sacrifices made and obstacles overcome.   (452925—$4.99)

☐ **SISTERS IN FANTASY 2 Edited by Susan Shwartz and Martin H. Greenberg.** From ancient spells unleashed upon our modern world to the equally powerfully thirsts for romance and revenge, here are all-original stories written especially for this volume by twenty-two of today's bestselling and award-winning women fantasists.   (455037—$5.99)

☐ **THE BOOK OF KINGS Edited by Richard Gilliam and Martin H. Greenberg.** Twenty original stories about kings and royalty, as seen through the eyes of queens, stable hands, mythical creatures and lowly peasants, written by some of today's finest fantasy writers including: Stephen R. Donaldson, Jane Yolen, Alan Dean Foster, and Judith Tarr.   (454731—$5.50)

☐ **DARK LOVE by Stephen King, Stuart Kaminsky, Ramsey Campbell and 19 others. Edited by Nancy A. Collins, Edward E. Kramer, and Martin H. Greenberg.** There is no safe hiding place on this fictional turf where burning desire and dark terror meet, where ecstasy merges with agony, and eros and evil spawn unholy horror. These macabre tales give new meaning to being madly in love.   (454723—$22.95)

☐ **THE GALLERY OF HORROR 20 chilling tales by the modern masters of dread. Stephen King, Eric Van Lustbader, Ramsey Campbell and 17 others. Edited by Charles L. Grant.** Some galleries specialize in the arts of painting, or sculpture, or crafts. But the gallery you are about to visit specializes in the most irresistibly riveting art of all—the art of horror. For connoisseurs of classic chills for whom no leap into unknown evil is too bold or too scary.   (454618—$21.95)

Prices slightly higher in Canada.

Buy them at your local bookstore or use this convenient coupon for ordering.

PENGUIN USA
P.O. Box 999 — Dept. #17109
Bergenfield, New Jersey 07621

Please send me the books I have checked above.
I am enclosing $_____ (please add $2.00 to cover postage and handling). Send check or money order (no cash or C.O.D.'s) or charge by Mastercard or VISA (with a $15.00 minimum). Prices and numbers are subject to change without notice.

Card #_____ Exp. Date _____
Signature_____
Name_____
Address_____
City _____ State _____ Zip Code _____

For faster service when ordering by credit card call **1-800-253-6476**

Allow a minimum of 4-6 weeks for delivery. This offer is subject to change without notice.